# Shine

## NOT BURN

## ELLE CASEY

Elle Casey
PO Box 14367
N Palm Beach, FL 33408

Website: www.ElleCasey.com
Email: info@ellecasey.com

ISBN/EAN-13: 978-1-939455-07-9

*First Edition*

# DEDICATION

To Mimi Strong.
An author friend whose name suits her perfectly.

**Want to get an email when my next book is released?
Sign up here:** http://eepurl.com/h3aYM

# OTHER BOOKS BY ELLE CASEY
*= *Coming Soon*

**(New Adult Romance)**
Shine Not Burn
Rebel*
Hellion*
Trouble*
Trainwreck*
By Degrees*
Don't Make Me Beautiful*
**(YA Paranormal Romance)**
Duality, Volume I (Melancholia)
Duality, Volume II (Euphoria)
**(YA Urban Fantasy)**
War of the Fae: Book One, The Changelings - *FREE!*
War of the Fae: Book Two, Call to Arms
War of the Fae: Book Three, Darkness & Light
War of the Fae: Book Four, New World Order
Clash of the Otherworlds: Book 1, After the Fall
Clash of the Otherworlds: Book 2, Between the Realms
Clash of the Otherworlds: Book 3, Portal Guardians
My Vampire Summer
My Vampire Fall*
Aces High (co-written with Jason Brant)
**(YA Post-Apocalyptic)**
Apocalypsis: Book 1, Kahayatle
Apocalypsis: Book 2, Warpaint
Apocalypsis: Book 3, Exodus
Apocalypsis: Book 4, Haven
**(YA Action-Adventure)**
Wrecked
Reckless

# Shine Not Burn

Elle Casey

# Chapter One

THEY CALL ME PARTY GIRL. That's who the invitation says I am, anyway.

*Yo, Party Girl! We. Need. You. Be at the airport tomorrow at 1pm on the dot at the Delta ticket counter or you will henceforth be known as Mud. We're not kidding. Don't let us down. And remember, you have permission to have fun and forget about your bullshit boyfriend PUKE because what happens in Vegas stays in Vegas. Over and out. Love, your best friend, Kelly. And no, Candice is not your best friend, I am. Love, Kelly. Your best friend.*

I put the invitation down on my desk. "No way," I said out loud into my office, "not gonna happen."

"What's not gonna happen?" asked Ruby, my assistant. Really she's more like a mother, next door neighbor, confessor, and general pain in the butt all rolled into one, but the nameplate on her desk says she's Ruby. Executive Legal Secretary at Harvey, Grossman, and Cantor, LLP. She came in carrying a piping hot mug of coffee, and like she does every day, earned my undying gratitude for her uncanny ability to know exactly what I needed when I needed it. Nine a.m. and I was ready to mainline the caffeine at this point. Bachelorette party invites do that to me.

"I'm not going to this stupid thing," I said, tucking the invitation under my desk blotter. I could already imagine what Luke would have to say about it. That would be Luke with an L and not with a P. My girlfriends weren't fans.

"For Kelly? Of course you are. She's your best friend. Do you want me to RSVP for you or are you going to handle it?"

I frowned at her, not quite snatching the cup out of her hands but letting her know she was making me cranky. "No, miss busybody, I do not want you RSVPing for me." I put the mug closer to my face so I could smell its contents, wishing the act of snorting coffee steam could get the caffeine to go in deeper or make its effects last longer. "I told you. I'm not going."

She pursed her lips at me in her patented Ruby-ain't-playin' look. "Mmm-hmm." Two head bob-n-weaves later and I was folding. She had serious guilt-trip power, and she wasn't afraid to use it on me regularly.

"But I don't want to go," I whined, getting my pout on and working it with everything I had. "I have two briefs to finish by Tuesday and three hearings this week on motions to dismiss and that's just the tip of my unholy awful iceberg." I kicked my desk lightly, wanting to do it harder but loathe to damage my Louboutins. They'd cost me almost a week's pay.

"You finished those briefs last week, as you well know, and you can send *Bradley* to the hearings." She said Bradley with that tone - the one that conveyed how irritating she found him. She always did. I had to really resist the urge to do it myself. He had this way of getting under a person's skin. Creepy crawly and seriously, ew. Gorgeous clothes and a pretty face could only do so much for a guy when his personality was so gag-worthy. Think snake crossed with honey badger and you'd be close to understanding his style.

I rolled my eyes. "You really need to stop snooping around in my computer files, Rubes."

"Why? How else am I'm going to keep up with you? If I wait for you to ask me for help I'll be old and gray before that happens."

"You already are old and gray," I said, smiling behind my mug. The glee I was feeling at this point was totally rude, but that's how I roll. Rockin the Louboutins while harassing senior citizens. Classy with a capital K.

She pointed a very long, very polished fingernail at me. "Girl, you are so lucky you're sitting behind that desk and not out there in that mess of secretaries with me, otherwise ..." She wrinkled up her mouth at me and shook her head slowly a few times.

"Otherwise, what? You'd mess me up? We'd throw down in the copy room?" My grin got bigger.

"Count on it, baby girl," she said. She turned to leave the office, her panty-hosed legs making loud swishing sounds like they always did. I swear one day the friction between her thighs was going to start a fire in the office.

"Who do I send the RSVP to?" she asked without even looking back at me. "Candice or Kelly?"

I sighed heavily, putting the mug down on the desk blotter.

Ruby wins again. As usual.

"Kelly," I sighed out. "Send it to Kelly's work email."

I spun my chair to the side so I could face my computer, clicking on the keys that would take me to my client files. The impending doom of Kelly's upcoming bachelorette party hung over my head. I was supposed to be figuring out how I was going to work my way around the 4th DCA's latest ruling, but the words on the document I'd just opened swam in front of my eyes.

My eyes glazed over and I was fifteen again, in a small back room of my mother's house with the hulking figure of her boyfriend standing over me, a belt raised above his head.

It crashed down again and again on my back, head, and shoulders. Nasty, hateful words streamed out of his mouth, dank ugliness that coated my skin.

I trembled not with fear but with anger. This had gone on for way too long. The bruises were taking longer to heal. I had to get away. With every beating the words had gotten more hateful, and the belt had come down harder. If I didn't find a way out of this mess I'd be dead and buried in the backyard before I hit eighteen. Wishing my mother would step in and help me was a waste of my time.

When he left the room that day, I'd drafted the first version of what became known as my lifeplan, the document that laid out the route that would lead me to my goals: independence, safety, and financial success. I couldn't depend on my weak, co-dependent mother to save me, so I had to save myself.

I shook my head, pulling it out of the clouds and bringing it back to the present. *No. I refuse to let those memories ruin my best friend's party.* I took a deep breath and expelled the ghosts haunting the recesses of my mind. I was twenty-five now and my lifeplan had gotten me this far. Taking a small break to go to Vegas wouldn't change anything. Taking a little two-day trip to Vegas with my best girlfriends presented zero risk to my lifeplan. I could do this. I would not allow Fear to be my constant companion anymore.

I clicked my mouse, bringing up the document that had to be finished before I got on the plane.

# Chapter Two

A CHORUS OF SQUEALS ROSE up as I walked over to the check-in area of Palm Beach International Airport. My best friends from college, Candice and Kelly, were standing near the Delta line.

"You made it!" yelled Candice, running towards me, paying zero attention to the bystanders staring at her. This was her usual way of making it through life. Oblivious. Loud. Ready to party at a moment's notice. She came on tiptoes, her shoes making any other type of walking impossible. She is the most lovable airhead I've ever known.

"*Ooph.*" Her surgically enhanced chest slammed into mine, knocking some of the air out of my lungs. "Miss me?" I asked over her shoulder, my eyes crossing just a little.

"Oh my god, yes." She squeezed me hard once and pulled away. "You hibernate in that office of yours all week long, every weekend, and then you spend all your free time with Puke. Of *course* I miss you."

"It's *Luke,* and I went to lunch with you just last week." I stepped back, picking up the overnight bag I'd dropped on the ground by my feet and putting the strap over my shoulder. "You know I have to make partner …"

"…By the time you're thirty. I know, I know, I know. It's going to be engraved on your headstone." She put her arm

5

through mine, leaning in and sniffing me. She did that all the time, always on the lookout for her next favorite perfume.

"Headstone? Hopefully, I'll be partner at the firm by the time I have *that* little depressing ornament over my head." I glanced sideways at her, smiling secretly over the fact that her lips looked like they'd been stung by wasps again. Once Candice discovered collagen a few years ago, she'd never gone back. One of her favorite sayings is 'thin lips sink ships' which makes complete sense to her; she doesn't care that it doesn't to anyone else. I've never asked for clarification of the 'ships' part of that equation because sometimes her thought processes give me headaches they're so asinine. But as goofy as she can be, she's still one-half of my best friend whole. Candice, Kelly, and I were known as the three amigas in college and that hadn't changed, even though our lives couldn't be more different now.

We walked over to the counter to join Kelly. She was having an animated conversation with the wispy-looking male ticket agent, first waving her arms around and then putting her hands in praying position. She looked like a regular church lady with her button down blouse and neatly-pressed khaki pants. Love had mellowed her out since college, but under that conservative, polished veneer was a crazy girl who used to dye her hair purple and do shots of tequila off male-stripper stomachs.

Candice snorted at the claim I was laying on my future partnership. "I've told you a hundred times. You won't make partner by the time you're thirty if you don't get out more. My cousin's cousin's husband's brother died of a heart attack when he was only twenty-eight. *Twenty-eight!*"

"You're cousin's cousin's husband's sister's ... whatever ... had a heart defect, and you've told me before he got chicken pox so bad he was hospitalized, so I'm pretty sure him *not* being a female lawyer working a few extra hours a week didn't contribute to his death."

"Just shut up and come with me. Kelly's trying to get us an upgrade."

I followed Candice to the counter and listened with amusement as Kelly tried to charm the obviously gay man into giving us an upgrade she didn't have the frequent flyer miles for.

"Please, pleasepleasepleaseplease pleeeeaaase? I swear we'll be good. We'll totally behave ourselves and not drink ten mini bottles of vodka on ice." She grinned like a movie star in a toothpaste commercial. She did have really nice teeth. Having a father as a cosmetic dentist made sure of that.

He gave her a perfunctory smile in return, which disappeared less than a second after it had appeared. "As much as it pains me to tell you this, I'm afraid I cannot give you the upgrade unless you have the points or the money to pay for it." He looked at his monitor. "To go from economy class to business class will cost you a total of one thousand two hundred dollars for the three of you. We accept all major credit cards." His nostrils flared slightly as he stared at her again.

Kelly's mouth dropped open. "Are you in*sane*? I could buy a shitty used car for that much money."

He smiled without humor. "But you don't get complimentary drinks in shitty used cars, now do you?" There wasn't a trace of sarcasm in his voice. Damn, he was good.

I walked up to the desk and rested my arm on it, giving him my best addressing-the-bench smile. "Hi there, ... Samuel. I'm Andrea ... Andie." I put my other hand on Kelly's arm. "It's my job to take this poor girl and give her the best two days of her life in Vegas before she ties herself down to a life of servitude and misery. I'm talking marriage here, and it's bad. It's *really* bad." I lowered my voice. "Her fiancé is a mortician."

"You're kidding me," he said, looking first at me and

then Kelly. His cold expression slipped just a little. We were used to the morbid curiosity when the subject came up, and I wasn't too proud to use it to our advantage. This was my best friend's bachelorette party, after all. Sacrifices would need to be made. Buttons would have to be pushed. Pride would have to be swallowed.

Kelly nodded, her eyes big and if I wasn't mistaken, a little shiny. *Nice touch*, I said in my nod at her. *Work it hard.* The sad thing is, I wasn't kidding about the mortician thing. She really was planning to marry Matthew Ackerman, otherwise known to us as Matty the mortician. Candice and I have asked her several times what she could possibly see in a man who deals with the dead all the time, and her answer was always the same: nobody's got good wood like a guy who works with stiffs all day. I'm still not even sure what that's supposed to mean, but I'm also pretty damn sure I don't want to know either, so I let it lie.

"You're going to marry a man who touches dead bodies every day? Cuts them open?" He leaned forward and spoke in a whisper. "Embalms them?"

She nodded. "Yes. We deal with death every day, the two of us. It's all very heart-breaking. This is my one last chance to let my hair down before I have to suck it up and be the wife of a mortician." She wiped a fake tear from her eye and turned away.

*And the Academy Award for Best Actress in a Non-Movie is … Kelly Foust!*

The agent looked to his left and then his right. His fingers flew over the keys, sometimes just the index finger pressing one key about twenty times. I wondered if he was really even doing anything. It was possible he was just messing with us by seeing how long he could keep us standing there believing we were convincing him to feel sorry for us before he told us to go get bent.

But then the sound of a dot matrix printer came from

under his counter and a few seconds later he was pulling six long boarding cards out with our names on them. "Business class upgrade? Why of course, ladies. We're happy to accommodate your business needs here at Delta Airlines. Here are your boarding passes for both legs of the flight to Las Vegas." He put them down on the counter and slid them over to Kelly. She grabbed them and squealed, her heels tapping the floor over and over as she simultaneously hugged Candice and jumped up and down with her. I put my hand on her shoulder to calm her down while giving my full attention to the agent.

"Thanks so much for helping us out, Samuel. That was really cool."

He smiled at me, the first genuine expression I think I'd gotten from him since I'd walked up to his counter. "Just be careful. They say what happens in Vegas stays in Vegas, but sometimes the trouble follows you home. Know what I mean?" He winked.

I nodded, even though I had no idea what he was talking about. I wasn't the kind of girl to get into that kind of trouble. I might drink a little wine now and then or a beer maybe, but I always remembered what happened the next day and I never went too far. I was all about self-control now that I was an adult and no longer goofing around in college. "Good tip. Thanks again."

"You're welcome. Thank you for flying Delta. Have a pleasant trip." He looked past me to the person next in line, so I took the hint and moved to the side.

Grabbing our carry-ons, we left for the security area, Candice and Kelly already making plans for our first night in Vegas. I heard something about slots and a night club before trying unsuccessfully to block out the rest. I let out a long sigh, realizing as each part of their plan was revealed that I had two days of adult babysitting to look forward to. It was no big deal, though. I'd had lots of practice in college being their roommate. I'd always been the responsible one, the dedicated driver, the girl who held their hair while they barfed over the toilet, the one who dispensed tissues and served up ice cream when boyfriends made them cry. *Two days in Vegas, running after my best friends and keeping them out of the kind of trouble that follows a person home. How hard could it be?* I had four years of practice at the University of Florida. This would be a piece of cake.

My phone buzzed after I went through security, and I read the text on the screen while we walked to our gate. The words glowing out at me didn't make the outlook for my trip any brighter. I considered turning around and dealing with the problem now so I could get it all over with, thinking I could hook up with my friends later. This was seriously going to ruin the trip for me.

"What's wrong, party pooper?" asked Candice, coming up beside me and putting her arm across my shoulders. She's normally only two inches taller than me, but with her stilettos, she had me by half a head easy. I'd worn lower heels today so I could be comfortable for the trip. It was more practical, and I was nothing if not that. Candice, on the other hand, abhorred practicality. She considered it the devil's influence and the road to a truly boring life.

I gritted my teeth, trying to contain my anger, trying not to let Luke ruin our bon voyage. "It's nothing," I said, acting nonchalant about it. "Just Luke." I went to slip my phone into the outer pocket of my purse, but Candice snatched it away from me.

"Hey!" I protested, reaching for it.

She handed it over to Kelly, keeping her grip tight on my shoulders. "Just relax. We're here to help."

"Oh my pink granny panties, did he actually just send this to you in a *text?* What a total douchebag McGee." She looked at me with her patented WTF expression. "Seriously, Andie, you *so* need to kick him in the balls when you get back."

"Whatsit say?" asked Candice, letting go of me and reaching for the phone.

"Read it and weep." Kelly gave me a pity frown as she handed the phone to Candice.

Two seconds later, Candice was typing something out on it.

"No!" I said, reaching for it. "Don't!"

"Too late! Too late!" she sang, dancing around in a small circle, holding the phone above her head.

I jumped up and snatched it away from her so I could read the very short conversation.

**Luke:** *I can't believe you're going. Have a nice life.*

**Andi's phone:** *Have a nice life yourself, assbag.*

"Wow. Thanks, Candice. That was awesome." My thumb hovered over the keys, ready to type out an explanation. An apology. Something.

Candice grabbed me by the arm and dragged me over to a group of empty seats inside our boarding area. "Listen to me, Andie. Before you send him another text, consider this..."

I sat down letting out a huff of frustration. I had already reached my vacation destination. Welcome to Sucksville! Next stop: Shit City!

Candice continued. "Luke's been sucking the life out of you for three whole years. Three years! And in all that time, what has he done, other than annoy the crap out of your best friends and make you cry? Huh? What has he done to deserve your undying loyalty? I don't get it."

"He's not that bad," I said, feeling a little guilty as I said it. My grandmother had always told me even little white lies were bad lies.

"Not that bad? Yeah, right. What did he get you for Valentine's Day this year? Oh yeeeaaah, that's right! A gift certificate towards liposuction! Wasn't that thoughtful." She rolled her eyes and threw up a hand for emphasis.

"Not," interjected Kelly.

"He knows I don't like my love handles on the top of my butt," I said, knowing as the words left my lips how incredibly lame I sounded. *Why do I keep allowing this stuff to happen? How can I call myself a strong intelligent woman when I act like a complete loser with men?*

"Right. Whatever." Candice was disgusted. "Talk about keeping a woman down. And what did he do the last time you went out of town for work? Oh, yeah. I remember now! He made out with his secretary at the office party!" She threw both her hands up and let them fall to slap the top of her thighs.

"He was drunk. They were both drunk. He told me about it, so it's not like he was hiding it." I remembered the sharp pain of humiliation over that one. It came back full force every time I thought about it, which was way too often.

Kelly sat down on my other side. "Please stop making excuses for that shitheel, would you? He confessed because everyone in the entire firm saw it, and he knew you were going to find out sooner or later." She put her arm around me and squeezed. "He's a crap boyfriend and a crap guy in general. Please just let him go and move on. Please, please don't go back to him. He's offering you a golden opportunity right now."

"That's easy for you to say. You're marrying Matty the mortician next week."

"Yes, well, if you recall, I kissed a lot of hairy, warty toads before I found my prince."

"Yeah. Remember Bruno from Italy?" asked Candice, giggling.

"How could I forget?" I asked, smiling too. Misery loves company. "Bruno, the one-balled wonder."

"Hey, he can't help it that he's missing a testicle," said Kelly, trying really hard to be offended but not quite hitting the mark.

"Uh, yeah he can, when he's the one who made it fall off," said Candice, snorting.

Kelly sighed with exaggerated patience. "It didn't fall off, okay? I've told you a hundred times, Candice, he had it surgically removed."

I couldn't stop smiling despite being pissed off about that stupid text and the idea that the first thing I'd have to do when I got back would be to pack up his crap and deliver it to his apartment ... although it would be nice to get my closet back. "And why exactly did Bruno have his own testicle surgically removed?" I asked, pretending I didn't know the answer.

Kelly shrugged. "I guess he had too much testosterone or something."

Candice snorted again, bending over a little with the giggles that were coming more uncontrollably now.

I sat back in my seat and crossed one leg over the other. "I thought he injected himself in the ball sack with some black market steroids and caused an infection down there that made one of them shrivel up and fall off."

Candice was laughing loudly now, her guffaws sprinkled liberally with very unattractive pig-snorts.

"Shut up, Andie. The guy almost died. You shouldn't be making fun of him." Kelly pressed her lips together to keep from smiling.

I reached over and pulled her into a hug. "I'm sorry. You're right. Poor old one-ball. He deserves our pity not our mockery."

I looked over at Candice and winked. She had to look away to contain herself.

A voice came over the loudspeaker: "Delta Flight eighty-seven to Las Vegas now boarding business class passengers only. Business class passengers only."

Candice and Kelly jumped up, Bruno One-Ball a distant memory.

"That's us," said Candice, picking up her Louis Vuitton make-up case. "Business class, here we come." She tiptoed over to the ticket counter, boarding pass out and big smile on.

"Seriously," said Kelly as we walked over to join our friend who was openly flirting with a man in a shiny silver suit, "you need to just let Luke go, at least during this trip. You need to be one hundred percent focused on having fun and enjoying this girl-time together. After I'm married and then have kids, I'm not sure I'll ever have time to do it again, at least until I'm like sixty."

I nodded. "I know. I'll just deal with him when I get back." The business of breaking up. And after a three year investment of time and serious future plan-making on my part, it wasn't going to be pretty.

"That's my girl," she said, hugging me with one arm. "Come on. Let's go drink all the vodka on the plane."

"Didn't you promise Samuel the ticket guy you wouldn't do that?" I said, handing the attendant my boarding card and moving to the passageway that would bring us to the plane.

"Nope. I didn't make any promises." She pulled my arm and tugged me along. "Promises are only promises if you say the word *promise*."

"I think it's the intent that matters, not the words." My feet dragged, my brain definitely not agreeing that Las Vegas was a good idea right now.

"You are such a lawyer sometimes," she said, frustrated with me. She jerked my arm. "*No* more lawyering. From this moment until the point that you get *off* the plane here in West Palm on our way home, you will not be a lawyer." She turned and faced me, standing in the doorway of the plane. "Promise me. Say the word. Promise you won't act like a lawyer the entire time we're gone."

I sighed heavily, watching the crowd of economy-class passengers coming down the gangway behind us. Kelly's stubborn. She'd stay there all day and make everyone wait

14

until she got her way.

"Fine. I promise. Andie the lawyer is staying behind in the airport." My shoulders sagged in defeat.

"Weeeee!" she squealed, taking me into a brief but strong hug. "Andie the party girl is now on board, airplane people." She smiled as she stepped into the front of the plane, looking out over the seats in business class. "Now someone show us to the vodka." She left me standing there, taking a seat next to Candice. They both squealed together like teenagers.

I followed along slowly, not looking forward to getting reacquainted with Andie the party girl. I'd left her behind in college and hadn't seen her in a long, long while. Andie the party girl did not fit into my plans of making partner, getting married, and having two point five kids by the time I'm thirty-five.

# Chapter Three

IAN MACKENZIE SADDLED UP ONE of his father's quarter horses and took off down the trail that would lead him to the back part of the far pasture. His older brother Gavin, otherwise known as Mack, was working there. The MacKenzies had a big herd that needed to be moved to higher ground because of some forecasted heavy rains, but it had to be done slowly. They didn't want the cattle to burn off too much weight before being sold by the pound. Loss of a single pound per head could mean the difference between feast and famine on the MacKenzie ranch.

Thirty minutes later, his older brother's musical whistling cued him in to where he was, just behind a large rock outcropping, under some tall trees. Mack had gotten farther in his mission to move the cattle, and the ride had taken Ian much longer than he'd anticipated. He allowed his horse to pick its way around the scrub brush and larger rocks, its sturdy legs and muscular frame well adapted to the area's rugged terrain.

"Yo, Mack!" Ian called out, making sure to announce himself so he wouldn't spook his brother or his brother's horse.

The whistling stopped abruptly. "Yo, Ian," came the response, albeit in a decidedly less enthusiastic tone.

17

Ian rode around the side of the large barrier, finding his brother sitting in the saddle and staring out over the gorgeous valley below, his reins loosely wrapped around the saddle horn. His leather chaps that he wore over his jeans looked as old as the hills themselves. Ian made a mental note to buy his brother new ones for his birthday.

"I'll never get tired of that view," said Mack, reaching up to rub his sweaty head by wiggling his cream-colored cowboy hat around, his longish dark brown hair curling up at the nape of his neck. The strong muscles of his arm flexed and moved, calling attention to the deep tan he'd acquired from working without his flannel shirt on. "Why would anyone ever want to live anywhere else?" He abandoned the head scratching and rested his hand on his thigh. Turning to his younger brother, he gave him the look that used to make Ian beg for forgiveness when they were younger.

Ian breathed out a sigh of annoyance. "Some people find other things to live for besides ranching and carrying on old and tired traditions."

Mack turned more fully to face his brother, his glowing, light blue eyes shining out from under his hat. This was the classic-old-West-cowboy-meets-GQ-model look that always got the girls in town all hot and bothered. Ian had spent a lifetime watching his brother duck and run from almost all of them. It was a damn shame, as far as he was concerned, that his brother was not only damn ornery but way too picky to boot. None of the girls in Baker City had measured up so far, and he'd pretty much run out of candidates. Even Hannah Pierce who'd been circling his brother's ankles and making herself a complete nuisance since junior high wasn't really in the running, much as she might like to think she was.

"Old and tired traditions?" Mack scowled. "Come on, Ian, that's not fair. Those traditions put you through school, not to mention set you up to get married to Ginny in style, just like she always wanted." He faced the beautiful view

18

again and adjusted his seat in the saddle, the leather creaking as it moved. Reaching down to gather up his reins in his gloved hand, he began whistling again, doing a unique rendition of the song *I'm Movin' On* by Rascal Flatts.

Ian knew the tune well. Their mother had been playing it everyday at home, wallowing in the sadness of losing her younger boy to the big city. Ian shook his head. Portland, Oregon was as small-town as a big city could possibly be, but his whole family was acting like he was going to the Big Apple never to be seen again. He and his soon-to-be wife Ginny had already promised to visit on every major holiday and two weeks during Christmas, but it hadn't done anything to ease his mother's suffering. All she could talk about was the grandchild who didn't exist yet that she'd almost never see.

"I bought you a ticket today," said Ian. "I came to tell you so you can pack and get in the shower before we leave for Boise. Plane takes off at four so we have to be there by three, no later."

"I told you, I'm not goin'. Gotta get the herd moved before next week."

"Boog already said he'd do it, and he owes you anyway, so just let him. And I need you, besides. You can take a break for once. You haven't had a vacation in ten years."

Mack urged his horse forward with a squeeze of his legs and a clicking sound inside his cheek. "You need me? In Vegas? Vacation? Yeah right, that'll be the day." The horse moved past the tree and along a grassy area below a tall hill - a mere bump compared to the mountains in the distance.

Ian gave his horse a light spurring, causing it to leap forward and cut his brother's mount off.

Mack scowled. "Cut it out, Ee. You know I don't have time to play with you right now. Stop acting like a fool."

Ian smiled, whirling his horse around so he could crowd his brother and get him to react. This cold indifference wasn't getting him anywhere. A challenge was the only way to get his brother to wake up and get involved in his life while he was still living it in Baker City. Ian saw this bachelor party in Vegas as Mack's last chance to leave this town and see a little bit of the world before he turned into a hermit, just like their father. Twenty-five years old and he acted like he was fifty. Responsible. Mature. Serious almost all the time. Ian felt the life draining out of him just watching his brother in the saddle.

"Bet I can beat you to the top of that hill over there." Ian lifted his chin once in challenge, knowing his brother wouldn't be able to resist. Mack always had to run the fastest, jump the highest, and whistle the loudest. He was nothing if not competitive, and yet, he always managed to do it Cool Hand Luke style, with no one fully realizing how much it mattered to him to be on top. Stealth ego. Mack MacKenzie was all about the stealth ego.

"When are you going to give it up, Ian? You know you're as slow as Methusela on a damn horse. All hat and no cattle. That's why you want to run away to the city so no one will know your shame." He chuckled. "There you can take the ankle express everywhere you need to go and forget about these pesky four-legged beasts."

Ian rolled his eyes at the tired expressions that their father had been using since before they were born. It was scary how easily they were rubbing off on Mack, now that he was taking on the mantle of ranch manager. "No, I'm *not* as slow as Methusela, I'm faster than you, and I can prove it. Why don't you put your money where your mouth is? Race me to the top of the hill."

Mack looked over at him out of the corner of his eye, his gaze dropping to take in the horse under Ian's saddle. Then he looked at the hill he'd have to climb, his eyes scanning the landscape between where his horse stood and there.

"What's the bet?" Mack asked, shifting again in the

saddle, getting a tighter grip on his reins, shortening them just the slightest bit.

Ian grinned, knowing triumph was nearly within his grasp.

"If I win, you go to Vegas. No bitchin', no whinin', no excuses. And you drink and you gamble and you womanize a little. Not a lot, just a little."

Mack's jaw bounced out a few times as he gritted his teeth, but he didn't say no. Instead, he smirked. "And if I win, you stay long enough to go to Mom's birthday party."

Ian's smile disappeared. "Aw, come on! That's not fair! You know I have to start work in Portland before that!"

Mack shrugged, a genuine smile sliding out to greet the day for the first time. "Not my problem, little bro. You do what you gotta do." He shrugged, all nonchalant, not a care in the world. "I don't have to race today. You know I'm going to beat your ass anyway."

"Screw that," said Ian, kicking his horse hard and snapping its hind end with the long end of his reins. "Heeyah!" The beast leaped into action, almost throwing him out of the saddle. He blew a stirrup, but there was nothing he could do but hang on and hope for the best.

# Chapter Four

MACK WASTED NO TIME, SENDING his horse off like a bullet. His little brother had gotten the jump on him, but it wouldn't matter. Mack was something of a legend in the area for his horse riding and cutting skills. People called him a *balance rider*, a guy so comfortable in his seat that no matter what the horse had a mind to do, Mack would go with it and not lose a beat. He hadn't fallen from a horse since he was five years old, and there wasn't a cow or steer alive that could outrun or outmaneuver his horse and lasso. Within seconds he'd drawn even with his little brother.

"Heeyah!" he yelled, mostly for his brother's benefit, but his own horse seemed inspired by it too. He left Ian's mare behind to eat his dust, leaping over the smaller rocks and the spring that ran across the property, landing smoothly on the other side and not even breaking stride as he surged up the hill.

Mack spun the horse so sharply at the summit that the gelding reared up and let out a whinny that echoed all over the valley. All in a day's work for Mack, he leaned forward casually, waiting for the horse to get back on all four feet and calm down. He patted his horse's neck, whispering his thank yous for the excellent work he'd done.

Ian came galloping up, sweat running down his beet-red

face, his horse with white foam gathering at the sides of her bit. "God*dammit*, Mack! Why the hell'd you go and do that? You know I have to get to Portland before the tenth!" His horse had slowed to a trot and Ian bounced uncomfortably in the saddle, never one for the work of a rancher.

Mack smiled again, feeling sorry for the horse. "Don't be a sore loser. You know Mom'll be thrilled that her baby boy's staying. Just don't tell her it's cuz you lost a bet though or I'll pound your ass."

"I should, but I won't." Ian scowled. "You suck, you know that? How am I supposed to have a good time at my bachelor party if my best man isn't even there?"

"You'll find a way, I'm sure." Mack wheeled his horse around and pointed it downhill. "Listen, I gotta go find some strays. You want to earn your keep around here and help me out?"

"No, I don't want to help you out. I've already earned my keep and I have to go take a shower now, my second one of the day, thank you very much. I have a plane to catch."

"See you when you get home," said Mack, not even looking back.

"The ticket's non-refundable!" Ian yelled at his brother's back.

"Shouldn't a-bought it in the first place!" Mack responded.

Mack pushed his horse into a trot, now in a hurry to get the job done. If he was going to make that plane for his little brother's bachelor party, he needed to hit the shower by no later than eleven-thirty.

He smiled, picturing the look Ian would have on his face as he watched Mack walk onto the plane. He and Ian weren't kids anymore, but that didn't mean Mack didn't still enjoy a good opportunity for teasing when it presented itself. Vegas was definitely not his idea of a fun place to go for any reason, but he couldn't very well abandon his kid brother on the last party night of his single life, now could he?  Besides, he'd be out there and home again in two days, back in the saddle without a hitch.  All he had to do was keep his headstrong little bro out of trouble and make sure he got back home in time to marry his childhood sweetheart.  And staying out of trouble should be easy enough.  He'd managed to do it his entire life.

# Chapter Five

"OH MY GEE WHIZ, WOULD you take a look at this place," said Kelly. She spun around to face Candice, a barely controlled grin making its way to the surface. "Did you do this?"

Candice grinned like the cheshire cat. "Of course I did. Who else would think to put you up in a gorgeous high roller suite during your bachlorette party, other than moi?"

I slapped her lightly on the arm. "What's that supposed to mean?" I dropped my bag just inside the door.

"Oh nothing ... other than the fact that if the planning had been left up to you, we'd probably be eating dinner at the Olive Garden right now and going home by ten."

I shook my head at her. "You are so lucky you're in heels right now."

She put her fingers up in the shape of a cross. "Stay back. I don't want you shaking my uterus around. I have plans tonight."

I barked out a laugh. "Your what?"

She sniffed, lifting her chin a little. "My uterus. I'm due to start my period any day, but I want to try and hold it off for as long as I can. I don't like having one night stands when I'm on the rag."

I grimaced, trying to make my way through the

quagmire that is her mind so I could figure out what she was actually thinking. "So your theory is that if I tackle you, I'll ... jiggle your uterus and start your period?"

"Exactly." She smiled with self-pride.

I shook my head in disbelief. "You really should have gone to medical school. With theories like that, you would have been something else."

"Andie, don't make me take my scissors out."

"That's not a very good threat," I said, wandering through the room, checking it out. "I'm due for a haircut."

Candice may be a totally brainless twit sometimes, but she was a hell of a beautician. Top of her class in coloring and styling. After making her parents pay for a four-year fashion degree at UF, she'd blown off the job market to go to cosmetology school. They'd loved that one, but no one can say no to Candice when she's on a mission. I really should visit her salon more, but I was always too busy. Boring ponytails had been my go-to hairdo for the past three years since graduating law school.

She quickly grabbed her bag off a nearby chair. "Go wet your hair. I've been dying to get my hands on that mess of yours for weeks. No, make that months. Years."

Kelly laughed. "I just love how much she enjoys her job, don't you?"

I shook my head as I walked to the bathroom. "I'm not going to say a word. I've seen how sharp her scissors are, and I like my ears the way they are." I was happy to let Candice have her way with my hair. *Why not enjoy a mini vacation and a mini spa treatment too while I'm at it?* I never pampered myself like that at home. I was always too busy.

As I wet my hair, I realized this haircut wasn't really about needing a trim. It was more symbolic than anything else. When I was finished and my hair was up in a towel, I pulled my cell phone out of my pocket and re-read the text from Luke, trying to give myself some inspiration.

*Have a nice life.*

I shut the phone down and put it on the counter, staring at it like it was a snake. *Deliverer of bad news. Traitor.* I took a deep breath and let it out slowly, trying to center myself. It was time to cut some of the dead wood out of my life. Take control. Do things a little more boldly and powerfully for a change. I was a bulldog in the courtroom, never letting go until I had wrung every last argument out of an issue. Attorneys feared going up against me, even when they had rock solid cases. But when it came to my personal life, I was a mess. A lamb to every man's inner lion. They chewed me up and spit me out, and like a total wienie, I just let them. Luke was just the latest in a string of really bad relationship decisions. Really, Kelly's One-Ball would be a step up for me.

I took the towel off and ran a brush Kelly had brought through my wet hair, staring at my reflection as I considered this little impromptu vacation. I was on a girls' night out, very far away from home. Maybe tonight with a new look I could walk out into the hot Las Vegas night and be a different girl. Even though it would only be for one night and a day, the idea held an almost magnetizing appeal. I was almost in a foreign land, where no one knew me. I could do whatever I wanted, and as long as I didn't get arrested, I'd be home free, back in the office being a kickass lawyer on Monday.

And single. I'd be single, but that could change. I smiled tentatively at myself. I have options; I'm not some ugly spinster that has nothing but a life of solitude and loneliness to look forward to. I leaned in closer to the mirror, evaluating my assets: greenish-gray eyes, brown hair with natural highlights, high cheekbones, decent chin, perfect nose or so my grandmother had always told me - not too small and not too big. My boobs aren't as big as Candice's but they're all mine, home grown. And I'd been told by most of my boyfriends that my best asset was behind me. I turned around, trying to get a look at it. My big, heart-shaped butt. I looked at my naked body in profile. Curvy is how I'd describe myself. I'd spent a lot of years when I was a teenager wishing I could be shaped more like a model with long legs and a well-muscled tummy, but lately I'd come to admire my more feminine silhouette. I nodded at my reflection and faced the mirror again. *If a guy can't appreciate what I have to offer, he can just keep on walkin'.*

I had some time yet. I was only twenty-five. My plans were still on track, even if Luke wasn't on board with them anymore. Junior partner by beginning of next year. Married by the year after. Babies a couple years after that. And then full partner at the firm. Bam. Done with all the hard stuff by thirty-five, and then smooth sailing from then on out.

I looked at my wet head in the mirror and shrugged, my hair several inches past my shoulders and grown-out bangs tickling my eyes. There are plenty of fish in the sea. There has to be one out there who'd want me and who'd find my lifeplan appealing. It was the perfect plan, I was sure of it. I'd carefully developed it and worked towards accomplishing it for over a decade. It was a life journey a million guys would love to be a part of. Now all I had to do was find the right guy. The one who would stick. I ignored the specters that tried to rise up out of my past to haunt me with the misery I'd worked so hard to leave behind. *Not today, bad memories. Today, I am invincible and I will have fun.*

I walked into the other room, noticing that Candice and Kelly were both out on the balcony with drinks in their hands. I joined them, my breath momentarily taken from me as the intense heat of the day hit me full force. It felt like walking into an open oven set at four hundred and fifty degrees. I took Candice's drink from her hand. "Don't drink and cut hair, that's my motto." I took a big swig of it and nearly gagged, the alcohol setting my throat on fire.

Kelly laughed before lifting her glass in my direction and taking a long sip of her own cocktail.

"Holy crap," I said, my voice severely strained, "what was that? Lighter fluid? Did I just drink lighter fluid?" I breathed out several times loudly and held my hand up as a caution. "No one light a match. I'll blow up or combust or something."

Candice waved my concerns away. "That only happens if you hold in your gas. Come sit down." She gestured to the chair in front of her.

My hand froze in the middle of putting the glass to my lips again. I pulled it away. "Uhhhh, what?"

Kelly was standing very still too, a confused expression coming over her face.

"You heard me," said Candice, sounding very confident. "If you hold in your gas, if you don't break wind, you can spontaneously combust." She looked at us like we were the stupid ones. "It's a medical fact, look it up."

"Again. A reminder of how your talents were wasted by you not going into medicine." I shook my head in sheer amazement. "Where did you learn this particular fact, may I ask?"

"Why are you asking?" asked Kelly, sighing. "You know you're not going to like the answer."

"If you must know, I saw it on Southpark," said Candice, lifting her chin in the air.

"Southpark," I deadpanned. I lifted up a finger and pantomimed cleaning out my ear. "We're getting our scientific medical facts from Southpark episodes now?" Candice scared me often. This was one of those moments where I wondered how she got through a single day without getting herself run over by a car or a person on a bike. Or a toddler on a tricycle.

"Hey, say what you want, but they bring up a lot of real world situations on that show and deal with them in a way that gets people talking." She pushed on my shoulder. "Now sit. I have magic to do here." She lifted up a lock of my hair.

"Desperate times call for desperate measures."

"Desperate?" I said, feeling like I'd just fallen down the rabbit hole. Thank God she was better with hair than she was with medical knowledge or I'd be seriously screwed. I took another big swig of the firewater.

"Yes, desperate. With a capital D. You just got dumped by a dick-for-brains, you're in Vegas," she looked at her watch, "and it's eight o'clock and you're still sober." She put her fingers on the bottom of my glass and pushed it towards my face. "Drink up, sister of my heart. Relax and let Candice the Great make you beautiful. We're going to help you find a *new* man tonight. A hot one!" She giggled a little too crazily.

I put my hand out, taking Kelly's fingers in mine. "Pray for me, Kells."

"Our father who art in heaven...," she said, drowning out the rest of her sentence with swallows of her drink. Her eyes crossed as the liquid burned its way down her throat, but that didn't stop her from going for more of it just seconds later.

I closed my eyes and drank the rest of my cocktail *and* the second round of it that Kelly put in my glass, listening to the snip, snip, snip of Candice's scissors near my ears. I prayed I wouldn't look like Pink by the time she was done because I so looked like a little man when I had short hair.

My mind strayed to thoughts of Luke, the motions of Candice moving my hair around making me totally relaxed and zoned out. The cocktail might also have had something to do with that feeling of floating, but I didn't fight it.

Why had I continued dating that turd after he'd given me the liposuction gift certificate? And the cheating thing? A kiss isn't that big a deal, but I'd been thinking for a while that there'd been more than a kiss for him to confess. I'd never pushed him to tell me more because I hadn't wanted to know the truth. Why? Because the truth would have messed up my plans. My crazy plans. Was I so dead set on seeing them to fruition that I'd force any old guy into the mold? Apparently so. How depressing. I hadn't even told Kelly and Candice everything there was to tell about Luke. About all the times he made comments about my hips. About how he was always trying to convince me to go blonde and get a boob job. They hated him enough without me giving them more fuel for the fire. I felt like crying, thinking about how much of myself I'd lost over the last three years. I'd forgotten what it meant to be strong and spontaneous and fearless. I'd let Luke mow me over so that he wouldn't leave me. So that we could still get married and have kids. *God, how pitiful can I possibly be?*

I was jerked out of my reverie by Candice's proclamation. "And I'm spent!" she said, putting her scissors down on the table next to my chair. "Behold. The new and improved Andie Marks. Party Girl is in the hizzy house."

"Party palace," said Kelly, lifting up her drink. Her arm swayed a little unsteadily. "Party girl is in the party palace. This is a *palace.*" Her arm swept the space in front of her as she spun, making it unclear whether she was referring to the hotel room or Las Vegas itself.

I stood, a little unsteady on my feet. "Whoa. Dizzy."

"Get her another drink," said Candice, handing my glass to Kelly.

"One more cocktail, coming right up!" Kelly banged past my chair and into the hotel room.

"She'd better slow down or she's going to burn out before the fun really gets going," I said, stepping into the room behind her. "Am I supposed to dry this or something?" I asked, reaching up to feel my still-wet head.

"I'll blow it out for you, but you need to shower first. Get all that hair off you and then you can change into what you're wearing tonight. I'll finish with a quick blow and then we can go to dinner."

I looked down at my jeans and flowy blouse. "I thought

this was what I was wearing."

Candice tsk-tsked at me. "No, no, no-no-no, you are not wearing that Bohemian get-up out for a night out on the town. No. A dress. A tight black one. And heels."

"But I didn't bring one." I pouted, feeling like Cinderella surrounded by well-dressed step-sisters.

"Not to worry. I brought back-up," said Candice. "I'll put something together for you while you're in the shower, don't worry."

I looked right at her chest. "I'm not going to fit into your clothes, Candice. Not unless I stuff an entire roll of toilet paper in my bra which I'm not going to do so don't even try it." I pointed a threatening finger at her and narrowed my gaze, just so she'd know how much I meant it. I wouldn't put it past her to try and force me to stuff my bra. She'd done it before in college, and the wet t-shirt contest that had sprung up spontaneously at the party we'd been attending hadn't ended well. I was scarred for life, in fact. I could never look at a wad of toilet paper again without seeing soggy boobs falling out of my t-shirt and landing on the ground at my feet.

"Just go shower and leave the details to me, okay?" Her smile was way too dangerous for comfort, but I suddenly realized I had to pee, so I left her standing there with her nefarious plans in favor of emptying my bladder.

"I'm not going to stuff my bra with toilet paper. I'm not," I mumbled as I made my way to the toilet.

# Chapter Six

"YOU MADE ME COME ALL this way and you didn't think to make hotel reservations?" Mack shook his head at his little brother. Ian's two friends were standing just behind him, too engrossed with checking scantily clad women walking by to care about not having a room to stay in for the night.

"How was I supposed to know the place was going to be so packed?" Ian scowled, hitching up his bag onto his shoulder uncomfortably. "There's like a thousand hotels in this town."

"Well, come on," said Mack, moving his hat around on his head a little. It was a nervous gesture this time, not just a sweaty, itchy head. "Let's at least see if we can talk one of these bellhops into looking after our bags while we get some grub."

Thirty minutes later they were sitting at a table for four, diving into plates piled high with all-you-can-eat buffet finds. Their bags were locked in a small room just behind the reservation desk, and the ticket to retrieve them rested safely under Mack's hat.

"Man, I ain't never seen so much food in one place in all my life," said Bo, Ian's best friend since grade school.

"That's cuz you've never been outside Baker your entire life," said Ian. "They have buffets like this all over Portland."

He shoveled a huge mouthful of potato salad in his mouth, not letting it get in the way of his conversation. "See, the difference is, here in Vegas? They got all kinds of food, like seafood, steaks, Indian food, vegetarian garbage. Anyone can come to Vegas and have a good time." He glanced up at his brother before spearing a hunk of beef. "Even Mack."

Ian's friends snickered.

"Laugh it up, boys, but I came here to do some business. I got plans." Mack took a bite of his overcooked steak and cringed. "Jesus Mary and Joseph, this meat is like jerky. Remember that jerky you made with Mom that one year, with the deer meat?" He poked the lump of meat he wasn't going to finish. "This stuff is worse."

"Oh, I remember that," said Dillon, Ian's other friend. "The dog wouldn't even eat it."

Mack pushed his plate away and drained his beer. "I have a date at the blackjack tables. Move it," he said to Dillon, elbowing him in the ribs.

"Aren't you gonna wait for us?" asked Ian, looking first at his brother and then at his half-full plate.

"You kidding? If I know you, you still have at least three more trips to the buffet before you're done. If I start now, I'll be up a grand before you're done with dessert."

Ian snorted. "Fine, mister high roller, go on with your badass self. After we're done tearin' up the buffet, we'll come find you. Just don't leave the casino here in the hotel." He stabbed his fork into five layers of various foods and stuffed them into his mouth, his cheeks bulging with the effort of chewing it all.

"I wouldn't dream of it," Mack said, standing and throwing some cash on the table. "Dinner's on me. Save room for beers. I'll see you at the tables."

He strolled away, tipping his best cowboy hat back a little on his head as he made his way to the blackjack pit.

# Chapter Seven

A DINNER OF SALAD AND a single breadstick wasn't exactly a gourmet meal, but with this tight black dress on and the stupid gel-filled boob propper-uppers Candice had forced into my bra, there was no way to fit a normal dinner into my belly, even if I'd wanted to. Thing was, though, I was too nervous to eat that much anyway. I found the firey liquid diet I'd been feeding myself since the haircut was more to my taste right now.

"God, all I had was a stupid salad and I feel like I'm going to bust a seam on this thing." I was walking on higher heels than I was used to, thanks to Kelly and her having the same size foot as me. "You guys conspired against me with this outfit, and don't think I'm going to forget it easily, either. We have at least two more bachelorette parties to plan in the future and revenge *will* be my bitch when that time comes." I flicked my hair back, trying not to smile. The haircut really did make me feel beautiful. It was totally Jennifer Anniston, and both Kelly and Candice said I was pulling it off well.

"What's she whining about now?" asked Candice, putting on lipstick using her tiny purse compact.

Kelly hiccuped. "I'm not sure, but I think she's complaining about the shoes again. Or maybe the dress. I can't keep track. I lost my brain about an hour and three margaritas ago." She rubbed her stomach and grimaced. "Can I go to bed now?"

"No, you can't go to bed." Candice snapped her compact shut and dropped it into her small handbag. "We're just getting started." She rubbed her hands together. "Okay, girlies, where to first? Poker? Slots? Craps?"

"Do you have to go to the potty? Because I do too. Good idea." Kelly tried to take Candice by the hand but Candice shook her off.

"What are you talking about? No one said anything about going to the bathroom."

Kelly frowned at her while I laughed silently. I loved watching my harebrained buddies try to have a grown-up conversation. The several cocktails I'd consumed since my haircut was making it even more amusing than usual.

"You said you were going to crap, so call me crazy, but in my world, that means we need to find a toilet." She smirked at Candice and then looked at me, rolling her eyes.

"If you had a functioning brain cell right now, you'd be dangerous," said Candice. "I said *do you want to play craps*, not *I have to go take a crap*. Jesus, I don't even use that word. You know I wouldn't say that, what's wrong with you?"

I decided to rescue my poor tipsy friend before she got too much dizzier trying to figure out what Candice was talking about. "Craps is a game, sweetie. Gambling. Where you throw the dice across the table and that guy has that hockey stick he uses to push and pull chips around? Like on TV where the guy's on a roll making a bunch of money and everyone's standing around cheering for him while he throws the dice?"

Seconds ticked by and then a virtual lightbulb went on over Kelly's head. "Ooooohhh, you mean the gaaaame craps. That makes waaaay more sense. It's true … you never say crap unless you're around people you want to impress and then you say that word instead of saying shit."

"No, I don't," said Candice, looking miffed or maybe a little embarrassed.

"Yes, you do," said Kelly, completely oblivious to Candice's mood change. "Okay, let's play this crap thing. This crappy crapper craps game." She giggled.

Candice rolled her eyes. "Do I want to get her another drink, Andie?"

"Yes and no," I said. "Yes, because it's her bachelorette party and yes we want her to get good and hungover later so she never forgets this trip and how much fun it is to be single … and no, because I hate it when people barf. It makes *me* barf when I see it. And if she drinks too much more…"

"…she's gonna barf," Candice finished for me.

"Exactly."

"Waitress!" yelled Candice, running after a barmaid with a tray.

Kelly and I watched her go. "What's she doing?" Kelly asked.

"Getting us drunk."

"Aren't we already drunk?" she asked, scratching her head.

I smoothed down the hair that was sticking up as a result of her confusion. "You are and I'm nearly there. But this is your party, little sis, so you must drink until you fall over or until you kiss a stranger."

Kelly looked at me in horror. "I did *not* come to Las Vegas to cheat on Matty!"

"Then you better start drinking," I said, handing her one of the cocktails Candice brought over.

"How'd you get these so fast?" I asked her, looking down into the glass, wondering if I was drinking something she found next to a slot machine.

"What can I say? Cleavage works." Candice raised her glass high. "Here's to winning big tonight and possibly getting laid in Vegas!"

"Here's to getting married!" said Kelly, raising her glass.

"Here's to getting getting married *and* laid in Vegas!" I said, clinking all of their glasses and downing my drink in one, giant, three-swallow gulp session.

Candice looked at Kelly. "Do you think she knows what she just did?"

"Nope." Kelly giggled, sipping on her straw.

"Shut up, buttheads. You know what I meant." As if I'd drink to getting married in Vegas. *Shuh, right.* That totally didn't fit into my lifeplan *or* my personality.

As soon as I finished my drink and put the glass down on a nearby shelf, we locked arms and walked into the casino area of the hotel. Having my girlfriends on either arm made walking in Kelly's ferocious heels way easier, so I was all for it, even though it made quite the barrier for people trying to get by. Whenever anyone scowled at us, I smiled big and said, "She's getting married. To a mortician. This is her going away party," and they'd turn their frowns upside down. It was like Vegas magic or something. It was impossible to be cranky here.

As we left the restaurants and lobby behind, we entered a darker area of the huge facility. The casino. Bells were dinging all over the place, lights of every single color of the rainbow were flashing and blinking, and thousands of people milled around. There were slot machines in groups with small passageways between them to get by and chairs filled with butts. People were dropping quarters like there was no tomorrow, pulling one-armed bandits as fast as the money clanged into place.

A group of tables were across the aisle from the slot machine section, all of them with green felt on top. The very first thing I noticed when we walked in that direction was a cowboy hat. And it had the most beautiful man I had ever seen sitting right under it.

"Oh. My. Good. Ness," I said, caught in some kind of

tractor beam, unable to look away. My foot lifted up, trying to walk that direction, but Candice held me back.

"I don't feel so good," said Kelly, pulling away from me. I let her go without a thought.

"Oh, shit." Candice let go of me too, leaving me to wobble a little on my own. "Come on, Kelly, come with me. I don't want you to barf on their nice carpet. Please don't yack. I hate it when you yack, you're so loud about it."

My brain barely registered what they were saying. I only had eyes for the god sitting on the stool just twenty feet away from me. *Jeans, dress shirt, cowboy hat, five o'clock shadow beard, muscles visible just below his rolled up cuffs, bronzed like he spent most of the day outside.* "Be still my heart," I said, talking to no one, to the wind, to the goddess of love who I was pretty sure had just shot an arrow into my chest cavity. I reached up and touched my hair, hoping it was perfect.

"Stay here while I take care of her," ordered Candice, her voice getting fainter as she got farther away. "I don't want you watching her and getting sick too or my whole night will be ruined."

"Yeah, okay," I said absently, walking towards the card table so I could get a closer look at the cowboy who'd taken my breath away and sent my brain on a vacation to Mars.

A cocktail waitress walked up to me when I was almost there and offered me a drink that someone had paid for but never picked up. I nodded and drank half of it down before I got to the table, hoping it was an offering from the gods, concocted specifically for the purpose of giving me the courage I'd need to say hello to this mystery man. He looked like he'd just stepped out of a magazine ad for Levis or a Bowflex or something.

I was nearly to his spot at the table when the toe of my borrowed heel caught something on the carpet and sent me flying forward. I watched in horror as my hand went out to help find my balance, sending the contents of my glass out in a stream right at the man who'd stepped out of my lustiest of dreams.

# Chapter Eight

I HALF STUMBLED, HALF RAN over to fix things. *Oh my god, oh my god, what have I done!* The former contents of my drink were now dripping off the top of his hat and down his cheek and into his shirt. He'd stood up and was staring down at himself in shock.

"Holy shit, I am *so* sorry. Oh my god, what did I do?! Oh my god..." I grabbed a bunch of cocktail napkins off the table, nearly spilling other people's drinks in my haste, using them to dab at his amazing, gorgeous, weather-lined face. He was even better-looking up close, which seconds ago I would have said would be impossible.

When he lifted his gaze to look at me, I nearly had a heart attack. I dropped the napkins with a plop onto his cowboy boots. It would have made Candice proud, the high register that I hit with my girly squeal. "Eeep!" *Those eyes!* They glowed out from under his hat a sky blue so bright they looked as if they were illuminated from inside his head.

"I'd say the drink is on me, but that would be way too corny and cliché," he said, his voice almost lazy the way it came out. But I barely heard what he was saying because his glowing blue eyes were piercing my soul or something. I'd never seen anything like them in my life. I could look at him all day long and never get tired of it.

43

"Huh?"

I cringed inwardly as soon as the syllable slid past my lips. The oratory skills that served me so well in the courtroom had abandoned me entirely. I doubted at this point whether I'd be able to string a coherent sentence together. His beauty combined with his slow-talking cowboy sexiness had completely robbed me of any intelligence. The drinks probably weren't helping.

"Never mind." He took his hat from his head and shook it a little off to the side, droplets of my former drink flying off to land on the carpet. His hair was longish, the ends curling up at his neck, which really surprised me. I'd been expecting a crew cut or a big bald spot under that hat to spoil the effect, to make him seem more human and not so supernaturally gorgeous ... but no such luck. He was *that* beautiful, managing to make every other man in the place look like dog meat. Every single one of them instantly ceased to exist for me, just like the memories of that guy I'd been dating for three years who'd broken up with me by text on my way out here. *What was his name again? Puke, I think?*

I looked down and noticed a wet spot on the front of the cowboy's jeans and all down the front of his shirt, and suddenly felt the desperate need to help. I'd caused this problem. I'd ruined his night. And if the stacks of chips in front of him were any clue, he'd been doing pretty well.

I grabbed the pile of cocktail napkins that the dealer had put down at his place and dabbed the whole wad of them first on his shirt and then on the front of his pants.

"I am *so* sorry. I have no idea what my problem is. Well, that's not true, I do know what my problem is." I snorted in disgust. "I'm wearing these ridiculous heels, which I knew were a mistake the first time I saw them, but against my better judgment, I put them on anyway." I was busy pounding away on his crotch, trying to soak up the alcohol, not really thinking about what I was doing, so wrapped up in my nightmare of a life. "I knew this was a mistake, I knew Vegas was going to be a problem. I don't know why I let people talk me into things like this all the time."

He grabbed my wrist and halted my movements. I stopped in mid stream-of-consciousness brain vomit and looked up at him.

"I think you'd better stop now."

"What?" I was totally confused.

He looked down at his crotch, still holding onto my wrist.

I followed his gaze and nearly had another heart attack. There was a distinct bulge going down the leg of his pants that hadn't been there before.

# Chapter Nine

"OH MY GOD, I'M *SO* sorry. Holy shit." I dropped the napkins on his boots again, my face going up in flames. I jerked my eyes to the ceiling, ready to cry with humiliation. I'd practically given him a hand job in front of no less than a hundred people. Someone nearby snickered. I decided a prayer to the universe was my only recourse. It couldn't possibly make things worse. "Floor, if you will please swallow me now, I promise to dedicate myself to feeding the homeless for the rest of my miserable life."

A hand gently grasped my upper arm. It was warm and big, the fingers going all the way around. "No need to sacrifice yourself to the Vegas gods on my account," said the cowboy. "I'll be fine. I'm just going to go wash up." He leaned in close to my ear and whispered, "Watch my chips for me, would you? I'm on a roll and I don't want to leave just yet."

I nodded, sitting down in the chair he'd vacated, staring at his wide back and trim waist as he walked away. *Holy shit, is this really happening?* I sat up straighter, turning to face the dealer. I picked up a few of the chips, reading the amounts on their faces. Assuming my math brain hadn't completely abandoned me in my moment of crisis and had allowed me to calculate correctly, there was over a thousand dollars sitting in front of me, and the cowboy had just walked away and left it with me. *Is he crazy? Am I being punked? No, I can't be in the middle of being punked when it's my own fault that I'm in this situation.*

I looked down at my feet. My *aching* feet. The heels were the problem. *They* were the cause of my complete humiliation. Not only did I let men run all over me in my pitiful life, I let my girlfriends do it, too. Kelly and Candice had insisted my practical heels were totally impractical in Vegas. The whole idea made me feel angry and sad and reckless all at the same time. I reached down and pulled the torture devices off, letting them drop to the floor beneath the stool. *Ha! Let that be a lesson to you, Kelly! I'm leaving them here! I will not wear heels that hurt my feet ever again! This is the new Andie taking over! No more railroading. No more bossing me around. No more telling me what to do.*

"Are you in or out?" asked the dealer. "If you don't place your bet you're going to have to leave the table."

My mouth dropped open as he stared at me. "Are you talking to me?" I squeaked out.

"Yes, I'm talking to you." He glanced at the chips in front of me. "This is a ten dollar minimum table."

So much for people not telling me what to do anymore. I picked up a couple chips, my fingers not really wanting to cooperate. Could I spend the cowboy's money while he was in the bathroom cleaning up my mess? Wouldn't that violate every rule of socially acceptable behavior ever written?

I put two chips down on the table, mimicking the actions of the person on my right. I had no idea how much money it was. The old man to my left gave me a smile, revealing perfectly straight dentures and bright pink gums. "Ever play blackjack before?" he asked.

"No. Never." I should have been scared out of my wits, probably. Gambling wasn't my thing and spending other people's money felt ten times wrong. But something about being here in this neon-glitzy place, my shoes off and my boobs pushed up to my neck made be feel bold. Daring. Ready to grab the world by the balls and make it beg for mercy. *Rawr.*

"Just get as close to twenty-one as you can without going over," he instructed.

"Sounds easy," I said, picking up my first card. I showed it to him. "Is this a good one?"

He nodded and leaned over to whisper in my ear. "Soft hand."

I held out my fingers in front of me, smiling. "Thank you. I use hand cream to keep them moisturized."

"Not your hand, the card. That's an ace ... possibility of a soft hand. It's worth either one or eleven, you can decide which. If you get a ten or higher - any of the face cards - you win. You get a return of a hundred and fifty percent of your bet." He glanced at the table. "You've put down two hundred dollars, so that could net you three hundred."

I stopped breathing for a few seconds as the blood drained out of my face. My voice came out an octave higher than usual. "I just bet two hundred dollars?"

He chuckled, flashing me more of the dentures. "That you did."

I looked around the casino, hoping the cowboy wouldn't come back and see the huge pile of money I was playing with. *Why didn't I look at the chips closer? Why didn't I check them first?*

"Insurance anyone?" asked the dealer.

I felt the blood drain out of my face even more. I was a ghost now. "Insurance?" My voice came out as a whisper.

"Dealer has an ace. He's giving you a chance to bet a little extra on the side. It pays two to one. If he gets a face card next, he wins automatically, so this can help offset your losses. You can bet up to half of what you have on the table right now."

"He wins, even if I get blackjack too?"

"No, then it's a push.   But you'd lose your insurance money, so you'd lose net."

"Should I do it?" I asked.

He shrugged.   "I can't tell you if you should or not. Gotta do what your gut's telling you." He examined his own cards and shook his head at the call for insurance.

"My gut's telling me to run and lock myself in the bathroom."

The old man shook his head.   "Better not.   Your boyfriend will lose his spot at the table and this dealer's treating him right.   He'll be taking a break in the next twenty minutes or so and then your boyfriend'll miss out on his run for good."

I gritted my teeth together and took a deep breath in through my nose, trying to ignore the spinning of the room. Too many cocktails. So little time. "Okay, fine. I can be bold. I can be dangerous." I shook my head at the dealer, trying to keep my game face on. "No insurance.   But thank you for offering.   That was very nice."

The dealer gave me a small smile.   "Rules of the house. I don't make 'em, I just play by 'em." He was kinda cute.

"Oh."   My face went red. Total rookie move. I slouched a little in my seat.

A cocktail waitress came up and stopped next to my chair. "Cocktail?"

"Oh, I don't have any money right now," I said.  I'd left my wallet and credit card in Candice's purse.

"They're on the house as long as you're playing."   She gave me a bored look.

"Well, okay then.  If they're free bring one for me and my friend." I winked at the man next to me and he nodded back. "Gin and tonic for me and …"

"Make it two," said my neighbor.

The dealer gave everyone else a second card.  He lifted

up the corners of own cards and then put them down, looking at the man farthest to my right expectantly.

The old man let out a hiss of air.

"What? What just happened?" I asked, looking at the dealer and then the old man again.

"Dealer doesn't have a ten or higher on that second card. Your bet is safe for now."

I watched the people around the table. They were all peeking at their second card and frowning.

I did the same, trying to mimic their technique of only bending up the very corner of the cards. Next to my ace sat another ace. My heart began pounding wildly. *What does this mean? Twenty-two? That can't be good. Twelve? That sounds too low.*

"Help," I whispered, wishing the gods of poker were on my shoulders in miniature, whispering in my ear and telling me what to do.

"What you got?" asked the old man, sounding amused as he leaned towards me a little.

I lifted up my cards so he could see them. "I think it's bad news," I said, dreading his response. I'd just blown two hundred bucks of someone else's money. I had to find an ATM machine, stat, so I could replace it before he found out. I had to find Candice and get my stuff! I looked around, but she and Kelly were nowhere in sight.

He let out a long whistle. "You need to split."

I jumped off the chair and looked around. "Okay," I said, wringing my hands, trying to figure out where to go and whether I should take all the chips with me or just abandon them to my shame.

He put his hand on my arm. "What are you doing? Take your seat."

I looked at him confused. "But you told me to take off."

He laughed, his round belly jiggling under his shirt. "No, missy, I told you to *split*, not take off. Split your cards into two separate hands and play them separately."

"What?" I slowly climbed back up onto the stool, not any less confused but at least reasonably sure I wasn't supposed to run off for the toilets or my room.

"You can choose to turn one hand into two. You have to double your bet, but in your case, it might be worth it."

I swallowed hard. "You mean, bet four hundred dollars instead of two hundred?" *Dollars. Of this stranger's money. Jesus, what the hell am I doing?*

"Yep." He looked at his own cards again. "You need to decide what you're going to do before you miss your turn." The old man nodded at the dealer.

I looked up to find the dealer staring at me expectantly.

"Um ... I ... uh ... need to split." My face was on fire. I needed a drink bad. Running to the bathrooms was sounding like a really good idea right now.

The dealer nodded. "Two hundred dollars."

I searched through my chips, turning them over and reading their faces. Once I realized they were color-coded, I found two more like the ones I already had out and put them on the table. The dealer reached over and split my two cards apart, putting two chips by each single card. He sent out another round of cards, and now I had four cards in front of me. I noticed the man to my right tickled the top of the table with his index finger and the dealer threw him a card. Then the man floated his hands above his cards and shook his head.

The dealer was back to staring at me.

I stared back, now getting a little irritated at him. "What?"

"Do you want me to hit you?" he asked.

I looked at him aghast, wondering what rule I'd broken so badly I needed to be physically abused over it. "*No,* I don't want you to hit me. Do you want me to hit *you?*" I stood up, ready to defend myself. This was the worst customer service

I'd ever experienced in my entire life. He was probably pissed off that I had half the aces.

The old man put his hand on my arm. "He wants to know if you want another card. That's a hit."

All the fight club went out of me in a big wave, leaving behind humiliation in its wake. This was worse than losing toilet paper boobs in a wet t-shirt contest. I sat back on my stool, pulling my dress down my thighs a little to keep from exposing my panties. "Oh. Sorry about that. I apologize for threatening you. Yes, please, I'd like a card for both of them."

"You need to give him a signal, not just words. Big Brother is watching," said the old man, pointing to a security camera inside a black globe on the ceiling. "People who lose like to claim later they said *stay* instead of *hit*, so they want to see your intentions really clearly."

I smacked a fist into my other hand. "Hit me."

The dealer laughed and looked away for a second, like he was collecting himself.

The old man chuckled too. "Just tap your finger on the table. No need to punch anyone."

"Oh." Another rookie move. I probably should have been more embarrassed about it, but the cocktails were easing the sting. I tickled the table with my fingers, once near each card pile.

The dealer nodded and threw two cards down. Somehow he was able to flick them right to where they needed to be, even while his hands barely moved. He was like a magician. And he was staring at me again. It made me want to growl at him.

"Look at the cards," said my helpful friend. "Try to get as close to twenty-one as you can."

I lifted up the card on my right side. It was a king. "How much is this?"

"That's ten. You need to stay."

I smiled. "Oh, I plan on staying, believe me. I have to

watch these chips 'til that cowboy guy gets back."

"No, I mean, you have to tell the dealer that you don't need anymore cards on that stack. Tell him you're staying with a hand signal."

"What's the signal?" I asked.

The old man waved a flat palm across the table, like he was trying to make something levitate off it.

I copied his motion.

The dealer nodded and then looked at my next stack. I followed his gaze and then jumped a little in my seat, realizing I had to look at the cards myself. I picked them up and saw a two as my newest addition.

The old man frowned. "You can either stay or ask for a hit."

"What should I do?" I felt the stress level rising. The glow from my earlier win was fading fast, and I hadn't even had a chance to celebrate it properly yet. I was pretty sure a victory dance was called for in this situation, considering I'd just won like three hundred bucks. That's an hour's worth of my time as a lawyer and I'd done it in five minutes without having to do any legal research. No wonder people liked going to Vegas.

"I can't tell you what you should do. Just consider that if the dealer busts, any hand that isn't already busted is a winner."

"Busted?"

"Over twenty one," he clarified.

"Oh. Okay." I counted up my card values. I had either thirteen or three. Neither sounded close enough to twenty one. "Okay, I want you to hit me." I stared at the dealer, waiting for him to comply. He stared at me like I hadn't just talked directly to him.

The old man nudged me. "Hand signals. Big brother. Remember?"

The guy to my right said nothing, but he demonstrated

the table tickle for my benefit all the same.

I wiggled three of my fingers on the table, like I was tickling the felt too. The old man chuckled and the dealer smiled. "That works," he said, throwing a card down on my second pile.

I lifted the corner. *Five. That makes seven plus the eleven. Eighteen.* I looked at the old man. "That looks pretty good to me."

He nodded, all seriousness now. "Looks pretty good to me too."

I waved my hand over the table. "I'm staying put, right here. Don't hit me anymore. I've had enough hitting."

I felt a presence behind me just moments before the heat of a large body standing very close came through my dress. I looked over my shoulder and saw the arresting good looks of the cowboy. I grinned, hoping my charm would keep him from being angry over the amount of money on the table.

He smiled back. "Looks like you've been busy." He lifted an eyebrow at me and then looked pointedly at the table.

# Chapter Ten

MY NIPPLES GOT HARD UNDER my dress and a zing of something electric went right down to my the space between my legs. I was too flustered to come up with anything even mildly intelligent in response. "Yes. Busy learning blackjack."

"Your girlfriend's a quick study," said the old man. He motioned the dealer for a hit. When he looked at his card he frowned and then flipped them both over.

I counted them up, letting the girlfriend comment just breeze on by. "Busted," I said, very sad that he'd lost. I pouted in his honor.

The dealer swooped up his cards and his money.

The old man nodded. "Busted, indeed." He stood and motioned to his chair while looking at the cowboy. "I'm done. Good luck to you both."

I spun around, my legs brushing up against the cowboy. I tried to ignore the way that simple touch was making my pulse hammer in my veins. "You're leaving?"

"Yep. Time to call it a day."

"Aw, that's a bummer. But thank you so much for your help." I hopped off the stool and grabbed him in a hug. He totally reminded me of my grandpa who'd died three years earlier.

He patted my back. "It was my pleasure, Lady Luck. Have a nice evening." He shook the cowboy's hand. "Take care of her. She's got lots of potential."

"I'll do what I can," said the cowboy, nodding once.

I watched my mentor walk away, wondering what he meant by that. It sounded nice. I liked the idea of having a lot of potential. There were people who'd known me for years who'd never say such a thing about me, but they weren't allowed to ruin my night. Not tonight. I pushed their ghosts out of my head.

The cowboy held the back of the stool I'd been saving for him. "Are you staying?" he asked.

I stood there, my face suddenly flaming red and my body screaming for more of him than just a blackjack partner or victim of my clutziness. *What the hell.* "Sure. I have to finish this game, right?"

He nodded. "Take this seat." He motioned at the one with his chips in front of it.

I took it, feeling the sweat break out under my arms when he claimed the seat recently vacated by my busted buddy.

"Do you want to see my cards? Your cards, actually?" I asked. I fingered the chips in front of me for a few seconds and then jerked my hands away, resting them in my lap.

"Hands on the table, please," said the dealer, frowning at me.

I threw them up to rest on the padded bar in front of the pile of chips, afraid I was about to get arrested for attempted cheating.

The cowboy lifted up first the cards on the left and then the ones on the right. He whistled his appreciation. "Well done, Lady Luck."

He was close enough that I could smell him. For the first time in all the years I'd known Candice, I fully appreciated her habit of leaning in to inhale people's scents. I wanted to get his man-scent up into my brain. It was doing something to me that I'd never experienced before.

*Pheromones.* My eyes widened. I was totally being drugged by this guy's manliness. How easy can a girl get? Maybe that should have offended my feminist self, but all it did was make me want to bury my nose in his neck. I glanced at him, biting my bottom lip in consideration. Am I tipsy enough to do it? He was leaning over looking at the cards, and it would be so easy.

I bent at the waist just the slightest bit and closed my eyes, inhaling deeply but slowly so he wouldn't hear it. When I opened my eyes, his face was just a few inches from mine.

"Are you okay?" he asked, humor tipping up the corners of his luscious mouth.

"Uhhh ... yeah. Are you okay?" I looked down at his crotch. "Did you take care of yourself in the bathroom okay?" Half a second later I choked on my own tongue. *Did I actually just say that?*

He chuckled softly. "I got my pants as dry as I could, all considered, if that's what you mean."

I nodded, afraid to speak at this point. Who knew what would come flying out of my mouth next. I was dangerous with this many cocktails in me.

The dealer distracted me from my embarrassment, turning over our hands and paying out or taking money. I looked at his cards. He had an ace, a three, and an eight. I counted furiously in my head. *Eleven, three, that's fourteen plus eight that's ... twenty-one? No! Twenty-two! Is it twenty-two?* I looked at the cowboy. "What's that mean?" I asked, pointing to the dealer's cards.

"He busted. Anyone not over twenty one wins, and you get a little extra for having blackjack."

I watched as the dealer pushed a pile of chips over in my direction. "Congratulations," he said. "Must be beginner's luck."

My mouth dropped open. "That's ... six hundred dollars," I whispered. I'd never won any money in my entire life. Every penny in my bank account was hard-earned.

"I hope you'll stay," said the cowboy, pulling six chips out from in front of me to put on the table. He put three in front of my spot and three in front of his.

"I don't have any money," I said. I'd left all my cash with Candice and it sure wasn't six hundred bucks.

He looked at the pile in front of me. "Sure looks like you do."

I smiled, my jaw a little off kilter as it dropped open. If this was his flirting game, I had to give him credit. It was original, even though it did feel a tiny bit like solicitation of prostitution. "That's your money, not mine."

He shrugged. "It's play money. Win or lose, the goal is to have a good time."

"Oh, I can have a good time in Vegas, trust me. And it doesn't even take a lot of money either." The cocktail waitress walked up with a tray and two drinks.

"Where's your friend?" she asked, looking at the faces around the table.

"He left. But I'll take his drink," I said, moving back so she could put them on the table in front of me.

"I'll take a Bud on your next trip by," said Mack.

She gave him a sexy smile and cocked her hip out at him. It irritated me more than I wanted to admit. "Coming right up. Can I get you anything else to go with that Bud?"

He looked right at me. "I have everything I need right here, thanks."

My throat closed up at the innuendo I prayed was coming out of his mouth. But he couldn't possibly be talking about me. The only thing he knew about me was that I was a klutzy chick who liked to spend his money. Not the best makings of a girlfriend candidate.

I wanted to slap my own face with the direction my mind was going. *Girlfriend material? What the hell is wrong with you? You're in Vegas for chrissake! Get control of yourself. Tonight is not the night for lifeplan action. But a one night stand? Maybe ...* I sat up straighter and looked at the table, lifting up my card at the corner.

He turned to face the table, but leaned a little closer to me than the stool would normally allow. "You okay?"

I looked at him, surprised to find his face so close again. I wasn't complaining at all, though. He had a pretty damn fine face, after all. "No, I'm great. Why?"

He smiled a slow, lazy smile that lit me on fire. "You look a little nervous."

I blew out a huff of air. "It's because you're too damn good looking." The second the words left my mouth I heard them and cringed inwardly. "Did I just say that out loud?"

"I'm not sure. What was it you thought you said?" he asked. He was teasing me. I could hear the smile in his voice, but I couldn't look at him. Then my humiliation would be complete.

I took a big breath for courage. "I am having a bit of a hard time acting like an intelligent human being with you sitting so close to me." I was losing my breath, and there was nothing I could do about it short of asking for oxygen or leaving his presence, and I definitely wasn't ready to do that yet. Talk about potential. This guy had the potential to be my Vegas fling. The wild and crazy sex Candice had talked about on the plane. The forget-Luke-and-move-on man. I looked at him really quick and then faced forward again. *Could I have sex with this guy? A total stranger who I know nothing about? Who I'll never see again? Whose name I don't even know?*

"My name's Mack, by the way. What's yours?"

Panic mode, level eight. *What is he? A mind reader? Okay, scratch the not-knowing-his-name part. The question is, could I have a one-night stand with a man named Mack who wears a cowboy hat to a casino?* He put his forearms on the table as he looked at his cards and waited for my answer. They showed lean muscles under tanned skin and golden highlighted arm hair sprinkling the surface enough to make me wonder what he had going on under his shirt. *Yes. I can definitely do this.*

I looked at him. He caught my eye and smiled at me, revealing just the slightest dimple in his left cheek ... and it was all over for any self control I might have possessed before coming to Vegas. "My name is Andrea, but my friends call me Andie."

"Andie it is, then." He draped his arm across the back of my chair, standing so he could get closer to me. "What are you going to do, Andie? Hit or stay?" He wasn't even looking at the cards. His piercing blue eyes were staring into mine, possibly daring me to take a challenge.

I didn't even look at my cards. "I could do either one right now and it would make me really happy." The thrill that ran up my spine was nothing compared to the electricity that jolted my entire body when he leaned towards me and put his face near my ear. His breath tickled my skin as he spoke.

"I meant on the table."

I smiled, the devil in me taking over. "Wherever, whatever. It's your call."

He tipped his head back and laughed, rubbing his hat on his head a few times while he grinned like a madman. "You're somethin' else, Andie, you know that?" He took the cocktail from the waitress who'd shown up behind us and handed it to me. I had three drinks now and I planned to drink every one of them. Once he'd gotten his beer and tipped the girl a few dollars, he raised his bottle in my direction.

"Here's to getting lucky in Vegas."

I grinned like a crazy fool. "I'll drink to that." I clanked my glass against his bottle so hard some of the drink sloshed out. He backed up really quick, pointing a finger at me. "You're dangerous. If I didn't know better, I'd think you were trying to get me all wet again."

I shrugged, sipping my drink as innocently as possible. Then my mouth opened up and more ridiculousness came out. "Turnabout's fair play."

He didn't say anything but he lifted an eyebrow. And I noticed for the next three hands of blackjack, all of which we both won, he got closer and closer to me, until I was turned sideways and one of his thighs was in between mine. If I scooted any closer to the edge of the stool, I'd be humping his leg, but I totally didn't care. I didn't even worry about where my friends were or what was taking them so long to find me. I knew Candice would return eventually, even if she had to put Kelly down for the night upstairs first. And I felt more than confident that Mack would take care of me until they came back. If I were being honest, I'd admit that while I waited for my friends' return, I sent up a few prayers to the goddess of love, begging that Candice not be able to find me for a really long time.

# Chapter Eleven

MACK GRABBED MOST OF THE chips in front of us and put them in a plastic cup with the casino's logo on it. He flipped a chip worth twenty dollars at the dealer. "You ready to get outta here?" He sounded surprisingly sober considering how many beers he'd drunk.

"But what about these ones?" I asked, touching to the ones he was leaving behind.

"Those are yours."

*He must be confused. Or maybe he's drunker than he looks.* I felt a little panicked when I realized maybe it wasn't confusion or beers ... maybe he didn't know that I'd been using his chips all along. I looked at the twelve hundred dollars of multi-colored chips in front of me. "Those aren't mine, they're yours. I kind of ... took some of your chips in that first round. I'm sorry ... I panicked. They said you'd lose your seat." I grimaced at him, wondering if I'd just blown my chance at a roll in the proverbial hay with the sexiest cowboy this side of the Mississippi.

"You won 'em fair and square. Let's just say I backed you for a little while, 'til you got on your feet."

I bit my lower lip as I considered whether I should insist that he take the money. I soon realized sitting still and concentrating like that was a mistake, though; the room was spinning way too much for well-reasoned, rational arguments. I decided it was more prudent to focus my energies on walking a straight line instead of denying any right to the money. I'd lost count of how many free cocktails I'd drunk in the last hour that we'd been playing, but I knew from the way the gambling pit was going round and round that I'd imbibed a couple too many. I stacked the chips up and fit them into the palm of my hand. Twelve hundred dollars was surprisingly light. "Thank you, cowboy. That's incredibly generous of you." I grinned like a drunk fool, which is exactly what I was. "I'll just have to find a way to pay you back, I guess."

"Come on, let's go get some fresh air," he said, holding out a bent elbow for me.

"Is that what they're calling it these days?" I asked sliding off the stool, and shoving my hand through the hole at his side. I only punched him in the ribs a little. It was when my feet hit solid ground and I got a better hold on my dizziness that I realized what a dork I sounded like. Talk about a mood-breaker. "I did it again, didn't I?" I asked, sighing. So much for the sexy black dress and the Jennifer hairstyle.

"Did what? I didn't notice you doing anything. Do you want to put your shoes on?" He pointed to the spot under my stool where Kelly's shoes lay in a small, spikey pile.

"If by saying shoes you mean the Devil's torture devices down there, then no. I definitely don't want to put them on." I frowned at the way-too-high heels, wondering how much trouble I'd be in if I just left them there.

He leaned over and grabbed them, crossing them over in the middle and holding onto them with his free hand. "How about I wrangle them for you 'til you feel like putting them back on?"

"Good plan. I should probably go up to my room and change into something more practical anyway."

"You're staying here? In the hotel?" He stopped, a few feet away from the blackjack table, causing me to bump into him.

"Yup. In a bitchin' suite."

"Humph."

"Aren't you?"

"Nope." He didn't offer any further explanation and I didn't ask for one. It didn't matter anyway, right? No need to complicate things.

He started walking again. Our bodies were side-by-side, his upper arm rubbing up against my right breast. Even that innocent bit of touching sent a thrill through me, especially as I wondered if it was intentional on his part. He didn't have to walk so close, but he was. Or maybe it was just me, clinging to him like a piece of seaweed clings to a rock. *God, please don't let me be seaweed!*

"I haven't heard that word in a long time. Bitchin'. I like it."

"Stick with me, cowboy. I'll show you all kinds of retro cool stuff. Like my Jennifer Anniston 'do. You like it?" I flicked my hair back and forth before glancing up to see if he was looking.

"It's pretty," he said, smiling a little. He turned and stopped, causing my arm to come out of his. He was just inches away, staring down at me. Putting the shoes in his other hand with the cup full of chips, he put his free hand on my shoulder, his expression suddenly going serious. My heart dropped with a thunk. *He's going to tell me he'll see me later. He's going to disappear. I knew it. The Jennifer Aniston hair flip was too much. Dammit!*

"Listen, Andie. I know you've had a lot to drink, so I kind of feel like the gentlemanly thing to do is give you a chance to walk away ... if that's what you want to do." He was staring at me with those damn glowy blue eyes of his, and I felt like I was being hypnotized by them. Being with him was so much easier to manage when I wasn't looking right at him; I could notch down the sexy to something manageable when his attention was anywhere but on me.

"Walk away? Walk away from what?" Playing a little hard to get seemed like the prudent thing to do just in case he was just being a good samaritan by hanging out with me. He sure sounded like one now, and in my experience, falling for a guy who has no interest in me is a particularly painful process.

He put his free hand on the top of his hat and moved it back and forth, making the curls in the back move too. "I don't know what I'm saying. That last Bud went right to my brain and addled it a little, I'm afraid."

"Addled. Good word. Are you coming up with me while I change my shoes?" I had zero fear of Mack being the wrong kind of guy to invite up to my room. He totally didn't come off as rapist material. Me, on the other hand, I wasn't so sure about. He was nearly irresistible, and if he got the ball rolling, I sure wasn't going to stop it from going straight downhill a thousand miles an hour. No matter what though, I didn't want to leave Vegas with any regrets. If he wanted to get all hot and sweaty together, then we were going to do that, no question. Screw second thoughts, screw ex-boyfriends who break up by text message, and screw complications. All I wanted was one night of reckless abandon so I could get all this craziness out of my system and go home with a clean slate, ready to kick ass, take names, and get on with my life.

"Do you want me to come up?" he asked.

*Screw playing hard to get.* "Yeah. Come on." I took him by the hand and half-dragged him over to a bank of elevators. "I think my friends are up there. I don't have a key so they'd better be." I pushed the up button, trembling a little over what I was doing, namely bringing an almost complete stranger up to my room an hour after meeting him so I could rip his clothes off and be a wild and crazy slut. I was so ready to be a prostitute right now. Twelve hundred bucks was definitely going to buy him a blow job. All I could think about was what he might look like under all those cowboy clothes and whether that bulge I'd seen going down his leg would measure up to my imagination.

"Your friends don't like to gamble?"

"Yeah, but one of them got too drunk so the other one was taking care of her."

"They left you alone in that dress?"

I tried really hard not to smile. "Kind of. Not really." One of the eight elevators dinged and opened. As I stepped in, I said, "I would have helped too, but I saw this totally hot guy in a cowboy hat and I got a little distracted." I cringed at the way my words were slurring together. I was trying so hard for cool, but was afraid I was getting closer to fool. Pressing the button for the right floor, I did my best to act like I hadn't just totally revealed my hand.

"Is that so?" he asked. "Do I need to go speak to him?"

I turned around, a sneaky smile on my face. I tilted my head, letting my hair hang down over my shoulder. "Maybe. What would you say to him?"

He moved closer. "I'd tell him he missed out. That I got there first and to step aside."

"Are you sure about that?" I asked trying not to pant like a bitch in heat. He was so close I could feel the sexy coming off his chest. My knees were turning to jelly over how tall and broad-shouldered he was. And that stupid cowboy hat … I should have hated it. It should have taken all the sexy away and turned him into a hayseed country bumpkin. But it didn't. It made him a wild thing. A dangerous stranger, untamed. Completely unconcerned with what anyone else thought, and comfortable in his own skin. If I hadn't been so drunk I would have been too intimidated to even talk to him. Instead, I was stepping forward to meet him halfway, my eyes drinking him in and not at all ashamed to be doing it.

His voice dropped to a near-growl. "The question is not whether *I'm* sure, but whether *you* are. Because I know exactly what I want, and I'm not the kind of guy who's afraid to go after it once I see it."

He dropped the shoes and the chips in a messy pile and was up against me wrapping his arms around my waist when the elevator dinged. We'd reached my floor. A second later the doors slid open.

His head came down slowly and the brim of his hat blocked out the light coming from above. We were in a cocoon of sexual energy, and I didn't want to stop long enough to get off the elevator. I put my hands on his chest, moving them up over his soft cotton shirt to his shoulders, reveling in the strong, lean muscles I felt there. Wrapping my hands around his neck, I buried my fingers in the curls at the back of his head when he bent down to meet my lips with his.

Our mouths connected and the passion that had been building flared up strong and hot. Nothing about our earlier flirtations and not-quite-accidental touches had prepared me for this. His lips were full and soft, but demanding in the way they pressed against mine and moved quickly to angle for more. I didn't wait for an invitation, opening my mouth and letting my tongue lick his lips, daring him to come out and play. He took my dare with a moan, his bold tongue charging out to tangle with mine. I'd never in my life been kissed like this.

The doors slid shut. Mack reached over and pushed the button for my floor again, but we were already going down.

"Shoot, we missed my floor," I whispered against his mouth.

His hands slid down to my backside and squeezed, send a thrill into my hottest of places, making me wet with anticipation. I pushed my hips towards his, wanting to growl with satisfaction over the hard length I found there. He moved against me while massaging my ass, making me want to scream with unfulfilled desire. If the elevator bell hadn't gone off at just that moment, I might have just yanked up my skirt and jumped on his offering. But it did go off, and then the doors opened, so I quickly pulled away and pushed down the bottom of my dress. Trying to look like I hadn't just almost screwed a cowboy in the elevator of my hotel was one of the hardest things I've ever done. I'm pretty sure I wasn't doing a good job of pulling it off.

"Going up?" asked an older couple, looking a little confused about seeing us standing there and not getting off.

"Uh, yeah," said Mack, having to clear his throat before he continued. "We're going up. All the way up."

I hiccuped loudly and threw my hand over my mouth, my eyes bugging out. *Not sexy! Not sexy!*

The woman put her hand on her husband's arm, stopping him from stepping onto the elevator with us. She glanced down at the chips all around our feet and then looked up. "I think we'll just take the next one. You kids go on ahead." She winked at us and shushed her husband when he started to complain.

The doors closed and Mack came after me without a second's delay. I welcomed him with open arms and open legs. As open as they could be, anyway, in the damn tight dress I'd been forced to wear. It was like a straightjacket when all I wanted to do was jump up and wrap my legs around him.

"What are we doing?" I said against his mouth. It was a stupid question, we both knew it. My mind was spinning and my hormones were raging. I needed him inside me, and I needed him there now. I'd never been so turned-on in my entire life. If Candice and Kelly were in our room, I'd just have to find a supply closet somewhere.

"Feels like we're about to have some fun," he said, not a trace of amusement in his voice. "I'm willing if you're willing." The elevator jerked slightly as it began traveling up again.

I pulled back, staring him in the eye, blinking to make the fuzziness go away. "I'm definitely willing. Definitely, totally willing."

We kissed again, and when he moved his hands down my back this time, he didn't stop at my rear end. He kept on going until he reached my thigh while simultaneously pushing me back against the wall of the elevator. Once he lifted my leg, my hot center was angled up to fully appreciate the hardness that he once again pushed against me. I wrapped my ankle around the back of his hips, moaning as I moved up and down, rubbing against him in a rhythm that I had no control over. Our mouths moved in perfect unison while my hips swiveled, bringing him closer with each thrust. My skirt was up around my waist, and my red lace underwear were soaked through when the elevator bell dinged again.

He dropped my leg and slid his hands down the sides of my hips and thighs, putting my skirt back to where it should have been when in public. He gathered up the chips and the shoes and stepped out into the hallway, pulling me with him. I tripped, getting tangled up in my own feet, but he caught me using his body and one arm. His hand holding the shoes dropped casually to my waist once I was upright again. "Which way?" he asked, squinting at the signs on the wall.

"Room two-zero-one-four," I said, sounding like a complete drunkard. I did some quick mouth exercises, trying to limber my jaw up so I could talk like the educated woman I am.

He caught me doing it and chuckled. "Could you hold these for me?" After he deposited all the chips and the shoes into my hands, I took a step down the hall, headed to my room.

"Whoop!" The sound came flying out of my mouth

when he surprised the crap out of me and swooped me up into his arms, carrying me in a cradle made of his strong arms. Long strides brought us down the hall towards the last room on the right while the money rattled away in the plastic cup. I was literally being swept off my feet, and if it hadn't been for the spinning of the hallway, walls, floors, and ceiling, it would have been the highlight of my night.

*Please let Candice and Kelly be on their way out!*

He put me down on my feet at the door and leaned on it with one hand, pulling me up against him with the other. I was breathless with the kissing that ensued, barely able to hold my thoughts together. Down the chips and shoes went again, scattered all over the floor and on my feet. I only opened my eyes a few times during the kissing to keep the spinning room under control.

"Wait, wait," I said, as a door down the hall opened and voices came floating down the corridor. I knocked on my door, desperation showing through in the rapid-fire tap, tap, tapping I was doing. I was incapable of playing it cool right now. *Cool? Say hello to Fool.*

"You don't have a key?" he asked.

"Where in this dress do you think I'd be able to hide a key?" My chest was practically heaving with all the heavy breathing I was doing. I was completely flustered and frustrated, my hands refusing to sit still. I could feel his six-pack through his shirt. His muscles actually rippled when I touched them. The bulge in his pants was huge. I needed to see this man naked soon or I was going to have a stroke brought on by pent up sexual desire. Like spontaneous combustion but without the gas or the fire parts.

He ran his fingers past my ribs to my back. "Hmmm, no key here." His fingers went down to my rear end. "Not here either." Putting his hand just under my right breast, he smiled. "And not here either." He grabbed my ass once and let go. "You're right. You don't have a key." He grinned, making me grab his face in my hands and kiss him all over again.

The door rattled and we jumped apart before I could start my next move, namely feeling up his bulge. I forgot Kelly's shoes were there on the floor and somehow got tangled up in them when I tried to turn around. I fell to the side as the door opened, landing in Mack's open arms.

"Well, well, well. If it isn't The Lady Gambler and her cowboy hero," said Candice, sounding a little put out and a lot mischievous.

I pushed off Mack's chest to get back on my feet and bent down to grab Kelly's shoes. When I stood up, I swayed on my feet, the room doing a full spin in front of me. Mack put his hand on the small of my back and stepped forward to put his body closer to mine. It was comforting to know that if I fell, he'd be there to catch me.

"Whoopsy. Sorry, lost my balance there." I grinned at Candice, trying to play off the fact that I'd shown up in our room with a random guy. "What took you so long?" I asked, walking past her and dragging Mack in by the hand. "I waited forever. Look what I won." I held up the chips he'd gathered off the floor for a second before dumping them on the table. Several of them rolled off an fell to the floor.

"Nice." She only had eyes for Mack. "And you won some chips too?"

I moved so I was standing next to him. "Ha, ha. I didn't *win* this cowboy, I *beat* him at blackjack." I snorted out a laugh at the frown on his face. I gestured to the cowboy and then at my friend. "Candice, this is Mack. Mack, this is Candice."

She shook his hand while raising an eyebrow. "Mack? Are you for real, that's your name?"

"Mack's a nickname. Short for MacKenzie, my last name." He grinned, and I saw the effect it had on Candice. Even her hard ass wasn't immune to his charms. I melted into him a little and he put his arm around me.

"Where's home?" asked Candice, sliding on her shoes. I noticed with a trace of bitterness that they were lower than the ones I'd been subjected to.

"Baker City, Oregon."

"You're a long way from home, cowboy," she said, standing up straight and pushing her boobs up in her bra.

"That I am, ma'am."

Candice's face fell and she ceased her wiggling around, her shoulders drooping down. "He just called me ma'am. I'm going to go drown my sorrows." She grabbed her little purse off the table and walked to the door, all hunched over.

"Where are you going?" I asked, mystified.

"I'm going out to find me a man. A younger one with a big dick. Keep an eye on Kelly if you feel like it. Otherwise, just lock her in. She'll be fine. She's sleeping it off in the bedroom on the left." She stepped out the door.

"But ... wait, Candice! You don't have to leave!"

She stuck her head in the door, her smile back. "Sorry, babe, but three's a crowd." She winked. "I'll catch you later, kids." The door shut behind her with a click.

"I think your friend just green-lighted me," he said.

I grinned big. "I think she did too."

He swept me off on my feet again, only this time the spinning wasn't nearly as bad since I was staring into his eyes the entire time. "Which way to the empty room?" he asked.

I pointed over my shoulder. "That way."

# Chapter Twelve

I SAT ON THE EDGE of the bed so I could watch the show.

The first thing he did was take off his shirt, button by button. I thought for sure that the cowboy hat was going to go flying first, or maybe that he'd set it down on the table before starting the strip tease. But no ... it was the shirt that he started with, and damn, was I glad for that. Never in my life have I seen a cowboy with his shirt off and his hat on, but I decided right then and there that I wanted to experience that on a regular basis for the rest of my life. It made me wish I had a video camera going so I could re-live the scenario over and over again. This event being just a one-night stand really started to suck in that moment.

The boots were next. After taking them off along with his socks, he was standing in the middle of the room in just a pair of well-worn jeans and a straw-colored cowboy hat. A large, brass-colored belt buckle rested at his waist.

"Good Lord have mercy," I said in barely a whisper, unable to look away. Somehow a southern accent had trickled into my speech. It just seemed appropriate, seeing him standing there in all his country-boy glory. I hiccuped again.

"That good, huh?" he asked, his grin going wide. He took several steps towards me, and I moved back just a little.

"Where are you going?" he asked, his voice low. I was reminded of a predator and its prey.

"I ... I don't know," I said, stuttering through my sudden attack of shyness. He was too gorgeous for words. I was afraid to be naked in his presence.

"You don't need to be afraid of me," he said, still advancing. He held out a hand, palm down, in a calming gesture. "Shhh, come here, babe. Let me just hold you. You don't have to do anything you don't want to."

His words warmed me to my toes. I had a feeling I now knew exactly how a skittish horse would feel in his presence. This man meant me no harm. Walking away would be the stupidest thing I could possibly do. No way was I going to live with that regret.

I put my hand out and let our fingers lace together. "I'm just a little nervous. One-night stands have never really been my thing." Okay, that was kind of a lie. In college they had been, but not since. Six years of dedicated relationships, all with total jerkoffs. I'm nothing if not consistent.

"It's the hat, isn't it?" He took it off and put it down gently on the floor near us, never taking his eyes off me.

"It wasn't the hat," I said, my voice feeling strained. *It most definitely was not the hat.* My pulse was picking up the pace and my fight or flight instinct was kicking in. Or maybe it was my fuck or flight instinct; that was probably more appropriate considering the look he was giving me.

"Is it the buckle?" he asked, gripping it in his fingers and angling it towards me.

"It's not the buckle," I whispered, staring at the letters engraved in the front of it ... something in Latin over a coat of arms, maybe. I was too distracted to give it much thought. He was getting too close for me to think straight. I was way too dizzy from all the alcohol, so I stood, hoping that would help.

He stopped just inches away, not quite as tall without the

boots on, but still so tall I had to angle my head up to look in his eyes.

"You are the prettiest lady in this entire town, you know that?"

I laughed a little, not falling for the schmooze but letting it warm me nonetheless. "I know that you drank about six beers in the space of an hour or two, so I have to think that may be interfering in your judgment."

He shook his head. "Nope. I've got all my faculties."

"Damn, you're just full of those quarter words today, aren't you?"

He pulled me up against his chest in one quick move, reminding me what a strong man he is and how much restraint he'd shown so far. "What's a quarter word?" He dipped his head down and kissed the side of my mouth.

"It's ... it's..." I tried to answer, but then I forgot the question. The small kisses he was feathering around my mouth were making me go air-brained.

"Hmmm? Quarter word?" he prompted.

"It's a ... big word ... worth twenty-five cents..." I opened my mouth and tried to turn and meet his lips, but he moved away, leaving me hanging. His mouth moved to my neck where his lips put a little suction to my skin. He licked the tender spot and then blew on it a little, making goosebumps come up all over that side of my body.

I strained to get closer to him, my breasts pulsing with need.

"I want to see you naked," he whispered, his hands going behind me to move my hair out of the way and slowly unzip my dress. His fingertips trailed behind the zipper, sliding along my skin from the top of my spine all the way to the small of my back. The cool air of the room whispered across my skin as the shoulders of my dress went slack and slid down my arms. The heat of my desire banked and my face burned with the fear of him seeing my body and judging it as less than worthy. I stood there in bra and panties, my face going bright red.

"Jesus, woman …" He pulled me against him roughly again, the hardness of his desire slamming into my pelvis. It was the sweetest pain I'd ever felt. A moan escaped my lips and urged him on.

He pushed my dress down until it pooled at my feet. I stepped out of it and kicked it lightly to the side, clinging to him the entire time. I didn't want us to get too far apart, but he had other ideas. He pulled back abruptly, pushing me away slightly by my upper arms. "Wait … just for a second. Let me look at you."

I dropped my gaze to the floor, unable to meet his eyes.

He said nothing for so long, I had to peek, unable to stand the pressure of not knowing. He was scanning my body from head to toe, and the dim light shining in from the attached bathroom told me nothing. His expression was serious. Dangerous, even.

"What?" I said, wanting to cross my arms over my body.

"No, wait … don't cover yourself. Please. Let me just admire you for a little while longer."

My face went red again. All I could think about were my too-small breasts with two rubbery booby-hikers hidden under them, my wide hips, and my big butt. "What are you talking about?" I felt like I was stuck halfway between feeling awkward and feeling sexy. I could have fallen over to either side with a single word from him.

He shook his head. "I thought bodies like this were only alive in my fantasies. I didn't realize they existed in reality." He ran his hand down my ribs and hip. "Curves everywhere." He looked into my eyes. "The body of a real, honest-to-God woman."

I pushed on his chest, laughter bubbling up from my throat as the fear disintegrated and then disappeared completely. *He likes curves!* "Get out of here, you lunatic."

He grabbed my hands and pulled me up against him. "Heck no, I'm not going anywhere. You lured me up here to your lair and now I'm going to let you take advantage of me."

My mouth dropped open in mock offense. "I lured you up here? Are you kidding me?" I tried to wrestle away, but he held on tight, walking us over to the bed.

"Don't play with my heart, Andie. Tell me you didn't bring me up here just to strip down to your gorgeous bits and then kick me out. I don't think my ego could take it. And neither could my ... other parts of me."

I lifted my chin to sass him back, but he took advantage of his height and came down to my lips, silencing me with his mouth.

The idea that he found my body so sexy lit some kind of fire inside me. Whatever misgivings I might have had about bringing a man to my room who'd I'd never see again after tonight? Yeah ... they went flying out the window and into the hot Las Vegas night. Any second thoughts that might have been brewing about my own attractiveness? Yup .. they joined those misgivings, leaving in their place a very horny, very excited *me*. Andie the party girl was definitely back. I shimmied out of my underthings as he kissed me and then stepped away from him when I was totally naked.

"Wow." He stared at me, his eyes taking in every detail of my body. "Talk about getting lucky. The blackjack table was nothing compared to this."

My heart soared with his compliments and a sudden surge of energy burst through me. "Woo hoo!" I yelled, pushing him down onto the bed and jumping on top of him. My leap was a little too enthusiastic though, because I misjudged my landing and fell to the side. I tried to catch myself on the edge of the bed but the stupid satin cover gave me nothing to grab onto. I tipped off the bed and fell onto the floor with a loud thud. I stayed there for a few seconds, waiting for the room to stop spinning.

"Holy shit," he said, trying to cover up his laughter as he leaned over the edge of the bed to look at me. "Are you okay?"

I jumped to my feet and smiled, determined to keep having fun regardless of the fact that I was a complete idiot. I held my arms above my head and stretched them to the ceiling. "How's that for a dismount?" I said, giving him a superstar smile.

He grabbed me around the waist and yanked me down onto the bed, jumping on top of me. "Gold medal worthy." His jeans pressed into my nakedness, ratcheting the erotic sensations up another couple notches. I had feared my goofiness would destroy the mood, but all it did was make me realize that we had the same sense of humor.

I pushed him over and scrambled to get on top of him. "I'm on top," I declared.

"Whoa, girl," he said, laughing while fighting to sit up. He grabbed me around the waist and flipped me over onto my back in one smooth motion. He was on top now and looming over me.

"Take off those pants," I ordered. "And stand there in the middle of the room so I can check you out. It's my turn to gawk." If I'd had a whip right then, I would have cracked it. Something about being with Mack tonight had gotten me totally fired up. If there'd been a bull in the room, I would have held up a red cape and waved it at him.

He backed up as he got off the bed, never taking his eyes off me. "Yes, ma'am."

Unlike Candice, I didn't mind being ma'am-ed. He could ma'am me all night if he wanted to.

Standing in the middle of the room near the bottom of the bed, he unbuttoned his jeans, slowly and carefully revealing an almost painful-looking erection. It was like Christmas morning and my birthday all rolled into one, the way his gift was revealed to me for my pleasure only.

My eyes widened at the sight of it. *Sweet Jesus, he's hung. That's some kind of magic, the way he somehow fits that thing into those pants.*

He pulled the jeans off the rest of the way from the bottom, dropping them on the floor next to him.

"No underwear," I said, still staring at his midsection. I couldn't think of anything else to say, save, *My god, you have a huge cock* ... but that didn't seem like the smoothest of moves, so I stuck with the basics.

"Too restricting," he said, coming towards me, his girth and hardness on display right at eye-level from my position on the bed.

I moved closer to the edge, dropping my legs over the side, fascinated by the size and shape of him. I became wet just imagining his length moving into me. The vision of it sent shock waves of desire though my body. I used to think foreplay was a really big deal, but I would have skipped all of it tonight and gone right to the heart of the matter without a backward glance. But then I saw his cock again and I just had to touch it. I reached out to take it in my hand, looking up at him to gauge his response.

His eyes were smoldering and his expression so serious, it would have been frightening if I wasn't so turned on and convinced of his attraction to me. I felt powerful and in control. "What do you want?" I asked, my voice barely above a whisper.

"Whatever you want to give." He voice was gravelly, thick with desire.

His jaw muscles clenched when I moved my hand experimentally, first stroking down towards the base and then up again to the tip with the lightest of touches. I didn't yet know if he was one of those men who like the light touch or preferred a firmer grip, but I was sure going to find out. A small flick of my tongue on the tip had him jerking slightly in response with an inward hiss of breath.

"Jesus," was all he managed to say before he closed his eyes.

I turned small circles of my tongue on his head to wet it down and then took him in my mouth as he rested his fingertips on my shoulders. I felt his fingers digging in a little as I did the one thing I knew I was really good at in the bedroom. I guess there's a benefit to dating a bunch of selfish losers ... it sure teaches a girl how to give a good blowjob.

His hips began to move in time with my rhythm, and his breaths came faster. I had my hand between his legs, fondling his balls. The way they were jerking up and then relaxing with every stroke of my lips, I knew if I kept it up for too much longer he'd be a mess, beyond rational thought and putty in my hands. The thought had no sooner crossed my mind then he pushed me back and pulled himself out of my mouth. My lips curved into a smile at the animal lust I saw in his expression.

"I need to taste you," he said in a half-growling voice. He pushed me back on the bed and dropped to his knees between my legs. They were hanging awkwardly off the edge and I wanted to move back, but I didn't have time. I started to say something but stopped when his mouth was suddenly on me, without preamble and with almost no warning. One second I was recovering from a tired jaw and the next I had this man's beautiful face buried between my legs, working some kind of crazy magic on me.

"Oh my god," I said, sounding almost like I was crying. The sensations that rocketed up from between my legs to my heart and brain and every other part of me were like nothing I'd ever felt before. A long, low moan escaped my throat and I arched my lower back, pushing myself into him, silently begging for more.

His tongue slipped inside me and did something that made me twitch with pre-orgasm excitement. A finger came up to replace his tongue while his mouth went up to my most sensitive of places and very gently, very softly made slow circles and up and down motions. I lifted my legs and shamelessly put them over his shoulders, using the leverage to get myself closer to his amazing mouth.

He took to the invitation eagerly, moaning himself as his movements came faster and harder. Normally I would have passed on this kind of approach, but I was completely and utterly gone. I'd fallen into a sexual vortex that had taken over every ounce of shame or fear that might have tried to rear its ugly head. I wanted to spread my legs as wide as they could go and feel every single bit of what he was doing to me. Andy the slut was in the house.

He moaned, a deep rumble against my most sensitive parts, sending delicate vibrations shooting up into the core of me and making me gasp with surprise and pure wanton joy. I could feel the wave coming ... the one that would take me to a higher place, the end of our wild ride. I desperately wanted the satisfaction, but then again I didn't want it ... not yet. I wanted the pleasure to last all night.

"You're close," he said, his tongue not stopping but his hand drawing away. He rested both palms on my stomach. They were warm and spanned my body's width. He stroked my skin and reached up to take both breasts in his hands, pinching the heavy nipples and making me cry out again. I strained against every part of him, needing more of all of it. I was greedy and totally shameless.

"Yes," I cried, breathing heavily and moaning. I couldn't help it. Everything was spinning out of control.

"I want to come when I'm inside you," he said huskily.

"Yes. Please, Mack. Come inside." Rational thought was gone. All I wanted was to feel him filling me completely, to enjoy the sensation of his cock stretching me to the limit. He was way bigger than any man I'd ever been with before, and I welcomed the new experience with open arms and open legs.

Suddenly he was gone from between my legs and I

heard a condom wrapper tearing. Then he was suspended above me with stiff arms, his palms planted on the bed at my sides. One of them slipped under my waist and dragged me closer to the top of the bed. I ran my hands up the bulging muscles of his forearms and biceps and snaked my arms around his neck, pulling him down to me. I reveled in the smell of our passion on his mouth.

His hard length pushed against me, begging to come inside as he lowered his body to mine. We kissed and tasted each other's tongues, the passion still as strong as it had been when he was between my legs.

I reached a hand down along with one of his, and together we guided the head of his erection over to my opening. I was completely ready for him.

"Are you sure?" he asked.

It seemed like a crazy question considering where our mouths had just been, but I guess he was just one of those guys who put the actual act of sex up on a different pedestal. "Yes, I'm sure," I said between tongue-heavy kisses, certain I wasn't risking anything. The cocktails probably had a lot to do with it, but I didn't care one bit. The passion had overruled any ounce of common sense I might have had, which explained what this sexy stranger who I'd just met was doing in my room right now. "Just put it in me, please." I was begging but I didn't care. Shameless would be my new middle name.

At first, there was some resistance, my folds so heavy with passion they were blocking his entry. He reached down once more to move the tip around, guiding it in slowly with an expert hand.

I cried out, spreading my legs and pushing my hips forward, urging him to come in deeper.

"Mmmm, just be patient," he said, a devilish smile forming under my kisses.

"I can't," I begged, "please."

He slid into me just the slightest bit more and then pulled out, deftly avoiding my attempts at getting him to go in deeper.

"You're teasing me," I said, waiting breathlessly for his next move. I both loved and despised what he was doing to me.

He pushed the head in a little farther this time. Leaving it there for a few seconds, he moved his hips in a small circle and then pulled back again. It was like he was dipping into a honey pot or something, just getting a taste and giving a taste and then disappearing. It was maddening and delicious.

"You're evil," I said, putting my hands on his hips. I was prepared to do whatever necessary to get him to do this thing all the way, including forcing him down on top of me.

"Oh yeah? You really think so?" He pushed into me, stopping when he was halfway in. He pulsed himself in and out in short little strokes before pulling out again.

"Yes. I really, really think so," I said, breathing fast as I anticipated his next move. I squirmed with anticipation, making myself mad with the not-knowing. Would this be it? Would this be the time he went in all the way, deep?

"Yesssss...," I hissed out as he slowly buried his full length into me. It just kept going and going, making me think for a few crazy seconds that it wasn't going to stop. I put my hands on his ass and pushed him in as far as he'd go, grinding myself into his lower abdomen and crying out with the sensations it created. Moving my hips in circles and bucking against him while he was buried inside me was what did it; it's what started me on the road to nowhere and everywhere all at once.

He drew himself out with agonizing slowness and then began the tortue all over again, burying himself to the hilt and pausing for several seconds before pulling out again in a dizzying stroke of pure sex, pure animal need. Over and over, I pushed against him while pulling his rear end down, forcing him to go deep, to increase his rhythm and give me the friction I needed.

"You're going to make me come if you keep doing that," he said, gritting his teeth with the effort of holding back. "Holy sh ... God, that feels so good." He finished sentence almost out of breath. "How are you doing that?"

I had no idea what he was talking about. All I knew was that a monster tidal wave of an orgasm was headed my way, and I was fully prepared and looking forward to drowning in it. The alcohol should have made this impossible; it should have made me insensitive and numb, but it seemed to be having the opposite effect. Or maybe it was just him. I'd never been with a man so amazingly sexy in all my life.

His strokes came harder and stayed deeper. My sensitive nub took the pounding of his body with pleasure. I welcomed it, meeting his every thrust with one of my own. Our rhythm was wild, untamed, raw ... a completely new experience in my carefully scripted life. His grunts and gasps of barely controlled excitement mirrored my own rising tide of passion.

"Oh, fuck, I'm going to come," he said, sounding angry and carried away by his lack of control.

It was a combination of his loss of control and the sensation of being filled with him that did it to me. The sensations that had been building rushed me all at once, taking me completely by surprise. I started yelling, crying, and gasping, with zero control over what my body was doing. I dug my fingernails into his back, not paying attention to what I was doing to his skin. I just didn't want to fall into the dark abyss that was calling out to me, worrying that once I was there, I'd never be able to get back. Mack would keep me safe. He'd keep me from drowning.

And then, when he shouted loudly and pushed into me with several short, sharp strokes, I fell; I fell into the velvet darkness that was swirling around inside my head. The sensation was entirely welcome. With this man filling me and pleasing me with every inch of his body, I had no other option.

Time stood still as we took the thrilling ride to the very top and then coasted down to earth again. The clock only began to tick again when our orgasms had totally played out.

Our bodies had melded together; I could feel every inch of him, even as he lost some of his hardness. He collapsed on top of me and rested his face on the pillow next to my head.

"Are you okay?" he whispered, the small wisp of his breath tickling my ear.

I nodded, not trusting my voice to work properly yet.

He pushed into me just a little.

I yelped with the shock that went through me.

He chuckled. "A little sensitive?"

"A little," I admitted, wondering if I should be ashamed about anything I'd done. I didn't think so. Anything that felt this good couldn't possibly be wrong.

Weird feelings rose up to smother me. My life plan felt really, really stupid and empty. This man would never fit into it, but now I wondered how I could ever go back to guys like Luke when I knew they could never make me feel this way.

Feeling his heavy body on mine, wallowing in the afterglow of the best sex I'd ever had, I questioned for the first time what the hell I was doing with my life. I tried to laugh at myself, having these thoughts during a one-night stand in Vegas, but the humor wouldn't come. This was real. This connection with this cowboy wasn't just a *thing*.

"What are you thinking right now?" he asked, sliding off to the side of me, his mostly limp cock sliding out of me and resting damply on my leg. He pulled the used condom off and put it on a piece of paper on the nightstand.

"Nothing. My brain isn't working yet." Hell-to-the no way was I going to tell him what was on my mind. He'd run for the hills and I'd never see him. *Do I want to see him again?*

*Yes. I think I do. No, I know I do.*

"You're lying," he said, running a finger gently from my forehead to the end of my nose. "I can tell by the way you wrinkle up your little nose that you're lying. Tell me what you're thinking."

"Oh, so I'm Pinnocchio now?" I tried to play it off, distract him from trying to get inside my head, but he wasn't falling for it.

"Please tell me."

He sounded so sincere, it made my heart skip a beat. How could a guy that good in bed and this gorgeous be so *nice?* Doesn't it defy the very laws of Nature? Maybe he was an evolutionary mutant. I turned my head, our faces only an inch or two apart. "Why do you want to know?"

"Because. I'm thinking lots of stuff too, and I'm wondering if you're thinking the same thing."

"You go first," I said, my heart picking up its rhythm for some stupid reason. No way were we thinking the same thing. *But wouldn't it be cool if we were?*

"Luceo non uro," he said. "That's what my dad always said."

"What does that mean?" I asked, pretty sure that even though I was still pretty drunk, he wasn't speaking English.

"It means that if I want to get lucky with you, I should just take the risk and tell you what's on my mind, because failing would be worse than never trying."

I grinned. "I'm pretty sure you already got lucky, but if you're looking for kinky sex, you're going to have to work to convince me it's a good idea." For him, I was pretty sure I'd do anything, but there was no way I was going to make it that easy by just telling him.

"It's not about the sex," he said, going all sober on me. "Well, okay, the sex might have been a little icing on the cake, but that's not it."

"You're being very mysterious," I said, now nervous as

hell. I really liked this cowboy. *Mack.* But I didn't know a single thing about him other than the fact that he doesn't wear underwear and he's got a big cock-a-doodle doo that he definitely knows how to use. *Yee haw.*

"I don't mean to be mysterious. I guess I'm not as bold as I'd like to be sometimes. Thing is …" He paused and then rolled onto his back, resting his hands under his head. "…I have something on my mind, and I want to say it to you, even though I know it probably won't make a difference and I'll probably never see you again."

The idea that we'd never be together again made me literally sick to my stomach, and I was pretty sure it wasn't the alcohol, even though the bed was spinning with its effects. Really, really spinning.

"Just say it," I urged, my words slurring a little. "You go first and then I'll go."

"Chicken," he teased, easing his arm under my neck.

"Guilty." I nestled in close to him, turning on my side so I could rest my head on his chest. I knew it was stupid, but in that moment, I felt cared for. Something I'd never truly experienced with the man I'd so recently wanted to call *Husband.* This was a very sad state of affairs, indeed. I was falling in lust with a man from Oregon, and I lived on the opposite end of the country. Our situation couldn't possibly be more complicated.

"Okay, well, here it goes. And if you want me to leave after I say it, then so be it. I'd rather say it and take the walk of shame than not say it and miss out on something."

"Alright already, say it." I faked a loud yawn. "I'm about to fall asleep over here."

He tickled my ribs with his free hand. "You're ornery. I like that about you." He leaned over and kissed my neck, sucking hard enough to leave a mark. I probably should have been mad, but when my nipples went rock hard over the sensation it created, I had the opposite emotion coming over me.

He left my neck and laid back down. "What I have going through my mind is that I don't want this to end. There's something about you that's just lassoed my heart or my common sense or something and I'm afraid I'm not going to be able to get it back until you let it go."

My heart seized in my chest. The beats just wouldn't come. And then I gasped, the need for oxygen too overwhelming. I'd been holding my breath without realizing it. "Really?" I croaked out. No one had ever said anything even remotely similar to me before. Even men who'd claimed to love me.

"Really. Does that make you want to run to Mexico?"

"Mexico?" I giggled.

"That's the farthest place from here I could come up with. Give me a few more minutes to sober up and I'll come up with something better."

I put my elbow up and rested my head on my palm. "Maybe it's just the beer talking. Maybe I'm not as awesome as you think I am in the sober light of day."

He pulled me against him and kissed me soundly. "No. It's not the beer. I might be a little out of it, but that doesn't make me deaf, dumb, or blind. You're something special. Didn't you feel it? The way we fit together so perfectly?" The expression on his face was vulnerable. Like this was important to him.

"Yes," I whispered, so thrilled to be hearing these things come out of his mouth that I couldn't speak properly. I couldn't even think straight. Bells were clanging and alarms were going off in my brain. *He likes me! A lot! He really likes me! And he's hung like a horse!*

"I'll tell you what ...," he said, pulling me on top of him, "...right now I want to do two things with you, but I can't decide which one to do first." He grinned up at me mischievously, my hair hanging down to create a curtain around us.

"What? Anal sex?" I asked.

He laughed loud and long. Then he spanked me on both cheeks before rubbing them and squeezing them gently. He pushed his hips up towards me, causing his semi-hardness to push into my folds. "No, you crazy girl, that's not what I was thinking. I'll take a raincheck on that, though." The dimple in his cheek came out for the first time since we played blackjack.

"Okay, so what were you thinking, then, if it wasn't the booty love?" I rubbed myself just slightly along his length and was surprised to find that the idea of another round of sex so soon wasn't entirely unpleasant. In fact, it was quite the opposite. He got harder with every passing second.

He reached down between us and angled his erection up, the tip teasing at my lower stomach. He said nothing; he just waited to see what I would do.

I positioned myself over him. Moving my hips in small circles, I eased the head of his cock into my warmth. I came down slowly, pushing past the opening to take him all the way in. I only stopped when I was fully impaled, his head pressing against the end of the road.

"Damn, girl," was all he could manage. He tipped his head back and closed his eyes as his hips moved in a rhythm that instantly threw all ideas of conversation out the window.

I was still sensitive and swollen from our last session, so it didn't take long for me to get close to orgasm. But the sensations were different this time. Sharp. Wild. A lot out of control. I needed speed and pounding, not soft and gentle strokes. I moved up and down his length, landing hard to give my body the ache it desired.

He met me thrust for thrust, his erection so firm it felt like steel. I screamed out a few times in my frustration, not able to get what I was seeking. Something … something … I didn't know what. It stayed just out of my grasp. I needed it but I didn't know what *It* was.

He growled once loudly and sat up, flipping me over onto my back on one smooth movement. Then he pulled out of me and turned me onto my stomach. "Put your ass in the air," he ordered, grabbing me under my hips and jerking my rear end up.

I complied without a sound. I wanted this. This was *It.*

He pulled my folds apart with his thumbs and buried himself in me once again. Scooting his bent knees in slightly under me, he used the top of my thighs for leverage as he pounded into me, heaving my body into the pillows at the head of the bed with every thrust.

I was angled up so far, I could feel his balls hitting my clit. Just the slight tap, tap, tapping was driving me wild. It wasn't enough. But his harsh thrusts were exactly what I'd needed, even though I hadn't known it until just now.

"Yes! Yes!" I screamed, not caring that they'd hear me out in the hallways and possibly on the floor below too.

"God, I love fucking you," he said between gritted teeth, the sound of our bodies slapping against one another echoing out into the room.

"Yes, fuck me, please, fuck me!" I was begging shamelessly, but it just felt so right. I wanted to be his, to be taken by him every single night of my life. I felt like I hadn't truly lived as a woman until this moment.

I was riding the crest of a wave I didn't understand. I was getting satisfaction from a hard fucking, something I'd never liked before. Where was this pleasure coming from? It had to be the most base, animal part of me. The passion was savage, carrying me away to another place and making me think and say and do things I never would have thought I was capable of.

"Aaaaarrrrhh!" he shouted, sounding like a wild man sending out his war cry.

"Aaahhhh!" I screamed. I was so close, so *close!*

He collapsed on top of me, trapping his hand under my body. His finger came up to rub my clit as he pounded into me with jerking motions, grunting and growling with every thrust.

That simple touch. Those two fingers barely touching me in the most inelegant way while he filled me completely. That's all I needed to disappear into myself, to fall into the passion that threatened to overwhelm and swallow me whole. I spread my legs as wide as I could, angled my ass back as much as possible, and rode the wave as high and as hard as I could, screaming the entire way.

He came inside me for the second time that night, and I experienced an orgasm like I'd never even dreamed of having, even with my very vivid imagination.

Minutes later, or maybe it was hours, Mack slid off me and fell to his side next to me. I looked up at him, my hair in a tangle over my face.

"What are you looking at?" I asked in a smartass tone.

"A beautiful woman who makes me think I can fly."

"So what's next?" I asked, fearing the answer. It was past midnight and Candice was sure to be back soon.

"I have a really wild, really crazy, really stupid idea."

"What, like having condomless sex?"

He grimaced. "Sorry about that. Is it… going to be a problem?"

"Don't apologize, it was my fault. And I'm on the pill."

"I'm clean if it makes you feel better. Doctor says so."

"Me too."

"Good. But back on track … that wasn't what I was talking about."

I got up onto my elbows, blowing my hair out of my face. "Okay, then, lay it on me, hot stuff."

"You sure?"

I pointed at my face. "Does this look like a woman who doesn't know what she wants?"

He tackled me onto my back, and forced a kiss on me. I let it melt into more heat for a few seconds before putting my hands on the sides of his face and pushing him away. "Stop stalling and tell me."

He jumped out of the bed and started pulling his jeans on. "Come on. We're going out."

I sat up, confused. "Out? I thought we were going to snuggle."

"Yeah. Out now, snuggling later." He picked up my dress and held it out in my direction.

I scooted slowly to the edge of the bed, holding out my hand for the dress. I took it when he brought it closer, not sure how I felt about this sudden energy burst and mystery trip *out*. The cocktails and sex were like a sleeping potion, and all I wanted to do was rest.

He didn't let the dress go, forcing me to look into his eyes. "Do you trust me?"

I nodded without hesitation. I shouldn't trust him. He's a stranger. I knew his body and the fact that he's a sexy beast, but nothing else. I almost laughed out loud at how ridiculous it all was. But the fact was, I did trust him. Implicitly. With him, I knew I could be myself. I could be confident and sexy and in control. I could dream of a life that didn't involve a plan that had to be followed for the next ten years. I could forget where I came from and who I'd left behind to become the woman I was now.

"Yes. I trust you," I finally said.

"Okay, then, get dressed. I have a surprise for you, and I hope like hell you're going to want to do it."

"Can I get a hint about what it is?" I asked, sliding off the bed.

"Sure. Here's your hint: *Shine, not burn.*"

When he smiled and winked at me, my heart melted into a puddle on the floor. I realized in that moment that I was falling hard for this cowboy stranger.

# Chapter Thirteen

I ROLLED OVER AND MOANED. My head was pounding, and I felt like I was going to throw up. The sound of snores pulled me the rest of the way out of my half-conscious state. I cracked a dry eye open and caught a blurry view of mangled blond hair next to me in the bed.

"Candice?" I asked. My voice sounded like a frog's. *What? Did I take up smoking last night?*

"Wha...?" she mumbled, her face buried in a pillow.

"Where are we?" I asked. I was afraid to sit up. The bed was spinning around the room too much for that.

"Vegas."

"Where in Vegas?"

She lifted up her head, her hair one giant knot hanging in her face. "Hotel room." She dropped her face back onto the bed. Moments later she was snoring again.

I rolled over onto my side away from her and stared at the nightstand next to me, trying to remember what the hell I'd done last night. My conscious mind wandered through the halls of my memories, trying to pick out facts and separate them from general fuzziness and the things that made zero sense.

I remembered going downstairs with Candice and Kelly. That part was very clear. I put my hands on my bare breasts, glad to know I hadn't fallen asleep with those gel booby-hikers on. My breasts would surely have fallen off due to lack of circulation after all this time. I noticed my nipples were tender.

*Sex. I had sex?* Visions of the cowboy came flooding back. "Oh my god. I had crazy monkey sex with a cowboy."

Kelly stood in the doorway. "What'd you just say? Something about having sex with a monkey?"

I sat up gingerly, holding my forehead when the effort was too much. "No. I said I had crazy monkey sex with a cowboy not a monkey."

"What made it monkey sex then, if there weren't any monkeys involved?" She sat on the end of the bed, wiggling Candice's foot. Candice pulled it away with a moan.

"Shut up. I have a splitting headache." I looked up at her through most likely very bloodshot eyes. "What did I do last night?"

She shrugged. "Don't ask me. I went down to the casino and ended up in the other bed this morning. I don't remember much myself."

Candice spoke in the pillow. "You got drunk, you lightweight. And I burned an hour of good man-cruising time taking care of your sorry butt. You barfed like three times."

"Oh," said Kelly, smacking her tongue and lips around. "No wonder my mouth tastes like kitty poo."

"What about me?" I said, nudging Candice on the arm. "What did I do last night?"

Candice sat up with a big annoyed sigh. "How am I supposed to know? You came up with the cowboy, I left when it got crowded, and then when I got back here you were gone. I went to sleep, *alone*, I might add. This town is totally dry for good men."

A tingle down between my legs said otherwise, but I didn't argue. I didn't have enough memory to do it properly.

Bits and pieces of my night in this room with the cowboy were trickling in piece by piece. My face pinked up at the memories. I stood, going into the bathroom and grabbing my cell phone on the way. "I can't remember a lot of what I did," I said, shutting the door.

"That may be for the best!" said Kelly, shouting so I'd hear her through the door.

I looked at myself in the mirror. I had a hickey on my neck. I put my cell phone down on the back of the toilet and lifted my hair to put it in a ponytail. Two hickies. Another one on the other side. *Great. Last time I sported one of these I was in eighth grade.* "Yeah. You're probably right," I responded.

I stripped down and stepped into the shower, soaping myself up while trying to put my memory back together. *I met the cowboy around nine last night ... what was his name? Mike? Mick? And then we came up here and had ... sex. Yes, we definitely had sex.*

I touched myself down there and noticed my sensitive parts felt used, like I might have had a really good time last night. Flashes of him naked, of him in a hat and jeans, of him holding me in his arms ...? Is that possible? All the memories were warm and made me feel ... loved. Had I taken X? Was I drugged? Damn if I could remember what came next, after the apparently happy sex had rocked my world.

I shampooed my hair and frowned in concentration. *Where is he now? Did he just take off after we did the nasty and say, 'See ya, thanks for the screw'? Where did I go after? Why wasn't I here when Candice got back? What was I doing and who was I doing it with?*

I didn't have the answers, and it bothered me on several levels, mostly because I felt like I really *should* remember. Like something important had happened, maybe even more important than crazy monkey sex.

Candice came in and sat on the toilet. "I feel like a warmed over cat turd," she said, slapping at the toilet paper roll, trying to make the paper spin off. It wasn't cooperating.

"You look slightly better than one, though," I said, the devil taking my tongue and torturing my friend with it.

"Yeah, well, hurry up and get out of there so I can have my turn."

"Isn't there another bathroom in this fancy suite?" I asked rinsing the conditioner out of my hair.

"Yeah, but it smells like Kelly-barf, so no thanks."

I squeezed the excess water out of my hair and grabbed a towel, wrapping it around myself. "Okay, here you go. I'm done." I got out of the shower and left her to her business. When I stepped out into the room, I found Kelly standing by the end of the bed looking at a little piece of paper.

"What's that?" I asked pulling some underwear out of my bag and sliding it on under my towel.

"Not sure." She flipped it over. "Some kind of claim check, I think."

I walked over and took it from her. All it had was a number on it, no other identifier. "Did we put our luggage or a coat or something somewhere?"

Kelly shook her head. "I don't remember doing it, but I guess it's possible."

I put the paper in my bag. "I'll keep it just in case."

Kelly shrugged. "Okay. I'm going to get dressed. When does our plane leave?"

I looked at the clock on the bedside table. "Three hours. Better hurry up. I need to eat something." I was hoping it would calm my stomach to put some food in it. I couldn't remember ever being this hung over. "Those margaritas or whatever they were kicked my butt."

"Tequila is pronounced ta-kill-ya. It's not a joke." Kelly left the room.

I stood there for a second in silence. The nagging feeling

that this paper Kelly had found was important wouldn't go away. I walked back over to the bag and pulled out the ticket. "Where did you come from?" I asked it. The ticket didn't respond.

Picking up the telephone, I hit the button for the receptionist. When a man with an Indian accent answered I used my best attorney-conducting-discovery voice.

"Hello. Hi. This is Andie Marks in room … oh, you already know. Okay, well, the reason I'm calling is I found a claim check I think in my room, and I was wondering if you could tell me what I asked you to hold there … in your baggage room, maybe? Last night is a little fuzzy for me."

"What is the number on the claim check, please?"

I read it off to him and waited on hold.

While I was listening to the hold music, a yelp and a scream came from the bathroom.

"What happened?!" I yelled at Candice through the door. I couldn't make the phone stretch far enough to go see her.

"I'm sorry, Andie, I really am!" Candice shouted back, her voice a little muffled.

"About what?"

"Shit! Shit! Shit! I just accidentally knocked your cell phone into the toilet!"

"Well, get it out!" I screamed. A feeling of dread crept over me. All my client contacts were in there and a million emails. I had them all backed up, but this would mean an entire day of being out of contact with my office. Talk about a nightmare.

"I did!" She stuck her head out the door. "But I think I killed it. I'm so, so sorry." She looked ready to cry.

I was about to give her a serious guilt trip, even though it was pretty much my fault for leaving the stupid thing on the back of the toilet, but the reception guy came back on the line so I just frowned at her sternly and waved her away.

"Ma'am, are you still there?" He sounded possibly

nervous.

"Yes, I'm still here." *Still here and now doubly annoyed.*

"Well … there appears to be a slight problem." Yep, he was definitely, positively nervous.

"How so?" I asked, feelings of misgiving washing over me. *What did I leave at the desk? Please don't let it be a monkey.*

"Well, some gentlemen came to reception this morning insisting that we held their bags for them yesterday, but they were unable to produce a claim check. We allowed them into the baggage room and, well …"

I sighed. "Spit it out. I'm not going to be mad." At least I didn't think I was going to be.

"Well, they identified what they claimed to be their bags and we allowed them to take them."

"What did the bags look like?"

He whispered to someone on his end before answering. "Four duffel bags, ma'am. Like athletic bags."

It was the ma'am that he used that made something click in my head. "Was one of them wearing a cowboy hat?"

"Yes! In fact, all of them were."

I nodded, sadness washing over me. He'd left. Without even a goodbye. Or maybe *with* a goodbye but not one I remembered. "It's okay. It was my friend's bag. You're cool, I'm not mad."

He breathed out an audible sigh of relief. "Oh, good, good, good, that is wonderful news. And for your trouble and stress, please allow me to offer you and your guests a free voucher for another night's stay with us."

I raised an eyebrow at that. "I'm leaving today."

"It has no expiration. Surely you'll be back someday, yes?"

*No.* "Sure, maybe. I'll come get it when I check out."

"Wonderful, perfect. Thank you, Miss Andie."

"You're welcome. Bye."

I hung up the phone, staring at the claim ticket. Why

did it bother me so much that the cowboy had taken his bags and gone? I looked at the trashcan and stretched my hand out to toss the ticket in, but at the last second, I didn't. Instead, I walked slowly over to my bag and shoved it into the side pocket.

Shaking my head at my own silliness, I went about the work of getting ready to leave. Our flight was leaving soon and we had breakfast to wrangle and a taxi to hire. I ignored the haunting memories that were telling me there was something I should be remembering.

# Chapter Fourteen

TWO YEARS LATER...

I FROWNED at the stack of messages on my desk. Each one was worse than the last, with phone numbers missing, names misspelled, sometimes with nothing *but* a name. I read the last one with disbelief as I pressed the button on my phone that would make the light blink on Ruby's: *'Someone called you about something related to the Blakenship file.'*

"Yes," came her clipped voice.

"Rubes, could you come in here?"

"The name is *Ruby*."

"Okaaaay. *Ruby*, could you come in here, please?"

"I'll be there in a moment."

That moment turned out to be ten minutes long, and I'd bet a box of doughnuts she pretended to be busy the entire time just so she could make me wait. These days, Ruby did everything she could to piss me off. It had to stop now, though. We had to have the confrontation that had building for months. I had too much on my plate to deal with her shit anymore.

She stood in the doorway, her back so stiff she looked like she had a pool cue up her big butt. She never relaxed around me anymore. It was all business, all the time. I wasn't even allowed to call her Rubes anymore.

"Have a seat, please." I motioned to the chairs in front of me.

"I prefer to stand," she said, lifting her chin a fraction higher.

I sighed loudly. "Ruby, please. Don't make me lose my temper again. I've had a really long day and a really long week, too."

A fake-confused expression bloomed across her face. "Oh, I'm sorry. Am I the one to blame for your temper now? I suppose I'm also to blame for you losing the Goldman motion and for you getting that speeding ticket on your way to work last week." She folded her hands casually in front of her ample waist. "What should I do now? Apologize? Or maybe you want me to resign." She raised both eyebrows at me, still with the fake innocence thing going. It made me want to slap the look off her face.

Her words hurt, cutting me through with their mean, serrated edges. I held up the stack of messages she'd taken while I was out. "You're to blame for a lot of things, but right now I'd just like to talk to you about these." I decided to save the conversation about letters never sent and forms mis-filed for another day. She was a handful when she was cranky and right now, she was definitely cranky.

She said nothing, she just stood there giving me silent attitude.

"Ruby, please don't make me ask again. Come inside, shut the door, and sit down."

She hesitated a few more seconds, just to let me know she could and would, and then she did as I asked.

Once she'd settled herself in the chair across from me, I let some of the heat out of my voice. "What's going on? Can you please just tell me? I can't take much more of the stress, I have to be honest with you."

She broke eye contact with me and stared at a

paperweight on my desk. "I'm not sure what you mean."

"Ruby, please look at me."

She looked at the ceiling, blinking her eyes deliberately.

"I want to know what happened."

Shrugging, she said, "You took a long lunch with *Bradley* and a lot of people called in while you were gone. I took messages. I don't know what else you want from me." She tapped her long fingernails on the arms of the chair.

"Do you have to say his name like that? He's my fiancé, Ruby. It hurts my feelings when you say it with such disdain."

She wiggled around in her seat a little but didn't respond. The fingernail tapping started again.

"I didn't mean the messages," I said, although that was one of the many symptoms of our problem. "I'm talking about what happened between us."

She finally looked at me, raising a cocky eyebrow. "Us? Whatever do you mean?" Again with the innocent act.

I wanted to scream, but I restrained myself. Anger just got Ruby going even more, making her more cold-hearted toward me than usual. "I mean *us*. You as Ruby, me as Andie. We used to get along. I used to love working with you, and I think you used to love working with me. But for a long time now, things have been going downhill." The tone of my voice rose up a notch. "And now they're to the point where I almost don't think we can work together anymore." I gave her my best pleading look. It worked really well on juries.

Her nostrils flared, but she didn't say a thing.

"Are you hearing me Ruby?" My heart spasmed with the pain of rejection. Ruby hated me, but I still loved and respected her. She had been so good to me once. Without her I'm not sure how I would have worked my way through learning to navigate the quagmire of civil procedure. She's an expert in her field, and I'm not the only young lawyer who she's helped mold into a litigating machine. But now instead of helping me, she seemed to spend every minute of her day trying to make me angry by undoing my work or making my work twice as hard as it should have been.

"Yes, I'm hearing you." She finally looked at me. "The question is, are you hearing *yourself?*"

I frowned. This, I wasn't expecting. "I think I am."

She shrugged just the slightest bit. "I think you're not."

"Explain," I said, curious.

"No, thank you." She put her hands on the arms of the seat as if to lever herself up. "Will that be all?"

I pointed to the chair. "No. Don't get up. I'm not done."

"Oh, and it's all about what *you* want, isn't it?"

Now we were getting somewhere. "Not *all* the time, but I am the attorney and you are my assistant. What's bothering you about our relationship?"

"If you're talking about being your assistant, then nothing's bothering me. Not one single thing."

"What if I'm *not* talking about you being my assistant?" I was fishing now. I had no idea what she was getting at, but I damn sure wanted to find out. If I could fix whatever was broken with Ruby and me, it would turn my life into a bed of roses again, especially considering how many hours I worked in this place. Or almost a bed of roses. Yes, there would still be some thorns, but I could live with *some* thorns. A girl has to live with some of those if she's going to marry a man. I'd accepted that as a simple fact of life. A necessary evil that went with being around a guy.

She clarified. "Not as your assistant? Okay then, if you're talking about us as two women who mutually admire one another, then that's a different story altogether. There's plenty bothering me where that's concerned."

That hurt my feelings. I prided myself in my people skills. I was known as the Rainmaker at the firm, single-handedly bringing in more new clients than any other junior partner for the last two years running. Everyone liked me. I got invited to all the parties and networking events. "How so?" I asked.

"I like my job."

I thought her response through for a few seconds, but reflecting on it didn't help ease my confusion in the least. "What does liking your job have to do with anything?"

"It has *everything* to do with everything. If it hadn't been for my need of this job, you wouldn't have ... done the things you've done maybe or I wouldn't be working here anymore."

I dropped my face into my hands, trying to keep myself from displaying the frustration that swirled around inside me. I didn't have any idea what she was getting at, but there was no way I could let this go until I had figured it out. She was finally talking to me after more than a year of the silent treatment or sometimes even straight up disrespect. It was time to put it all to bed.

My voice came out muffled as it battled to make it through my fingers. "Please tell me what the hell you're talking about, Ruby."

"See, that's one of the problems right there. Your mouth."

"My mouth?" I lifted my head and looked at her again.

She pursed her lips and shook her head. "Hm-um. I'm not saying anything more. I need this job."

"Are you saying that you feel like you can't talk to me because if you do, you'll get fired?"

She gave me a tight smile. "That's exactly what I'm saying. See, you're a smart girl." She stood. "I have files to work on, so if you don't mind…"

I was angry now. "I do mind. Sit."

"Don't you talk to me like that! I'm not your dog!" Her southern accent came out towards the end, the one she worked to keep out of her voice at work when surrounded by us lawyers.

I stood up, my voice louder than it should have been. "I

know that, Ruby! I *know* you're not my dog! I'm just asking you to sit down and have a civilized conversation with me for a change!"

The door opened and Bradley's head popped in. "Trouble, sweetie?" he asked, not even looking at Ruby.

"No," I waved him away, "I'm fine. Just give us a few minutes."

"Yeah, sure," he said stepping into the room.

Out of the corner of my eye, I noticed Ruby rolling her eyes.

"I just wanted to firm up our date at the country club with The Coral Group? Tomorrow at seven sharp. We can't be late."

"Yes, I remember. It's in my calendar."

"Okay, great." He flashed me his good-job grin, the one that used to make me feel all warm inside but now just made me want to slap him. I immediately felt guilty. A girl probably shouldn't feel that way about the man she was going to marry in just a couple weeks.

"Do you mind?" I said, trying not to sound as annoyed as I felt. "We're having a little meeting right now. If you need to chat, I'll be out in a minute."

"Oh, you want me to leave?" He looked at Ruby. "What's the matter, Rube? You screw something up again?" He gave her his best cheesy, movie-star smile. When Candice and Kelly were still talking to me, they said it was too perfect. At the time I'd argued. Now, seeing him here kind of harassing Ruby, I wasn't so sure.

Ruby got halfway out of her seat before I intervened. "Bradley, come on, just give us a break, would you?"

He put his hands up. "Hey, it's just a joke. Come on, ladies, lighten up." He backed out of the room and went through the door in reverse, stopping when everything but his head was out of my office. His voice went from jocular to businesslike. "Ruby, seriously, though ... let me know when she's free so I can stop by and chat with her, would you?"

She didn't even acknowledge him. Bradley left after winking at me, giving me a thumbs up and pointing at Ruby's back. He probably thought I was going to fire her. To say he and Ruby do not get along would be a massive understatement.

"Okay, so where were we?" I asked.

"I was telling you I'm busy and you were excusing me from this meeting."

"No, that's not where we were." I left the space behind my desk and came around to join her, taking the chair on her left. She turned away from me, facing the wall of bookshelves that ran next to my desk.

"Ruby, if you're worried that being honest with me will cause you to lose your job, I want you to know that it won't happen. I'd never let you go for being honest. Besides … the senior partners love you. You have total job protection here."

She swiveled her head slowly in my direction. "Can I get that in writing?"

"Shit, Ruby, you know the law as well as I do. Your job is safe. Come on, talk to me."

She sighed. "I don't want to upset you." Her tone wasn't quite as harsh. It was the kindest thing she'd said to me in six months, and it gave me hope.

"Please, if it will help get us to the bottom of this mess, I don't care. Upset me."

She stared at me long and hard before exhaling in a really long, really sad-sounding sigh.

Just that alone made me want to cry. I almost didn't want to hear what she had to say now, knowing she was preparing herself to deliver some very bad news.

"Okay, I'm just going to come right out and say it, because this is something you need to hear. And since you don't talk to your friends anymore, it's on my shoulders to do it." She pressed her lips together and sat straighter. Then she looked at the ceiling before muttering, "Lord Jesus, please forgive me for being so bold and honest, but you know I'm doing it for the right reasons and my heart is true."

My own heart skipped a few beats. I threw up a prayer of my own. *Dear Tiny Baby Jesus, please give me the strength to not bite Ruby's head off, because I have a feeling I'm going to want to before she's done.*

Ruby's expression was part compassion and part anger. "You've changed and not for the better," she blurted out. Her eyes went wide and she blinked a few times. A half smile moved across her lips. "Well, that just came out all bold didn't it?" She laughed nervously. "What I mean to say is, ever since you got back from Kelly's wedding, you've changed. Your whole life has changed. You stopped talking to your friends, you stopped talking to me, you took up with that *Bradley...*"

"There you go again ... saying his name in that tone again. You know that sets my teeth on edge, Ruby." Tiny Baby Jesus had abandoned me in my hour of need. Ruby's head was already in danger of being removed and she'd only just begun.

She leaned in and looked me dead in the eye. "*He* used to set your teeth on edge. Remember that? We both hated that man." She poked me in the arm. "Now it's just everyone else hating him and you ... sleeping with him." Her lip curled up in disgust. "And now you're talking about *marrying* him? Have you done lost your mind, baby girl? How could you do that to yourself? He's not even close to good enough for you. He's not even good enough to wash your car."

I felt ashamed, angry, and sick. "I love him, Ruby." I almost choked on the words. They didn't want to come out.

She scowled. "Oh, fiddle sticks. You don't love that man. You love the idea of being married to *a* man. *Any* old man will do."

My face flushed an angry red as I sat back in a slump. "I can't believe you're saying these things to me. What gives you the right?"

She reached out and grabbed my wrist, pulling my hand into her lap and making me lean forward awkwardly. Her speech was passionate. "I'll tell you what gives me the right … I care about you, Andrea Lynn. You are a *good* girl. You are a *great* lawyer and a *strong* woman. But that *Bradley*? … I'm sorry, but he just sucks the life out of you, girl. He's got you on a leash like a tamed lap dog, and I'm not just going to sit back and let you tie yourself to him for life without knowing what you're getting into. It's my duty as your friend to tell you the things you need to hear. And if you want to go find yourself a new assistant, I'll understand. But good luck finding one here. You have a reputation now, you know." She nodded slowly, ever the wise one of the office.

I tried to pull my hand back but she held on with a grip of iron.

My tone was fury contained. "I know what I'm getting into, Ruby. I'm a grown woman." The words tasted sour, like unripe fruit on my tongue.

"Maybe on the outside you're full-grown, but on the inside, you're still a young girl looking for love and taking terrible substitutes instead. Why can't you see what I see and what Candice and Kelly see? You're smart, you're beautiful, you're strong … why do you have to act so deaf, dumb and blind when it comes to men?"

I laughed bitterly. "Wow. A veritable trifecta of awfulness. A hat trick of sucking. Thank you for that."

"No." She shook her finger in my face. "No, ma'am, you are not going to play that game with me."

"What game?" The guilt was almost overwhelming; she'd busted me attempting to use my litigation skills on her - a friend, a woman I respected. I was desperate not to hear her truths.

"You know what I'm talking about. That *game* you play. Where you go all cold and calculating and do the things that *Bradley* taught you. He is a bad influence, Andie. A very bad influence. He's changed you into a cold person who doesn't care about other people's feelings. You don't even know what's important anymore." Her expression and tone went a little desperate. "Can't you feel it? I know you can't see it, but can't you at least feel it?"

I yanked my hand away. "I know what's important. I've had a carefully crafted lifeplan guiding my actions since I was fifteen: go to college, go to law school, make partner, get married, have children. It's absolutely normal and fine. All those things are important and valuable to any sane person. It makes complete sense on paper."

Ruby cringed. "Do you hear yourself? Your life cannot be written out on paper! People with hearts and brains don't function like that!"

I stood up. "Of course I hear myself! I'm proud of what I'm saying and what I'm doing and have done! I'm the youngest junior partner this firm has ever had. I'm the rainmaker for Chrissake!"

She shook her head in disappointment. "No. You are a girl who's lost her way. A snake in the grass hissing a lot of new dirty words she learned from another snake in the grass." She snorted in disgust. "That *Bradley*, he is the King Cobra of snakes." She stood up and turned her back on me to walk to the door. Just before she left my office, she blasted me with her parting shots. "Maybe before you say, 'I do' to the King Cobra, you should ask yourself these questions: why did all your friends - all those *good* girls - abandon you? Why are you more alone now than you've ever been before? Shouldn't you be full of joy and sharing that joy with others when you're about to be married, instead of making up a guest list full of strangers?" She shook her head. "Your marriage is going to be more like a funeral, and I for one am not going to be a part of it."

The door shut behind her, and I stood there in the middle of my office with tears coursing down my cheeks. I hadn't wanted to listen to any of *that* garbage. I'd just wanted to know why she was doing such a horrible job as my assistant and why she'd stopped being my friend. Instead I'd gotten a pile of shit dumped on my head and my heart cracked in two.

I shoved the chairs back into position, ignoring the fact that the legs weren't put back in the indentations of the carpet they always rested in. Making my way around the desk, I shook my head in disgust. Ruby was so full of shit. Bradley had done nothing but advance my career and my stature at the firm. We joined the country club together and played tennis every weekend with other couples. We ate out all the time and even talked about moving in together before the wedding. I'd held off for some stupid reason, but now I couldn't remember why. Bradley was the only one who got my lifeplan and was totally on board with it. He's just like me: organized, driven, smart. We both know what we want and we're not afraid to go after it. Too bad for the rest of the world. If they don't understand the value of planning and drive, screw them. I didn't need anyone or anything but Bradley and the firm.

I ignored the physical pains that sliced through my chest at that thought.

The ring of my phone told me Ruby was calling in. I leaned over to the far corner of my desk, grabbing the handset, fully expecting to hear her apology. I planned to be gracious and act like the things she said hadn't cut me to the bone. Then we could go on as before, but with her doing a better job. A tight smile took up residence on my face.

"Yes?" I said, cold pride filling my voice.

"Line three is for you. Someone from the courthouse."

"Who is it, Ruby?" I asked, instantly irritated. She had a

hell of a lot of nerve giving me one of her bullshit call transfers after our little discussion. She knew at a bare minimum I needed a name, a department, and case file reference. *Jesus, what is her damn problem?*

Ruby's voice was so calm, so casual, it was as if we hadn't just had a come-to-Jesus meeting two minutes before. "I don't know who it is," she said. "Someone from the marriage license division."

"Oh." I frowned, the wind going completely out of my sails. "Why would they be calling me now? My appointment to pick up the license isn't until later this week. They never do things that fast or ahead of time."

Ruby just breathed in her handset.

"Put them through," I said, giving up on having a civil conversation with her.

I waited for the call to connect, my mind racing with questions. Bradley was in charge of arranging the catering, and I was in charge of the legalities and the band. Our guest list was mostly our top-value clients and fellow employees, so that meant there could be no skimping and no mistakes. If I didn't get that license in time, we'd be totally screwed. Nothing could be rescheduled without losing a lot of money and causing a lot of headaches.

The connection clicked through. "Hello, this is Andy Marks. How may I help you?"

"Hi, Ms. Marks, this is Latisha. You the one who applied for a marriage license? Annnnndrea ... uh ... Marks. Sorry, I can't really read your writing. You really should write neater on these forms."

I ignored her scolding. *Shuh, right. As if some minimum wage clerk down at the courthouse is going to give me lessons in filling out forms. Raise your hand if you went to law school.* "Yes, that's correct. That's me."

"And your middle name is Lynn and your social security number is 078-05-1120?"

"Yes, that's also correct. Is there a problem?"

"Yeah. That's why I'm calling. There's a question on the form you've answered incorrectly, so I need you to come back and do another form and include your divorce decree with it. I can't process it until it's complete, and without that decree, it won't work. The system won't even accept it, so I'm not even going to try. And don't ask me to change it for you, because that's not how it works."

"Wait … what?" My brain was misfiring, trying to put together her nonsensical words into a sentence that would mean something to me.

The woman sighed loudly. "Don't play. Seriously, I don't have time to play lawyer games today, okay? I got fifteen … no sixteen forms to process before I leave for the day, and if I don't get it done the team leader will be all up in my business, know what I'm sayin'?"

"Yes, I do … but no, I'm not playing. I'm serious. I've never been married in my life." A huge pit opened in my stomach, and that pit was filled with molten lava. *This cannot be happening to me.* Bradley will totally shit a hamster if there's a glitch. He's planned a bachelor's golf party and everything, with fraternity brothers coming in from all over the world to attend.

"Are you sure you're not married?" she asked, sounding doubtful.

"Positive," I said, sincerely irritated with this jerk in the courthouse who obviously hadn't gone anywhere after high school except maybe to McDonalds' hamburger university. "Believe me, I'd know if I was married to someone other than my fiancé."

"You ain't never been to Nevada?" she asked, an evil-sounding smile in her voice.

My ears burned as memories washed over and threatened to drown me in fear. I almost couldn't get the word out. I have been to Nevada. *Oh fuck me, I have been to*

*Nevada!* "Maybe. Once."

"When? Any chance it was about two years ago?"

My heart was pounding like a really loud and fast bass drum. I could literally feel the pulse in my neck without even touching it. "Maybe?" My voice was only capable of squeaking at this point. *Two years ago. That was Kelly's bachelorette party! No, this can't be happening!*

"Says here in my system you married a man by the name of … Gavin MacKenzie, on April tenth, two thousand and eleven. The signature matches the one you put on the form, maybe a little more messy, but it's the same one. That name ring any bells? Gavin MacKenzie? What is that? Scottish?"

My brain and heart both felt like they were going to explode now. My vision went fuzzy and my jaw dropped open as all the blood drained out of my head.

"Ma'am? Are you still there?" she asked, sounding bored and far away.

The phone dropped from my hand and hit the desk. A tiny voice came from down near my blotter. "Ms. Marks? Are you there? Are you okay? Hello? I'm gonna hang up this phone, you know. I don't have time for these games, I already *told* you."

The room started spinning and I blinked my eyes several times, trying to get my vision to come back. But it just kept narrowing down, a long gray tunnel with eventually just a pinprick of light at the end.

That's the last thing I remembered seeing before I woke up again on the floor with Ruby's worried face hanging over me.

# Chapter Fifteen

THE PLANE TOUCHED DOWN AT lunchtime in Boise, Idaho, the closest airport to Baker City, Oregon. I'd spent a sleepless night yesterday at my apartment. I begged off going with Bradley to the pub after work, telling him I had to attend to an emergency client meeting out of town that I couldn't put off. Luckily we worked in different departments and he wasn't privy to all of my client files, otherwise he would have known I was full of crap. I was also fortunate that Ruby had zero issue with hiding things from *that Bradley*. She'd been almost too delighted to make my plane, hotel, and car rental reservations. The feelings of guilt were turning into an ulcer, eating through me from the inside out.

The memory of Ruby pressing her good luck troll doll into my hand made me smile weakly, easing the pain somewhat. "Take this," she'd said after I'd sat in my chair like a zombie and tried to explain the huge error I had to go fix out in Oregon of all places. I had less than a week to get an annulment or divorce and fix the license garbage at the courthouse, or I was done. Single once again. Lifeplan in the dust. "It'll bring you luck," she assured me. "I had it in my pocket when I met my Michael, God rest his beautiful soul." She tilted her head back to stare at the ceiling for a few seconds, a contented look on her face.

I didn't ask her why she had a lumpy, plastic, ridiculous-looking troll doll in her pocket when she met her future husband. It was irrelevant, and I had to save all my energy for relevant facts only. I'd stared down at the thing in my hand, its ridiculous blue and purple hair sticking out in all directions, and almost shut it up in my desk when she turned around. But instead, I threw it into my purse and dragged it along with me on this fool's errand.

I sighed heavily, looking for the signs that would direct me to the car rental agencies. This had to be a mistake; it just had to be. How could I possibly have married a man in Vegas and not remembered any of it? This stuff doesn't happen in real life.

Only, it kind of does. It happens often enough that I've found myself part of a statistically valid group. I slogged through the airport as I recalled what I'd uncovered, my feet and legs moving through virtual mud or quicksand or something. I was so not motivated to deal with this shit.

After I'd gotten up off the floor of my office and convinced Ruby I didn't need an ambulance, I'd gone into research mode. No one can conduct discovery like this girl can, no one … especially when I was this focused on finding a loophole. While looking up my alleged husband's name and vital information provided on the faxed-over marriage certificate, I'd run across several newspaper articles about these twenty-four hour wedding chapels in Las Vegas that catered to the too-drunk-to-remember crowd. One of them was the one I'd been inside. And there was no doubt about it; I *had* been inside. My signature on the form was real. Yes, it was sloppy. Yes, it was crooked. Yes, it was even smudged. But it was definitely mine.

The signs for Enterprise car rentals appeared above my head. My hand shook as I wiped my upper lip. Boise was hotter than I would have guessed it could be this time of year. I continued down the hallway, lugging my overnight bag over my shoulder.

All my research had not been able to uncover one important fact: whether or not the marriage had been consummated. I wasn't even sure if I'd remember what Gavin MacKenzie *looked* like. The law firm's resources were pretty strong in the area of conducting background checks, but nothing had brought up a picture of the guy. I had his driving records - spotless - but no DMV mug shot.

I wanted to sob with anger and frustration. This whole mess flew in the face of my lifeplan. If Bradley ever found out that I'd kept this from him or that I'd even done such a stupid, irresponsible thing, our wedding would be canceled. And then I'd be one of *those* girls: the ones who get left at the altar. *Ugh. Shoot me now.* My rainmaker title would surely be gone soon thereafter. Who wants to do legal work with a girl who tries to become a bigamist on the sly? It's sick how quickly bad news makes it around our town. No one would believe me if I tried to convince them I didn't know I was married. Even as a skilled litigator, I was certain *that* was an argument I'd never be able make convincingly.

"Welcome to Enterprise. Can I help you?" asked the man at the counter.

"Yes. I have a reservation." I handed him the papers Ruby had given me. They were all so neatly organized and labeled. She was back on her game in a major way, even giving me a hug and kiss when I left the office. I guess that was one small consolation in my craptastic life. She didn't even scold me when I dropped the F-bomb no less than five times.

The rental agent typed some things into his computer, gave me some forms to sign, and then handed over some keys and a small black box. "Here you go. Enjoy your stay in the greater Boise area. Do you need a map?"

"No, I'll just use the GPS." I looked at the tiny device he'd given me, not feeling overly confident that it would do the job, but I was terrible with maps.

He smiled and nodded, my dismissal clear when he spun his chair around and faced the opposite direction.

I walked out into the parking lot and found the space he'd written on the rental folder. I frowned at the bright yellow and black machine that sat there waiting for me. *What is that? A riding lawnmower?* "This can't be right," I said to no one. I was the only one out there, so I don't know who I thought I was talking to, but having a thousand conversations in my head over the last twenty-four hours was making me question my own sanity. Probably talking out loud to myself wasn't any better, but what the hell ... might as well change up the crazy every once in a while to keep it fresh.

I pressed the button on the key ring and the headlights flashed on once, proving this was not a mistake. "A *Smart Car?* Are you kidding me?" It looked like a giant, wasp-yellow roller skate. Maybe not even a giant one; maybe just a large-ish roller skate. Surely looking like a giant wasp flying down a country road was a bad idea for a girl with a sting-allergy...

I debated in my head whether I should go and argue for one of the other fifty full-sized cars on the lot, but then gave up on the idea five seconds later. "Screw it," I said, annoyed as hell. "Might as well get eight hundred miles to the gallon, right?!" The tone of my voice had drifted a little over to the hysterical side, but there was nothing I could do about it. I was barely hanging on, the stress almost enough to send me to the looney bin. I just kept picturing Bradley saying, "You got married? To a complete stranger? In Las Vegas? When you were drunk? By a guy named Elvis?" It was too horrible to fully fathom. He'd dump me just for humiliating him in front of all his clients and his frat brothers and his parents. There were so many people expecting me to be the perfect fiancée.

I threw my overnight bag in the passenger seat and

drove off the lot, wishing I could peel out and really express my anger in a satisfyingly loud and obnoxious way. But I quickly learned that a Smart Car doesn't know how to peel out; it's not equipped to do much with its lawn-mower sized engine. It just knows how to deliver me from Point A to Point B on a very small amount of gas with almost zero elbow room. I felt like a clown buzzing around in her little circus car. The only things missing were a little face paint and some floppy shoes. At first I thought I was also missing one of those brass honky-horns that clowns carry around, but then I pressed on the steering wheel and found out differently. Yes, it's true. The Smart Car comes equipped with a clown honky-horn.

I arrived in Baker City, Oregon a little over two hours later and checked into my hotel room. Sitting on the bed in the tired old room, I stared at the ugly wallpaper. The folder sitting next to me on the nightstand was full of information I could use to help me find the mysterious Gavin MacKenzie. Now I just had to build up the nerve to use it. Then I could take off, ask a few questions of some strangers, track him down with their clues, and have that conversation with him. The one where I ask him if he remembers sleeping with me and then possibly marrying me too. My stomach was in knots.

# Chapter Sixteen

MY FIRST STOP WAS THE local diner.   Baker City's a smallish town, so I figured it would be like all the small towns I'd seen in the movies.   Everyone goes to the diner for a coffee and pie right?

I sat at the counter and ordered a decaf, getting the lay of the land before making my first move.   I skipped the pie because I didn't trust my stomach right now; it was way too full of a large contingent of very anxious butterflies.   My phone buzzed in my bag, but I ignored it.   Bradley or whoever it was would just have to wait until I got some direction.

My first goal was to work up enough nerve to ask some of the most ridiculous questions I'd ever asked in my life. Here's how I pictured that conversation going:

Me: *Do you know Gavin MacKenzie?*

Country person:  *Who's askin'?*

Me:  *His wife.*

Country person:  — *vacant look — crickets —*

There was no way I was going to be able to track him down without a story.   I needed a *good* story that wouldn't humiliate both of us.   A nice fat lie.   I picked up a sugar packet and emptied it into my cup as I thought about my options.   *I'll say I'm a lawyer and I'm tracking him down for an inheritance.* I frowned at my coffee cup, picking up the teaspoon to stir in the sugar. *No, that won't work. They'll want to know relatives' names and I don't have anything like that with me.* I stirred and stirred and stirred. *I'll say he's won some money in a contest. No, that's stupid. What am I ... Publisher's Clearing House?* I shook my head, grabbing more sugar. I ripped the packet open sloppily, spraying small white crystals all over the counter. *I'll say that I'm a relative from another city and I'm tracing my genealogy.*

"How're you doing over here?" asked a woman's voice. My waitress was staring at me from behind the counter, waiting for my response.

The words came flying out before I could stop them. "I'm looking for Gavin MacKenzie, do you know him?" *Oh, shit. Did she say* how *are you doing or* what *are you doing?* My skin flamed up a burning crimson, and I had to restrain myself from fanning my face with the napkin. I could *not* believe I just blurted that out. What happened to my kickass plan to play it cool? *Argh,* I totally hate myself sometimes.

"Of course I know Mack. Everyone knows Mack. But no one calls him Gavin except his mother and his grandmother." She smiled, the happy emotion not quite making it to her doe-brown eyes. Her name tag said *Hannah.* She was cute, even though her blonde hair was a little too brassy and her skin a little too heavily made-up. I guessed her to be a couple inches taller than me and about the same age, maybe a couple years older. The only thing keeping her from being a totally cliché diner waitress was bubblegum-smacking. She reminded me of a country version of Candice. My heart pulled uncomfortably at the thought of my friend. It had been way too long since we'd spoken. I blamed it on work, but Ruby blamed *that Bradley.*

"Can you tell me where to find...Mack?" I asked.

"Who are you, and what do you want to find him for?" She stood there with the coffee pot in her hand, her hip cocked, fully prepared to remain there until I confessed.

My ears burned with the shame of the coming deception. "I'm ...uh... Andie. And I'm looking for him so I can put together my genealogy chart."

"What's that? Like a school project or somethin'?"

"Yeah," I said, a lie sparking up in my mind and quickly turning into a roaring wildfire of bullshit. "I'm taking this special college course and we're learning how to put together our family tree and stuff and his family ...the MacKenzie's... they're in my tree. I think. The MacKenzies of Baker City to be exact."

A gravelly voice came from behind me, making my hair stand on end with fear.

*"Luceo non uro!"*

I spun on my stool. "Wha...!" I banged my coffee on the way around and sloshed it all over my hand and the counter, but I didn't bother with cleaning it up because I was too busy worrying that I was about to be eaten by a giant man-bear-pig.

*"Luceo non uro!"* he yelled again and then laughed. His mouth was completely covered by a gnarly, unkempt beard. I caught glimpses of teeth and tongue which made me feel just a tad bit safer. The idea of a toothless man-bear-pig somehow scared me more than one with proper dental care. I was obviously not functioning with all my brain cells online.

"Yeah, that's about right," said the waitress, snorting a little.

My voice finally started working again when I realized he wasn't about to attack or eat me. He was just standing there looking down at me from very high up and speaking Latin. There was a slight chance he was even smiling, but it was impossible to tell with the brown shag carpet he was wearing as face decoration.

I cleared my throat, giving it a little jump start. "I'm sorry, but what did you say?"

His voice came out gentle then, and smooth. He could have been a book narrator when he wasn't growling at women in diners. *"Luceo non uro.* It's the MacKenzie clan motto."

"MacKenzie *clan?"*

He cocked his head. "You know what a clan is, right?"

I gave him my best you-must-be-kidding look to cover up for my ignorance. "Of course I do. Don't be ridiculous. I'm doing a project."

"So I heard you say. What school are you attending? It sounds like a very interesting project." His tone suddenly went from man-bear-pig to cultured academic.

I decided it was a distinct possibility that I'd either fallen into the same rabbit hole as Alice or been slipped something illegal on the flight over. "Just a community college. In Florida where I live. It's pretty small, I'm sure you've never heard of it."

"Could be I haven't … could be I have, though," he said, putting his hands behind him and rocking a little on his heels, waiting expectantly. "Won't know until I hear the name."

"Palm Beach State College?"

"Are you asking or telling?" he said. His beard moved. I took the upward shifting of the hairy mess as a smile.

"Telling." I turned partway back to my coffee, using my napkin to dab away at my mess. "So, what was that motto again?"

*"Luceo,* which means *shine .. Non,* which means *not*…and *Uro,* which means *burn."*

"Shine not burn," I said, almost to myself. Why was that ringing a bell? Why did I think I'd heard that somewhere before?

"Kinda cute, huh?" asked Hannah.

Sounded more sexy than cute to me, but I smiled and nodded anyway. I had to get in good with the locals if I wanted to get this mess taken care of ASAP.

"That where you're from?" asked Hannah. She set the coffee pot down on the counter in between us. "Florida?" She was ignoring at least three people waving at her for more of the caffeinated goodness.

I nodded. "Yes, I live there. I'm just here for research."

"Long way to come for research when you could-a just called," she said, chewing her lip like she was trying to figure me out. It made me nervous to think that Diner Barbie was hot on my trail of lies. I was getting the distinct impression she'd be really happy to bust me.

"Yes, well, I tried to call but the MacKenzie group is hard to get in touch with that way, apparently."

"Who'd you try to call?" she asked.

Her questions were taking on an intense mood to them that made me less inclined to share. "I can't remember. I don't have my notes with me." *Lies, lies, and more lies.* The leather messenger bag at my feet had exactly one troll doll and everything I'd been able to find on the MacKenzies. Unfortunately, all I had for an address was a post office box in the middle of town and a phone number nobody ever answered.

"Why are you looking for Gavin?" she asked. Her tone had taken on a proprietary air, and I realized I could very possibly be looking at Gavin's *other* wife, since apparently only special people called him by his given name. *What are the chances that I've stepped right off the plane into a pile of horse shit?* I looked at her slightly mutinous expression and knew the answer. *Out here, probably good.* Checking her finger, I saw no ring there. I let out a slow breath of relief, hoping she and the man-bear-pig still behind me wouldn't notice now nervous this conversation was making me.

"I'm headed out to the MacKenzie place if you want to hitch a ride," said the grizzly man.

I turned back around to face him, but not before catching a scowl move across Hannah's face.

"Really? That would be great. I could follow you in my car."

He looked out the front windows of the diner directly at my Smart Car.

"I wouldn't recommend it," he said simply.

I imagined myself trapped in a vehicle with this man and decided there were certain risks I was willing to take and others I just wasn't. "I'll be fine. That little car has a lot of spunk ... you'd be surprised."

"Whatever floats your boat. You ready to go now?"

"But she hasn't even finished her coffee," said Hannah. She sounded very upset about it, too.

"I can wait," said the man.

I stood. "No need. I put too much sugar in it anyway." I put some money down on the counter, enough to cover the coffee and a generous tip. "Thanks, Hannah."

She frowned at me. "How'd you know my name?"

I looked pointedly at her name tag. "Uhhh, I guessed?"

"I got my eye on you, Abbie," she said in a threatening tone, narrowing her eyes.

"That's *Andie*."

"Let it go, Hannah Banana," said the man-bear-pig, sighing at the end of his plea.

"Shut up, Boog! You don't tell me what to do anymore, got it? And stop calling me that name."

I picked up my satchel, very happy to be leaving the unhappy Hannah Banana behind. She obviously had an issue with strangers, so it was time for me to leave. Besides, if I could get lucky and find this MacKenzie place before dinner, I could very possibly be home by noon tomorrow. A grin spread across my face as I pictured myself sewing this little problem up and tucking it away in a little box no one would ever find.

"Come on, follow me. I'm in the blue truck out there. We've got about a thirty minute drive ahead of us."

I stopped walking as his words sank in.    "Thirty minutes?" I asked.

He didn't answer.  He just went out the door of the diner, leaving me to follow.

# Chapter Seventeen

THE FIRST PART OF THE trip was a breeze. Fifteen minutes of smooth driving and beautiful weather had my windows down and my voice soaring out into the wind. *Walking On Sunshine* came on the radio, and I yelled the lyrics as loud as I could, rejoicing in the seratonin that was bleeding into my brain. *Life is good! Life is awesome!* I was on the road to traveling towards my lifeplan again! I pictured myself on the plane with my signed annulment papers in my lap and a smile on my face. There was even a cocktail on my tray in this vision of glory. Maybe I'd even upgrade to first class.

Just as my song was finishing, the man-bear-pig, a.k.a *Boog* turned off the two-lane paved road and onto one with only a single-lane of dirt. Calling it a road was generous, though. It was more like a path than anything else. It made me happy I was driving a clown car when I saw his big tires going off into the weeds on both sides.

That happiness faded quicker than I would have thought possible. My life went from smooth-sailing to Nightmare on Elm Street in five seconds flat. Literally *flat*. Like, flat-tire flat. I was so busy trying to see Boog through the cloud of dust his giant truck was kicking up, I didn't see the huge pothole in the road. My tire fell into it and then didn't want to come out. The whole vehicle was sitting off-kilter, the passenger-side lower than the driver-side.

I pressed on the gas pedal and the car rocked a little, but then nothing but the sound of spinning wheels greeted my ears. The clown car and I were done.

Looking up, I saw Boog's truck getting smaller and smaller in the distance. He didn't seem to consider the craters in the road a reason to go any slower than he'd been traveling on the highway. I pressed on the clown car's honky-horn several times to get his attention, but he didn't seem to hear it. He soon disappeared in a cloud of dust.

I got out of the car and walked around to the other side of it. The front tire was flat and resting deep in the hole. "What the hell!" I screamed, kicking it and hurting my toe in the process. "Ow-ow-ow-ow-OW!" I yelled, hopping around on one foot, now worried that I'd broken not only the car but a toe, too. I was jumping around like a lunatic yelling cuss words when a horse and rider appeared out of the nearby trees and bushes.

# Chapter Eighteen

"LOOKS LIKE YOU'RE IN SOME trouble," said the man on the back of the horse.

I couldn't decide which of them was prettier. The horse was a patchwork of colors and the man was broad-chested and thick in the thighs, wearing a pair of those leather pant cover thingies that cowboys have on over their jeans in commercials. If I were to guess, I would have said he was younger than me by a few years. He reminded me of someone I'd seen before, but who it was exactly escaped me. It crossed my mind that it was some movie star I'd seen in some indie film a while back, maybe. This would be a good place for celebrities to hang out. No paparazzi would bother coming all the way out into this wasteland for a stupid photo.

"What kind of car is that, anyway? Is it electric?" He rode the horse up closer, walking around to inspect my clown car.

"It's not electric. It's a Smart Car. Are you from the MacKenzie clan by any chance?"

"Could be," he said. "Depends on who's asking." He got down off his horse and walked over to stand by my out-of-commission tire, crouching down and putting his hand on it.

"My name's Andie, and I'm here to find Gavin. Is that

you?" I was fairly sure it wasn't him. Surely I would have recognized something about the man I allowed into the golden palace and *married*, for God's sake. This man was a stranger to me.

He stood, still looking at the tire but shaking his head. "Nope. I'm sure as hell *not* Gavin." He got back up on his horse in one smooth maneuver, swinging his leg over the saddle like he did it every day of his life. With a creak and shift of the worn leather, he used the reins to turn the beast's head in the direction Boog's car had gone. He make a clicking sound with his tongue and jabbed his boots into the horse's sides. It moved off with a flick of its tail.

My mouth dropped open as my brain computed what my eyes were seeing. *Is he...is he leaving me?* I couldn't believe he was actually riding away, but that's exactly what he was doing, without even a backward glance.

"Are you just going to leave me out here?" I asked in a raised voice.

He didn't answer, so I started running after him. "Hey! I'm talking to you! Are you just going to leave me out here to die?!"

"House isn't that far," he said calmly, not looking back. "You won't die."

His horse's giant ass-end was the last hope of transportation I saw on that road for the next hour. It wasn't, however, the last *living* thing I saw on that road.

"Ack! Jesus!" I yelled a half hour later, jumping to the side at the sound of rattling coming from a pile of rocks about five feet from the side of the road. My voice became a half screech, half whisper when something moved out from a crevice and started slithering towards the road. "Rattlesnakes?! Are you kidding me?!" My heels were the world's worst running shoes, but running shoes they became. My satchel banged against my hip as I took off sprinting down the road, heedless of the rough terrain and my sore toe, thinking only how I'd definitely miss my wedding if I was chock full of snake venom. I could totally picture myself a bloated, poisoned mess on the side of this road, and that vision gave me a speed I hadn't known I was capable of reaching in three-inch heels.

I fell to my knees twice before I was hurt enough to have to slow down. I was being beaten to death by my own purse every time I bit the dust, which wasn't helping. "Dammit," I growled, bending down and holding onto my ankle as I tried to stand, while my bag once again whacked me in the side of the head. I'd twisted my foot good when the front of my shoe ended up balanced on a rock instead of the dirt road. I looked up through the strap of my bag and blew my hair out of my face. Everything was the same color out here - golden brown - and it was impossible to see what was rock, what was road, and what was a frigging pit to fall into.

"Ooohhhh mmmmm rrrrr." I moaned like a wild woman, trying to force the pain out of my foot and into the atmosphere. It wasn't working. I tried to limp with the shoe on, but that wasn't working either, so I took it off. It wouldn't fit into my bag, so I just held it. "Baker City *sucks!*" I shouted at the snakes and the spiders and the horses' asses I'd met so far. "I can't wait to get out of this hell hole and back to the East Coast where all the *normal* people live!" I pulled the troll doll out of the bag and looked at it. "You were supposed to be good luck, you little bastard." I arched my arm back, ready to launch the little traitor out into the dust, but at the last minute I held back, thinking about how Ruby had looked up to the heavens when talking about the damn thing. She'd never forgive me. I started walking again, the troll doll gripped tightly in my hand.

The sun beat down on my head and neck, making me wish I'd brought sunscreen. I could feel my skin frying, the smell of my roasting skin nauseating for the pain I knew I'd be in later. I put my satchel on top of my head as a temporary shelter for a few minutes but eventually gave up. It was too heavy and I had my stupid shoe and the troll to carry, which left me one-handed. Eventually I gave up trying to carry the bag on my shoulder and just dragged it in the dust behind me.

It was when I'd reached the point where I'd estimated my chances of survival at less than twenty-five percent when I caught a glimpse of a building ahead. A house, maybe. Or a barn. It was tough to tell in the wavering heat with my blurring vision. Whatever it was, it had a roof on it and probably a faucet inside. "Water," I said, holding my shoe out towards the house as I limped painfully along. I heard more rattling sounds behind and to the sides of me, but I could no more run from them than I could conjure an ice-cold lemonade out of thin air. Oh, what I wouldn't have given for such a thing right then. I would have chugged it down and then thrown the glass at all the snakes probably right behind me on the road, a giant league of them just waiting for me to fall one last time.

I made it almost to the gate of the fence that circled a large plot of land around the house before I took my last trip down to face-plant alley. My toe caught another rock or pit or snake or something and the road rose up to greet me in a very unwelcoming way. I got a real up-close and personal taste of what Baker City, Oregon has to offer. I was spitting a mouthful of it out when I rolled over onto my back in the middle of the road.

Above my head was a giant archway of wood with a crest in the middle of it. There were flames and a rope carved into it, and above it all were three Latin words: *Luceo non uro.*

I whispered them aloud. *"Luceo non uro.* Shine, not burn." I closed my eyes and drifted off, remembering a man wearing a cowboy hat and a pair of jeans with a brass-colored belt buckle riding around his waist. That phrase was the last thing I remember that cowboy saying to me.

*Shine, not burn.*

# Chapter Nineteen

"WELL, PICK HER UP THEN, dammit," said a woman's voice. "What's wrong with you, son, you know better than that!"

"Aw, she's fine. She's just being dramatic. What's that thing in her hand?"

"Look at her dry lips, fool. She's dehydrated and she's hurt her ankle or her leg. Look at the bottom of her foot there. *Tsk-tsk*, that one without the shoe is bleeding." The woman sounded very concerned and caring, unlike the male voice.

"Mack should be the one out here hauling her around. She came out here for him, not me."

"We'll hear all about that later, but right now I want her out of the sun and in the living room, pronto. And if you sass me again, you're going to be on branding duty alone for the next three weeks."

"For shit's sake, Ma, you don't have to get ugly about it! I didn't say I wasn't going to do it, I just said it should be Mack taking care of his problems, not me. I'm tired of taking care of his problems."

The sound of a face getting slapped made me smile in my half-conscious state.

"Don't you dare, Ian MacKenzie. You might think

you're a grown man, but I have absolutely no problem getting my spatula out and serving you up a heaping helping of bare butt flap jacks, you hear me?"

A loud sigh preceded a subdued, "Yes, ma'am."

"Now do what I told you to do, and be nice to her. She's going to think all the MacKenzies are a bunch of savage retards."

"Ma!" said the man, trying to talk but laughing instead. "That's not nice at all, is it? Calling your children savage retards... Jesus."

"I call it like I see it. I'll be waiting for you inside. Now get to it."

The sound of gravel-crunching footsteps faded in the distance, leaving me alone with the savage retard, Ian MacKenzie.

"I see you smiling down there. You can stop playing possum with your little purple-haired friend and help me get your big butt up off the ground any day now."

My eyes flew open. "Excuse me? Did you just insult my butt?"

He shrugged, zero expression on his face. "I call it like I see it and make no apologies."

I wanted to get up now just so I could give him a heaping helping of whatever his mother had just promised him. "I don't need your stupid help," I said, struggling to stand. I slapped his proffered hand away. "Don't touch me, you savage retard."

"Oh, that's nice. Demeaning people with handicaps by using their condition as an insult." He backed away, giving me plenty of space. "Go ahead then, take care of yourself. I'll just stand over here and shoot that rattler that's behind you."

I spun around, screaming, "What?!" I tried to back up at the same time as I turned, and the combination of movement I'm woefully not qualified to make while wearing one heel sent me once more to the ground. I crabwalk-dragged and scrambled my big butt across the road to put as much distance between me and the serpent as possible.

"Where is it?" I asked breathlessly, staring desperately first into the bushes and then up at him.

The bastard was laughing.

Realization dawned. "There wasn't a rattlesnake there, was there?"

He shook his head while he laughed at me, tears coming to his eyes. "Damn, girl, you sure can scoot when you have to."

I whacked him in the leg, making my hand sting from the slap against his leather pant covers. "Help me up, jerk. My ankle's messed up and now my clothes are ruined too, thanks to you." Not even crazy drycleaner magic was going to be able to save this suit. And I'd just bought it last month in my favorite store, too. They should put a slogan on the sign coming into town: *Baker City, The Dustiest Place on Earth.*

Ian bent down and grabbed me under the armpits. One smooth yank and I was on my feet in front of him. Damn, he was strong. His shoulders were about a mile wide.

"Put your arm over my shoulder," he ordered, dipping it down a little and reaching his hand out.

"No." I pushed his hand away.

He had been about to step forward with me next to him, but then he stopped. "Why not?" He turned to look at me. Up close I could finally get a good look at his face. He seemed so familiar. *Must be because I'd accidentally married his brother.*

"Are you and Gavin twins?" I asked, before I could put the brakes on between my brain and my mouth.

"Nope, not even close." He ducked his shoulder again and forced it into my armpit. "Come on, I have to get you inside before my mom skins my hide."

"Aren't you a little old for the Aunt Jemima treatment?" I asked, deciding not to fight his help anymore. I really couldn't walk without it. It wasn't so much the twisted ankle as the possible sun stroke.

He chuckled. "You don't know my mother, do you?"

"No, I don't know any of you." I limped along, appreciating his support but loathe to admit it out loud.

"If you don't know any of us, then what are you doing out here asking for Gavin?"

I battled with myself, wondering if I should tell him the truth or go with my genealogy story. It made little sense that I'd be tracking just Gavin down for a family tree project, but the lie was easier to go with than reality. Even standing here on his family's land within arm's reach of my goal, real life was just too big and scary.

"I'm doing a project researching my family tree, and his name came up. I'm just following leads." I told myself it wasn't a complete lie, hoping to assuage the guilty feelings that were making my face burn. According to the records of the State of Nevada, I am officially part of the MacKenzie tree ... sitting right next to Gavin on one of its branches, in fact. If I really was doing a project, all of this would make complete sense. Kind of. Except for the marrying-someone-and-not-remembering-it part.

"Huh. Sounds interesting," said Ian, but not like he really meant it. "Did you go to Utah first?"

"Why would I do that?" I inhaled sharply when my bum foot accidentally dropped down and caught the edge of the road, twisting it back.

Ian slowed down to accommodate my pain and mumbled cussing. "I thought that's where all the best genealogy records were kept."

Since I'd been talking out of my butt this entire time, I had no idea if he was right about that or not, but I figured there was no harm in shining him on. "Yeah, well, I just did it all online. But you're right about Utah. I might go there next."

"So you're just flying around all over the country following family tree leads?"

"Yeah, something like that."

"Don't you have a job?" We'd reached the porch and my ankle was throbbing at this point. I turned to face him where he was standing one step below me.

"Yes, I have a job. I'm an attorney."

He snorted. "Why does that not surprise me?"

"Do you really want an answer to that question?" I asked, ready to let him have it. I'd reached the end of my patience with this idiot.

"Who's this?" asked a male voice behind me.

I turned around and almost had a stroke over the glowing blue eyes that bore into me from under a straw-colored cowboy hat.

"Mack," I said in a strangled whisper, memories rushing over in a giant tsunami to drown me in raw emotion.

"Andie," he said, his face set in angry lines.

# Chapter Twenty

"WHOOP, THERE SHE GOES AGAIN," said Ian, catching me as I tilted backwards. He lifted me up like a baby and carried me into the house, dropping me onto a couch from a couple feet up.

My head lolled around as my body bounced up off the cushions. I was so dizzy, I feared I was going to yack in their living room. When my body finally settled into a still position, I stared at the ceiling, swallowing several times to get control of my stomach and throat. *Do not throw up, do not throw up!*

A woman who looked to be in her fifties and wearing a well-worn denim dress appeared, standing over me. Her dyed brown hair was pulled loosely into a bun and a pair of sunglasses were pushed up to the top of her head. In her hand was a glass of fluorescent yellow liquid. "Here, sweetie, take a drink of this." She sat on a coffee table just next to me.

"What is that? Antifreeze?" I asked, my voice muddy with fatigue and nausea.

She hooted loudly and then smiled. "Anti-freeze? Now that's a new one. I've been accused of a lot of things, but never poisoning a houseguest with automobile products. Come on now, drink up your Gatorade. You're dehydrated."

I smiled weakly. "Oh. Gatorade. That's good." I put

the troll doll down on the tabletop and took the glass with a shaking hand, drinking the entire serving of watery sourness in about five swallows.

"Good," she said, patting my arm and taking the glass back before standing. "Come on, Ian. Let's let this young lady have her peace with Mack."

"I'm not staying," said a deep male voice from across the room near the entrance.

"Yes you are, dear," said the lady, leaving my side and walking over to Mack. I could just barely see him by tilting my head all the way back into the pillows at the end of the couch. He stood there in jeans and a black t-shirt, his hat and belt buckle proclaiming to the world that he's a country boy. The beautiful cowboy I'd thought I had imagined had risen from my dreams and nightmares like a specter to stand before me, a ghost who was not only haunting my past but my present and possibly future now, too.

The older woman patted him on the upper arm as he looked down at her with an unreadable expression. "She came all the way from who knows where, and from the looks of it, walked a lot of the way. She deserves a couple minutes of your time, at least."

"She's already had a couple minutes of my time and it was more than enough, trust me."

"Well, then, just give her a few more for me. Make your momma happy." She left the room and dragged Ian with her. He said nothing, just stared at his brother and then at me for some reason. His eyes were still drilling holes into my head as he disappeared around the corner.

I tried to sit up but only got partway there before my brain was spinning again with the dehydration or whatever, so I laid back down. "Would you mind coming a little closer? I can't really see you over there." My stomach was in knots being in the same room with him, but I'd come this far and put up with snakes, spiders, dirt, and a man-bear-pig leaving me to die. It was time to woman-up, bite the bullet, and get 'er done. I had no idea where my satchel was, but it had to be close; I'd made it all the way to the front gate before dropping it. Those annulment papers were all ready, and the only thing I had to do was explain so he would sign on the dotted line.

Mack took a few steps into the room, stopping about ten feet away from me in the center of the space. He said nothing.

My heart ached with how handsome he was standing there. I might not have been able to remember everything of the night I met him, but his face I could never completely forget. I knew that now. When I'd met him I'd thought him the most gorgeous man I'd ever seen; but now I knew I'd been wrong then. *Now* he was the most gorgeous man I'd ever seen. The two years had been good to him. His face was a little lined and his tan deeper, his expression more severe. But those eyes … those glowing eyes were as brilliantly blue as ever. They drilled right into my chest and seared holes into my heart. He was angry, and he was making it very clear I'd been the one to cause his pain. He was probably furious that I'd put him in a position to have to explain to his family the ridiculous thing he'd done on a crazy weekend in Vegas.

I tried to smile, but I could feel it was coming out more like a grimace. My face didn't seem to want to obey my commands at this particular moment. I gave up on forcing it when one side of my mouth started to twitch. "I'm sorry to come out here without any notice, but I did try to call first."

His smile was definitely of the bitter variety. "That's interesting."

"How so?" I had a feeling there was more to that response, and I wasn't disappointed when he finally explained half a second later.

"I thought maybe you didn't know how to use a phone. That's what I told myself, anyway."

I frowned. "What? Of course I know how to use a

phone. The problem is *you* apparently don't know how to *answer* one. I called your house here like ten times in the last couple days." I struggled to sit up. *I'll be damned if I'm going to be insulted lying down.* Swinging my legs over the side of the couch, I was finally able to present a more serious appearance, battling nausea but determined to win. *Time to get down to business.* "Listen, I don't want to waste your time or cause you any problems with your family or girlfriend or whatever, but I'm about to get married and we have a problem. In the process of applying for a license, I discovered a little issue with the records in Nevada. I just need to get them straightened out and I'll be out of your hair forever, I promise."

"A little problem. With the records." He said it so coldly, it made me flinch.

I cleared my throat and continued, boldly ignoring all the body language in front of me that said I had a very angry cowboy on my hands. "Yes. A problem. The State of Nevada seems to be under the mistaken belief that you and I are actually *married*." I tried to force a laugh, but it sounded more like a goose being strangled so I quit immediately. "I just need you to sign off on the papers I brought so we can fix it."

"Papers." He was like a parrot the way he kept repeating what I said. It was highly irritating. I tried not to let my annoyance show in my voice but it was pretty much impossible.

"Yes. Annulment papers. Or divorce papers. I brought both." Thank God I knew attorneys in Nevada through my own networking who I could contact privately. No way could I have used the firm's connections without alerting every single employee there that I was married to some dude out in Oregon. What a mess that would have been. No ... secrecy was the only way to handle this. Bradley could not find out what I was doing out here. He'd never understand. I'd tell him after we're married for a few years, when it wouldn't matter anymore. Not that it mattered now...

"One set of papers wasn't enough, you needed both?"

I squirmed uncomfortably on the couch. Here came the part where I felt like Andie the super-slut. "Just in case ... you know..."

"No, I don't," he said very calmly. "That's why I asked."

My face flamed red. "If we didn't consummate the marriage, well, we can just annul it. But if we did, then, a divorce is just quicker."

He just stared at me, his own face going red too. Only *his* high color probably wasn't the result of being embarrassed, judging by the way he kept tensing his jaw while glaring at me.

"I'm not going to sign," he finally said, before turning to leave.

"What do you mean, you're not going to sign?" I wasn't sure I was completely understanding or even hearing properly. Maybe all that sun exposure had given me a stroke.

"I don't believe in divorce," he said. He walked out of the room and the house without another word, slamming the front door so hard behind him it made the curtains shake and some glass things tink together in a china cabinet.

I stood to run after him, but quickly fell sideways onto the couch when my feet got tangled in themselves and threatened to take me down onto the coffee table. My hip hit the cushions, sending a whoosh of air up into my face. I blinked a few times getting my wits back before sitting up.

"What. The. Hell." I said out into the room. I was at a complete loss as to what I should do now. Run after him? Nope, legs were not cooperating. Yell at him? Nope, he was already too far away to hear anything. Wait for him to come back? Not sure that I had any other choice.

I leaned back into the cushions and stared out into nothingness, my mind swirling around with the implications arising from this unexpected circumstance. Never in my wildest of imaginings had I pictured him saying no to signing the papers. The worst thing I'd come up with was another woman in the mix, and while it had been uncomfortable to think about, it wasn't as awful as this. At least a jealous girlfriend or even a second wife would have provided some kind of motivation for him to execute the papers.

*Dammit! What am I supposed to do now?* I looked around the room, my mind zooming all over and not making much sense. But then my eye landed on a group of photographs and my brain zeroed in on one of the faces I saw there. I slid off the couch and crawled on hands and knees over to the table that showed off the family's loved ones in frames, not trusting my feet to get me there without tipping over.

I reached up and took down the one I'd seen from across the room. I smiled when I saw the faces there and the postures held by the people in the photo that told me this was something I could use to my advantage. "Bam. I gotcha now, cowboy."

I put the framed photo back and crawled back to the couch, deciding that in order to have my ducks in a row and the energy that I'd require for the upcoming fight, I'd need all my strength back. A nap was in order, and the couch was just too comfortable to pass up. I eased my aching feet up to hang just over the edge and laid down on my side. Grabbing the silly troll doll and tucking my pressed-together hands under my cheek, I told myself it would just be a cat nap. The troll's hair tickled my chin, but I left the doll there. My only friend in a great big state full of dust, snakes, and angry cowboys. *Just long enough to get the dizziness to pass and to put together my plan of attack.* All of my court cases had been won with a combination of planning and skill. I could do this, no problem. I'd be out of Baker City with signed documents in less than twenty-four hours. I just had to be at the top of my game the next time I saw Mack, so I could convince him that denying me what I wanted was futile. I would get him to sign those papers if it was the last thing I did.

At some point I sensed someone coming in and putting something heavy on me that I snuggled under happily. And then I was finally awakened by the sounds of dishes and glasses hitting one another and silverware scraping on plates. Distant voices told me that a large number of people were very close by. I set the troll doll down on the coffee table and went to investigate.

# Chapter Twenty-One

I GOT UP SLOWLY, MAKING sure not to put too much weight on my bum foot, and snuck out into the hallway where I found a bathroom. Stepping inside, I emptied my bladder and did the best I could to fix my hair. It was pretty much a hopeless case. I had no brush to smooth out the lumps and bumps, and when I took my elastic out to try and tighten the ponytail I'd put in earlier, it broke.

"Dammit." I stared at it, wondering if I could knot it back together and try again.

"Hello?" came a voice from the other side of the door. It was the woman who'd given me the Gatorade. "Andie? Can I get you anything?"

"Uh, no, thank you. I'll be right out." I rubbed a wet finger over my teeth, trying to get rid of the sour sleep taste in my mouth, and washed my hands. Before walking out the door, I took one last look at myself; I was a sunburned, tangle-haired mess. Why Mack wasn't rushing to sign the papers was some kind of weird mystery. If I were him, I'd be doing everything I could to get my sorry-looking butt out of here.

I walked out of the bathroom to find the older woman waiting patiently in the hallway.

"There you are. Did you sleep okay?" she asked.

"Um, yes. Sorry about that." My face went redder with embarrassment. "I only meant to take a little catnap to get rid of that dizzy feeling, but I must have really dozed off."

She put her hand on my shoulder and gently but firmly guided me down the hallway in the opposite direction of the living room. "You were all tuckered out. It's perfectly fine for you to take a nap here, it's not a problem at all. We were just sitting down to an early dinner and thought you'd like to join us. My name's Maeve by the way."

I stopped dead in my tracks. "Dinner? With your family?"

"Well, yes, sweetie. We eat as a family here, every night." She smiled warmly. "It's kind of a tradition. Our boys have always been the type to run out the door with friends and work and everything else, but one thing we always insisted on was dinner at home, all of us at the table with no television, no phones, and no radio. Just eating and talking and hopefully laughing but sometimes a little bit of yelling happens too." She gave me wry grin. "Comes with the territory of having all men in the house."

I smiled, despite my panic. "That's nice. The eating together part, anyway."

"We like it." She pushed on me to make me move, but I stayed put.

"I'm sorry, is it your ankle or your foot?" She looked down at it in concern.

"No, it's mostly fine now. But I don't think I should eat dinner here, though. I appreciate you inviting me, but I think I'd prefer to just get a bite in town."

"Oh, no, I insist," she said, pushing me more firmly.

I moved because to do otherwise would have been rude. Besides, it was very possible that I'd need this woman to intervene on my behalf, so getting on her bad side would be seriously counterproductive. "I guess if it isn't any trouble..."

"No trouble at all. I've never learned to cook for less

than ten people."

"Ten?" I squeaked out. The closer we got to the next room, the louder the voices became. *Are there ten people in there?*

"Sometimes we have that many. Tonight it's just the four of us, Boog, and you. But since I cooked for ten again, we'll have leftovers for tomorrow's lunch. I hope you like ribs."

My stomach chose that exact moment to growl like a bear. Ribs were one of the guilty pleasures I allowed myself about once a month from a local eatery that specialized in authentic pit barbecue.

She laughed. "I'll take that as a yes. Come on. I've put you across from Gavin."

We turned the corner together and my feet slowed as I took in the scene before me. Maeve and I were the only females in the room. The rest of the space was taken up by giant men. Not one of them could have weighed less than two hundred pounds, and Boog himself was almost twice that, with hair enough for a couple wookies.

It was easy to see where Ian and Mack got their good looks. They were a perfect combination of their parents, getting their large frames and square jaws from their father and their hair color and smiles from their mother.

As soon as they realized I was in the room, the smiles disappeared. The talking stopped and all eyes were on me.

Boog turned around to see what the silence was all about. He was the first to speak. "Well, there she is. Sleeping beauty rises from the dead." He chuckled and went back to gnawing on the bone he held in his hand.

I walked over to the empty seat next to him and stood behind it. "No thanks to you. Appreciate you leaving me out there to die with the rattlesnakes." I tried to sound mad, but the food looked and smelled so good I couldn't concentrate on my anger enough to make it believable.

"You recall that I tried to offer you a lift…" He turned to

face me and I worked at not feeling sick over the pieces of rib schmeg stuck in his beard. He looked like a complete and utter savage, making me wonder what Mack's family could possibly be thinking by wanting him here at their table.

I looked across the table at Mack and then quickly shifted my gaze to the mashed potatoes when he caught my eye. *Those damn blue eyes. Why do they affect me like this?* I felt like I had a fever, my skin suddenly going sensitive and the heat rising up inside me. My master plan to use the girl in the photo to force his hand seemed flimsy. He definitely wasn't coming across as a man who could be easily intimidated. Why did I remember him being so much more easygoing? Was it because I was so drunk or because he'd changed?

I turned my attention back to Boog. Looking down at him from behind my seat was like taking a visual cold shower, helping me get a grip on my emotions. "Yes, but you failed to mention when you offered that lift that the road was straight out of Baghdad and not suited to travel by a Smart Car."

He snorted. "Foreigners." Taking a bite of his rib, he continued to speak, not letting the fact that he had a mouthful of meat bother him in the least. "I got news for you … a Smart Car isn't suited to travel anywhere around here, not even the highway. With all the four-wheel drive trucks around, you could get yourself hurt if you got in an accident. Better leave the Smart Cars on the golf course where they belong."

Mack shifted in his seat and I looked up at him again. I felt the heat rise in my cheeks as the muscle in his jaw pulsed out a few times. I was affecting him as much as he was affecting me, only I think my presence was making him angry whereas his was making me think stupid, stupid things that girls who are engaged to other men should not be thinking. I pulled the chair out and stood in front of it at the table.

Boog continued. "Next time a gentleman offers you a ride, you should take him up on it and not be so big city independent about it."

"The first time one does, I will." I smirked, taking my chair at the edges and pulling myself up closer to the table. I was so distracted from Boog's scolding and my own witty comeback, I sat down from higher up than I intended and my butt made a loud slapping sound on the wood. I blushed again, too embarrassed to look at anyone. There was already at least one guy at the table who'd noticed my big back yard, but now the whole family was aware of the fact that my butt-cheek to chair-seat ratio was a little butt-heavy.

"Welcome to the ranch of Clan MacKenzie," said the big man at the head of the table, sitting just to my left.

I jerked my head in his direction, glad for the distraction. "You're the patriarch, I take it." I held out my hand. "My name's Andie. Andie Marks." His grip was firm and warm.

I snuck a glance in Mack's direction in time to see his jaw bouncing out a couple times as he clenched his teeth together, but then he put a rib up to his mouth and covered the lower half of his face, making it impossible for me to tell what he was feeling.

"I'm Angus," said Mack's father. "My boys are Gavin - he goes by Mack - and Ian. My wife over there is Maeve, and this is Mr. Atticus Boegman, but everyone just calls him Boog."

I nodded at everyone. "Nice to meet you all." *For the second time, some of you.* Mack was doing a great job of acting like he couldn't give a flying fudge about me being at the table sitting directly across from him, with his casual nod and sudden interest in the arrangement of his peas on his plate. I watched distractedly as he pushed them around in different formations.

Angus handed me a big heavy bowl of mashed potatoes with little green and black flecks in them. "So, Andie Marks, tell us what brings you to Baker City. I take it you're not from around here." He smiled, and for the life of me, I couldn't detect a trace of mockery there in his expression, despite the fact that Boog had done a fine job of setting me up as the out-of-town big city girl goofball. Or maybe it was me who'd done that. It didn't matter either way; I was out of my element and definitely a foreigner. The quicker I could get out of here, the better it would be for everyone.

Angus's question sent me into panic mode. I scooped out potatoes and plopped them onto my plate with as much concentration as I could muster, trying to appear as if I couldn't serve and talk at the same time. I had to stall and come up with a plan. *Why am I here in Baker City?* This was nothing like the courtroom. There I always told the truth, but here in front of this judge and jury I had to decide whether to keep up the family tree charade or just come out with the whole sordid tale. Las Vegas or bust.

I cast a glance at Mack and caught him shaking his head slightly, possibly warning me off. It made me feel sick with embarrassment and shame. I felt like I'd been a bad person or something, falling for him in Vegas, but what was even worse was how *that* idea made me so sad. None of this was making any sense, from start to finish. Even sitting here at this table was nuts. I should already be headed back to the airport with signed papers in my hand.

Angus was waiting for a response, so I opened my mouth and let some words fall out. "Well, you're right, I'm not from here. I'm from Florida."

"Florida!" he exclaimed. "Well, I'll be. You're a long way from home now, aren't you?" He picked up a rib and bit into it, his eyes sparkling with happiness or mirth, it was hard to tell which.

I was glad to see he was much neater at eating ribs than Boog. I couldn't help but smile back at him. He was so nice, despite being almost as big as a grizzly bear and nearly as intimidating. "Yes, Baker City's a long way from home in more than one way."

Everyone laughed politely except Mack. He just chewed his food very methodically and stared at the saltshaker between us. He was so handsome it made my heart ache.

"How long have you been in town?" asked Maeve.

"Just today. I arrived around lunch." I put some peas on my plate, the smallest portion I could manage and still officially be eating them. Peas and I are not generally on speaking terms.

"And what have you seen so far?" She handed me a basket of dinner rolls, bypassing Boog entirely. He took it all in stride, not even missing a beat of his rib-mangling.

"Well, let's see ... I've seen my hotel, the diner in the center of town, aaaand the road out here with its rattlesnakes and spiders."

"You've hardly seen anything yet," she exclaimed. "Please don't judge Baker by just those little bits. This town is one of the most beautiful places on earth."

Ian snorted in disgust.

"Ignore him," said Angus. "He's not a fan of ranch work or Baker these days."

"Damn straight," mumbled Ian, jabbing his fork into a pile of peas. They rolled everywhere, like they were purposely trying to escape being speared.

"Don't get him all riled up, Angus, please." Maeve sighed heavily. "Just ignore them, Andie. Tempers are high tonight because we have a lot of extra work right now. Everyone'll be all smiles and laughter in another couple days once all the calves are taken care of and we have our annual picnic."

"I'm sorry I'll miss that," I said, taking a bite of the most delicious mashed potatoes I've ever eaten in my entire life. I scooped up another forkful and indulged in more of the starchy goodness, ignoring the call of my pre-wedding diet.

"How long do you intend to stay?" asked Angus, resting his forearm on the table next to his plate. "We'd love to have you here for the picnic. We'll have people from all over the area attending, lots of family and friends. It's quite an event." He pointed his fork at Mack. "You'll get to watch my boys on the broncs. That's something you don't want to miss."

I swallowed and took a sip of water before responding, because the image of Mack in full cowboy regalia being thrown around on the back of a horse was surprisingly sexy. "I'm only here for a day or two, then I'll be heading back home." I picked up my knife and fork, preparing to attack a rib. "But thanks for inviting me." I looked up at Mack, my heart skipping a beat when I realized he'd been staring at me. He looked away before I did.

"I thought you were going to Utah after this," said Ian, his tone accusatory.

"Ian," said Maeve, her tone friendly but sharp, "get that bee out of your buns right this instant before you curdle my milk and upset the hens."

"I'm just asking. She's the one who said she was going there." He scowled at me and then his plate. He looked much younger than his actual age which I guessed to be around twenty-six or so.

I shrugged. "Maybe I'll go to Utah, maybe not. I haven't decided yet."

Angus's gaze dropped to my plate and a confused expression appeared. I froze in mid-rib-spearing, suddenly self-conscious.

Boog caught Angus's expression and followed his gaze to my knife and fork. "What are you doing?" he asked.

I looked at him like he was slow, raising my knife up a little. "Cutting the meat off the bone?"

He smirked, grabbing a rib from his plate with his fingers and biting into it like a caveman. "Foreigners," he said, his mouth already full.

Mack blinked a couple times and may have smiled just the slightest bit, but then his face became a mask again and I was back to knowing nothing about what was going on in his head. It was beyond frustrating.

I probably shouldn't have cared; his signature was the only thing that should have been taking up headspace in my life. But right now I wanted to know what he was thinking more than anything else in the world.

I blinked a few times, attempting to focus my thoughts on why I was here and visions of my upcoming nuptials. But trying to conjure images of Bradley was not working to get Mack out of my brain. All it did was make me compare the two and that was really stupid, really dangerous ground to be walking.

"Leave her alone," chided Maeve. "Not everyone eats with their fingers." She picked up her knife and fork and proceeded to cut meat from her ribs too. It was awkward for her, I could tell. It made me want to hug her the way she was trying so hard to make me feel welcome. Then I felt guilty, not being truthful with her or Angus. They hadn't done anything wrong; they didn't deserve my lies.

"So, I understand we're related somehow, is that right?" asked Angus.

Mack cleared his throat loudly and picked up his glass, preparing to take a drink of his water. "Dad, why don't you just let her eat?" he said, not sparing me a glance.

"I'm just curious." Angus waved his fork around absently. "Ian mentioned she's doing some genealogy research. Came here looking for you, in fact." He turned to me. "Why Mack, specifically? Why do you think his name came up in your research and mine didn't?"

My mouth opened but the words wouldn't come out. "Uhhhh ... I don't know?" The guilt was weighing heavily on me. I was lying to these nice people, and it was making me lose my appetite.

"There she goes again," said Boog. "Asking a question instead of telling the answer." He wiped his mouth and beard off with his napkin in big swiping motions.

I motioned to a couple spots where he'd missed chunks of food, grimacing at the sight of it.

"What? Did I miss something? Get it for me, would ya?" He moved in close to me with a devilish grin that moved his facial hair-bush up, revealing a row of bright white teeth.

I leaned way back and gave him a disgusted look, unable to find the right words to respond with.

"Boog, leave her alone," said Maeve, trying not to laugh but failing miserably. "You'll have to excuse our friend. He delights in teasing the ladies. That's why he's so popular in town."

I nodded sagely, sitting back up normally again. "Oh, yeah. The old dig-food-schrapnel-out-of-my-beard move. Sexy. I'll bet he's got the chicks lining up out the door."

Angus let out a really loud whoop and then laughed so hard, he started choking on something. Mack had to jump up and whack him on the back several times to get him breathing correctly and able to talk again. I sat demurely in my seat, working very hard at not gloating over getting one over on the man-bear-pig.

By the time Mack took his seat, the table had finally calmed down, and I enjoyed a small sense of triumph over bringing Boog, the butthead who'd left me in the dust with the rattlesnakes, down a peg or two.

"They are lining up," said Boog, pouting, not ready to let it go.

The whole table erupted in laughter again, even Mack and Ian joining in. My heart skipped at beat at Mack's expression. I remembered seeing one just like it in Las Vegas. He'd been happy then with me. And I must have been happy with him too, otherwise there's no way in hell I would have married him. Even drunk, I must have been able to sense right from wrong. The big mystery wasn't so much why I married him anymore, but why I didn't remember something so momentous the very next day and why he had just disappeared after becoming legally bound to me. Did he forget too?

I stole a glance at him as he spoke with his father about something, I hadn't heard what, too lost in the memories to pay attention. He'd given me every reason to believe he *did* remember what we'd done, and he seemed even more unhappy about it than I was. Maybe it had to do with the girl in the picture. I made it a plan there and then to find out as soon as possible. I'd probably have stay a day longer than I'd originally planned, but it would be worth it to get this over with. This family was like a drug I could easily get addicted to.

"What do you think, Andie?" asked Angus with a twinkle in his eye.

"About?"

"About Boog doing that online dating stuff. Think he'd catch him a fish or two?"

I opened my eyes wide and moved them around vacantly, trying to picture what the ad would say. "I suppose there are women out here who wouldn't mind dating …," I looked sideways at Boog, "…a guy like him."

"D'ya hear that, Boog?" asked Ian. "She says there're girls out here who'd date Bigfoot."

"Aw, come on now," said Boog, dropping a bone on his plate. "You know I have a lot to offer the right woman. I'm just picky."

I snorted and then hid my mouth behind a forkful of peas as the conversation carried on without me.

I felt light-headed and happy to be a part of the friendly, raucous meal until dessert, when I caught Mack's eye again. And then the reason I was sitting at the table across from him came crashing back into my reality and erased the smile off my face. Instead of feeling light-headed now I was nauseous. He was, simply put, the most attractive man I've ever seen in my entire life. Part of it was his looks, obviously, but the other part was his family. Angus and Maeve were incredibly kind and welcoming, the type of people I've never known personally. Maybe it was a country thing to be so damn nice, but I'd always just assumed people like this lived only in the movies.

Bradley's family were cold fish in comparison. They smiled but the warmth never made it to their eyes. I'd perfected the same smile myself, and that thought scared me more than anything else. Was Ruby right? Was Bradley a bad influence on me?

I shook my head, getting it out of the clouds. I had to harden myself to their charms and not get comfortable here in their little love nest. Mack himself was chock-full of flaws, and a pretty face meant nothing when you added it all up. He's obviously an asshole deep down. He had to be. I mean, what kind of guy gets a girl so drunk she marries him, and then abandons her in a hotel room in Vegas? Not the kind of guy I want to be married to, that's for sure.

Bradley was way better than Mack for marriage material. He was driven at work, upwardly mobile, competitive, and a socializing machine. Sometimes his schedule was even too full for me, but that was the price I had to pay to be with someone focused on moving up in the world and making a name for himself. Bradley was perfect for me in almost every way. *No … every way. He's perfect for me in every single stinking way.*

I ignored the self-doubt that kept banging on the door of my thoughts, insisting it be let in so it could have its say. I moved back my chair so I could step out of the room to go call him. I'd hear his voice, tell him my plan to stay another day, and everything would be fine. I'd be back on track and focused on my goals.

Maeve put a big, thick apple pie down on the table, interrupting my inner dialogue and my exit. "You can have your pie with or without vanilla ice cream. I recommend *with* … I churned it myself this afternoon."

I scowled at the dessert. *Damn you, apple pie.* Apple pie à la mode is my favorite dessert of all time. I'd been planning on making the call and going back to my hotel until she'd set it down and started all that crazy talk about home made ice cream. Who makes home made ice cream anymore? This could be my last chance to ever have it.

Maeve frowned. "You don't like apple pie?"

My eyes bugged out, embarrassed I'd been caught staring daggers at her dessert. "No! I mean, yes! I love apple pie. Sorry … I was just thinking about how I don't have time for a piece and have to go back to my hotel."

She beamed. "Of course you have time. It'll only take me a minute to scoop you out a piece."

"She said she doesn't have time, Ma." Mack looked only at his mother, not me. It made me want to kick him under the table for some reason. I had to tense my leg muscles to keep my foot from striking out at him.

She frowned at her son. "Don't be rude, Mack. She's our guest. If she wants a piece of pie I'm going to make sure she gets it." Turning to me, she flipped her frown upside down. "And besides, you're welcome to stay here tonight." She paused to look at her husband, "Isn't she Angus, sweetie?"

"Well, of course she is. We have plenty of room here for family." He nodded once, as if it was a done deal.

My face flushed with the idea of sleeping under the same roof as Mack. I'd done that once before and look where it had gotten me. "No, I couldn't do that, but thank you so much for the offer. I have a … phone meeting later. I have to get back to my hotel for it." Hopefully they wouldn't ask me what time the meeting was since I had zero clue what time it was now.

"We have phones here," said Angus. He'd put his fork down and was staring at me, some of his good humor gone.

"Yes, but ... I have my numbers back at the hotel."

"She'd obviously rather stay at the hotel," said Ian. "I don't know why you guys are trying to bully her into staying when she obviously doesn't want to stay."

We all responded at the same time.

"They're not bullying me."

"We're not bullying her!"

I stood, unable to take the strife I was causing. "Really, it's okay. I appreciate the offer, but I should go." I chose that moment to put my weight on my injured foot and realized too late it was a mistake. "Ah! Shit!" Teetering to the side, I fell against Boog, one of my hands slapping right into the side of his head when it reached out to stop my fall.

He sat there unmoving, just blinking rapidly several times.

"I'm so sorry," I whispered, hopping onto my good foot to regain my balance. I reached out and patted his head and ear gingerly. "That must have hurt." My own hand was tingling from the contact.

"Oh, that's all right," he said, ignoring my fluttering around his head while he cut away a big bite of pie from his slice. "You don't hit very hard, even for a girl." He continued to eat his dessert, ignoring the snickers around the table. " 'Course, you did just slap the man who was your only ride back into town."

"I thought you were staying," said Angus. "We need your help, Boog, you know that." He sounded stressed. It was really awful compared to the happy-go-lucky Angus who'd been so kind throughout dinner.

"I know that, but she left her little three-banger out in a pothole back down the road, and I know she can't ride a horse, so what do you want me to do?"

"I can bring her back," said Mack, sighing heavily.

"No, son, you know we can't spare you right now." Angus was angry now.

"It's only an hour." Mack pushed his plate away.

I felt terrible. Bringing me back to town was obviously a huge problem. "Never mind," I said, hurriedly. "I'll figure something else out. How about a taxi? I can take a taxi."

Maeve gave me a smile of pity. "I'm afraid our town's taxi service leaves something to be desired. But I'll try and give them a call if you like."

I nodded. "That would be great. I'm sorry to put you out over this." I stared down at my pie. Its sugar-glossed crust and warm gooey brown apples had lost a little of their appeal. I wasn't sure my stomach could handle all that happiness.

"It's no trouble at all, I promise," assured Maeve. "How about you eat that pie, and I'll go make the call?"

I nodded, not trusting myself to speak. For some reason I felt like crying. These people were being so nice to me. I wondered what they'd do if I told them the truth. Probably kick me out the front door and tell me to walk back, rattlesnakes be damned.

"I made the crust myself using real butter. You let me know if you like it." Maeve winked and left the table.

I dared a glimpse at Mack. He was steadily eating away at his dessert, his eyes glued to the task. No way was he going to reveal what he was thinking, that was obvious. It was a miracle I met him at the blackjack tables that night. He should have been at the poker tables; he was probably really good at that game with his ability to hide what he was thinking. I know I was completely in the dark about what was going on in his head, and I'd been studying him surreptitiously all night.

"What's the important phone call all about?" asked Ian.

"Lawyer stuff?"

I looked up sharply at him. He was smiling, clearly thinking he'd caught me in a lie. *Little shit.*

"Yes. Lawyer stuff."

"You're a lawyer?" asked Angus. "What kinda lawyer?"

"I'm a litigator."

"She likes to argue. Why doesn't that surprise me?" asked Ian.

"Shut up, Ian," said Mack.

"Why don't you make me, Mack?" Ian dropped his fork loudly on his plate and threw his napkin down next to it.

Mack followed suit and stood, his chair scraping the floor behind him. "Come on, then. It's been a while since I've beat your behind. Looks like you're long past due."

"Boys, sit down," said Angus, sighing and shaking his head. He seemed relatively unconcerned about the idea of his two grown sons assaulting each other. "They're always full of piss and vinegar during B and C."

"B and C?" I asked.

The two brothers smiled devilishly, first at their father and then me, twin gods - so alike and yet so different - arresting my heart for a full two seconds. *Adorable? MacKenzie be thy name.*

"B and C's just a little nickname we have for branding and castration," said Ian.

My stomach turned over, all visions of the MacKenzie gorgeousness fading to be replaced by the idea of burning skin and sliced body parts. "You actually *do* that?"

"Yes, we actually do that," Angus said, smiling patiently, "just like ranchers all over the world." He stood. "Come on, Boog. I've got something to show you. You too, Ian. I'm putting you on the tails."

"I prefer the heads," said Ian, his good humor gone. He walked out of the room with his father and Boog behind him.

Angus's voice faded out into the air on the porch. "Well,

when you're in charge, you can be wherever you want. Tonight you're on the tails."

Mack and I were left alone in the dining room. I opened my mouth to speak, but he turned to follow them before a single word had come out, effectively cutting me off. I huffed out a sigh of frustration and put my hands on my hips. Annoyance and hurt gave me the courage to speak even though it was clear he had no interest in listening. "You're just going to go without saying anything?" It was making me crazy how he was acting like this whole situation was something he could just ignore. *How can he be so unaffected and casual about everything when I'm not even sure which end of my world is up anymore?*

"I have work to do." He didn't look at me; he just stared out the glass doors to the back porch, absently pulling a well-worn baseball hat out of his back pocket.

"Yeah, well, I have a wedding to get to, so if you don't mind, I'd like to talk to you about our divorce." The last word almost got stuck in my throat. The idea of divorcing a man like him felt completely wrong, which is absolutely crazy, ridiculous, and stupid beyond measure. But I could no longer fight the feeling than I could change the fact that I'd somehow, for some reason I didn't yet fully understand, married this man after only knowing him for a few hours.

He faced me, putting his hands on the back of his chair and letting the hat dangle off to the side in his fingers. His tone went cocky. "I don't think we need a divorce, actually."

I lifted an eyebrow at him. "Oh yeah? How so?"

He shrugged. "Because I don't think we're married. No marriage, no divorce."

I snorted. I might be waffling around about my feelings or emotions, but I know my legal paperwork. There was no denying what's in black and white as much as we might want to. "Oh, we're married, trust me."

"Says you."

I bristled, lifting my chin in defiance. "Says the State of Nevada and your signature on the marriage license." *Dumbass jerk butthead cowboy redneck sexy person. God, why does he have to be so sexy!*

"Could be forged."

My jaw dropped open at the accusation that lay beneath his words. "Why on *earth* would I forge your signature to a marriage document when I don't even know you?"

His eyes burned into mine. "I think the better question is why would you even marry me in the first place if you didn't know me?"

The room went dead silent. A cuckoo clock started doing its thing in the next room, the clacking sound of the little bird's door following each of its cries.

*Cuckoo!*

*Cuckoo!*

*Cuckoo!*

*Cuckoo!*

*Cuckoo!*

*Cuckoo!*

Mack was right. So was the damn clock. We both had to be completely crazy to have done what we did in Vegas. My pie threatened to make another very unpleasant appearance, my stomach burning with embarrassment, anger, and something very much like sadness. We were crazy two years ago. *Crazy in love.* The words haunted my soul and refused to be buried in the darkness anymore.

"Like I said," he continued in a softer voice, "I have to get to work. Maybe we can chat later."

He left me standing at the dining room table with tears shining in my eyes.

# Chapter Twenty-Two

"AWW, SWEETIE, WHAT'S WRONG?" ASKED Maeve, coming into the room and stopping at my side.

I hurriedly wiped the tears away. "Oh, nothing. I got pepper in my eye."

She pulled her head back in confusion. "Pepper? How'd you get pepper in your eye?"

I waved her question away, trying to distract her. "Did you find a taxi for me?"

She shook her head sadly. "No, I'm sorry, but I guess they're all full right now." She went around the table picking up dishes and leftover food. She left me alone in the dining room, carrying everything into the kitchen.

I grabbed a couple plates and followed her, limping the whole way, too afraid to put all my weight on my foot again. "The taxis are full? What do you mean, full?"

"They only have a couple cars and they're on call for all kinds of things. I think tonight there's a dance at the high school, so they'll be busy all night shuttling kids around."

"Wow," I said. *What are the chances that the one time I'd need a taxi in Baker City there'd be a prom going on?*

"That's small-town life for ya," she said. She didn't sound upset about it. "You take the good with the bad."

"Well, aside from that amazing dinner and dessert, I

haven't seen any of the good." I regretted the words as soon as they were out of my mouth. I blamed Mack for getting me all messed up in the head and causing me to forget my manners. Him and Ian both, two butthead peas in a pod.

"Oh, it's not all that bad." There was a smile in her voice.

I breathed a sigh of relief that she hadn't taken offense to my careless words.

"You've only seen the hotel and the road out here, and believe me, that's no way to judge our little town. You stay the night tonight, and tomorrow I'll pack you and Mack a nice lunch. He can take you out for a ride and show you a little bit of the hills and some of the other nicer areas. That way when you go back home you can have a nice well-rounded picture of the Baker City MacKenzies for your research."

"A ride? As in on a horse?"

"Unless you prefer a four-wheeler." She piled up dishes next to the sink.

"I don't even know what that is, but wheels sound better than horse legs to me."

"We prefer the horses, actually. They don't cost any gas money so they're better for the wallet and the environment. And they can go just about anywhere. Some of the places I'm sure Mack would want to show you are impossible to get to any way other than on horseback." She looked at me and winked. "You'll miss half the fun not being on a horse."

"I'd probably get killed if I tried to ride a horse." The idea was both thrilling and terrifying at the same time. I'd always been fascinated by the beasts but never considered they'd be a part of my life. As far as I was concerned, horses were for movies and weird rodeo channels on TV.

"You've never ridden before?" she asked, sounding like she wouldn't believe me if I said yes.

"I was close enough to touch one once."

"I'm sensing a story here. What happened?"

I ran my finger along the edge of the counter and got lost in the memory of being in a barn at a summer camp when I was ten. "I remember thinking how beautiful he was. Huge. Proud or something. The person I was with told me to pet him on the nose. When I finally worked up the nerve to do it and reached my hand out, he lifted his head up in one big jerk and whinnied so loud I peed my pants."

Maeve burst out in musical laughter. "Oh, Andie, that's priceless. How old were you?"

"Nine or ten. Old enough to remember with distinct clarity the humiliation of having peed my pants at an age where a girl isn't supposed to do that anymore." I pulled my hand off the counter and put it behind me awkwardly. I felt like the girl with wet pants all over again.

She patted my arm with a soapy hand. "Not to worry. Mack would never let a mean old horse cause you to lose your water. You'll be as safe as a bug in a rug with him there." She handed me a wet dish. "Would you mind drying this off for me?" She gestured with her chin to a towel on the nearby counter.

I took the plate from her, frowning at it. "Don't you have dishwashers in Oregon?"

"Sure, they have them all over, but we're simple folk out here. I don't mind doing things by hand. I find it relaxing."

I rubbed the towel on the plate until it squeaked. Noticing my reflection in the white surface, I smiled. There was something to be said about doing a routine, basic task in the company of someone you enjoyed talking to. It was almost relaxing or meditative. Maeve had an easy way about her that made me feel like I could just be myself standing next to her here in this kitchen. Glancing at her profile, I wondered if she would totally hate me if I told her what Mack and I had done in Las Vegas. It made me sad to think that she might, which was silly because I'd be gone in just a day or two and then I'd never see her or Angus again. Or Mack.

My stomach clenched uncomfortably. Why did the thought of never seeing him again bring actual, physical pain? I should have been breathing a sigh of relief over it. No way would Bradley be okay with me being here, let alone spending time with a guy like Mack. My fiancé wasn't stupid. He'd sense something was up right away. It was all part of his killer instinct ... he could smell underlying emotion in others like a shark could smell a drop of blood in the water. It's what made him such a successful lawyer; he always got to the bottom of things, even when the people he was up against did everything they could to keep them secret.

My guts churned with the realization that the chances of me keeping this whole mess from Bradley were very, very slim. I wondered if his feelings for me were strong enough to forgive me. I wondered how much I really cared, too, and that worried me more than anything else.

"In the cupboard over there, on your right," Maeve said without looking up from her task.

I put the plate away, leaving the door open since another one was about to join it.

We stood in the kitchen doing dishes in companionable silence for another five minutes before the next comment floated out there in the air between us.

"So tell me about this research you're doing, Andie."

I glanced at her, but the expression on her face showed nothing but curiosity and dedication to the task of washing. She'd moved onto the serving dishes and silverware.

"Well, I was doing some research and I ran across ... something that told me I might be related to a MacKenzie, so I thought I'd come out here and see if it was true." My fingers trembled with the stress of giving her half-truths. She didn't deserve to be lied to. She'd done nothing wrong.

"What kind of research was it, exactly?"

I decided a little more truth was in order. It was the only way I could keep on speaking; the lies were getting caught in my throat. "Well, actually, I'm getting married."

She stopped scrubbing the pot she had in the sink before her and waited for my next words.

"I was applying for the marriage license and there was this document the courthouse came up with, so I decided before I got married, I'd come out and see what it was all about." My heart rate had picked up, causing me to breathe faster. Any minute I was going to start sounding like I'd just run a mile if I didn't get a hold of myself. *Calm down, idiot!*

Maeve's hand moved in slow circles, round and round the bottom of the pot. "You're getting married."

"Yes. Back east. In just over a week."

"Have you been together long?" She tipped the pot over to scrub the sides and bottom.

"Not quite two years. Long enough."

She looked at me briefly, a small smile on her lips. "Not that a person can have a timetable for something like that."

"Oh, I do." Now I was on firm ground. We'd moved away from talking about the MacKenzie clan and on to my lifeplan. Maeve seemed like a pretty down-to-earth person. I was sure she'd get where I was coming from.

She stopped scrubbing again and turned to face me. "Really? You have a timetable for love?"

"Well … sure. Kind of. I mean, I don't have it on a calendar. Okay, maybe I *do* have it on a calendar but not in that way." I was getting flustered trying to explain.

"I'm not judging, Andie, I'm just trying to understand."

"No, I know that. It's just hard to explain I guess. See, ever since I was young, I've had this plan."

"Mmm-hmmm…" She nodded, rinsing off the pot.

"And in the plan I decided that I had to reach certain goals by the time I was twenty one and then twenty-seven and then twenty-nine and finally thirty-five." I took the pot she'd rinsed and put it on the counter, using its support to dry the inside.

She chuckled. "You stopped the plan at thirty-five. Is that when you retire?"

"No," I smiled back, glad she wasn't mocking me too hard. "It's when I'll be done having children."

"So what happens if you don't meet one of your goals?"

"I don't know. It hasn't happened yet." I grinned at her with a little personal pride shining through. "I don't know why I'm so goal-oriented. Meeting goals makes me feel like a success. Like everything is going to be fine in my life."

She soaped up several forks at the same time. "Was there a time in your life when things weren't so fine?"

A loud ringing started in my ears. The pounding of my heart got so loud I worried she'd hear it. "Maybe when I was young things were a little crazy. But that was a long time ago." I cleared my throat to get the frog out of it. I never thought or talked about my childhood with anyone. Ever.

She remained silent for a while. When she spoke it was with a gentle tone that made me want to cry. "Sometimes when our lives are out of control, the only thing that makes us feel secure is to swing in the opposite direction. To control every last detail."

"Maybe," I said, not sure that I agreed with her assessment. My lifeplan was a result of several years of wasted time, the result of a series of poor choices. Once I had a lifeplan in place, I started making smart decisions - decisions that amounted to investments in my future. A drunken marriage in Elvis's chapel of love notwithstanding, my lifeplan had served me well. I was totally on track to be married by my deadline.

"So tell me about your fiancé," she said, thankfully moving past the discussion of my goals.

"Well, his name is Bradley. He's two years older than me and we're very compatible."

She smiled again. "Compatible. That sounds romantic."

I nudged her good-naturedly. "It is. Seriously. We work in the same office, we're both lawyers. He's very driven and goal-oriented. He has the same ideas about success that I do. He wants to have two children, a boy and a girl, just like I do. He went to Yale, and his parents are attorneys too. We're a perfect match."

"Do you love him?"

I accidentally dropped the handful of forks I'd just picked up to dry. Her question made me instantly cranky. "Of course I love him."

"I was just wondering because you didn't mention that part."

"I do love him. I do." It felt like I was trying to convince myself, but that wasn't necessary. Of course I love Bradley. He and I are a perfect couple.

"What do your friends think of him?" she asked.

I stopped in the middle of gathering the forks back up and turned partway to look at her.

She finished washing out the sink and turned off the water to look at me. "Did I say something wrong? Am I prying too much?" Her face fell. "I'm sorry. Angus tells me all the time I pry too much."

I put my hand on her arm and squeezed gently. "No, it's okay. It's just a sore spot, actually." I sighed, my vision drifting off to scenes of my friends' reactions to Bradley's behavior. "Truth is, none of my friends like him. Even my secretary at work hates him."

"Why do you think that is?" she asked, putting her rag down and taking the towel from me to finish drying the silverware.

I shrugged, leaning back against the counter. "I guess he can be pushy. I used to really dislike him myself. Two years ago I used to mock him behind his back." I frowned. "That's really terrible, isn't it?"

"How did you go from dislike to love and marriage? Seems like a pretty big leap."

I really didn't have a good answer for her. Even hearing the path to loving Bradley in my head made me kind of cringe. After two years of putting everything I had into love, I'd gotten dumped by Luke in a cold and casual way. I'd gone to Las Vegas and had a wild fling with a hot stranger. Then I'd returned home on a mission to get my life back on track. Bradley just seemed to fit the mold so perfectly, and he'd asked me out when I was feeling lonely and lost. The timing was perfect, or so I'd thought at the time. Why hadn't I examined this more closely before? Had I been so focused on my lifeplan that I'd missed something? "I don't know. It sounds silly, but I guess … I guess it started when I got back from Las Vegas."

"Las Vegas?"

"Yeah." I wasn't looking at her. I was staring at the floor, lost in the memories. They were coming in clear for some reason, like it had just happened last week. It was the first time in two years this had happened. "My best friend Kelly was marrying a mortician."

"A mortician?" Maeve chuckled like I was joking.

"Yes, seriously, she was marrying Matty the mortician. So my other best friend, Candice, organized a bachelorette party in Las Vegas. I was dating a guy named Luke at the time and I was really busy with work, so I didn't want to go, but they guilted me into it. Or Ruby did."

"Who's Ruby? Is she another friend?"

"No. Yes. She's both. She's my assistant but she's also like a mother, neighbor, and girlfriend all mixed up into one big ball of fire."

"She sounds like fun."

I nodded, warming with the memory of our last few hours together. They were so much better than the last year had been. "Yeah, she is. She is *so* sassy. But she's real and she's honest and she is the best damn legal secretary in the business."

"Probably very valuable for a busy lawyer," Maeve suggested.

"Yes, absolutely. She's not only valuable, she's also pushy. And she guilted me along with Candice into going to Las Vegas, so I went."

"Sounds like fun. Girls' night out in Las Vegas." She kicked some shoes over in my direction. They looked like moccasins. "Here, put these on. Let's take a walk."

I slipped my feet into the comfortably worn leather and followed her out the back door and down the porch stairs, only limping a little now. My ankle felt much better. The air was warm enough that I didn't need a sweater, but Maeve handed me one that I put over my shoulders.

"So tell me about Las Vegas," she said. "I've never been."

I walked next to her down a path, headed towards the sounds of cows mooing. "Well, it's loud and there are lights everywhere all day and night. And there's this air of excitement, like anything can happen and anything *will* happen." I couldn't stop the smile from blooming on my face. "It's kind of a magical place in that way."

"What did you do there? Gamble? I hear the buffets are fabulous."

"We didn't see any buffets, but we did gamble. Or I should say, *I* gambled. My friends ended up in the room most of the night. I guess it wasn't much of a girls' night out in the end."

"They were in the room all night without you?" Her smile disintegrated into an expression of worry.

*Shit. Why am I telling her this?* "Um, yeah. I was alone for a while that night, but it was okay." *It was more than okay. I had company.* My heart clenched at the memories.

"You said you gambled. Which game did you play?"

I swallowed hard. Maeve's questions were starting to feel more like an interrogation, but it wasn't because of something she was doing. She was just getting too close to the part where her gorgeous son entered the picture.

"I played blackjack."

"Oh, that's Mack's favorite. He went to Las Vegas with his brother a couple years back, for Ian's bachelor party, as a matter of fact. He won over a thousand dollars ... used it to buy a new horse. Funny thing about that, now that I think about it..." She turned to me with a weird expression on her face for a few seconds. Then she smiled and the weird look fell away. "Hey, maybe you were there at the same time."

I tried to smile, but my lips were trembling too much. Luckily the sun was in her eyes as it dipped closer to the horizon, making me think she couldn't see me very well. "Maybe," I said.

Maeve sighed. "That was a tough time for our boys."

The sadness in her voice made me intensely curious, but it felt wrong to push her for information when it was very possible my interactions with Mack may have influenced the situation. He'd spent at least part of the night with me. If he'd been there for the purpose of celebrating his brother's last nights as a single man, Ian would have been pissed to not have him around. *Maybe Ian knows what happened. Maybe that's why he's so rude to me.*

I was just about to ask her for details when we turned a bend in the path and came upon a huge group of cows, fences, and men, and the men were in the process of doing things that were making the cows very nervous.

# Chapter Twenty-Three

MAEVE MOTIONED FOR ME TO sit with her up on a fence that gave us a good view of what was going on but wasn't actually close enough to get in the way of what the men were doing. I climbed up next to her with a little difficulty, my ankle not excited about lifting my weight like that. Once we were settled, Maeve began to explain what we were watching.

"All these calves need to be treated with vaccines, branded, and castrated before they get too big, so that's why the men are working so late and Boog's here to help. We have several hundred head to get through, and it's exhausting work."

The smallish animals were being led down a path between metal rail fences with encouragement from Ian to a small, square, fenced-off area set up where Mack was waiting. When the calf made it into that area, Ian would shut the entrance to trap the calf inside a smaller box made of bars. Mack pulled levers to trap their head and then their body.

My heart leaped into my throat as I watched Mack move another lever and flip the entire calf over on its side in the contraption. The show of brute strength was unexpected and thrilling in a pure animal lust kind of way. "Oh my god," I half-whispered, unable to tear my eyes away. "What is he doing?"

"He's getting the bull calf into position so they can do the work on him. That metal box he's in now is called a squeeze chute. Believe it or not, it calms most calves to be held in it like this."

"What work are they going to do on him?"

"You'll see…"

Mack opened up a small door near the calf's neck. Ian came in at the same time and grabbed the calf's back leg, pulling it out straight.

Angus walked over next with something in his hand, standing over the calf's neck.

"What's Angus doing?"

"He's going to vaccinate the calf and then brand him."

"Does it hurt?" I asked, ready to cry on the animal's behalf.

"The vaccination? No, not at all. They inject them just under the skin, like the vet does with a cat or dog. The branding might hurt a little. Usually they just lie there, but sometimes they bawl a tad or kick once. It's normal. They get up and move on like nothing happened right after, though. They're tough little buggers. It's the castration that hurts, but not as much as you might think."

"Who does that part?" I asked, feeling sick to my stomach again.

"Boog. He gets paid in testes, and he's as gentle and skilled as they come. We're lucky to have him and so are the animals."

I swallowed with effort, my voice coming out strained. "I think I might have misunderstood. I thought I just heard you say you pay him with *balls*."

She chuckled and patted my knee. "No, you heard right. You'll see why soon enough."

I didn't respond because I was quite sure I would never see how testicles could be considered a paycheck. Besides, arguing would be a waste of breath; they obviously worked on a different set of values around here.

The calf kicked a little and then seemed to give up, relinquishing his will to that of the men who held him down. Mack's forearm muscles flexed under his skin and his thighs bulged through his jeans with the effort of flipping the calf and operating the machinery. He had the baseball hat on instead of a cowboy hat, and somehow managed to make it look sexier than I would have thought possible. I was definitely sick or something. Every time I looked at him I felt dizzy and out of sorts.

"What's the matter, Andie?" Maeve was staring at me.

"Oh, I was just thinking I might have a fever or something. I feel a little light-headed."

"It's probably just the idea of castration. It's not exactly after-dinner conversation, is it?"

Angus walked up with something on a cord and stopped at the animal's back end.

"What's he doing now? And do I even want to know?"

"Branding. Some ranchers use ear tags, but we find them a problem when the animals get too high in the mountains. Lots of branches and things for them to catch on, and then we get maggot problems. Plus, they're easier to remove by rustlers. Branding is easy, quick, and less likely to cause problems later, so that's what we do."

Angus pressed the end of the iron into the side of the calf's upper hip. A huge cloud of smoke rose up to surround Angus's head, making me really glad I wasn't close enough to smell the burning hair and flesh. "That poor baby," I whispered, my hands curling into fists. I pressed them into my mouth, unable to tear my eyes away from the operation. Angus stood and moved out of the way.

"We take good care of our animals and branding is part of that," explained Maeve, pride in her voice. "Without it they'd be easily stolen, and people who steal animals generally don't take very good care of them."

I wanted to stay mad at Mack for holding down the calf and allowing it to be hurt like that, but the simple fact is that I like hamburgers. My sense of fairness and accountability told me it was wrong to hate the process and participants when I was a willing beneficiary of it all. "I suppose if you do your best by the animals when they're in your care, that's the best you can do."

"We follow the Temple Grandin methods out here as much as we possibly can. We're big believers."

"Temple Grandin?"

"She's a brilliant scientist who's done a lot to contribute to the livestock industry and animal husbandry. You should check her out online. She's a pretty amazing woman."

"Soooo ... she has rules or whatever about how to do things?"

"Not rules, per se. See, she's autistic, and has a special sensitivity to the world around her, much like cows do, in fact. So she's able to see the world through their eyes, something ranchers never seemed to be able to do in the past. In our world, cattle are a means to an end. At least, that's how it used to be. But thanks to her insight and contributions, we've been able to find ways to make the animals' lives here as pleasant as possible while also making a living at raising them for food. It's a delicate balance, but we like to think we're getting it right."

"It sounds fascinating." I wasn't lying either. I'd never heard of such a thing, and the fact that it was a woman doing the work of understanding cows for the benefit of ranchers was empowering even just to think about. It seemed like such a man's world out here. This Temple person must have had an uphill battle on her hands. I admire kick-butt women in general, so I made a mental note to Google her later.

"It is fascinating, it truly is. I suggest you start with the movie that was made about her. It's powerful. I guarantee you'll need tissues when you're watching it. Her work sure caused a lot of heads around here to think differently. Started with Angus many years ago and bled over to several other operations, and the movement grows every year. Right now over half the cattle in our country are raised using methods she discovered and taught."

"That's ... amazing. Really, I mean it."

"Yes. Temple is an amazing person. Brilliant and compassionate. She reminds us that animals deserve our respect, a decent life, and a painless death. It's the least we can do. I've seen her speak live before. It was quite a whirlwind of energy and information. She's a real fireball. Makes you proud to be a woman rancher." Maeve stared out over the operation and nodded silently.

A lump developed in my throat that wouldn't go away. I turned to face the men and watched as Boog bent over at the animal's rear legs near its stomach.

"He's castrating the bull now," said Maeve in a soft voice. "This part hurts them, but he's good and he's fast. It'll all be over in a minute."

"Why do they do it?"

"It makes the animal much less aggressive towards the men and the other animals, so it's a safety issue. And it makes their meat better. They're being sold for food, so that's an important thing."

I nodded absently, focused on Boog. I couldn't see exactly what he was doing, but after about a minute he straightened up and dropped what he was holding into a bucket near his feet.

"What was that?" I asked.

"Testicles. He'll fry them up later and eat them. We'll have some at the picnic so you can give them a try." She looked at me. "You're coming, I hope."

"You said it's in a couple days, but I'll be gone by then." I left the eating-of-balls comment alone because it would be an ice-cold, snowy day in hell before a calf testicle passed through these lips of mine.

"It sounds like you work a lot of hours, being focused the way you are on your lifeplan and all."

Her change of subject threw me off a little. "Uhhhh … yes, I do work very hard. At least sixty hours a week."

"Wow, that *is* a lot. When was the last time you had a vacation? Maybe you're due."

I had to think about it for a little while. "I guess it was a couple years ago. And it wasn't really a vacation."

"Your trip to Vegas?"

I nodded. "Yeah. I was only there for a day and a half and … I didn't do a lot." *Except get married. Gah! Another lie. When will it end?* I felt positively twitchy over my half-truths.

"That's the last time my boys went out of town too. Well, that's not exactly right. That's the last time Mack went anywhere. Ian left for a little while and had plans to take a vacation, but they fell through."

"That's too bad. Where was he going to go?"

"Hawaii." Maeve smiled, but it wasn't the happy kind; it had too much sadness laced in it.

"Hawaii sounds nice." My tone was prying, but I didn't care. I was curious. If anyone needed a vacation it was Ian. Maybe it would help him change his attitude to go surfing or snorkeling somewhere.

"He didn't really much care for the idea of Hawaii. He's not much of a beach person, but it was Ginny's dream to go there, so he agreed to go."

"Is that his wife?"

Maeve sighed heavily. "No, Ginny was *going* to be his wife, but they ended up canceling the wedding just days before it was supposed to happen."

"Oh. That sucks." Mack had been to Las Vegas to celebrate that upcoming wedding. It gave me a bad feeling to know I'd been around just before the big breakup.

"It was terrible. A very emotional time for everyone, but especially Ian of course. He still hasn't recovered."

"Is that why he's..." I rolled my eyes at myself. I'd almost said, *such a rude jerk*. Talk about a rude jerk ... yeah, that's me, the girl sitting here completely oblivious to the feelings of the lady who probably cried a thousand tears over that little left-at-the-altar event.

She patted my arm. "That's why he's so *sharp* is how I like to put it. He wasn't like that before. He's a sweet boy underneath the hurt."

"I'll take your word for it. I've seen glimpses."

She stood, like she was shaking off the memories. "Come on. Let's go take a closer look."

I followed her off the fence, not positive I wanted a closer look but loathe to be rude to such a nice lady who was working so hard at making me feel comfortable. If things had been different between us, I was sure we could be friends. She reminded me a bit of Ruby.

She went to stand at the gate near where they were letting the calves in one-by-one. I stood next to her, just a few feet away from Mack. He turned sideways, giving me a great view of his face in profile, and I couldn't stop staring.

"How many left?" asked Maeve.

Angus answered without looking over. "About a hundred, give or take."

"Will you finish tomorrow?"

"Maybe. Maybe not. Depends."

She nodded. I was curious what it would depend on but not enough to ask. I'd already learned way more than I'd ever wanted to about cattle ranching.

I tried to be mad about what I was seeing - the animals' pain and the almost barbarian practices of branding and castration - but I couldn't work up that emotion. Instead, all I could feel was admiration and envy. Maeve made it clear that they did their best to make the business of raising cattle for beef a humane operation, respectful of the animal and its sensitivities. I was jealous of the loving teamwork I saw happening here, and the easy way they had about them.

Comparing what was going on here to my life back home, I found my world coming up short. The law firm was a highly competitive environment with people just waiting for me and everyone else to screw up, it seemed. Deadlines were strict and ever-present, and the workload was enormous. The little demon on my shoulder was ponking me on the side of the head, reminding me that my personal life wasn't much better. For some reason, being honest with myself was really easy out here, despite all the near-lies I was telling Maeve.

Whenever I went somewhere with Bradley, I constantly had to watch what I said, what expression I showed on my face, what impression I was giving off. Here I had a feeling it wouldn't matter; the MacKenzies were going to like me if I was nice and respectful and that was that. It wouldn't matter what clothes I was wearing, where I went to school, how much money I made in a year, or how many hours I billed last month. It was only me they would care about and how I treated people.

It made me sad to imagine them finding out about what I'd done with Mack and about the lies I was telling them about it now. They'd think I'd used Mack and then left him in the dust. They'd tell me to get off their ranch and never come back. I realized as I stood in front of the fence in the twilight-lit evening that I wanted to be liked by them, even though I knew I'd never see them again. The idea that they'd hate me for something I couldn't even remember doing made me physically ill.

"I'm going to get your room put together. I just need to put some sheets on the bed." Maeve pushed away from the fence.

"I'll help you," I said.

"No, stay. I'll come get you when I'm ready. I think the boys like having an audience." She nodded in their direction and I followed her gaze. Ian was flexing his right arm, trying to get his brother to compare biceps with him. Mack just shook his head and turned away.

I nodded, not even looking at Maeve, fascinated for some strange reason by the scene in front of me. Four cowboys - make that three cowboys and one wookie - were gathered inside a pen that had a calf running around in it, kicking up his heels. The little guy was apparently very happy now that he was free of their squeezy machine, even though he'd left his testicles behind. Ian was still flexing, now with his other arm. Mack was shaking his head, laughing a little. Boog and Angus were talking quietly about something. If I had a camera I would have shot fifty photos of them right there. It was like the cover of a magazine. The article would read: Ranching life in the heart of the mountain valley of Baker City, Oregon ... Idyllic. I lifted my eyes to the peaks that surrounded the city. They were majestic, barely visible now in the waning light.

# Chapter Twenty-Four

THE BABY CALF WANDERED OVER in my direction and stopped at the fence, interrupting my thoughts. His big brown eyes stared out at me and locked onto mine. I couldn't have looked away if I'd wanted to. But I didn't want to. He was beautiful. Looking for signs of distress, I saw none. I held out my hand, wanting badly to touch his forehead but a little afraid. Maybe he'd jerk his head really hard and moo at me and make me wet my pants.

A long pink tongue snaked out of its mouth and licked my finger.

"Oh my god," I said, laughing a little over being taken by surprise. It felt like the roughest sandpaper in the world. "Aren't you a bold little monster."

He pumped his head up and down several times as if nodding and happily agreeing with me. His long eyelashes made him look like a pretty little girl cow.

I grinned, rubbing his wet pink nose with my hand. His tongue came out and grabbed my index finger, pulling it into his mouth. I gasped, thinking I was about to lose my dialing finger to Jaws, the killer calf, when he began to suck on it instead. He was sloppy and loud and had a hell of a strong suction going for him, making me wonder if it was possible to get a hickey on a fingertip.

"Cute little bugger, isn't he?" asked Mack.

"Yeah. He's sucking my finger like it's a cow's udder." I laughed a little at the ridiculousness of it. The calf didn't miss a beat. He was way too happy about the idea of finding some milk in my hand to worry about the big bad cowboy coming up behind him.

"They're like little pigs. They'll eat all day if you let 'em." He pushed the calf's head away and my finger came out with a pop.

I looked down at it and saw it was covered in calf drool. Some of my good humor evaporated. "Ew. That was a bad idea, I think."

Mack pulled a bandana out of is back pocket and laid it flat in his hand. He grabbed my wet finger and slowly pulled the soft blue cloth down, drying it off. "Hungry and messy. Every last one."

I wanted to come up with something funny to say, to respond in a way that was both cool and casual. But I couldn't, because he was touching me. Even that little bit of cloth between us wasn't enough to keep the feelings from rising up to take over my common sense.

"We need to talk," I said, sounding like someone was strangling me.

He was so close I could see the fine wrinkles in the skin around his eyes telling me he smiled a lot when I wasn't around.

"We will," he responded softly. Staring over the top rail at me, he put the bandana in his pocket while resting his other hand on the fence just inches from mine. My gaze dropped to the strong, sun-bronzed hand and thick fingers that were huge in comparison to mine. I became obsessed with the thought that I could shift my hand to the right just a little and touch him ... if I was bold and stupid and willing to risk throwing my lifeplan in the garbage.

I closed my eyes and counted slowly to three, getting a

grip on myself. My hand stayed where it was. I've been working on my lifeplan for way too long to throw it away so easily.

"When can we talk, do you think?" I pressed. "I really have to get going back home soon." I was trying to choose between crying and smiling after the words came out. He was so close and yet so far. I shouldn't even want him to be close, but I did and that was nothing but a recipe for disaster. Up until now I'd been thinking that the only thing standing in the way of me marrying Bradley was a piece of paper and a signature. Now I was starting to think it could be much more than that.

"We'll talk tomorrow. I have to get back to work." He turned to go, his hand sliding away from the rail.

I grabbed it and held on. "What about later tonight?" I was afraid if I waited too long, I'd do something entirely stupid and ruin everything I'd been working towards. Something about this place was messing with my head and making me forget what was important, including the future I'd planned for myself.

His fingers curled around mine and gripped my hand gently for a few seconds before they slid away. "I'll be working until after midnight, and then I'll be too tired after. Just catch me after my chores tomorrow morning."

"What time?" I asked, hating that I sounded so desperate and needy and anxious about getting everything over with. Instead of feeling like the smart thing to do, hurrying him towards divorce felt cold and heartless. I definitely had a fever. I was sick. Heartsick.

"Nine o'clock." He walked back to the other men.

I might have argued more, but I suddenly had a really great view of his backside and it rendered me momentarily speechless. I was like a dog getting distracted by a small animal running by. *Squirrel! Fine ass!* I made a mental note to find out where the gym was in this town. If I was going to be staying for a few days, I'd need to work out. He obviously did.

*Stay a few days? Where'd that come from?*

My mind was spinning in so many different directions I didn't know whether to laugh, cry, or eat a fried calf testicle.

"You ready?" asked Maeve, coming up behind me.

I jumped in surprise, yanked out of my weird thoughts by her unexpected arrival. "Yep." Glad for the distraction, I followed her into the house. Part of me was relieved to be getting away from Mack. Seeing him made me lose focus, forget what I was supposed to be doing, forget Bradley, even. But another part of me was kind of wishing Maeve hadn't come so soon. Watching Mack work was doing something to me. I don't know what it was exactly, but it was pleasant. Just touching his fingers brought back the ghosts of warm, dangerously sensual memories. So many of my memories were unpleasant, the kind I wanted to never bring back. It made the good ones extra special as a consequence.

"I've got you just down the hall from Mack. Normally he stays in town, but lately he's been back in his old room. It saves him a bunch of sleep hours not having to travel."

"Does he live alone?" My hands clenched into fists as I waited for her answer. I didn't know what I wanted it to be. Either one would complicate things.

"No. He has a roommate. I suspect that's another reason why he's been here so much lately."

I got dizzy again and instantly melancholy over something that made zero sense. Why did I think he'd still be single two years after being with me? He's gorgeous, smart, comes from a good family and has a ranch business. He's more than a great catch; he's ... *my husband.* Anger and jealousy and sadness all washed over me at once, threatening to push me to tears. *That girl in the picture. It's her. That's who he lives with.*

Maeve climbed the step into the house and then the

stairs from the foyer, giving me time to collect myself. By the time she started talking again, I was back to my new normal - confused and angry at myself.

"We normally just grab a bite to eat and a coffee before we do some work around the place, then we sit down and have a real breakfast around eight thirty or so."

"Mack and I were going to have a chat around nine. I guess we'll do that after breakfast."

"Oh, that's nice." She walked down a hallway and stopped at an open door. "Here you are. Bathroom's just there down the hall, and if you need anything, you can either tap on Mack's door there or find my room downstairs off the dining room."

"I'm sure I'll be fine." My face went red as I pictured myself tapping on Mack's door. *Like that'll ever happen.* I stepped into the room, noticing my satchel sitting on the end of the bed and the troll doll on the sidetable. *Good. I can call Bradley and get my head on straight.* Taking in all the baseball memorabilia on the walls, I quickly realized where I was. "This is Ian's room," I said.

"Yes, how did you guess?" Her smile told me there was no point in answering. "He was a superstar in high school, but he wasn't interested in doing it in college. We never could figure that one out. He had offers."

"I don't want to put him out." All Ian needed was another reason to not like me.

"No, he doesn't sleep here anymore. This room has been empty for a few years now."

There were several of the photographs around the room that had someone missing out of them. Whoever it was had been cut out roughly with scissors. I picked up the nearest one off a dresser. Ian looked about ten years younger, fresh-faced and not as tall or as broad. He had one arm around a taller boy and the other over an empty space that used to have a person in it. "Looks like a bad break up." I said, putting the frame back down.

"Ginny. They were together forever. Engaged to be married and then … well … not. It ended right after he got back from Las Vegas."

I moved farther into the room. "What happened? Or is that too personal a question?"

She sighed. I glanced back and caught her leaning on the doorframe as she crossed her arms and looked at the carpet.

"I wish I knew. Ian's not that open about his relationships and things he has going on outside of his life here on the ranch. I'm not even sure Mack knows. I know Angus doesn't." She pushed off the doorframe and dropped her arms to her sides. "It's neither here nor there, though. It's over and they've both moved on as best they could." She gave me a brief smile to try and cover up the sadness that had descended. "Is there anything else you need?"

"A towel maybe?" I hated putting her out, but I felt like I had Baker City dust particles in every single crack and crevice of my body. A shower sounded like heaven. Maybe it would wash away my confusion too. My failure to push Mack into signing the papers was definitely due to exhaustion.

She smacked her forehead lightly. "I'm so sorry. Of course you need a towel. In the bathroom, under the sink. Take any one you like. There's a robe on the back of the door, a small white one we keep for guests. Feel free to use that too. I laundered it just the other day."

"I don't want to steal anyone's robe."

"It doesn't fit any of my men, so you don't need to worry about that." She tapped the doorframe with her palm a couple times. "Goodnight then, Andie. It was nice meeting you, and I'll see you in the morning."

"Yes, thank you for everything. See you tomorrow."

I closed the door behind her and walked over to sit on the bed. Scanning the walls and shelves around the room, I counted no less than twelve pictures with Ginny's face cut out of them. I wondered how much the trip to Vegas had messed up Ian's life, just like it had Mack's and mine. I also considered how much better off we all would have ended up if the trip had never happened.

I reclined back on the bed and tallied up all the effects on my life, courtesy of Las Vegas: Without Vegas, I wouldn't have this marriage to dissolve. Without Vegas, I wouldn't be sneaking around behind Bradley's back out here in no-woman's land with rattlesnakes and dust up my ass. Without Vegas, I wouldn't be sitting in a strange man's bedroom looking at his life in tatters. Without Vegas, I'd be dining at the private Mar-A-Lago Club with Bradley, talking with a disinterested group of so-called friends about how much we were paying for the flowers and cake. Without Vegas I wouldn't have met Mack. I wouldn't have seen him sitting there, played blackjack with him, rode the elevator up to my room with him, and had crazy monkey sex with him. Without Vegas, I wouldn't be married to a stranger in a cowboy hat. I rolled over onto my side with a loud, sad sigh and took the troll doll off the sidetable, tucking it under my chin.

So why, oh why, didn't Vegas feel like a mistake? And why did it feel like the only smart thing I'd done in the last ten years?

# Chapter Twenty-Five

THE SOUND OF CLOMPING BOOTS on the stairs woke me up. I sat bolt upright, trying to figure out where the hell I was and what was going on. Looking down at myself I saw that I was still fully dressed in not only clothes but the thick layer of sweat and dust that had turned into an uncomfortable stickiness all over my body. The troll doll was clenched in my fist. *Oh shit. I forgot to call Bradley.* I put the doll on the night stand and grabbed my satchel off the bed, pulling my phone out. *Dead. Shit. And I left the charger in my hotel room.* A sense of relief went through me, and it scared me to realize it was because I was happy to have a decent excuse for not calling. I had zero desire to talk to him, and it wasn't just because I didn't want him to know what I was doing. All I could think about was how much he hated Ruby and how much I really loved her as a friend. There's something seriously wrong with anyone who hates Ruby. *Why didn't I think about that before?*

A door opened somewhere and then closed shut softly. I got out of bed and tiptoed silently over to the entrance of my room. Opening the door and peeking out into the hallway, I saw no one. There was a light on underneath a door on the opposite side of the hallway. Maeve had said that Ian doesn't stay here in the house anymore and the master bedroom is downstairs, so it had to be Mack I was hearing. I pulled my head back in the door and stood there, listening for sounds of his intentions. I wanted to use the bathroom, maybe even take a late-night shower so I could sleep comfortably, but if he still needed to use it I didn't want to interfere.

After several minutes had passed, I looked out again. The light no longer glowed from under his door. My heavy bladder wasn't going to let me chicken out, so I left the room and tiptoed down the hallway, trying not to make a single sound. Once in the bathroom, I shut the door and locked it.

A fluffy pink towel was under the sink as promised, and the edges of the tub had several hair and soap products that promised to rid me of the Baker City grime. I quickly stripped off my clothes and stepped into a hot shower, my eyes closing automatically as the warmth washed over me and tickled my skin. The liquid trickling through my thick hair and seeping down to my scalp gave me goosebumps.

I picked the shower gel that smelled like roses and squeezed a generous amount into my hand. I'd worked up a serious lather to scrub the dirt off my legs and feet when I heard a sound outside the curtain. It seemed to be coming from way too close to not be inside the bathroom, but I was certain I'd locked the door. I froze in place. "Who's there?" I said softly.

The door shut. *Oh my god! What happened to the damn lock!*

I crossed my soapy hands over my breasts. Everything was slippery and covered in bubbles, the showerhead placed well behind me and not in a position to rinse my body off prematurely. Earlier it had been a good thing, now not so much.

"Is someone there?" I asked. I should have grabbed the curtain and checked around the edge of it, but I couldn't move. The idea that I was standing in the shower naked while a man was on the other side of the thin curtain was both frightening and sensual at the same time. There was only one person it could be. But he wouldn't do that ... break into a locked bathroom when I was naked in it. *Would he?*

"You said you wanted to talk." His voice was deep and not loud, but it wrapped itself around me like chains and held me captive. I should have run. I should have been angry and offended. But I didn't and I wasn't and the words wouldn't come anyway.

"I'm ... I'm in the shower." I squeezed my eyes shut, embarrassed that this was the best I could come up with. I should have been yelling at him to get the hell out.

"I can see that. But I have to run an errand in the morning after chores, so I figured you'd want to talk now rather than wait around another day."

I nodded rapidly, his reasoning making perfect sense ... except for the fact that I was naked in the shower and it was the middle of the night. "Okay." I hesitated, my hands still over my chest. "But no looking."

"Fine. Even though I've already seen you completely naked and *then some*."

I heard movement and backed into the water a little. The soap I'd put on the back of my neck was running down to travel between my butt cheeks. The slipping of the bubbles past my sensitive parts and Mack being on the other side of the curtain gave everything an erotic feel. Even my own hands on my breasts felt sexually charged.

I stepped forward and peeked out of the curtain. He was shirtless and bootless, wearing unbuttoned low-riding jeans and leaning against the counter. I swallowed hard, trying to focus on my response instead of his thick chest, six-pack abs, broad muscled shoulders, and adorable face. "What's that supposed to mean ... *and then some?*"

He shrugged, giving me a lazy, sexy smile. "*And then some* means you were naked, I was naked, and we were both doing things to each other's naked bodies that leaves nothing more to the imagination. I know how you feel *inside*." His lips curved up even more, and I swear I remembered in that moment what his tongue felt like between my legs.

I threw the curtain closed to hide my burning face, and covered my chest with my hands again. "Wow." It was the best I could do. No other words would come to mind. My ears were ringing and my legs were feeling weak enough that I worried I might fall. I held onto the soap holder with one hand just to be sure I wouldn't.

"I'm sorry ... is that too forward for you?" he asked. He was obviously perfectly cool with everything, not showing any emotion other than slight amusement in his tone.

"Maybe," I admitted. *Definitely. Holy shit, how is he turning me into a virgin ninny-boob by just standing there in jeans and flirting a little? What is my damn problem? Is he really flirting?*

"I don't see why it should be too forward, since you claim we're married. Married people do things like we did all the time."

Now we were getting on more solid ground. Arguing I can do, especially when I have the evidence to back me up. "We *are* married, I'll have you know, and yes, that's true, married people do those things. But when we did those things we weren't yet married, so technically it was never consummated. And right now, I'm engaged to be married to someone else so..." I wanted to finish that sentence with a threat, with a demand for propriety, but the words wouldn't pass my lips. They would have been lies and I'd already told enough lies for one day.

"So ... what? You're engaged, so I should leave?"

"Yes," I said, lifting my chin. It was easier when he said the words and I just had to agree. *Chicken shit.*

"And I shouldn't get any closer to the shower, right?" His voice wasn't coming from the sink area anymore.

Without hearing his footsteps, I knew he was standing just on the other side of the curtain from me. My nipples ached with the knowledge that he was just an arm's length away from touching me.

"No," I said in a half-whisper. "You shouldn't get any closer."

"And I shouldn't take my clothes off and get in there with you, I suppose."

"Not under any circumstances," I said, breathing heavily, proud that my words were finally serving me again, but ashamed to admit that I was hoping he'd ignore them. I was a bad person. Everything my mother's boyfriend had predicted for me was coming true. *Liar. Slut.*

He didn't respond. I waited several seconds for his next teasing comment, but it didn't come.

"Mack? Are you still there?"

The curtain flew back, and I screamed in shock.

"Ahh! Oh my ... *holy shit!*" I crossed my arms over my body in several different formations, doing everything I could to shield myself. "What are you doing, you maniac?!"

He was standing there in the middle of the bathroom completely naked, his cock like a missile pointing right at me.

He grinned big. "I'm getting in the shower with my alleged wife." He stepped in next to me, crowding me into the heavy stream of water.

"You...!" The water was bubbling out of my mouth, making me sound like a crazy mermaid. I brushed it away while I tried to argue. "You can't come in here! I'm naked!"

"Yes, you are," he said, closing the curtain behind him. Then he turned to me and put a hand on my waist.

I slapped it away. "Don't touch me or I'll scream!" I could have pushed the curtain to the side and stepped out. I could have kicked him or thrown soap into his eyes. There were any number of other ways I could have escaped his grasp, but I didn't do any of them. I just stood there with the water running over my head, face, and shoulders as he moved in closer, hoping he would touch me again. It was wrong, wrong, wrong to be here with him and be wanting this, but denying it was ridiculous. Emotions this strong are impossible to deny.

"Screaming could be fun. If you really, really want me to stop touching you, I will. I swear it." He put his other hand on my other hip, his fingers digging in and encouraging me towards him. "But if you want me to *keep* touching you, all you have to do is say please, and it'll be done. I'll touch you all night. All you have to do is ask." He didn't smile. He was making me a promise, that much was clear.

We were close enough that his erection was poking me in the stomach. He shifted to make it rest sideways against my stomach and pulled me even closer.

I was too stunned to speak. Some of the soap was still on my skin, and his hands had gathered some of it. His fingers were sliding up my back and down to my ass, massaging my skin with heavy, commanding strokes. A hot wetness come from inside me to lubricate my folds, almost like a release, as if from the moment I'd laid eyes on him today, the passion had been waiting to be unleashed.

"We really shouldn't be doing this," I said in a hoarse whisper, staring at the hair that was growing damp around his face and curling at the ends.

"Why?" he asked, bending his head down to lick my ear. With just that simple touch, goosebumps came up again, all down that side of my body.

"Because…," I said into his chest, my hands leaving their protective positions and dropping to rest on his upper arms, "…I'm engaged." *To a man I don't care enough about, apparently. I'm a terrible person.*

He yanked me up against him roughly, his cock pressing against my abdomen. "No, you're not," he growled into my neck. "You're married. To me. *We* came first, not him."

His biceps flexed heavily under my fingers. They were bigger than I remembered. Thicker. "There's nothing wrong with sleeping with your husband," he insisted.

I moaned, unable to stop the sound from coming out. He was offering me forgiveness even though it wasn't his to give, and I was letting it influence me anyway.

His lips went from my ear to my mouth, leaving a trail of kisses on the way. I moved my mouth towards his eagerly, hungrily, more than ready and willing to feel his lips on mine. But just as they were about to meet, he pulled away. We were touching at the waist, but his torso was leaning back now, leaving my breasts alone and heavy, the nipples aching to be sucked and rolled between his fingers.

He just stood there staring down at me.

"What are you doing?" I asked.

"I'm waiting for you to say the word."

My nostrils flared and my chin came out mutinously. "No." I pushed on his chest, but he didn't move.

"No, what?"

"I'm not going to beg you. This is wrong."

He grabbed me by the back of the head with one hand and forced my lips to his, opening his mouth and sending his thick tongue in to invade mine. My arms flew up to wrap around his neck as I pushed my hips into his. I sighed against his mouth. *So much for resistance.*

The soap on my breasts made moving against him so easy, so wet and slippery. All I had to do now was angle my lower body up somehow and I'd find that sweet relief that I knew only he could deliver. Memories of his heavy body on mine assailed my mind, making me admit that nothing had ever been as good since that night in Las Vegas.

"Say it," he growled against my lips.

"No," I growled back. "I won't." It was wrong, what we were doing. I wasn't going to make it worse by begging. In the back of my mind I was thinking if I didn't beg, I could blame all of this on the passion, on the confusion that muddled my brain any time Mack was in the same space as me. I couldn't help it. I couldn't be blamed. I was just a sorry little slut who couldn't control her libido.

He grabbed one of my thighs and lifted it up, hiking it over his hip. He guided his cock down to my folds, and I nearly wept with joy when it made contact. He slid the head up and down, moving it across and around my entrance, giving small pulses forward as a tease when he reached the center.

"Just one word, that's all I need," he said. His voice was so calm and assured. It was maddening in its business-like tone. He had nothing but control, and yet I was barely holding on. The only thing I could do was refuse to beg, but otherwise, I was all-in. Lifeplan be damned.

He put his other hand on my lower back and pulled me towards him while holding himself out and ready with the other hand. The tip slid in with zero resistance, completely covered in my slippery wetness that the shower hadn't managed to wash away.

"Oh my god," I said, holding onto his shoulders, looking down at where we were joined. "What's happening?"

"I'm going to come inside you now," he said.

I looked up to see a fierce expression bearing down on me. His nostrils were flared wide and his jaw clenched. His blue eyes were stormy with passion, his hair drenched and hanging down over his forehead. I was swept away in all of it - the dark mood, the challenge, the commanding presence of this man who'd invaded my shower, my private places, seizing what he wanted and demanding that I cave in. One simple word. That's all it would take.

"No," I said.

But we both knew I didn't mean it.

His cock went in slowly, slowly. I thought he was going to stop, a vague memory of our last encounter telling me that was how he did his thing ... but he didn't stop. He kept going, filling me until there was nothing left.

I ground into him awkwardly, trying to get as close to him as I could. The shower was too small and there was nothing to hang onto. I grabbed for the curtain when he pulled out and came back inside, and managed to yank the whole thing down on top of our shoulders.

He shoved the plastic off to the side and kept going, not letting the water or the mayhem even cause a stutter in his rhythm. And the whole time he was plunging into me, he never looked away; he stared into my eyes like he was driving home a point. And I felt that point he was making with every thrust. He was taking possession of me, laughing in the face of whatever plan I'd made before coming here. He was calling the shots, not me.

He picked up the speed of his rhythm, our wet bodies making slapping sounds when they came together. I didn't care. The act was even more erotic knowing we were making a mess and being loud about it.

As I felt the heat building between my legs and coming out from my core, I suddenly felt the need to protest. No one had ever made me feel this way and it was wrong. It had to be wrong. It made my other experiences with other men seem boring and faked. He was going to ruin everything.

"We need to stop. We shouldn't..."

With every thrust, he gave me his response. "You. Are. My. *Wife.*" The last word came out as a growl.

I clung to him, no longer caring whether it was right or wrong. All I wanted was for the feeling to keep on going forever. I'd worry about the consequences later.

He stopped suddenly when he was fully buried inside me and leaned over. Shutting off the water, he bit my neck at the same time.

"Ow!" I squeaked. "What are you doing?"

"Get out of the shower," he said, pulling out of me in

one smooth, quick stroke.

I immediately felt empty and abandoned. "What?" My brain was going in about five different directions, completely confused as to what he was doing.

He got out of the shower, his hard-on completely engorged. "Out. Put your hands on the counter and bend over."

My eyes bugged out a little, but I didn't argue; I was beyond any of that foolishness. I stepped out, gingerly avoiding the curtain, and did what he said. I turned my back to him, the cool air making me shiver. My nipples turned rock hard as he stepped up behind me and I bent at the waist.

"What are you doing?" I whispered, looking down at the sink. It was a silly question. We both knew what he was doing. I was playing the innocent victim and he the marauding conquerer. It worked to assuage the guilt.

"Shhhhh. Just stand there, and when you're ready to say please, we'll finish. Until then, be quiet while I touch you." His big hands came around and slid across the sides of my breasts, taking them fully into his palms and squeezing them once he reached the front. My nipples were in between his fingers, and he pinched them together while squeezing my breasts over and over. A low moan escaped my throat and I closed my eyes, lost in the sensations that zipped out of my chest to other places on my body, making me wetter than ever. My insides throbbed with the need to feel him in there, stroking, sliding.

His erection was between my cheeks. I pushed into him, hoping he'd finish what he started. One hand came away from my breast to angle his cock down. It was between my legs now, and as he leaned over to pinch my nipples again, it slid in between my thighs toward the counter. It was close enough to tease but not close enough to give me any satisfaction whatsoever. It was maddening.

"You're torturing me," I said, leaning my head back

against him as he dropped his lips to my neck and sucked. He bit and then he kissed. He licked and sucked again as he squeezed my breasts. I put my hands on the wall on either side of the mirror, giving him better access.

"The torture can stop anytime you want it to. Just say please."

I shook my head languidly, refusing once again. "Never." I sounded and felt drunk.

He dropped a hand and then the head of his cock was angling up to massage my entrance. "Never say never, babe. Never do that."

"Never," I whispered, stuck in some wonderland where he was almost filling me again. I already know what it was going to feel like and I couldn't wait to experience it again.

He pushed down on my upper back between my shoulder blades, forcing me to bend over farther. I went down gladly, opening my legs wider and offering my ass up for the taking. He came to me then, rubbing the tip around my folds, getting it wet and slippery.

"You feel so good," he said. "And your ass. My god, I love your ass." He squeezed one of my cheeks and slapped it. The sting felt way better than it should have.

"It's too big," I said, dropping my head, pushing back a little, silently begging him to come inside. This waiting was killing me.

"Let's see about that." He grabbed me by my hips and pushed himself inside my slippery entrance, pulling me back against him to sheath himself completely with my heat. "Oh, god, yeah." He squeezed my hips. "That ass. *Mmm!*" He smacked my cheek once more before grabbing my hips again and forcing me forward and back. His arms flexed and extended, moving my lower body to slide back and forth over his full length. "Oh, no, babe." He pumped his arms faster, pushing his hips forward and back with the rhythm. "This ass is perrrrfect exactly how it is."

His balls were hitting my clit, making me whimper with unfulfilled need. I pulled my hand away to touch myself and he stopped moving. Grabbing me by the wrist he hissed, "No. You keep your hands where I can see them." He forced my hand to the edge of the sink and pushed it down, not letting go until I wrapped my fingers around the edge of the counter.

He went back to pumping himself into me, squeezing my hips in his iron grip and forcing me to stay right where he wanted me. I was at his mercy, halfway to pleased and most of the way to frustrated, all the while loving the way he was taking command and making me do things I was pretending I didn't want to do.

"Touch me," I demanded.

He slammed into me harder, our bodies slapping louder with the impact. "Beg me," he challenged.

"No," I said, but with a lot less strength of conviction this time. The heat was building and his shaft was getting bigger, thicker. He was close. We were both close. But he was going to get there first.

"Do it," he growled. "I can't hold on much longer." He was breathing hard. "Jesus, your ass is fucking amazing. God*dammit!*"

My nub was pulsing with need, swollen to the max and begging for his touch. My mind swirled with the implications. We were screwing like animals in his parents' bathroom, and I was supposed to be already gone back to Florida. But his body felt like it was made for me and we fit together like it was meant to be. This was what I wanted. Nothing else in the world mattered right now but finding release with this man inside me.

I was breathless, barely able to get the words out. "Please, Mack, please. Okay? Please." My surrender was made complete with that one simple word. *"Please,"* I said again, nearly whimpering with need.

He pulled out with a yank and spun me around roughly.

"What?" I cried, thinking I'd been had.

I didn't have time to figure out what he was going to do before he'd lifted me up and sat me on the sink, spread my legs, and put his cock back into me.

Now we were face to face, eye to eye, and nose to nose. His blue eyes bore into mine, the passion and emotion impossible to miss.

"You're my wife," he said, only inches away, his hot breath flickering over my lips. "You married me in Las Vegas two years ago."

"Yes."

"And I'm your husband."

I nodded, tears slipping out.

He gritted his teeth and growled out, "And this is *us*, consummating our marriage." He buried himself inside me and pulled me close by my lower back, making sure I was pressed nice and tight up against the base of his cock. He moved in and out, banging into me and filling me, sending me over the edge in four sharp strokes.

"Oh, Mack!" I screamed, holding onto him by the shoulders.

"Ahhrrrrrr! Fuck!" he roared, hunched over and bucking against me, his hair tickling my nose as he bit into my shoulder.

I dug my nails into his back as I rode wave after wave of orgasm. Just when I thought it would be over, he'd push inside me again and send me into another spasm of pleasure. I was lost and didn't want to come back. I was dizzy and confused, wandering around a kaleidoscope of colors in my mind, not even sure where I was or who I was anymore.

He wrapped his arms around me held me in his strong arms. He shuddered several times, breathing heavily in my ear, sounding like an angry bull or a freight train. I let the emotion take me away, hearing only the sounds of his breathing and nothing else. It was comforting. Dangerously alluring.

What seemed like a long time later, when he'd finally stopped moving and my body had stopped betraying me, my cries of passion faded into whimpers and then dissolved into tears.

He took a deep breath and lifted his teeth from my skin, resting his forehead in my neck as he sighed heavily. "I love you," he said simply, his breath tickling my ear.

My heart spasmed painfully in my chest. "Please don't say that," I whispered, tears threatening.

"Yeah," he said, his voice rough with emotion, "I get it." He pulled his softening length out of me and turned around, his hand already on the door.

"Where are you going?" I asked, my voice revealing sorrow and confusion. I sagged back against the mirror.

"Away. I'll talk to you tomorrow at nine."

And then he was gone. The door shut behind him, leaving me alone in the passion-torn bathroom. For a long time I just sat there, finally realizing what a broken heart really feels like. I'd thought before that I'd known. When Luke broke up with me by text message, when other people had let me down as a child, it had hurt. A lot. But I'd been wrong about those painful moments. They had bruised my heart, yes. But this right here? This was real pain. This was true heartache.

I knew without a doubt that I was watching the only man who could ever make me feel this way walk out the door to go sign our divorce papers, and it was true sorrow like no other. I would look back on this trip to Baker City, Oregon and know that Gavin MacKenzie was the man who cracked my heart into a thousand pieces. And I was just going to let him do it. I had no other choice.

I got down off the sink and moved slowly over to the shower to put the curtain back up, my heart going numb with pain. I rinsed off, jumping when my fingers touched the now overly-sensitive parts between my legs. Everything was thick and swollen down there still, and I realized for the first time as I tried to wash everything away that we'd had sex without protection.

*Oh, Jesus, how stupid can I possibly be?* I stared at the ceiling as the tears dripped down and filled my ears. *What am I going to do now?*

# Chapter Twenty-Six

I DON'T KNOW HOW I slept. Maybe it was the leftover sun exhaustion or the buckets of tears I cried, but my eyes didn't drag themselves open until well after nine. I jumped out of bed and shimmied back into my dirty clothes. Running down the stairs after only a cursory glance in the mirror, I went from room to room looking for Mack. Last night was a mistake. I had to just tell him that. I had to tell him that we had to let go of unreasonable expectations and live the lives we'd been born to. His was here and mine was across the country. We were completely incompatible.

"Well, good morning, sunshine," said Angus, leaning against the counter and drinking what looked like a cup of coffee. He pointed to a machine next to the sink. "Help yourself. Mug's are in the cabinet above."

I shuffled over and got out a cup. "Is Mack around?" I asked, pouring myself a cup of dark coffee. Today I'd be skipping the cream and sugar; I needed straight-up harsh caffeine going right into my veins.

"Nope. He went into town."

I spun around. "But … we had an appointment."

Angus chuckled. "We don't generally do appointments out here."

"Okay, well we had an agreement to meet at nine so we

could talk."

"About your genealogy business?"

I nodded, taking a sip of my coffee. According to my sleepy brain, nodding wasn't exactly lying.

"You can ask me questions if you want. I'm available for the next half hour, and I'm a MacKenzie."

"Don't you have cows to de-testicle?"

He laughed again. "Nope, not yet. I need Mack for that and he had to go."

"Where did he go? Do you know when he'll be back?"

Angus looked into his mug, frowning a little. "I'm not exactly sure."

I could tell Angus was lying, but it was probably true that none of it was my business. I was just the girl trying to detach myself from Mack's animal magnetism and get back to my real life.

"Is there any chance I could get a lift back to town so I could get my phone numbers and charger and things?"

"Actually, all your things are in the front hall. Boog brought them over early this morning."

I put my cup down without saying a word and walked out of the kitchen towards the front door. My jaw dropped open at the sight of all my things sitting there on the floor. *How in the hell…?*

Angus stood behind me. "Got your car towed to the garage. You've got a bent axle. It's gonna be a while before it's fixed. Since you didn't have any transportation, we figured you'd want to have your things while you're here. Boog knows the girl at the reception desk, so she let him into your room."

I spun around to face him, not even sure what I was going to say. The expression on his face made me stop the words that were about to fly out of my mouth. He looked … sad.

I frowned in confusion. None of this made any sense.

"Yup ... so ... I'm going to head out to the barn. Maeve'll be in the kitchen in a few minutes. She just went to gather some eggs." He left me standing there in the hall.

I kept everything where it was except my phone charger, which I brought up to Ian's bedroom and plugged into my phone and the wall. As soon as there was enough juice to power the phone up, I checked my messages. There were four texts from Bradley, one from Ruby, and one from Candice. I didn't even bother checking the ten voicemails. I checked Candice's text message first.

**Candice:** *I hear you're out in Oregon??? Call me, bitch.*

**Candice:** *Okay, you know I was only kidding about the bitch thing, right? Call me. Bitch.*

I smiled as I pressed her number. Bradley could wait. The office could wait. I hadn't talked to my best friend in months.

"Hello? Is this really you?" Candice said, nearly yelling.

"Yes, it's really me." I didn't realize until just then how much I'd missed her craziness.

"And you're calling me from Oregon and Bradley's not with you, right?"

"Yep, that's right."

"Squeeeeee!!!" The phone dropped and I heard a loud bang and then some rustling around. "Oops, sorry about that," she said, now slightly breathless. "I just lost my shit for a second there. Did you break up? Are you running after twooo wuvv?"

"What are you talking about?"

"Ruby told me everything. Come on, fess up. What's he like? Did he flip his cowboy hat when you showed up?"

My heart was racing. "Hold on a second, Candice. How do you know all this stuff? No one knows about this, not even Ruby. All she did was make my travel arrangements."

She snorted. "As if. Have you forgotten who you work for?"

"Umm… no." What could my law firm have to do with any of this?

"Ruby. You work for Ruby. Ruby knows all, Ruby sees all, Ruby tells me all. Ruby has the password to your computer files, duh."

I closed my eyes and sighed, putting all my frustration, worry, and feelings of helplessness into it.

"Are you pissed? Don't be pissed at her. She was just doing you a big, fat favor, believe me."

"What did she do?" The words would barely come out.

"Nothing. She just told me and Kelly what's what so we could, you know, help if necessary."

I rested my forehead in my hand. "Believe me, your help is the last thing I need."

"Please don't hang up," she begged. "I finally got you back, I wouldn't be able to take it if you dumped me again."

"Dumped you?" I sat up again. She was making no sense.

"Yes. Dumped me." She felt very strongly about this apparently. "Ever since you started dating *that Bradley*, you dumped all your friends. Or did you not notice that you have zero *normal* people in your life anymore?"

Putting Candice in the category of normal was like putting Ruby in the category of shy privacy-respecting people, and that was a load of cow poo. "I did notice that you and I haven't had lunch in ages."

"Ages? Try a year, my friend. A full fucking year. And now look … you made me cuss! You totally made me break my vow not to cuss this week. I hope you're happy. Anyway, enough of that … tell me about your man."

I felt like crying. "He's not my man. I'm waiting for him to sign the divorce papers."

"So you really did marry him," she whispered. "Oh my god, that's so romantic!" She squeed again, but thankfully this time not right in my ear.

When she came back I clarified. "It's not romantic, it's awful. It's terrible-awful." Tears rushed to my eyes.

"Oh, sweetie, what's wrong? Why are you crying?"

"I'm not," I insisted, wiping tears off my cheeks. "I'm just frustrated."

"Talk to me. Tell me what's going on. I'm sure I can help."

"You can't, you really can't. It's just ... very complicated."

"Tell me! I'm good with people. I can help you un-complicate it, I promise. Please-please-please-please-pleeeeaaase?"

She wore me down with her begging, and I really did need to get the secret off my chest. It was killing me to have no one to talk sense into me. "Okay fine. Apparently I married him two years ago, after you left us and we had crazy monkey sex."

"Oh, man. That must have been some pretty amazing stuff to make you go marry the guy."

"I know, right? I have no idea what happened though, because the next day he was gone."

"Where did he go?"

"I have no idea! I found a claim check in the room and called the front desk. They said he came and got his bags from downstairs and left with them. I never heard from him again, so I don't know anything else."

"And since you didn't remember getting married, you did nothing."

"Right. I mean, I was kind of sad he didn't call or anything, but I moved on. You know I had the Luke thing to deal with and then ... well, life got in the way."

She snorted. "You mean your stupid *lifeplan* got in the way. When are you going to throw that thing in the shredder and get on with your real life? Life *unscripted?*"

"I don't know," I said in a weak voice.

"Well, hey now, that's progress! That's the first time I've ever heard you even consider shredding the Dark Forces. Good for you! I think maybe Oregon is good for you."

I laughed. "Dark Forces?"

"Yes," she said with conviction. "That damn lifeplan has done nothing but lead you down the wrong path since day one. Dark Forces. Devil in disguise."

"It got me into college and law school."

"Granted, it got you into college which is where you met me and Kelly, but other than that, pooey. What did law school ever do for you other than turn you into a cold-hearted, analytical bitch?"

I nearly choked on my outrage. "Hey! That's out of line! Even for you, Candice."

"Hey! I'm just giving you the tough love you've needed for years. Now listen up, because I know my time is about to be cut off. This is hard shit to listen to, but you need to hear it. You have terrible taste in men because you're always trying to get them to fit into a box. You fall in love with potential instead of reality. You are attracted to characteristics on paper instead of the real man underneath. Stop putting men into categories. Stop making checklists and measuring men up next to them! Luke was a puke and Bradley is a turd sandwich. He doesn't care about you; he cares about what his friends *think* about you. He's obnoxious, and one day he'll be kicked out of the Bar because I'll bet he cheats. I'll bet he cuts corners! You're too good for him and all those other buttheads you've gone out with. But maybe not this cowboy. Maybe this guy is the real deal." She finished in a softer voice. "He sure seemed nice when I met him."

I'd begun crying halfway through her speech and now I just sat there, numb. The pain was terrible, not so much because the words had come from the mouth of someone I cared about, but because they were all true. I knew they were true, but I also knew I wasn't strong enough to do anything about it but ignore them.

"Thanks for the call, Candice. I have to go now."

"Oh, no you don't! No way am I going to live with another friendship dry spell! Talk to me. Tell me what you're thinking right this second!"

"I'm thinking that I have to go."

"No. I don't accept that. Try again."

I let out a long, shaky sigh. "I don't know what you want from me, Candice."

"Honesty. Tell me right now, in all honesty, how you feel about the cowboy. What's his name, by the way?"

"His name is Mack. And how I feel about him? I don't know. It's confusing."

"Give me a bullet list. You like lists."

"Shut up."

"No, I'm serious. Bullet list. Go."

"Fine. You want a bullet list? Here it is: Sexy. Handsome. Smart. Sexy. Magnetizing. Compelling. Muscles. Good family. Confident. Polite. Sexy."

"I'm getting the impression that there's some chemistry going on over there." I could tell she was smiling by the tone of her voice.

I took another shaky breath, afraid to admit what I'd done but knowing it was relevant. I really wanted to confess my sins to Father Candice.

"Tell me what you're not telling me," she insisted.

"You're a mind reader now, too?"

"Yes. I always have been. Did you sleep with him?"

"In Vegas? Yes."

"No, dummy, in Oregon. Don't play games with me. I have a color and cut in ten minutes."

"Go ahead and go. I have to call Bradley. He's left me a ton of messages."

"I can get on a plane and be out there in less than six hours." She was threatening me.

"*No.* Stay put. I already have enough trouble juggling what's here. I don't need to add you to the mix."

"Then tell me. You had sex again, didn't you?"

"Promise you won't squee in the phone again."

"Squeeee!! You totally did it, you big fat ho!" She was laughing out loud, probably in the middle of her salon.

"Yes. Last night. It was amazingly erotic and the wrong thing to do and ... shit, Candice! I don't know what the hell I'm doing!" I felt and sounded like I was on the edge of sanity.

"Of course you do! You're going with your heart and your vagina instead of your head for a change! Good for you! It's about time. Damn, when we were in Vegas I thought you'd finally figured it out. But then we got back and you put your head right back up into your butt. Ruby and Kelly and I thought you were a goner. But now you're back, baby, you're *back!* Don't quit on us now. There's too much riding on this."

"Too much of what?" I was smiling through my tears. Candice had such a way with words.

"Too much happiness, sweetie. I think this cowboy could make you happy. Why don't you give him a chance?"

"I can't," I whispered, looking up at the pictures on Ian's shelves.

"Why not?" Candice sounded like she was going to cry right along with me.

"Because I think he has a girlfriend. I think she's his roommate."

"Well," Candice said, sparking up again, "then she's gotta go. You got there first, you're his wife."

"It's not that simple."

"Sure it is. If he had a girlfriend who meant anything would he have slept with you last night?"

"Maybe not. Or maybe he slept with me to teach me a lesson."

"A lesson? A lesson about what?"

"I don't know. He seemed mad at me from the moment he saw me."

"Did he remember you were married?"

"Yes, I think so."

"But he was mad at you, even though he took off and never called."

"Yes."

"Hmmmm... Well, how come you never called him? Weren't you even curious why he disappeared?"

I shrugged, sitting alone in Ian's room, trying to remember back to that day two years ago in the hotel room. "I couldn't."

"You couldn't what?"

"Call him. I didn't have his number."

"Are you sure? You blacked out for half the night. You blacked out during a whole damn wedding. Surely he could have put his number in your phone and you wouldn't have remembered that either, right?"

My face burned right along with my stomach. "I ... I don't remember seeing a strange number on there."

"*Pfft.* You have like a million numbers on your phone. Didn't you even think to look for his name?"

A memory came rushing back. "I couldn't!"

"Why?!"

"Because you dropped my damn phone in the toilet, don't you remember?!" I was gripping the bedsheets, feeling like I could shred them with my nails.

"Oh, crapski. I *do* remember that. Oh, maaaan. And all your contacts had to be loaded on to a new phone when you got back to your office."

"Except for the one that was added in Las Vegas, since it wasn't in my office back-up," I said sadly. "Assuming there *was* one added in Vegas."

"I guess you have a mission, then," said Candice. "You need to ask him if he gave you his number. Maybe you were supposed to call him, and when you didn't, he got mad."

"But why wouldn't I have given him *my* number? If he wanted to talk to me, he could have just called me, right?"

"You'll never know until you ask." A stranger's voice spoke softly next to Candice. "Shit, I have to go. My next client is here. We'll talk more about this later. Promise me you won't disappear!"

"I promise." I wanted to curl up in the bed and sleep the day away. This was a royal mess, and now I realized on top of everything else how I'd basically almost thrown my best friendships in the garbage. When the man-crap hits the fan, girlfriends are the only ones who can make things better. Why had I let them go for Bradley?

"Good. Chin up, gorgeous girl! We'll figure this out. Meanwhile, I'll bring Kelly into the loop and get an update from Ruby."

"No! I don't know what Ruby's doing over there, but Bradley *cannot* find out what's going on here!"

"Uhhh, it might be too late for that. Gotta go, lovebugger. Tah-tah!" The line went dead.

# Chapter Twenty-Seven

MY FINGERS SHOOK AS I dialed the phone. If Ruby had told Bradley, my ship was sunk. Not only my lifeplan ship but my work ship, too. I'd built up a reputation as a professional, hard-working woman, and the rumor that I'd gotten married to some guy who I didn't even know out in Vegas during a drunken party binge would destroy all of it. *Poof!* Six years, out the window. Back to square one with zero plan for the voyage and shame as my baggage.

I didn't even wait for the receptionist to finish her introduction to the firm. "Jackie, can you pass me to Ruby? This is Andie and it's kind of an emergency."

"Sure, Andie, hold on a second for me." I got no indication that she knew anything about what I was going through from her tone, but that didn't mean anything. Jackie was as professional as they come. She could be in on who assassinated the president and she'd still sit there with a bland look on her face and act clueless.

I waited for what felt like forever before the phone connected again.

"Andie?"

My heart sunk. The voice was way too deep to be Ruby. "Yes...," I squeaked out, barely more than a whisper.

"Andie, this is Bradley. Where in the hell are you?" He

sounded both worried and angry.

I swallowed hard. "Pretty much in the middle of nowhere. Where are you?" I wanted to smack myself on the forehead. *Way to sound confident, Andie!*

"What do you mean, where am I? I'm at work, where you should be."

"But what are you doing answering Ruby's phone?"

"I heard it was you and I intercepted. I don't know why you're calling her and not me. Something's going on, Andie, and I want to know what it is."

I could hear Ruby's voice in the background now, and she didn't sound happy. Thank God for Ruby. "I just need to talk to Ruby about some paperwork and then I'll call you. My phone was dead and my charger wasn't available, so that's why I haven't called." And I was with another man. *Ahhh! This is horrible. I'm going to hell for sure. I need to confess.* My ears burned with the idea of coming clean, but it was the only way to handle this now. Lying was wrong and unfair and not who I am.

Bradley was not happy. "Ruby's threatening to impale me on her fountain pen, so I have to go. Call me immediately, Andie, I mean it. As soon as you're done with her."

"Okay, I'll call you as soon as I'm done with Ruby. I promise. We have to talk."

"You're damn right we do. Here." He passed the phone away and Ruby's voice came on the line.

"I'm filing a complaint, Bradley. You hear me? An official complaint. You've gone too far."

Bradley responded, but I didn't catch the actual words.

"Ruby?"

"Yes, Andie, I'm here. Can you believe the nerve of that man? Picking up my calls on my phone and putting his nose in my business? He's going to pay for that one. I've had it up to here with him."

"Ruby, calm down. You can't report him for that. He's

upset with me, it's my fault."

Ruby sighed heavily. "When are you going to learn that you are *not* responsible for the behavior of the men you date? He's a big boy. He makes his own decisions."

"I haven't called him in over twenty-four hours. He was worried, especially when the first person I called wasn't him."

Her voice dropped lower. "Good for you! Does this mean you're finally going to get rid of his sorry behind?"

"No. Maybe. Shit, Ruby, I don't know. That's not why I called." My hands were shaking so bad, I clenched my free one in a fist and hit the bed with it a few times.

"Mmm-mmm-mmm, you still haven't cleaned up that language, I see."

"Stop. Seriously. Did you go into my computer and look at my files?"

Silence.

"Ruby, I know you did. I already talked to Candice. What did you see?"

"Well..." She stopped there.

"Come on, Ruby. I don't have all day."

"Fine. I saw your...," she lowered her voice to a loud whisper, "...marriage license." She raised her voice again. "Is it real? Did you really do that?"

Tears threatened. "Yes, I really did do it. I don't know what the hell I was thinking, but I married a practical stranger two years ago at that stupid bachelorette party *you* made me go to, and now I'm out here trying to unwind the mess before my wedding to Bradley."

"You're blaming me for this?"

"No. I just put that in there to make you feel guilty."

She snorted. "Huh, like that would work. I'm proud I did it. I'm *glad* I did it. Anything to get rid of *that Bradley* is a good thing."

"Listen, Ruby, he didn't do anything wrong, okay? He's been a good boyfriend. I was set to marry the guy for ...

poop's sake."

"*Were* set to marry him?  As in past tense?"  She was back to whisper-yelling at me.

I shook my head and took a deep breath, ready to bawl again.  "I don't know what the hell I'm going to do.  I have to talk to Bradley, and I have to talk to Mack.  It's pretty much out of my hands at this point.  My lifeplan is swirling down the toilet as we speak."

"Who's Mack?  Is he your husband?"

My heart lurched at the word *husband*.  *Mack is my husband.*  The idea gave me chills and brought gobs of fear along with it too.  "Yes.  He is."

"Oh my dear Lord … this is a problem, isn't it?  Do you want me to start canceling things?  Maybe we can get some of your deposits back."

"No! No, don't cancel anything.  Just transfer me over to Bradley's line, please.  And Ruby?  Please don't say anything to anyone else.  Candice is fine, but no one else can know.  It'll ruin everything at work."

"Oh don't worry, baby girl.  Your secrets are safe with me."

I rolled my eyes.  "Yeah, right.  Bye, Rubes.  Talk to you later."

"Please hold," she said in her professional secretary voice, sending me over to Bradley's line.

# Chapter Twenty-Eight

"BRADLEY."

THAT ONE WORD SAID it all. Strong. Firm. Take no prisoners. He never cared who he trampled over to get what he wanted. It's what attracted me to him eventually, that he made no apologies for who he was. He was so driven and in control. I was jealous of that for a long time until I became that. Now I knew it had been a mistake. I'd lost *me* somewhere along the way, right along with my two best friends and the respect of my colleague, Ruby.

Time to finish destroying my life. "Hi, it's me, Andie." The line went silent for so long I thought I'd lost him. "Bradley?"

"Still here. Just waiting for an explanation."

His voice was so cold it made me ill. I'd hurt him. He was a prick sometimes, but that didn't mean he deserved to be cheated on or lied to. "I have something to confess. Something big."

"You're with another guy, aren't you? How long has it been going on?"

I sighed, trying to work up the bravery to come totally and completely clean. I saw my future crumbling into tiny fragments right in front of my eyes, my lifeplan and all the solidity and security it offered disappearing into the wind.

My future was now a cloud of dust motes floating away to clog up some stranger's nostrils...

"Andie, I'm not going to sit on this line forever. I have work to do."

"Sorry. I'm just ... never mind." I cleared my throat. Time to do the right thing. "Do you remember when we started dating?"

"Of course. I'd been trying to get you to go out with me for months. Getting that first yes out of you was a real coup."

I smiled sadly. "I think ... I might have said yes for reasons that weren't necessarily all the right ones."

"What's that supposed to mean? Are we going to be talking in riddles now, Andie? Because I really don't have the time or the patience for it."

Typical Bradley. He was doing me a favor being harsh. I just needed to get this done with. "Two years ago I went to Las Vegas with Candice and Kelly."

"The bimbos."

"No, Bradley, they're not bimbos."

"I beg to differ. Anyway, as you were saying..."

"I went to Las Vegas with my two best friends. And while I was there, something happened."

"You broke up with Luke and got laid. It's no big deal, Andie, people do it all the time."

The way he said it gave me a weird feeling, like he was being defensive instead of understanding. I shoved it aside because all this garbage had to be said, and I was on a roll. "Yeah, well, it was more than that."

"What? You fell in love with the guy? You want to get back together with him? Please, what a bunch of horse shit. You've been with me for *two years*, Andie. I've invested two long years of my professional and personal life with you. Do you know what two years is like in my life? They're like dog years. Multiply them by seven and that's how long we've been at this thing together. Fourteen years is too long to play games. Just tell it to me straight, because right now I don't get what you're trying to say."

*Dog years? Since when did our relationship get measured in dog years?* "I'm trying to tell you, but you keep interrupting." He was irritating me now, making me see some of the things Ruby saw in him, reminding me of the things that used to bother me about him before we started dating.

"I'm sorry," he said, toning down the jerk a little. "Please continue. I'll wait until you're done before I comment again."

"Thank you. As I was saying ... I went out to Las Vegas. Luke broke up with me by text on the way out, as you might recall. I got really drunk and met this guy named Gavin. He's from Oregon, and yes, we had sex. And then the next thing I remembered was waking up in the hotel room with Candice next to me and Kelly in the other room. The guy was long gone and I never saw him or heard from him again."

"So?"

"So, when I applied for our marriage license last week, I found out that there's a marriage license with my name on it out in Nevada."

"What? What does that mean?"

"It means I married him. I married the stranger."

"You said you fucked him."

"Well, I didn't say that exactly, but yeah, that's the idea."

"So he wasn't a stranger. And you're with him now, too, right?"

"Yes. I came out here to get him to sign the divorce papers."

"Okay, fine. So get the asshole to sign the papers and then get your butt back here. We have a wedding to put together."

I held the phone out and looked at it, not really believing what I was hearing. How could he be so casual about it? I frowned. Probably because he didn't know the worst part yet. *Deep breath. You can do this.*

"Did you hear what I said?" he was asking as I put the phone back to my ear.

"Yeah, but ... I don't think that's going to happen."

"What do you mean it's not going to happen? We've been planning this for six months! People have plane tickets in hand. Non-refundable ones."

"I know but ... I'm sorry, Bradley ... I ... *shit*," I pressed my fingers into my forehead and crushed my eyes closed. "I slept with him again. Last night." I let out a huge breath. "I'm so, so, so sorry. You didn't deserve that. I'm a total jerk, I know." I had to swallow several times to keep the bile down. Admitting to being a slut with zero morals is quite a step down for me. I had expected it to be somewhat cleansing, but instead I just felt dirty.

"Did you go out there to do that?" His tone had calmed down considerably, which made it even scarier than his anger would have been.

"No. Hell no. I came out here to get divorced, that's it."

"That's interesting, don't you think? That you went out there to get divorced and instead fucked him?"

"Bradley, please don't." I sighed shakily. This was going to be ugly. I deserved it, so I sat there, preparing myself to take it in. My punishment.

"Why? Why shouldn't I just come right out and say it. It's what everyone else is going to say. Bradley couldn't hold on to his woman. She married some dumb fuck redneck out west and left his ass at the altar."

"No one's going to say anything, because the only ones who know are you, me, him, and Ruby."

"Oh, I'll bet Ruby's dancing a goddamn jig over this one." I could picture Bradley running his hands through his short hair in frustration. He did that when he was upset and only out of the view of other people.

"She's not, Bradley. She might be glad that we're

breaking up, but she's not happy that I hurt you."

"Breaking up?    We're not breaking up.    Don't be ridiculous."

My eyes nearly crossed. "What?"

"You heard me.   We're getting married.   This doesn't change anything."

"Are you insane?    Of course it changes things!"    I laughed a little hysterically.

"It doesn't have to."   He went from angry to courtroom convincing in the space of half a second.    "Listen, let's be honest … we're perfect for each other.   We both have the same goals, the same drive, the same reputation."

I wanted to argue that last point, but he talked right over me.

"So you made a mistake.   We all make mistakes.   I know I've made a couple.   That's life.   But once we say the vows, we know that the fun is over.   We'll be monogamous, dedicated to our goals as a couple.   We put another five years in at the firm, then we either keep going if the bonuses are good or we start our own firm.   Right now we could take half the place with us.   Then you pop a couple kids out, we buy a place in Colorado for ski season and *bam*, we're all set."

"You've got it all figured out, huh?"   My voice went all weak and I hated myself for it.   He was offering me an out. Blanket forgiveness for all my sins.   And I, in return, would have to offer him the same.   I wondered what his sins might be, considering how magnanimous he was being.   I was sure I didn't really want to know.

He sounded excited now.   Almost endearing in a way. "Yeah, I've got it all figured out.   That's why you love me, right? Lifeplan, babe.   You're the one who turned me on to all of that stuff.   Am I or am I not the *only* guy you've ever been with who can appreciate the lifeplan?"

I nodded sadly.   "Yes, you are.   And I think that's why we have to break up."

"What?! Fuck that. No, I don't accept that. We're not breaking up. Being apart is not an option."

"Bradley, don't make this harder than it needs to be. Seriously. I screwed up big time ... too much to fix it. You deserve better than me. I don't love you like I should. I've come to admire you and look past your issues, but that's not enough."

"You don't marry someone you just *admire*. You love me, Andie. You've said it a thousand times. And you agreed to marry me."

"I don't think I knew what love meant when I said it, though."

"Until now? Until you screwed that redneck? Please."

"He's not a redneck. Listen, I have to go."

"I'm coming out there, Andie."

My heart stopped beating for a full three seconds. "*No!* Do *not* come out here Bradley."

"Either you come home so we can get this wedding over with, or I'm coming out there. Don't worry ... I'm sure I can convince the guy to give you a divorce once we're face-to-face."

"Bradley, *no*. I'm not kidding. This is non-negotiable. We're through. I'm sorry to have to say it over the phone, because I know how much that sucks, but I'm serious. We are *not* getting married and you *cannot* come out here."

"You're not yourself, Andie. You've been under a lot of stress, and that's my fault. I take full responsibility, putting all the planning in your lap and bullshitting around with ... stuff. But I'm not going to let my investment in *you* and in *us* go down the drain. I'm booking a ticket. I'll see you tomorrow."

"NO!"

My shouting was in vain. He was already off the line.

"Shit fuck shit fuck," I moaned, desperately pushing buttons on my phone. "Come on, Ruby, pick up, pick up, pick up..."

*"Hello, you've reached the voicemail for Ruby, assistant to attorney Andrea Marks..."*

I hung up the phone, dialing Candice next.

*"Hi, this is Candice, you know what to do! —BEEP—."*

I threw the phone down on the bed. "Dammit!"

"Anything I can help with?" Maeve was standing in the doorway, and I had no idea how long she'd been there.

# Chapter Twenty-Nine

QUICKLY BRUSHING THE TEARS OFF my cheeks, I looked up at Maeve standing in the doorway of Ian's room. "Oh, hi. I didn't see you there." I cleared my throat to get the frog out of it.

"I just got in from collecting eggs. I have to head into town to get some things for the picnic. Would you like to join me?" Her expression told me nothing about whether she'd heard any of my conversation.

I looked around the room and at my phone, Bradley's threat weighing heavily on my mind. *What if he really comes out here? How would he find me? I'm out in the middle of nowhere.*

Underestimating his determination would be a mistake, I knew that. I had to be on my way back to the East Coast before he got here. It would be the only way to avoid a huge, ugly scene.

"I think I'd better stick around here," I said. "I need to talk to Mack."

"Well, Mack's in town, so if you want to talk to him, best come with me." She left the room before I had time to argue. The conversation Mack and I needed to have wasn't one to engage in with his mother standing nearby, but the idea of waiting around the ranch for him to show up who-knows-when was even less appealing. If I found him in town, maybe I could make him take me somewhere private where we could finally end this thing as painlessly as possible.

I grabbed my satchel, slipped on the moccasins Maeve had loaned me last night, and followed the sound of her footsteps going down the stairs.

"I'm just going to throw some other clothes on," I said.

"I'll be outside," she responded from the porch.

I grabbed my overnight bag from the floor and pulled out a t-shirt and shorts, slipping them on in the bathroom. I brushed my teeth and did what I could with my hair before joining Maeve outside.

"You have a car?" I asked as I walked to the driveway, making my way over to a pickup truck that Maeve was already getting into.

"We have a couple cars here, but I guess you could call this one mine. It's the one I drive most often."

I stopped at the passenger door, my fingers resting on the handle. "I probably could have asked you for a ride last night instead of Boog, huh?" It was the closest I could come to scolding her for not offering without being a complete jerk.

"You could have asked, but I would have said no, unfortunately." She slammed her door shut and reached for her seatbelt. "I can't drive from dusk on. I have night vision problems." She smiled ruefully at me as I climbed in next to her.

"Oh. Well that's … inconvenient." I put my seatbelt on and scanned the dashboard. There was dust all over it. I clasped my hands in my lap to keep from wiping it off. Instead, I busied myself with getting the small brush out of my satchel and working the knots out of my hair.

"No, not really." She started the engine and it roared to life. "When I go out at night, I'm always with Angus or one of the boys, anyway. I prefer it when they drive. Then I can just ride and look at the scenery." She backed out into the yard and turned onto the dirt road leading to the property's entrance gate.

I lifted an eyebrow but kept my mouth shut about the so-called scenery, refusing to let my bad day ruin hers too. As far as I could tell, the entire landscape consisted of scrub brush and dirt. There wasn't much to miss, except maybe the mountains off in the distance.

"Hey!" came a voice from the side of the house, just as we were reaching the gate.

Maeve stopped the truck and rolled down my window. Boog was just coming around to the front where all the trucks were parked.

"Where you headed?" he asked.

"Into town. Grocery store. Need anything?"

"You could grab me some chew and I wouldn't complain."

"I'll see what I can do," Maeve promised.

The window went up as Boog pulled a cell phone out of his pocket and started a call before going back around the side of the house and out of sight.

We rode down the dirt road that had almost killed me yesterday, the truck's shock absorbers doing little to keep my teeth in my gums. I had a headache by the time we reached the main road.

"I sure hope you'll be able to stay for the picnic. It's a big event for the family, and since you've got some MacKenzie connection somewhere in your line, it would be nice for everyone to be able to meet you. We have MacKenzies coming in from some other counties, not just the immediate area."

*Great. More people to witness my shame.* "I really can't. I have to get back to work as soon as possible. After I talk to Mack, I'll be heading out."

Maeve frowned but said nothing in response.

After a little while, the silence started to eat at me. "So, do you know why Mack had to go into town?" I was trying to sound friendly-casual about it. "He'd told me we could sit down and chat at nine, so I was kind of surprised to hear he wasn't around."

"I have an idea why, but I'm not sure it's right."

I bit my lip. "I hope it wasn't an emergency. I mean anything bad." I cringed at my complete lack of finesse.

Maeve didn't seem to notice. "He just has some loose ends back in town that he's been putting off taking care of. I guess he decided it was about time and got a bug up his buns to do it right away."

"With Hannah Banana?" I did it. I totally went for it. And now that my mouth had leaped in front of my brain once again, I was just going to have to live with the fallout. I waited on pins and needles for Maeve's response.

She looked at me sharply before turning back to face the windshield. "How did you know about Hannah? Did Mack tell you about her?"

I shrugged. "I saw her at the diner when I was in there yesterday for coffee, and then I saw the pictures of her and Mack in your living room. I just put two and two together." Stupid jealousy was eating me alive. Before, Hannah being in Mack's life had just been a suspicion, something I planned to use to force his hand into signing the papers. Now it was something else entirely. *Does he love her? Does he want to marry her? Why do I care?*

Maeve sighed deeply. "Hannah is ... how can I say this nicely ..." She pressed her lips together for a few seconds. "Hannah has been hanging on to the idea of her and Mack being together since she was fourteen years old."

"That's..." I paused to estimate the years.

"A long time," Maeve finished for me. "And in all those years, Mack never reciprocated the feeling."

"But don't they live together?"

"Yes, but not as a couple."

I snorted. Mothers could be so clueless.

Maeve frowned at me for a split second. "No, really. I'm not privy to all of their private moments, but I know my son."

I nodded noncommittally, not believing a word of it. Maeve believed it, but that was just a mother's naiveté, what she wanted to be true. A man like Mack and a woman in love with him for over ten years couldn't possibly live together and stay just friends. He would have had to beat her off with a stick, and he was too nice a guy to do that.

I shook my head, battling tears. It figured. I had the best sex of my life with a man who was already spoken for, and the sex education he'd provided me was enough to make me realize that the man who'd I'd planned to marry was not the man for me. Or maybe he was. Maybe I was better off with a guy who was cold, calculating and absolutely sure of how I fit into his life.

Nothing made sense anymore. I was so confused. The divorce papers in my bag were either my ticket to happiness or my doom; I had no way of knowing. Investing in a Magic Eight-Ball when we got into town seemed the best plan of action at this point. Asking it to solve my problems would probably put me on a better track than I'd be able to manage for myself.

"When they were growing up, Hannah was always on the outskirts of my boys' games. She watched them doing their rodeos when they got older, went to their sporting events ... but never once did Gavin give her the time of day. He didn't respect her is what he always told me. She married another man - a friend of Gavin's - and then ended up in a bad way a couple months back, so he offered her a place to stay. He did it at his friend's request, not Hannah's. He's just being a good friend."

"Mmm-hmm," I said, staring out the window. Maeve was pushing a knife into my chest with every word. Next she'd probably tell me how they had to share a bedroom, all because Mack's such a good guy. A veritable saint in form-fitting jeans and a cowboy hat.

"You should talk to him about it. He'll explain."

"He doesn't need to," I said, trying to keep the sadness out of my voice. "It has nothing to do with me."

"Are you sure about that?" Maeve had stopped in town at a red light. She glanced at me before driving forward through the cleared intersection.

"I'm sure." I said, knowing it wasn't true. Mack and Hannah had lots to do with me. He's my husband, but he belongs with the girl who's loved him half her life, not the one who couldn't even remember she married him. Standing in the middle of that wouldn't be fair. Great sex does not make a relationship, and besides, we were opposites in every way. He's a cowboy, I'm a lawyer. He lives in the dust and I live on the asphalt. He rides a horse and I drive a clown honkey-horn having Smart Car.

Maeve pulled into a parking lot. "Here's the grocery store. Come on in with me and we'll grab a few things before we head on over to the party supply place."

I got out of the truck and followed her in, my eyes staring at the ground in front of me as I mulled over my situation. I didn't see Hannah until she was almost on top of me.

# Chapter Thirty

"WELL, IF IT ISN'T THE foreigner. Fancy meeting you here. How're you doing there, Annie?" Hannah sauntered over in a pair of denim short-shorts and a red blouse tied at the bottom *à la* Daisy Duke, abandoning her grocery cart near a pile of books set up in a display near the front doors. The only thing she was missing were ponytails on either side of her head; instead, her hair was left curly and loose. It appeared less brassy than the last time I'd seen it, making me think she'd just spent some serious dough at the beauty salon. I glanced down towards the bottom of her long legs at her cute, multi-colored embroidered cowboy boots. Where I came from, she would have been laughed at for looking like a silly hayseed redneck. But out here, the whole get-up made her look like a country-western singer. A really pretty one. Maybe even sexy, too. My heart sank, suddenly seeing her through Mack's eyes. She was like every cowboys' wet dream right there in the flesh. She probably knew how to bake pies, too. I wouldn't know the first thing about doing that. I'm more the buy and defrost kind of girl.

"Her name is *Andie*, not Annie," corrected Maeve. She looked deceptively calm and casual about being approached by the girl we were just talking about in the truck in a not very complimentary way.

Hannah dragged her eyes from me to acknowledge Maeve, who wasn't standing more than three feet away from her. "Oh, hi, Miss Maeve, I didn't see you there. You acting as tour guide for the visitor?"

I glanced nervously around the immediate area, wondering if Mack was shopping with her. Part of me wanted to see him because he made me punch drunk with his sexiness, but the other part of me - the part that had a functioning brain - wanted a few States separating us. Especially with Hannah Banana around, staking her claim and making me feel like an advertisement for Nerdgirl Monthly in my plain t-shirt, shorts, and borrowed moccasins.

"I guess you could say I'm a tour guide." Maeve smiled at me. "We're just stocking up for the picnic." She turned a less smiley gaze on Hannah. "You're coming this year, I assume."

Hannah grinned so big she looked like she was trying out for the part of The Joker. Her eyes even sparkled. "Wouldn't miss it for the world. I've been to every single one, since I was just a kid. I love being part of the MacKenzie family."

My nostrils flared at the idea, and the kitty claws came out before I could think to sheathe them. "Are you a MacKenzie? Like, officially?"

Hannah's smile went tight at the corners. "I'm one by osmosis. I've spent my whole life at Mack's side, so yeah, I'm pretty much a MacKenzie."

I swallowed back the retort that was my first response and let out the one that would be most likely to get me home with my eyeballs *not* scratched out by a jealous waitress. "That's nice."

She put her chin in the air. "It is, actually. Mack's a really good guy. Are you going to be staying in town long? Maybe you and I could have lunch sometime."

Maeve pushed her cart forward. "Andie, I'm going to

check out those cookies I mentioned to you if you want to come take a look."

*Cookies? What cookies?* Understanding dawned a second later, and I seized the escape Maeve was offering. "Yeah, I'm coming." I stepped away, looking over my shoulder at Hannah as I left. "I'm only going to be here another day or so, so I'm going to have to skip lunch. But thanks for the offer."

"I won't see you at the picnic?" The hopeful gleam in her eye was impossible to miss.

"Nope. Gotta get back to work."

"Awww, that's too bad. Have a nice trip back, though!" She whirled her cart around and pushed it down the first aisle at a fast clip. I was pretty sure she had just added champagne and cake to her shopping list so she could really celebrate my departure in style.

"Thanks for that," I said to Maeve as I pulled up next to her and her cart. We turned down Aisle Five.

"Don't mention it. Hannah, that poor misguided girl, sometimes just gets a little ahead of herself."

"What … ? You mean you *didn't* sign up to adopt Hannah as your long-lost daughter?"

Maeve chuckled. "No. Definitely not. She's a sweet girl when she wants to be, but she's got her claws dug so deep in my boy's arm, it gets me a little hot under the collar sometimes. But I'm just the mom, so I have to keep my opinions to myself."

"Maybe Mack should just give in," I suggested, sad about the idea but thinking I had to be mature about it. "She seems really dedicated to him."

Maeve stopped pushing the cart. "Give in and go with a girl he doesn't care about? What's he going to do when the girl he's *meant* to be with comes along, then? Sounds like a life of sorrow to me." She shook her head. "No thank you. I don't want that for my boys. Life's too short to settle for second best."

"Maybe she's the right girl for him, though. She sure seems to think so."

"Just because a person is obsessed with the idea of something, it doesn't make it right or even good for them." She slowed down and started scanning the shelves for something specific. "Unfortunately, obsessed people are also deaf, dumb and blind most of the time, so it rarely works to try and help them see the light. Mack is too kind. He has a hard time just coming right out and saying what needs to be said sometimes."

Her words were like giant Liberty Bells gonging around inside my head. Whether she realized it or not, she wasn't just talking about Hannah. She was talking about me and my stupid obsession with my lifeplan. Why had I put so much of myself into the idea that I could carefully script everything out?

I knew the answer. Just like Maeve had said yesterday, sometimes when a person's life is so out of control and scary, the only thing that can give it any sense or meaning is structure. My life as a teen had been such a mess, I'd done what I had to do to get out with my sanity intact. I'd created a new reality for myself so I could survive when survival was the bare minimum I could ever hope for.

I exhaled heavily. As hard as I'd worked at keeping it from happening, my past was still managing to creep into my present to cast its dark shadow.

"Why the big sigh?" asked Maeve, reaching the end of the cookie aisle. She pulled two boxes off the shelf and held them up while winking at me.

I took one from her and stared at the label, not really seeing what was there. "I was thinking about my mom." I was lost in my memories and had just started talking without realizing what I was saying. *Dammit. Too late to take it back.* I hated sharing my past with people. It was embarrassing and made me feel second class to quality people like Maeve and her family. Shame burned my cheeks pink.

"Are you close with her?" She took the cookies from my hand and put them in the cart, either not noticing I was flustered or politely ignoring my distress. Either way I was grateful for it.

I looked across the aisle at the cereal, pretending to be interested in one of the sugary breakfast foods. "No, we're not close at all. We were when I was younger, but she dated a guy who ... came between us. I haven't talked to her in years."

"Oh, that's too bad." Maeve sounded like she really meant it and wasn't just being polite. "Where is she? Does she live near you?"

"No, actually, she lives closer to you than me. In Seattle, last time I heard."

"Well, why don't you stop by for a visit before you go back East?" Maeve put her hand on my upper arm. "No matter what happened in the past, I'm sure she'd love to see you. Mothers never stop missing their kids, even when they're just in the next town over."

I grimaced. "No thanks. She's not someone I want to spend my time with." I almost shuddered, but stopped myself. No need to pull those particular skeletons out of the closet. I was already making a hell of an impression so far.

Maeve dropped her hand. "That's too bad." She pushed the cart forward and turned the corner, banging into something loudly.

"Oh!" she gasped, and then her tone turned to one of anger. "Hannah, what are you doing skulking around over here?"

"Skulking? I'm not skulking. I'm just getting my groceries!" Hannah Banana was the picture of innocence, her eyebrows so high they were practically at her hairline.

"Is that so?" Maeve looked pointedly in Hannah's cart.

The entire basket was empty, and Hannah was already three quarters of the way through the store. I got nervous, wondering how much of my conversation with Maeve she'd overheard.

"Yes, it *is* so. I'm here to get barbecue meat for tonight's dinner. I've got the old group coming over. Mack, Ian, Ginny, and me."

Maeve snorted. "Are you throwing a party or a funeral?"

Hannah's jaw dropped open for a second before she recovered. "What's that supposed to mean?"

Maeve shook her head, maneuvering her cart around Hannah's. "Nothing. Nothing at all. Did you check with my boys before you made your plans? Because we have calves to work."

"Not yet, but I'm sure they'll come. I have a surprise for them." Her cocky smile made me want to slap her. I got the distinct impression that she thought her influence over the MacKenzie men was stronger than their mother's. I didn't know them that well, but I couldn't imagine that this was the case.

I caught up to Maeve in time to see her rolling her eyes. She was already moving down the next aisle. "Okay, well, enjoy your party," she said without looking back.

Hannah looked at me, a saccharine smile stretching her lips as she spoke up loud enough for half the store to hear. "I'd invite you, Angie, but I have a really small place and Mack is not really into hanging out with strangers much. He likes to just keep it simple, you know?" Her head cocked to the side, as if she expected me to answer.

I stopped halfway down the aisle. "It's *Andie*, not Angie. If you'd invited me I would have declined anyway. I'm leaving town after I talk to Mack today."

"Awww, bummer. Okay, well, have a nice flight." She wiggled some polished acrylic fingernails in my direction and pushed her cart away, disappearing around the end of the aisle.

Maeve was muttering to herself when I caught up with her.

"Anything I can get for you?" I asked, holding lightly onto the edge of the cart.

"No, I'm about done here. Just got the last ingredient for my famous lemon bars. Come on, let's get out of here before I say something stupid to someone I should be ignoring. I'll grab the cream cheese on the way out."

We made our way to the front of the store through the refrigerated aisle and paid for the groceries. Maeve refused to let me contribute, saying, "You're our guest, and guests don't pay," even though I was already at least two meals into her hospitality and would probably have one more before leaving.

The happiness over her generosity only lasted about five seconds. As we were walking out the door, I noticed a familiar figure striding towards the front of the store. His swagger was impossible to miss.

"There he is." Maeve waved him down. "Mack!"

The man in the cowboy hat turned his head and smiled. Then he caught sight of me and the smile disappeared.

*My god, he is so gorgeous it should be illegal.* Ten thousand butterflies took up residence in my stomach and started a little rodeo when the memories of what we'd done last night came rushing back to greet me.

# Chapter Thirty-One

"WHAT ARE YOU DOING HERE?" asked Maeve, giving her son a hug.

He glanced at me as he answered. "I had to do some packing and shopping. What are you doing here?"

"Picnic supplies. But didn't you have plans to talk to Andie this morning about her project?"

Mack hid his surprise well. "Um, yeah. But I had to do this other thing first."

"Well, I'll tell you what ... why don't you bring her back with you so I can run by the party supply place and then the dry cleaner? She'll get bored being with me all morning, and I think she said she needs to get back to work. Best get your business together worked out as soon as possible, right?" She patted him on the cheek and then put her hand on my upper arm. "See you back at the ranch, sweetie."

I smiled. "Back at the ranch. I've always wanted to say that."

"Go ahead then." She stood there waiting.

"Okay. See you back at the ranch, Maeve." I couldn't keep the grin off my face.

"Hope to shout." She walked off and left us standing there, Mack's expression telling me nothing.

"What'd she just say?" I asked.

"Hope to shout." He turned away from the store. "Come on with me, then. I'll get you back to the ranch."

"What does hope to shout mean?" I shuffled along behind him in my sexy moccasins.

He walked up to another truck, this one red and brand new, pressing the button on his keychain to open the locks. "It means I sure hope so or something close to that."

"Huh. I've never heard that before."

"It's pretty country. Probably not your cup of tea."

I climbed up into the truck with the help of a step that was attached to the side. "I wouldn't say that." I had to go back down when one of my shoes fell off. I grabbed it with my hand and just carried it in. Buckling up, I watched him get into the truck, waiting for him to look at me.

He studiously avoided looking in my direction, acting like he was very busy with adjusting mirrors and checking for traffic. He didn't respond either.

I had my work cut out for me. Mack was my captive audience, unable to avoid me whether he liked it or not. Now I just had to get him to talk. My heart was pounding and the adrenaline was rushing into my blood stream. Everything in me was telling me to run back home and forget this ever happened, except that one little part of my brain that said we needed to get this over with. Before Bradley showed up. Before my life completely imploded. I was already looking at the nightmare of canceling a wedding and sending back a pile of gifts. Luckily, I had a feeling Ruby wouldn't mind helping me clean up that part of my mess. She'd probably throw a break-up party in Bradley's honor. The question I still hadn't even begun to answer was what I was going to do with myself after it was all over. Something told me life according to Andie's Lifeplan wasn't going to be enough anymore.

I did a fake cough to get the ball rolling. "So … we were supposed to meet this morning at nine to talk. I get the feeling you're avoiding me." *Oh good! Right out of the gate just confront him like that! Smooth move, Ex-Lax Andie.* I wanted to slap myself in the forehead for being so confrontational. This was no way to get anywhere with Mack. He was too proud for that. The only reason I was sitting in his truck was because his mother had made him take me.

He pulled out of the parking lot and onto the main street. "I'm not avoiding you. I'm actually doing the opposite, but since you can't read my mind, I'm not surprised you misunderstood."

"You could have said something." I had to hold back the pout that wanted to take over my face. Mack always seemed to have this effect on me where I forgot I was a professional businesswoman who should have been above the sillier emotions like disappointment and bruised feelings.

"You were sleeping, and you'd had a hard day. I decided it would be kinder to leave you there rather than wake you up just to give you a message."

"I'll bet you have paper and pen at your house. You could have left me a note."

"Too impersonal."

I shook my head in disbelief. "And disappearing without saying anything isn't?"

A tiny smile snuck out before he could hide it.

I pointed at his face. "What was that?"

"What was what?"

"That smile! I saw you smile, don't try to hide it. You like this, don't you?"

"Like what?" He was all innocence.

"Like torturing me, that's what." I was grumbling now. I've never felt so out of my element and at a disadvantage as I did now. I hated myself for being such a wiener. If we were in the courtroom, I'd have Mack on his knees and the judge shaking his head in pity. But in this truck, wearing his mother's slippers and my former dorm-wear, I was the one being made a fool of. And the saddest part was, I was doing it to myself.

He said nothing to deny it. His tiny smile slid away to make his expression once more unreadable.

We drove in silence for a while, my stress elevating with every passing mile until I couldn't take it anymore. "Listen, all joking aside, I have to talk to you. It's really important."

"So talk. I'm sitting right here."

"I really need you to sign those papers."

"No."

I huffed out a big breath of frustrated air. I'd been expecting a run-around but not a flat out refusal. Time to change tack … "You don't love me, Mack."

"How do you know who I love and who I don't love?"

"You don't even know me! How can you possibly love me? That's just … stupid. Asinine, even."

He glanced at me, his expression dark. "I know you better than you think I do." His brows turned down as he focused on the road, and his hands tensed on the wheel.

"Oh, yeah? I doubt it." No one knew the real me. Not even Bradley. People who said you needed to be yourself when you were with your soulmate didn't know the real me. If they did, they might change their perspective on that little happy thought. Some things were just better left unsaid, and some pasts are just better left behind.

"Okay, how about this … I know you grew up in the northeast and your father left when you were very young. I know your mother dated a bunch of men who were big partiers, before moving in with one who eventually abused her. I know you feared for your lives for years, and finally convinced your mom to leave him when you were in high school, but that she went back to him right before you started college. I know he almost killed her once and you saw the whole thing happen." He paused and looked at me for a few seconds. "How am I doing so far?"

My heart-rate went through the roof and my mouth had

gone suddenly dry. *How could he possibly know all my secrets? Is he a mind reader? Did he do a background check on me?*

He continued unraveling my secrets, not waiting for a response from me. "I know you started working on your, uh ... lifeplan ... I think that's what you called it, when you were fifteen and have been following it to the letter ever since. Except for that little side-trip you took from it in Las Vegas, everything's been going according to plan. You've only dated guys who fit the mold and want the same things you want, and when they stopped fitting into the plan, you dumped 'em and found another candidate."

"More like they dumped me," I mumbled. My ears burned with shame. I felt like that teenager in the hospital again, signing off on documents I didn't read, telling the doctors to go ahead and do whatever they could to save her.

"Dumped, got dumped ... that's all just semantics. I'm not done yet. So, then this guy asked you to marry him, and you checked all the boxes to make sure he fit, and when you realized he did, you said yes. And that's when you decided to finally give me a call and take care of the little problem you started two years ago."

I lifted my arm and rested it on the windowsill, the opposite hand pressed into the seat next to my left thigh. I felt like I was being attacked, only he was doing it in a normal tone of voice without a hint of malice. If the truck had been stopped, I probably would have jumped out.

My voice was shaky when it finally started to work again. "I didn't start any problem, you did. And how do you know all that stuff about me? Have you been spying on me?"

He laughed bitterly. "Hardly. I didn't even know where you were until you showed up in town looking for me. When Boog called and described you and told me what you'd said to Hannah, I knew it was you. It's the first time I've even come close to you in two years." He didn't sound happy about that at all.

"That doesn't explain how you know my personal history. I don't share that with anyone. Not even my best friends."

"Sure you do. You shared it with me." He sounded proud, the jerk.

"No I *didn't*." My voice went higher out of panic.

"Are you calling me a liar?" He glanced at me as he turned onto another road.

"No, I'm just saying … you must be mistaken or something. I don't share my past with anyone, not even good looking cowboys."

"Well, you shared it with me. And I'm not just some guy. I'm your husband. You should share that stuff with your husband." He glanced at me once more. "You didn't share it with that guy you're engaged to, did you?"

"Would you stop saying that?" Sweat had broken out on my upper lip and under my arms.

"Saying what?"

"That you're my husband!" I screeched. He was being too calm about everything, like his hand wasn't hovering over the bright red button on my console that would set off all the nuclear missiles I kept under lock and key.

"The truth bothers you that much?"

"No, the *joke* bothers me that much. This is all just a big joke, don't you get it?" I was panting, not able to get enough oxygen to my brain. *Dizzy. I'm dizzy. Why am I so dizzy?*

The muscles in his arms jumped a little. "No, I guess I don't get it. Explain it to me." He pulled onto the dirt road that had ended my Smart Car.

My left hand came up and started doing chopping-down motions as I explained. He absolutely had to understand this, because if he didn't, I was going to implode. My voice went up and up, getting nearer and nearer to hysterical proportions with every sentence. "Okay, Mack … here it is. Two years ago I got dumped by a guy and was feeling vulnerable. I had

too much to drink and I met you and you were all … you …
and I got carried away. We both got carried away, I guess,
since you don't seem the type to go off-plan much either. The
next day I woke up, you were gone, and I went home. Okay?
Do you get it now? Life went on for *both* of us, not just me. I
started dating Bradley, you started dating Hannah, and now
here we are, two years later needing a divorce." I took a deep
breath and let it out, trying to release some of the stress. I felt
like my head was going to explode.

"I'm afraid you're missing part of the story, there,
counsellor." A country drawl was flavoring his words a little
and tempting me to smack him upside the head in a very
violent way.

"I don't think so," I said through gritted teeth.

"I know so." His phone rang and he picked it up,
frowning at the screen. He put it on the seat and ignored it. I
glanced down and saw Hannah's name there.

"Why aren't you answering it? She's your girlfriend,
and I get the impression she wouldn't appreciate being blown
off."

"She is not my girlfriend. I don't know who told you
that, but you should probably not listen to that person
anymore."

"It was Hannah who told me, and the fact that you *live*
with her was kind of just a bonus, I guess."

He blew out a huff of air. "You definitely shouldn't ever
listen to Hannah. And I don't live with her. She lives with
me, temporarily since I was doing a favor for a friend, but
that ends today. She's all packed and ready to go."

I laughed bitterly. "I think you forgot to mention that
little fact to her. She's in love with you, you know."

"Bullshit. She's in love with my family's ranch, with our
money, with my truck, and very possibly my little brother,
but she's *not* in love with me."

"If she was, would you go out with her?"

"Hell no. She's not my type."

I found that really hard to believe, since Daisy Duke was every country boy's type and she wasn't that far off. "What *is* your type, then if it's not Daisy Duke?"

He took a few seconds to answer. "Head strong. Smart. Beautiful. Funny. Good at blackjack. Maybe a little more conservative than Hannah Banana." He glanced at me, smiling devilishly. "I like a little mystery to my women. I think the song lyric says it best: *Lady on the street but a freak in the bed.*"

I whacked him hard on the arm, my faced burning. "Shut up. I am not your type. And I am not a freak anywhere."

He reached over and took my hand in his warm one, pulling it against his leg. "I'm your type too, you know."

"No, you're not." I tried to pull my hand away, but he had a hell of a grip.

"Sure I am. I'm educated, business-minded, sexy - you said so yourself, so don't try to deny it - and I can make you scream like nobody else can." He lifted my hand and put it on top of his leg, very near his crotch.

My heart was hammering in my chest now, making me feel like I was going to start panting like a dog any second. *Control yourself, Fido! He's just a guy!*

I pulled my hand back more insistently this time, and he let it go. "Sex isn't love. Don't fool yourself into thinking it is." Memories of my mother flashed before my eyes. She was always in a dreamy state after being with her boyfriend in the bedroom at night, but it never stopped him from smashing her in the face later.

"You're not her, Andie. You're not your mother."

"Shut up! You don't get to talk about her to me!" My shouts echoed around the small space of the truck's cab, making my ears ring. My face burned with embarrassment over losing my temper. "Sorry for shouting. Just ... don't talk about her, please. She's off limits."

"Sounds to me like you'd be better off talking about her rather than pretending she doesn't exist, but I'll leave it alone for now." He reached over and put his hand on mine, stroking the side of it with his thumb. "I got some things for us so we can take a little ride this afternoon."

"A ride? Where?" I asked, suspicion ruling my emotions. "I don't want to take a ride with you." The words came out, but the feelings weren't backing them up.

"Up into the hills a little bit. I think we need some privacy so we can talk this out and get things straight. I know you have a lifeplan to follow and all, so no reason to delay anymore."

I couldn't tell if he was mocking me or sad or anything else. "I'm surprised I met you that night," I said.

"Oh yeah? Why's that?"

"Because with that poker face of yours, I'll bet you could make a lot of money at the poker tables instead of the blackjack tables."

He smiled, sending a shock of attraction right through my chest and down to the space between my legs. "I do like to play poker now and again, but I always warm up with a little twenty one first." He patted my hand before putting his back on the wheel. "Glad I did that night, I can tell you that."

I said nothing, not sure whether he'd changed my life for the better by playing blackjack that night or doomed me to a life of misery.

# Chapter Thirty-Two

I SAT ON THE PORCH waiting for Mack to come around to the front. He'd told me he was getting our transportation. I leaned against one of the posts holding up the porch's roof, my feet resting on the steps. My mind wandered as a cool breeze moved bits of my hair around my face, tickling my skin.

I couldn't remember the last time I'd sat in the sun and just let my thoughts wander. It was nice, making me wish Mack wouldn't come back too quickly. Right now, I'd willingly pay big money for a spell that would make time freeze so I could sit here and just breathe for a while without worrying about Bradley or Hannah or my future. It was all such a mess.

Replaying the things Mack had said to me in the truck was helping me piece together what had happened in Las Vegas. Not all of it was making sense, but some of it was. Obviously, the first thing that had gone wrong was my complete lack of self control. Mack's sexual energy was like a magnet, pulling me in and making me do stupid things like forget my plans and all the things I'd sacrificed to leave the past behind and accomplish my goals. Just the idea of abandoning what amounted to my life's work made me scared senseless, like I'd be floating in the wind with no direction forever - a complete lack of control. And on top of all that, in the space of maybe six hours, Mack had somehow convinced me to unload all of my personal garbage onto his shoulders to carry around. The skeletons that used to live in my closet had come out to dance in the hot, Las Vegas night.

Even so, he still acted like being married to me wasn't the worst thing that had ever happened to him. He'd said the L-word while we were in the middle of having shower sex, but that kind of declaration can't be taken seriously. So he wasn't in love, but he wasn't in a hurry to divorce me either. What was he, exactly?

A small smile played across my lips. Him loving me was too ridiculous to even consider part of my reality. People don't fall in love with strangers. Strangers could be anything, anyone, with an unlimited amount of awful baggage no one would ever want to bear. How could he know I wasn't a serial killer or mother of eight kids or already married? He couldn't. Smart people like us don't do stupid things like get married at twenty-four-hour chapels by a man named Elvis. That's what irresponsible people who have nothing to lose do.

*Right?*

I sighed, drawing a heart in the dust next to me. Looking back and seeing things from the view of this porch, I wasn't sure anymore that I'd had much to lose back then. Two years ago I was freshly dumped by Luke the Puke, vying for a coveted junior partner spot at a firm that was sucking the life out of me, and getting ready to kiss my friendships goodbye for another guy. That didn't sound like something to strive towards.

All my grandiose ideas of who I am fell apart when I received that document from the Nevada State vital records department. Apparently, smart, responsible people *do* sometimes do stupid things like get married at twenty-four hour chapels by a man named Elvis; either that, or I'm at least ten times dumber than I thought I was.

The problem wasn't so much that I'd done it, but that for the first time since figuring this all out, I was wondering which was worse: getting married to a stranger in Vegas or scripting my life out and expecting to be happy at the end of the production. My life was like a play with actors and scenes and lines I'd written, with a happily-ever-after I couldn't even visualize. Instead of working towards a clear vision of happiness, I'd been head down, moving in the direction of ... nothing. A big cloud of smoke I couldn't see through. I drummed it into my own head, this mantra of success, success, success ... but where was the happiness? Where was the love? And why hadn't I realized this before?

As I sat on the porch trying to envision myself as an older woman, all my brain would conjure was an image of an older Mack sitting across the dinner table from me, smiling in that knowing way of his. Looking back now, the plan I had laid out for myself seemed not only stupid, but dull. Empty. Safe, but in the end, very very dangerous for how it could cause me to lose the real me entirely. *Who have I become? And what is it about this ridiculous, dust-covered snake haven that's causing me to re-think my entire life?* Maybe I did get bitten by that snake after all. *Can poison do this to a person?* I looked at the back of my ankles for the telltale double puncture wounds.

"Ready?" Mack's voice came to me from down in the yard.

I pulled my head out of the ether and stared at him and his transportation. When my voice came back it got away from me a little. "No fucking way, Mack." I shook my head. "Excuse my French, but that is *not* going to happen."

He grinned, holding two sets of reins in his hands. "Sure it is. You'll be fine. Come on over here so I can give you a leg up." He stood between a brown horse with a black mane and a blonde one with a pretty cream-colored mane.

I didn't care how pretty she or it was, I was not going to ride it. "Give *yourself* a leg up. I'm not riding a horse anywhere. Those things bite. Bring me the four-wheeler or whatever you call it."

"Can't. It's out of gas." He was still smiling, obviously very pleased with himself.

I ignored the beauty of it, refusing to let him charm me into my death. "You're lying." I stared him down.

He lost the grin and put on his innocent-as-a-lamb expression. "Nope. Dry as a bone. Come on, I brought you an old nag." He gestured to the brown one with his chin. "She couldn't buck you off if she wanted to, and I promise, she won't want to. And she doesn't bite either." His elbow came up to greet the teeth of the blond one who had swooped its head in towards his waist. He didn't look like he'd hurt it, but he'd done a good job of blocking its moves.

"Ha! That one just tried to bite you!" I backed up a little, making sure I had plenty of room to maneuver if it decided to come after me next. The thing was huge, towering over Mack who was pretty damn tall himself.

"This one's feisty, I admit. But I'll be riding her and you'll be riding her momma, so you'll be fine. Cross my heart," he said, making an X on his chest.

"Your heart's on the other side."

"I know," he said, winking. He held up crossed fingers. "Got all my bases covered, just in case."

My mouth dropped open at his casual dismissal of my well-grounded fears. "You don't have to kill me by horse, you know. All you have to do is sign the papers." When he looked at me quizzically, I explained. "People die on those things every day."

"Not on my horses they don't." He held out his hand. "Come on, wife. Come take a little ride with me. Let me show you all the things you'll be missing when you go back East and leave me here with a broken heart."

My heart melted just a little bit in that moment, and I was pretty sure I'd never get it to go cold again. It wasn't just the things he said but how he said them. He swung so easily between strong, sexy cowboy and soft-hearted loverboy, he was making me dizzy with it. Maybe even a little love-drunk.

I stood, grabbing his hand petulantly and scowling at him, doing my damnedest to not fall for his charms. "You're not going to have a broken heart, you big dummy."

He put his hands on my waist and leaned down, putting his lips near my neck and ear. "It's already bruised." And then he lifted me up all of a sudden, causing me to whoop with fear.

The horse he was putting me on didn't bat an eyelash, but the other one jumped to the side and made snorting noises at us. From my new perspective on top of the two-story horse, I could see the blonde one was very agitated.

"Oh my god," I whisper-squealed, forgetting about everything else, "I'm on a horse!" My butt muscles clenched so tight, my whole body raised up about three inches. Sweat broke out all over my body and my heart doubled its pace.

"Just relax," he said, adjusting a stirrup and putting my foot in it when he was done. He walked around the horse and did the same on the other side. "She's as gentle as a baby. You won't have to do anything. She'll just follow my horse wherever she goes and all you have to do is enjoy the view."

I snorted. "Yeah, right." My hands and thighs were trembling.

He came to my left side again and put the reins in my hand, leaving his fingers on top of mine. He stared at me as he gave me a quick lesson. "If you want to go to the left, just move your hands like this." He dragged the leather strips to the left. "The bit in her mouth and the reins on her neck and head will let her know what you want to do. If you want to go right, take the reins and do this ... see?" He went the opposite direction, reaching over the horse's neck to demonstrate, waiting for me to nod my head before continuing. "When you want to stop, just pull back gently. Not too hard, she has a sensitive mouth. Try not to raise them up high, just keep them at waist-level. When you want to go, loosen the reins and give her a kick or squeeze her with your legs and click your tongue and she'll go."

"I thought you said I was just going to follow you and I wouldn't have to do anything." Sweat kept pouring down my sides and back. The heat had nothing to do with it; it was all plain old, garden-variety, paralyzing fear.

"I'm giving you instructions, just in case," he explained.

"Just in case *what?*" The pitch of my voice came out way too high, but I couldn't control it.

He didn't answer me until he was on his horse's back. "Just in case my horse bucks me off and throws me to the ground, knocking me unconscious."

"What?!"

He shot me a grin and pulled his reins sharply to the left while kicking his horse and talking to her. "Get-up there, girl."

I was so busy watching him ride away, I was totally unprepared for my horse to follow. She jerked me to the side and then backward as she moved to follow Mack's horse, and I had to grab the saddle horn sticking up in front of me to keep from falling off. My reins dropped to her neck and hung down limply on the sides in big loops.

"I lost my thingies!" The right words wouldn't come out in my panic.

"What are thingies?" he shouted, not even looking.

"The leather things! The reins!"

"Pick 'em up."

I held onto the saddle with a death grip in one hand and reached out with the other to grab the knot holding the two thin straps together. As soon as I snagged it, I pulled back on the reins, anxious to get control of the horse.

The horse stopped going forward.

I panicked, watching Mack get farther and farther ahead, worried my horse would run to catch up and dump me on my sorry butt. I'd probably fall right onto a snake, and with the way my luck was going, I'd land on him while he was sunning himself fang-side-up. My whole body tensed into a human-shaped board of solid fear.

The horse snorted and began walking backwards.

I yanked on the reins some more, trying to get her to stop, but she wouldn't listen. She just kept going faster the wrong way.

"Mack!" I shrieked. "It's broken or something! It's in reverse! It's going in reverse! How do you make it go into drive?!"

He twisted in his saddle and started laughing.

I was torn between laughing with him and crying, my whole body trembling, even my lips.

"Stop squeezing her sides and let the reins loose. You're telling her to go backward with your conflicting signals!"

I immediately shot my legs away from her sides, sticking them straight out like Hawaiian canoe out-riggers. I dropped the reins to her neck again and held onto the horn with both hands. I would have slid right off and saved myself from the nightmare of riding this beast if I'd thought I could land without dying.

The horse moved forward and ambled over to where Mack was waiting. The bulk of my rear end was pushed up off the saddle by two very tense ass-cheek muscles.

He couldn't breathe for a little while, due to all the laughing he was doing. I, on the other hand, was sweating-hot and cranky, wondering what had possessed me to listen to this idiot and get up on this monster when I knew damn well it would be a mistake. He could charm the fangs off a snake if he wanted to. "Can we go back now? I think I've seen enough scenery."

Mack leaned over and grabbed my horse's reins, pulling the animal up next to his. "Get over here, girl," he said, wrapping his hand around my neck and pulling me closer. He leaned in and kissed me right on the mouth.

I squealed against his lips, fearing I was going to fall too much to appreciate their warmth.

"I gotcha," he said, putting his arm around my waist and steadying me. My horse shifted under the saddle, but she didn't move away.

I let him kiss me this time briefly before pushing him back. It felt too nice not to. "You're going to make me fall," I said, pushing him away.

He smiled, all kinds of happiness lighting up his eyes. It made me think of sugary sweetness and vulnerability, things I never showed anyone. Things I'd removed from my repertoire a long time ago. *He's braver than me.*

"I think you're going to be a natural in the saddle," he finally said.

I tried to hit him, but he was too far away. "*I think* when I finally get off this thing, I'm going to kill you. I hope you can run fast." I plucked the reins off the horse's neck and held them in a slightly-less-shaky grip.

"Is that a promise? Cuz if it is, I can run extra slow and give you half a chance of catching me." He winked and clicked his tongue, sending his horse forward and leaving me behind again. He spoke to me without looking back. "Pick up the slack in the reins, but don't pull on them. Rest your toes in the stirrups but don't squeeze the horse with your legs. Just pretend you're straddling a log. Find your center balance."

"Straddling a log," I grumbled quietly to myself. "Why don't you go straddle a log, you big dope." I gathered up the reins and pictured myself riding a stupid log over a stupid rushing river, letting my stupid moccasined feet just hang down.

The horse moved forward instead of backwards, and after a while I was surprised to find her pace calm and relaxing. The rocking motion soon worked its magic on me, lowering my blood pressure and dispersing the images of death that had crowded my mind. I took a deep breath and exhaled, letting out all the tension that had gathered. As my butt cheeks took a vacation from turning into rock, I settled lower into the saddle and found the process of riding the horse almost pleasant.

We wound our way through some trees and piles of rock, steadily moving uphill towards a near mountain range. Sitting high up on the tall horse, I could see everything normally blocked to me when on foot, the vista spreading out before us like an impressionistic painting done entirely in nature's most beautiful shades of green, brown, and blue.

Neither of us spoke, making it easier for the sounds of the wild West to trickle in and take over my normally busy-with-words mind: a hawk screeching; wind blowing through branches; leather squeaking and creaking on the saddle; the horses' footsteps over rocks and crunchy plant debris ... *swish, clop, swish, swish, clockle, crack ... swish, clop, clop, crack.* A bark announced the arrival of one of the ranch dogs, who raced past us and took the lead on the path.

Maeve's words came back to me, how she liked to let the men drive so she could enjoy the scenery ... how Baker City was one of the most beautiful places on Earth. I'd argued with her then in my mind, but right now I wasn't, and I knew I never would again. It was wild here and untamed for sure, but its savage beauty was something I'd never seen before in real life, living in cities and their suburbs. *Majestic* was a word that came to mind as I scanned the landscape around me. *A spiritual place.* It made sense that Native Americans had chosen to settle in this area of the country. I felt really connected to the Earth for some reason.

It was crazy to be feeling this way when I was a city-girl

at heart, but denying it would do me no good. The irrational, emotional part of my brain might be claiming that I'd suffered a nervous breakdown over my destroyed wedding plans or the fallout that awaited me back home, but the fully functioning rational brain inside me and my heart too were both telling me the truth: that this place isn't just a city on a map. It's a home - a place where a person could be herself, and surround herself with people who loved her and respected her and laughed with her.

With that realization came the understanding that sometimes you can't appreciate the true beauty of a thing until you've experienced it for yourself; no amount of words or pictures will do the trick. And no amount of planning could make it happen. Sometimes, we just have to go where the wind takes us and see where we end up.

I sighed with both happiness and melancholy. The wind had blown me to Baker City, Oregon and by being here I'd found a place in the world where I could very possibly discover peace, for the first time in my life. But this Eden was inhabited by one of the biggest mistakes I'd ever made in my life, and because of that, I would have to leave.

There was just too much negativity wrapped up in the situation to consider staying: a drunken, blacked out marriage that was neglected for two whole years; a girlfriend waitress who maybe wasn't a girlfriend but she sure seemed to think she was; an angry younger brother who may or may not blame me or Mack for his failed wedding plans; and the fact that I'd poured my heart out to this stranger and shared pieces of me that I'd been trying to lose for over ten years. It was hopeless.

# Chapter Thirty-Three

"YOU'RE BEING AWFULLY QUIET BACK there.  What're you thinking about?"

Mack's question startled me out of my reverie and reminded me I was sitting up way too high off the earth.  My body tensed for a few seconds before I could get a grip on myself again.  "Nothing."  *Better to just let it lie, right?*  Sometimes the truth just needs to stay in darkness.  The problem was that it felt like if I hid the truth from everyone, I'd be hiding myself there too, and I wasn't a fan of the dark.

"I don't believe that for a second.  I get the feeling you're always thinking about something."

"What are *you* thinking?" I asked, trying to turn the tables over to safer topics.

He glanced back at me.  "About how bad I want to see you naked again."

My face pinked up.  "Be serious."

"I am being serious."  He turned to face front so I was looking at his broad back once more.  "That's not all I'm thinking, but it's high on the list."

I sighed, sad because I wanted to see him naked again too, and in the light of day for a change, but that would be stupid.  Sex would only complicate things more.  "We're not going to do that again, okay?  The two times we've done it were both mistakes."

"Two times? Boy, you're not very good with math, are you?"

"What's that supposed to mean?"

"Well, according to my math, it's more like five or six. Not that I was counting or anything."

"What? You're crazy." I wondered what else I'd forgotten from that night, other than the wedded-by-Elvis part.

"Believe me, I don't forget things like that."

I snorted. "Right. How many women have you been with?"

He twisted around and grinned. "You jealous?"

"No." *Maybe. Yes.*

He shrugged. "Not many. I'm picky."

"I find that hard to believe."

He stopped his horse. My horse kept going until it was next to his.

"It's true," he said in a more serious tone. "I don't just sleep with any girl."

"You slept with Hannah." It was a total shot in the dark, but I waited breathlessly for his response.

"No, I did not." He sounded offended. "Who told you that? I've never slept with that girl nor would I ever."

I shrugged. "I heard it in town somewhere."

His jaw was set and hard as he stared off ahead of his horse. I figured I'd already gotten him upset once, might as well go all the way.

"You slept with Ginny." Another shot in the dark. This one right into the heart.

Mack kicked his horse and it took off running, leaving me and my horse behind. Apparently she didn't appreciate it, because she took off right after them. She didn't go as fast, but the pace was accelerated enough to cause me to turn into a bouncing piece of human popcorn on the saddle. My butt slapped the leather seat over and over making the most embarrassing sound … *Whap! Whap! Whap! Whap!* My yell came out with every bump telegraphed in it. "Ah-uh-ah-uh-ah-uh-ahhhhh! Mack! Wait-uh-ay-uh-ayyyyt!" My teeth clacked together when I stopped talking, giving me a headache.

I whap-whap-whapped my butt around a windy trail through a cover of trees and out into a blindingly bright meadow full of wildflowers before we finally slowed. Mack was standing still again, his horse just on the outside of the field. He slid down off the back of the animal and started unbuckling some packs that were strapped to the back part of his saddle. My horse drew up next to his and then dropped her head sharply, jerking the reins out of my hands.

I stared at him, wondering if he really had slept with his brother's fiancée. I really hadn't thought it was the truth, and I don't know why I said it. But his reaction made me doubly curious, and it also made me wonder if I'd misjudged him. He didn't seem the type to do something like that … something like I had done by sleeping with him while engaged to Bradley. *God, I'm such a terrible person. Why would he want to be with me? Is it because he's a cheater too?* The very idea made me sick for some weird reason. I wanted him to be a better person than me.

"You can get down now if you like," he said, not looking at me.

"I'd love to," I said, sarcastically.

He stopped what he was doing and stared up at me with stormy eyes. "So what's stopping you?"

"The two-story drop to my death." I looked pointedly at the ground.

He went back to his unpacking, ignoring me entirely. I gritted my teeth together as I watched him pull out a thick blanket and then a few brown bags with things in them I couldn't see. It looked like a picnic that would be much better enjoyed on the ground.

My horse took a few steps forward, her head staying down so she could yank up a mouthful of grass. Mack busied himself with putting out the blanket and setting things down on it. I held onto the saddle horn for a while but eventually gave up on waiting for his help. Leaning over the front of the saddle while hanging onto the horn at my chest for dear life, I swung my right leg over the back of the horse and slid down its side to the ground.

Surprisingly, I landed on my feet and not my butt, which was a good thing considering how sore it was at the moment.

I walked out into the field and left him behind, feeling a little lost and alone over the idea that he wasn't as perfect as I'd built him up to be in my mind. When I got halfway in, I stopped and looked around. Butterflies flitted among the petals of the wild flowers at my feet and beyond. Birds chirped in the nearby trees. Dandelion fluff or something soft and white floated in the air. My sense of wonder was complete. If fairies existed, they would definitely live in this place.

Footsteps crunched and swished behind me, but they were of the two-legged variety, so I didn't look back. Mack stopped at my side, staring out into the flowers with me.

"I brought a picnic."

"I saw that." My throat was sore from unshed tears. I refused to cry over a guy who hadn't measured up to my impossibly high standards. Even if he was my husband.

"I didn't sleep with Ginny either."

"That's nice. For Ian." I hid my relief well, letting out a long breath in a very quiet stream through my nose. He wasn't a cheater. Why that mattered to me - a cheater myself - made no sense ... but there it was.

"But I did cause them to break up."

I turned to look at him. His expression was nothing less than tortured.

"What happened?" Now instead of feeling angry or relieved, I just felt sad for him. It was clear this had hurt.

He cast his eyes down, his hands hanging loosely from his front pockets. "When we went to Vegas and I pretty much disappeared all night with you, it got the guys pretty pissed off. They looked for me all night, I found out later. When we got back, the story got told around town that I'd disappeared and they'd all assumed it was with a woman."

"What's that got to do with Ginny?"

"I'm getting to that." He sighed, looking off into the distance. "Ginny was at a store in town and overheard someone talking about how Ian's bachelor party was a bust because one of the guys disappeared with some woman and caused a big fuss. She asked who they were talking about and no one could tell her."

"Why not?"

"Because I'd sworn them all to secrecy. They did it - kept their mouths shut - for me. Mostly shut, anyway."

"What? I'm sorry, but I'm completely lost. Are we still talking about Ginny?"

He sighed heavily. "Yes, in a roundabout way, we are. What happened is that the guys found me in the lobby where I was waiting for you, and they took me to get our stuff, and we went home. On the way back I told them everything and made them swear not to tell a soul. I wanted to surprise our parents when I introduced you." His voice got rough at the end.

"I don't get it. I'm sorry, Mack. I know I sound like an idiot and I sure feel like one, but I think I'm missing parts of the story."

He looked at me, his expression tortured. "You really don't remember?"

"No, I swear to God, I don't." I put my hand in his large one, holding it gently. "I'm sure it's not because I wasn't really feeling whatever it was I was feeling at the time. I just

… drank way too much, I think."

He nodded once, walking back towards the horses and pulling me along with him gently. I tried to take my hand back, but he just held tighter.

"Do you want me to tell you the story the way I remember it? Start to finish?"

"Yes," I said, "please do that. And what I remember, I'll fill in too." The anticipation of learning the truth was great, but so was the fear that I wasn't going to like what I heard.

# Chapter Thirty-Four

"COME SIT ON THE BLANKET with me and we'll talk while we eat the lunch my mom made for us."

"Aww, she made lunch for us? That's so cute." I never used that word for moms, but there was something about Maeve that made it the only word that would fit.

"She likes you a lot."

I felt ashamed about that … having her like me when I was just going to break her son's heart. "How could she like me? She doesn't even know me."

"I think she can tell how much I care about you, and that means something to her."

I had no response for that, so I kept my mouth shut. I wanted it to be true, as implausible as it seemed.

I settled onto the blanket and Mack did something to tie the horses up so they could eat too. He joined me, lying down on his side next to me as I sat up with my legs crossed. I took a long blade of grass from nearby and played with it as he told me his story, keeping my eyes on my task so he could recount our shared past without feeling embarrassed.

"Okay, so here's how I remember it. I was sitting there minding my own business at the blackjack tables, trying to win a little money to give to my brother for his wedding gift. He and Ginny were planning to go to Hawaii and it was taking a pretty big chunk of change from his savings."

"Your mom told me."

"I was up about a grand when a pretty little girl in a tight dress came over and threw a drink on me."

"Guilty." I raised a finger for a few seconds before letting it drop. I found that I liked being called the pretty little girl in a tight dress for some reason.

"After spending a little time with her and thinking about nothing but wanting to know her better in every way, we went up to her room where I did just that. I got to know her, and for the first time in my life, I felt like I was with someone I could really relax with. Be with." He rolled over onto his back, lacing his hands behind his head. "It sounds crazy to say it out loud, but I distinctly remember thinking when I saw you sitting at that blackjack table that you were the girl for me." He shifted his head to look in my direction, so I lifted my face to look at him too. "Maybe even before that. When you threw the drink on me ... I think I knew it then." His piercing blue eyes slayed me, sending a heat right into my veins to warm up my whole body.

"That's crazy," I said in a slightly breathless voice. "That doesn't happen in real life."

"It does in mine." He looked back at the sky. "Anyway, I fell for you like a ton of bricks and we made love, which only sealed the deal for me." He got a weird grin on his face. "And then we laid there and talked." He sounded like he didn't believe it himself. "Everything you said just spoke to me on a really deep level." He looked at me again. "You might find this hard to believe, but I generally don't have conversations like that with people."

I smiled sadly. "I got that impression." I loved knowing I was special in his life, but I hated knowing it was only temporary. It sucks more than anything in the world to see a dream of who you *could* be and know you have to walk away from it to be something less. Living up to the expectations of others was beginning to feel like it was the path to destroying my soul.

"So I got this wild hair up my ... hat ... and asked you to come on an adventure with me. We went to a bar where I flirted outrageously with you and then asked you to marry me."

I swallowed with difficulty. "You did? You actually asked me?"

"Yeah. Got on bended knee with a flower that some guy sold me and everything."

"Oh, God, I wish I could remember that part." I felt like crying.

"Yeah, it was pretty bad. But I somehow managed to convince you it was a great plan, and off we went to the chapel. We had to wait in line for a while. I had to keep reminding you we weren't in a hotel room anymore."

I dropped my head into my hands. "I'm not sure I want to hear this part."

"Why not? It's the best part." He was grinning again, I could tell by the tone of his voice, but I refused to look at him.

"What did I do?"

"You couldn't keep your hands off me. I had to take your hands out of my pants about ten times."

"Oh, Jesus ... no wonder you wanted to marry me!" I tried to keep the images from entering my head, but it wasn't working.

He reached over and pulled one of my hands away. "Come over here. You're too far away."

I yanked my hand back. "No. Stay away. I'm too embarrassed."

He sat up and wrapped his arms around me, pulling me down with him until I was lying partly next to him and partly on top of him. I didn't fight him at all, I just let myself be force-cuddled.

"You have nothing to be embarrassed about. It was the

best night of my life and not just because you kept calling me King Dong."

I laughed. I couldn't help it. "Oh, how far I've fallen."

"Shush, I still haven't told you the whole story."

"So tell it.   And try to skip over the parts where I humiliate myself time and again."

"I'll try, but those were the fun parts.   The other parts that came later are the sad part of the story."

My heart clenched up in my chest. "Tell me."

He remained silent for awhile, but I didn't push him.  I was busy enough with imagining our night together that I didn't need him to continue right away.

"Where was I?" he finally said.

"We were in line at the chapel."

"Yeah, okay.  So we got to our turn and we didn't have rings.  They offered to sell us one, but you said you didn't need one.  We said the vows, which you made up, and then we signed the documents."

"Do I want to know the vows?"

"They were very creative."

"Don't tell me.  I don't want to know."  I was trying to keep my humiliation from becoming complete.

"You sure?"

"Yeah.  Tell me the rest of the story.

"Alright, so after the deed was done, I finally took a look at my phone and saw about fifty texts from my brother and his friends.  While we were waiting for them to come, we talked about what we were going to do."

"What do you mean?"

"We talked about our future."

"Oh."

"You were going to go back to your room and stay with your friends and call me in the morning.  You wanted to get pretty or something, you said.  Letting your boobs breathe, I think was another concern.  I was just going to hook back up with my brother for a few hours before we had to leave and then re-connect with you by phone first."

"And then what? We were going to live apart as a married couple? This doesn't sound like a very smart plan or anything I would have been a part of, even drunk out of my gourd."

"Me neither. But at the time, it made perfect sense. We'd both been drinking, so even though I knew what I was doing, I might have suffered a little bit of fantasy-thinking at the time."

"Fantasy-thinking. Hmmm."

"Yeah. Anyway, we got to the hotel lobby and I left you at your room telling you to meet me downstairs later. When I went back down to the lobby, my brother was already there, fuming. He was pissed I'd missed the whole night with him and his buddies, and it didn't help that he'd lost all his money gambling. We got our bags from the desk and he went to the airport, but I stayed there in the hotel, waiting for your call."

I swallowed hard. "I didn't call you."

"No," he said quietly. "You didn't call me." His arms went tighter around my body.

"How long did you wait?"

"Until lunchtime. Several hours. I called the number you gave me eventually, but it wasn't your number."

"What number was it?" I asked, confused.

"I have no idea. Some guy named Deacon kept answering."

"Luke Deacon?" I asked in a small voice.

"Yeah. Something like that. Do you know him?"

"He was my ex." I looked up at the sky, my face flaming red again. "Oh, man. I am such a loser. I gave you my ex's phone number by mistake."

"You sure it was a mistake?" he asked. He was looking at me again, his expression unreadable.

"Of course it was," I said, not sure I believed myself. Maybe some part of me got married to him because of Luke's recent and overly cold rejection. There was nothing more opposite to rejection than a marriage proposal, after all. Talk about a rebound.

"The last plane was leaving, so I had to go. I went up to your room to see what was going on, and the maid was there cleaning up. You'd already gone."

"You thought I just ditched you, didn't you?"

"Pretty much. I didn't want to believe it at first, but you weren't in your room, you'd given me a bum phone number, and finally when I went to the front desk they confirmed you'd checked out. And I never heard from you again. You never called me once. Believe me, I watched my phone like a hawk for weeks. Months."

I reached out and took his hand. "Candice, the girl who I was staying with that you met, knocked my phone into the toilet that morning when I was in the shower. My SIM card was destroyed. I had to get a new phone and a new card and load everything on it from my computer back-up. That's why I didn't call."

He lifted my hand up to where he could see it and played with my fingers. "Would you have called me when you got back ... if you hadn't dropped your phone in the toilet?"

"Yes. Maybe." I had to think about it for a few more seconds. "I'm not sure. I didn't remember we were married. And when I got back ... I guess I just tried to start my life over. Get it back on track."

"You had a plan, you said. You talked about it a lot that night."

"Yeah." I smiled bitterly. "My lifeplan. I thought it was the answer to everything, but now I'm starting to think it destroyed any chance I had at being happy."

"You're only twenty-seven."

I pushed on his hand with mine a little. "How do you know how old I am?"

"I know you were born on the fourth of July and consider all fireworks being set off in your honor. You are an only child. Your mother lives in Seattle and at some point spent a lot of time with men who made you a very unhappy person. And I know you used that lifeplan to get your life on track and headed in a direction that made you feel good about yourself."

My stomach clenched with fear. Having someone know me this well was nothing short of terrifying. Why was he still with me? Why hadn't he told me to get the hell out of his life? "You know a lot. You *remember* a lot. I know this sounds terrible, but the only thing I remembered about you was your eyes, your face, and your hat. Oh, and that belt buckle you wore."

"Well, that's better than nothing, I guess." He smiled sadly, making me want to punch myself.

"*Luceo non uro,*" I said, struggling to find something to make him feel better. To lessen the hurt I'd caused. "I remembered those words. And then when I saw them on your ranch gate out there, I remembered waking up in my room that morning without you. I thought you'd left me."

"Shine not burn. Ain't that the truth."

"How so? What does it mean?"

"Literally? *Luceo non uro* means *I shine, not burn.* To me, though, it means that I have a choice. I need to balance the bad with the good, make sure to avoid the things that could burn or scar me but get close enough to the heat that I feel life and really experience it. Until I met you, I'd never really embraced that idea. I walked around my life just being there, but not really feeling it or being actively involved in making it worthwhile. Then there was you, and suddenly it all made sense. I grabbed onto what Fortune was offering me that night and ran with it. I was shining that night, for sure.

Brighter than the Vegas strip."

"And look where it got you." I was so sad that I'd somehow been involved in him getting eventually burned by my carelessness. "Burned." I stroked my thumb over his hand, wishing I could undo the pain for him.

"I don't regret it," he said, lifting my hand and kissing my fingers. "It might have felt like getting burned for a while, but you're here now. If I hadn't done what I did, we wouldn't be getting this second chance. It feels like shining to me, not burning."

I pulled my hand away and sat up, tears close to the surface. "It's not a second chance, Mack. It can't be."

He sat up next to me and pulled me to his side with his arm across my shoulders. Touching his head to mine he spoke in a low voice. "Yes, it can. We're still married. Why can't we just take a shot at making it work like a real marriage?"

I felt and sounded desperately freaked out. "Maybe because we live across the country from each other?"

"That's just geography."

"But I have work and a life."

"So, I'll come live with you."

I pulled my head away and stared at him, my heart slamming in my chest. "You'd give up all this for me?" I looked around the meadow and up at the mountains in the distance. Heaven on earth.

"Sure. In a heartbeat."

Tears sprang to my eyes. This was such an impossible situation. "I couldn't let you do that."

"The hell you couldn't." He stood and took me by the hands, leveraging me up to stand. Once I was in front of him, he took me into his arms. "I'd go live in a trailer park in the middle of the Mississippi swamps if it meant I could be with you and give this a shot."

"That sounds miserable," I said, laughing sadly into his

chest.

"You're right. But I was just trying to make a point. I don't care where I am, as long as I'm with you."

My mind shifted to practical matters so I could keep the reins tight on my runaway heart. "But where would you work? There aren't any ranches around where I live."

"I have an MBA in finance. I could get a job without much of a problem, I'm sure. I've been managing the business of this ranch for years, and it's a big operation. That translates into all kinds of other work."

My tears went on pause and I pulled my upper body back a little so I could look up at him. "You have an MBA? From where?"

He gave me a sad grin. "Does it matter?"

"No." I answered automatically without thinking because that was the polite thing to say, but on further reflection I realized it didn't matter because we couldn't be together anyway. Him having an MBA didn't change anything.

"What about your brother? You haven't told me how his wedding figured into this whole thing."

Mack released me and turned to stand side-by-side, lacing our fingers together and tucking my arm up under his. "Okay, sorry ... got side-tracked there. Where was I? Oh, yeah. Getting back ... I came back from Vegas after swearing Ian and his friends to secrecy. But the story got around somehow that one of us was off with some girl all night, ruining the party."

"Who told?"

"I don't know for sure, but I think Boog was somehow involved. He wasn't there, but he was on the phone with everyone before and after. He's kind of the town gossip."

"Boog?" I couldn't believe it.

"Yeah. Boog. The guy's a granny gossiper. Makes my mom crazy."

"But the story wasn't complete. Why didn't the gossipers say it was you?"

"Oh, they did eventually. But whoever Ginny was eavesdropping on didn't specify or she missed that part, so she flipped out thinking Ian had cheated on her and came after me."

"You? Why you?"

"I don't know. I guess she expected me to be supervising or something since he's my little brother. She confronted me at my house in town. I brought her inside because she was making a scene on the front porch. She was hysterical, and when I tried to tell her it wasn't Ian, it was me, she didn't believe me. She must have thought I was just covering for him."

"Couldn't she just have asked him? Why was it all on you to take care of things?"

"I guess when she first found out, she tried to call Ian and discuss it, but he wouldn't talk to her about it. He got defensive when she came right out and accused him of messing around on the trip and refused to talk to her. They used to fight a lot like that - she'd go off the handle on him and then he'd shut down and give her the silent treatment. He doesn't do well with shouting and she's definitely a shouter. Then he wouldn't answer his phone. By the time she got to my place she'd decided he'd slept with some other woman and we were all in on the plan to keep it hush-hush. I think she had revenge on her mind."

"What do you mean?"

"She came after me. Like trying to come-on to me."

"Oh. Wow. Ick. What'd you do?"

"Tried to get her off me and get away."

"Did you succeed?" I wasn't sure I wanted to hear his answer.

"Yes, I succeeded." He frowned at me. "Do you really think I'm the kind of guy to sleep with my brother's fiancée?"

I shook my head. "No. I never would have thought that about you." I was so relieved he wasn't that kind of guy I was giddy.

He sighed, looking off into the distance again. "Anyway, people saw her coming in all hysterical and being in my house for a while and let Ian know. He asked me what happened, and I told him. Small towns love the gossip." He sighed heavily. "That's one thing I wouldn't miss leaving here."

"You *told* him?"

He nodded, his jaw set in a hard line. "Yeah. I told him. I've wondered many times if I should have just kept it all a secret, but I'm glad I didn't. Even though Ian got hurt, it doesn't change the fact that lies are like acid. They eat everything away eventually - your integrity, your heart ... your soul. It's not worth it."

I nodded. "What does your brother think about all of it?"

"He was really angry at me for a long time. He didn't speak to me for months."

"But it wasn't your fault."

"I'm the one who disappeared that night in Vegas and started the rumors. Ginny made a mistake overhearing only part of a conversation and letting it get the best of her, but if I hadn't done all that, it never would have happened."

"But she was totally wrong for coming on to you. I mean, come on. She doesn't deserve that much of a break."

"Let's just say she showed her true colors that day. Ian never forgave her. He canceled the wedding, tore up the honeymoon tickets, and mailed her the pieces."

"Is he okay with everything now?"

"No. He's just surviving day-to-day, drinking too much, partying way too much in town. He hates it here. He had a job all lined up in Portland, working as an architect in this new firm. His first job out of school. But after the Ginny thing, he just couldn't deal. He blew them off, blew off all his plans for the future ... he's just been riding out his time at the ranch, drinking almost every night with his buddies. He's in a bad way, but right now he's not really accepting any help from anyone. Boog keeps an eye on him for us, but that's about all we can do."

"I feel terrible." My heart ached for both of them and their parents. I could tell they were all suffering for it. It made me so sad to know that I had something to do with it.

"Why do you feel terrible? It's not your fault."

"It is too. If it hadn't been for me, you would have been with them all night and then there wouldn't have been a rumor. No rumor, no upset fiancée, no funny business in the back room."

He turned to face me, pulling my shoulder around so I was facing him. "Oh, so you're like a spider who lured me in to her web and I had no choice in the matter? I can tell everyone I was just an innocent victim?"

When he said it that way it made me feel silly, but I still wasn't ready to walk away without taking any of the blame. "Yes, that's what happened. I lured you into my web." I stepped closer and hugged him to me. "I wore booby-pusher-uppers that night and that tight dress and heels. You fell right into my trap. You had no choice."

He hugged me back tightly and leaned down to inhale the skin of my neck. "You're right about that. Once I saw you, I had no choice. I was done for good. You're the last woman I ever want to be with." His hands slid down my back and squeezed my rear end as we lifted our faces to gaze at each other.

The combination of his touch, his words, and the way he was staring at me with love shining out of his eyes made my whole system go haywire.

"We're going to have sex again, aren't we?" I asked softly, the wetness building in an instant.

He gave me a wicked smile. "Hell yes, we are." And then he lowered me to the ground.

# Chapter Thirty-Five

THE WEIGHT OF MACK'S HEAVY body pressed my back into the soft earth beneath the blanket. His breath was sweet and his mouth insistent, the scratchy surface of his shaved upper lip giving me a thrill as it slid across the sensitive skin of my lips and neck. His hat tipped off and fell into the grass next to my head.

"What if someone sees us?" I asked, feeling his growing need pressing into my leg.

"No one's out here except you, me, and the horses, and they don't care what we do, so long as we let them eat in peace." His lazy smile arrested my heart. "Just relax and let me love you." He dipped his head down and kissed the hollow of my neck, pulling the neckline of my t-shirt down to expose my skin and kiss there too.

I closed my eyes and ran my fingers up and down his back, loving how the muscles bunched up and relaxed as he covered me in his affection. He was such a strong man. I felt safe with him. Turned on just at the thought of him.

"Do you like this?" he asked, nuzzling my ear and giving me chills.

"I like everything you do," I said softly. "Everything feels amazing."

He came back up to my face and kissed me on the mouth

hard before pulling away. "Get up."

"What?" The fog that had started to take over my conscious mind quickly dissipated, leaving me confused.

"Stand up and take your clothes off for me. Strip, sexy girl, I want to watch."

I giggled. "Get out of town." My face flamed at the idea of him seeing me in the broad daylight like that.

"No, I'm serious." He leaned down and pressed a kiss against my lips, forcing them apart and pushing his hot tongue inside. My nipples went rock hard. I reached for him blindly as my eyes slid shut, but he pushed my hands gently to the side and pulled away. I opened my eyes and pouted.

"Nope. I want to see you naked," he insisted. He sat up and bent his legs at the knees, letting one leg fall to the side and leaving the other upright so I had a perfect view of his jeans-encased crotch. He rested his forearms on his knees and winked at me, lifting his chin in a gesture of encouragement. "Go for it."

"I want to see *you* naked," I responded, challenging him with my grin.

"You first." He moved his eyebrows up and down in a promise of future play.

I felt energized for some reason. Daring. I got up from the blanket and stood a couple paces away.

"What should I take off first?" My cheeks were still burning with embarrassment and anticipation, his focused, serious gaze causing a flush to come over my chest and neck too. He was so gorgeous, sitting there in his jeans and t-shirt, looking so carefree and oblivious to his charms. His hair was rumpled, curling around the edges from the heat and sweat. Keeping my hands off him took monumental effort.

"Shoes," he ordered. "Take 'em off."

I kicked the ugly moccasins off and they went flying over his head.

He grinned. "Shirt off. Show me what you got."

I pulled the t-shirt up from the bottom and let it slide down my arm to drop at my feet. An answering wetness started between my legs when he reached down and put his hand on his crotch, pulling at it a little and adjusting it. I'd never before been turned on by the idea of a man touching himself, but yep, it was happening now. Big time.

"Bra." He dropped to his side on the blanket, one hand propping up his head and the other stroking the front of his jeans. The bulge underneath was impossible to miss.

I raised an eyebrow at his command. I thought for sure the shorts were going to be next. I shrugged. If he wanted to see me naked from the waist up, who was I to argue? Reaching behind me, I unclasped the only thing keeping my naked breasts from being exposed to the whole world. I'd never been without clothes in public before and I expected to hate it, but as the air touched my skin, I suddenly felt wild and free; like I was taking a risk and loving every minute of it.

"Jesus, you have a nice rack."

I laughed. "A nice *rack?* Wow, that's sexy. What am I, a deer?" It *was* kind of sexy, having my womanly parts referred to in such a man's way. I reached up and put my hands underneath them, pushing them up a little and rubbing the last vestiges of heat away.

"Better stop doing that," he said, his face going dark, his hand stilling its movements on his jeans. The muscles in his jaw tensed, and he looked like a lion considering whether to attack its prey.

My hands froze. "Why?" I asked the question, but I already knew the answer. I just wanted to hear him say what his expression was already telling me.

"Because I'm not done with the strip tease, but if you don't quit doing that I'm going to tackle you."

I couldn't stop smiling. "Fine." My hands fell to my hips. "What's next?"

"Shorts. But turn around. I want to see that ass."

I spun, losing my balance a little and giggling as I worked on the button and got my feet back under me. Once they were unzipped and on their way down, sliding over the roundest part of my rear end, I looked at him over my shoulder.

He was hypnotized, staring at me with his hand rubbing his crotch slowly. Maybe I should have been shocked at his blatant male behavior, but instead, I was turned-on beyond rational thought. To think that he was getting so turned on just by seeing my naked body was blowing my mind. I'd always gotten undressed in the dark, self-conscious about my flaws. Here with him in this bright meadow, I felt like the goddess of sex.

The shorts hit the ground at my feet and I stepped out of them.

I was facing away from him again, wearing nothing but my panties.

"What's next?" I asked, my voice carrying out into the clearing in front of me.

I heard a rustling, and before I could react, he was behind me on his knees. His face was against my lower back, kissing me while he held onto my hips with his strong hands. My legs trembled as his thick fingers hooked into the top of my panties and slowly dragged them down.

"I want... I want..." I tried to use words to express my desires, but they wouldn't collect in my head properly. Every time I attempted to form a coherent thought, he licked my skin and then kissed it - sometimes with a feathery lightness and other times with a strong suction that would leave a mark - leaving me senseless once again.

"What do you want, sexy girl?" He turned me around by the hips, forcing me to face him.

I looked down at his face, burying my hands in his hair at the sides of his head, running my fingers into the thick, sweaty, wavy mass. "I want … you." My face was flushed with passion. Seeing him down there and fully dressed with nothing between his mouth and my naked lower body was enough to make me have a heart attack.

He moved closer, wrapping his arms around my backside and leaning in towards me. I gasped as his tongue touched my folds, going right inside without hesitation to sear me with its wet heat.

"What are you doing?" I whispered, looking down at his head, feeling it move under my hands as he worshipped my body. My legs shook and I went from holding on for pleasure to holding on for support. I would have fallen without his strong shoulders to keep me up.

I moaned as his tongue found my most sensitive places and my folds became swollen with need. Slick wetness gathered, prompting my desire to feel more of him between my legs. "Mack … please."

He leaned back and spoke in a dangerous voice. "Lie down."

My breath hitched as I realized things were about to get real. This is what my body needed … to feel him inside me, filling me, taking me on the ride that would end with me screaming and lost.

I gathered what was left of my wits and did as he said, walking around him to lie on the blanket. I reclined onto my back, my breasts relaxing down towards my ribs. I opened my legs and bent my knees a little, waiting to see what he would do. My hand moved to my folds where I touched the wetness he had caused.

He stood and pulled off his t-shirt in one quick move, revealing the rippling, lean muscles beneath. He didn't say anything. He looked angry, but I knew it wasn't that emotion that was going through his mind and heart as he stood before me. Passion looked a lot like darkness on him. It made my blood run hot.

His boots, socks, and pants came off next. That's all he'd worn to our little picnic and now in the bright sunlight I was finally able to fully appreciate the man I'd married in all his muscled glory. Shadows from the curves of his muscles highlighted their dense structure. Even without the hard physical work he did on the ranch, he'd still have a body to die for, but with all that cattle management came a big payoff, and I felt like the luckiest girl in the world to be enjoying it right now.

And my luck didn't stop at his totally built physique. His cock was a marvel too, its length and breadth something that shouldn't have worked; how it was able to fit inside me was some kind of miracle. It stood out in front of him, making it perfectly clear what he wanted to do with me. I spread my legs a little farther and ran my fingertip over my clit, making it burn with need.

"I like it when you do that," he said, his voice husky.

"I like it better when you do it to me," I said, never breaking eye contact with him.

He pulled a condom from his pants pocket and put it on. When he was finished, he walked over slowly, his hard length swaying with every step. Bending down, he grabbed my wrist, pulling it away from my wetness and moving it to a spot over my head.

"I'm going to make love to my wife now," he said, his voice deep and soft, a sexy promise I was ready to beg him to keep.

A thrill ran through me to be called that word ... *wife* ... and to be promised that joy, even though it was wrong. Even though I shouldn't have encouraged him to see me that way.

"We shouldn't," I said, one weak, last-ditch effort to help him let me go. I was so terrible at doing the right thing. My heart just wasn't in it. I wanted it all; I wanted to have him for mine and live just for this moment for the rest of my life.

"Bullshit." He let my hand go and angled his cock up to

enter me, using his hand to guide it. Once in position, he put his hands on either side of me and stared deeply into my eyes.

I gasped when he entered me, my head falling to the side as the sensations washed over me and the anticipation of what was to come grew.

"Don't look away," he said. "Look at me."

I turned my face to do as he demanded. His brilliant blue eyes bore into me, causing my heart to fill with overwhelming emotion. He moved inside me, slowly, in and out, all the while never looking away.

I closed my eyes, the passion growing.

"Open your eyes, Andie, look at me. I want to watch you come."

I forced my lids up even though they wanted to shut out his beauty. I'd never watched a man make love to me, and it was too deep. Too much. Because it was Mack.

Tears welled up, even as the heat did too.

His rhythm picked up and my breasts bounced as his thrusts became more insistent, faster. He never broke eye contact with me, even though his face showed the extreme control he was exercising over his need. He was holding out for me, waiting so that I could come with him. I angled my hips up even more, taking him deeper.

I was mesmerized. He was branding my heart, showing me that he was going to love me whether I liked it or not and that I was his and no one else's. I'd never had anyone insist on loving me before like this. Tears slipped out of my eyes and dripped down to my ears as the orgasm built. I was on the precipice of a big chasm, a place where I could easily get lost and never find my way out of.

"I love you, Andie Marks MacKenzie. I'm not letting you go."

I sobbed, but still didn't look away. Sweat dripped down from his neck and landed on my breasts, tickling my skin as it slid down to my ribs. I drew my legs up and moved my hands to his ass so I could push him deeper into me. I wanted to feel every last inch of him filling my need. I couldn't help it. We were becoming one in that moment, and I didn't want to miss any of it. This would be the one and only time I would have this in my life. No man could ever measure up to the standard that Mack set.

His expression became stormy. His eyebrows drew together and his lips pressed into a thin line. Sweat broke out on his forehead and dripped down his face and onto mine. He groaned, his body moving fast, his shaft getting thicker.

The sensation of being stretched and the smooth gliding into my core, combined with his intense concentration and words of love were too much. Too much for my body and too much for my soul.

The heat and fluttering sensations between my legs where our bodies were joined took over, leaving all my reticence, self-doubt, and worries behind. I clung to him as I screamed out his name, crying the entire time.

"Look at me!" he growled, going down on his elbows and grasping my head on either side in his huge hands. I was trapped in his life, his face just inches away.

"I can't! I can't!" I gasped out, my face contorting with the effort of managing sorrow and orgasm at the same time.

He crushed his lips to mine and then stiffened, his entire body going rigid for a second before he began pounding into me with short hard thrusts. His mouth became too hard against mine, forcing me to turn my head.

"Andie! God*dammit*, Andie!" He was breathing against my face like a freight train as he came inside me.

Anything else he might have said didn't register. I was too far gone to hear or say anything of substance; all I could do was feel. I was drowning. Love and pain and hope and loss mixed into one big maelstrom of emotion. "Mack!" I cried, hanging onto his back with every ounce of strength I had, bucking underneath him until I couldn't take the sensations anymore. My cries turned into silent tears and I just let them fall.

He collapsed on top of me, suffocating me with his weight and distracting me from my sadness. When it got to the point where I had to struggle to breathe, he fell off to the side, pulling out of me abruptly. I reached over and slapped him gently on the face.

"What was that for?" he asked, reaching over to wipe the tears from my cheeks.

"That's for leaving me and being so mean like that."

He grabbed me as he rolled over onto his back, pulling me with him. I was lying on top of his chest, looking down at him and his passion-flushed face.

"You're the one who's leaving and being so mean, not me."

I frowned, my heart stung by his words. "Don't say that." Leaving felt so wrong; it was killing me to imagine myself on a flight out of here.

"Stay." He reached up and gently pushed a lock of hair out of my face. "At least for the picnic. I want you to meet the family before you go."

The knowledge that he'd accepted my departure as a foregone conclusion hurt. The masochist in me wanted him to keep fighting for me to stay. I guess I hadn't caused either of us enough pain yet.

I sighed. "I don't know if that's a good idea."

"Sure it is. What's one more day going to do? Just stay. My grandma wants to meet you and my mom needs your help."

I stared into his sneaky blue eyes, frowning at him. "Low blow, Mack."

He shrugged, not smiling. "I'm going to use whatever tricks I have up my sleeve to keep you here."

I sighed, not wanting to let him or his mom and

grandma down. It was a great excuse to put off my heartbreak for one more day. "Fine. I'll go to the picnic, but that's it. After that, I have to go back." What I was going to do when I got there was still an unknown. The only thing I *did* know was that I wouldn't be getting married to Bradley. This little tryst in the meadow had solidified that decision in my mind.

Mack came off me with a push-up and stood, reaching for my hand.

I gave it to him and let him guide me to my feet. "What are we doing now?" I asked, falling against him as his arms wrapped loosely around my back.

He dipped down and gave me a quick kiss on the lips. "Now, we play tag."

I frowned, going still, not sure I'd heard him correctly. "What?"

"You heard me." He grinned and pushed me away from him, reaching around to smack me lightly on the butt cheek. "I'm It. Better run."

I laughed for a second. "What are you talking about?" A tickling sensation started in my stomach as I pictured him taking me down by the heels.

One of his eyebrows went up in a devilish challenge. "Better run. If I catch you, you're going to get thrown into the lake that's just behind those trees. And I have to warn you … it's pretty cold this time of year."

A huge dose of adrenaline shot into my veins, and I took off running without a second glance at him. The horses lifted their heads as I zoomed by heedless of the snakes that might be waiting for me, only knowing I had to get away from the crazy man who was going to turn me into a human popsicle.

His pounding footsteps came up behind me, causing me to scream and laugh at the same time. Hysterical giggles bubbled up out of my chest and echoed around the clearing.

"Gotcha!" he shouted, grabbing my upper arm.

I twisted away and ran around him, shrieking again when I saw him go into a crouch, his muscles bunching up in preparation for attack.

"No, Mack! *No!*" I flew over the grass and flowers, my heart racing and my arms pumping.

"Yes!" he growled, hooking me around the waist from behind and lifting me up in his arms.

He strode across the meadow and into the trees with me in his arms, clamping down on me so hard, all I could do was struggle mutely, barely able to move my arms or legs.

"Please don't throw me in," I begged, mostly meaning it but partially thrilled with his caveman act. I was so used to being in charge in my life, this was an erotic twist in our relationship I hadn't expected to like. But there was no denying that I was hoping his next move would be to drop me to the ground and do that thing that he does oh so well, all over again.

Shimmering bluish green water came into view and I pleaded with renewed vigor, imagining how cold it would feel against my hot skin. "Please, I'll do anything. Please don't put me in there, Mack. I hate cold water!"

He stopped abruptly. "You'll do anything?"

I nodded without hesitation, my chest heaving. "Yes. Anything. Name it."

"Stay. Stay for the picnic..."

I smiled. "I already said I'd stay."

"...And let me sleep with you tonight. I want our last night to be spent in your bed, inside you."

A shiver ran through me as I imagined his hard, hairy body next to mine in the small bed of his parents' house, while we did things we shouldn't be doing. I looked over at the lake and its cold, deep waters. The decision was a no-brainer.

"Fine. Deal."

He dropped my legs and put his hands on either side of

my face. "I knew I'd get you to see reason." He kissed me passionately for several seconds before surprising me by turning me around to face a tree. "Now do me a favor and bend over."

"Why, what are you going to do?" I held my breath waiting for his answer.

He leaned in and spoke softly next to my ear. "I'm going to fuck you from behind." He ran his hand up my spine from my rear end to my shoulder blades, pushing forward on my upper back.

A thrill shot through me like an electric shock, and I was instantly ready for him. I smiled, barely containing my excitement as I spread my legs and leaned over, grabbing the trunk of the tree. My breasts hung down, the cool air tickling their sensitive skin as my fingers dug into the rough, hard bark. His velvety hard length came up to touch my swollen place and he gripped one of my hips in his strong, warm hand.

I couldn't stop moaning as he pulled my hips back and slid into me once again.

# Chapter Thirty-Six

OUR RIDE BACK TO THE house went a lot faster then the ride out to the meadow. The sun was getting nearer the horizon and my belly was full from the food Mack had fed me with his own hands as the ranch came into view.

My brain was going a thousand miles an hour, trying to find some kind of fall back plan for my life or something. The connection Mack and I had made today had done nothing but complicate things even more. A glimmer of temptation was keeping me from just putting my foot down and insisting he let me go. All I could see down that path was loneliness and despair, and for once I didn't feel like I was going to be completely happy following the script I'd written so long ago.

"You're thinking too much again," said Mack, not even looking back.

"Shush, you have no idea what I'm thinking."

"You're trying to figure out if you should make me sign those damn papers or just go with the flow and see where it takes you."

"I never go with the flow," I said, feeling grouchy.

"You said you'd stay through the picnic so you have to stay. I already texted my mom and she's counting on you to help."

"Dammit, Mack, that's playing dirty." He was getting

family members on his side, making it harder for me to leave, and he knew it.

I kicked my horse a little to get her to move up to Mack's side. His horse flinched away a little, but stayed on the path.

"I do what I gotta do to shine, babe. That's all I'm doing … shining not burning."

"Screw that. You're being sneaky and manipulating my heart and I don't like it."

He looked at me with all traces of humor gone. "All's fair in love and war, and I plan on winning, no matter what."

My nostrils flared. Time to drop the big bomb. "Bradley's on his way out here."

Mack did a double take. "Say that again?"

"You heard me. He's coming out. I tried to stop him, but he wouldn't listen."

Mack actually grinned. "Sounds like my kind of guy."

I shook my head. "You just don't get it. He's not your kind of guy and he's going to come here and cause a big fuss. I need to be gone when he comes or it's going to be not only ugly but embarrassing."

"Not for me, it's not. And it shouldn't be for you either." He reached over to touch me but I flinched away.

"Hands off. I'm not kidding. You're not going to charm yourself out of this one. He's coming, and when he realizes I've been sleeping with you, he's going to make a big stink and everyone will know that we're both cheater assholes."

Mack laughed. "Cheaters? How can we possibly be cheating when we're married?"

I growled. "Rrrrrr, you know what I mean! Don't try to make me feel better about what I've done."

Mack leaned really far over and snatched my hand, refusing to let it go. "You've done nothing wrong, you hear me? Love is what it is and love does what it does to survive. It's an instinct. Technically you were cheating on me with him, but I don't look at it that way. I know you didn't remember, I believe you. And now you know you're married to me and you're sleeping with me as my wife. Nothing wrong happened. Nothing."

I was too angry to guard my words. "It's not love, okay? Stop calling it that."

He dropped my hand and stared straight ahead. "Is that so." It came out like a statement. I'd hurt him. But I couldn't stop myself from burying the knife in deeper.

"Yeah, that's so. It's just lust. You'll get tired of it soon enough, and then I'll have to go back with my tail between my legs and beg for forgiveness from everyone."

Mack shook his head. "Girl, you really need to get your head out of your keister if you're ever going to find happiness in life." He kicked his horse and surged ahead, leaving me to follow in his dust.

I think my horse was as shocked as I was. She just plodded along, as if Mack and his mount weren't getting tinier and tinier in the distance. The house was close - I could make out its roof less than a mile away - but still ... I was fuming about being left behind by the time we entered the front yard. Boog was waiting for me, a bland look on his face.

"What are you looking at?" I asked, pissed at him for being such a gossip.

"City slicker. What are you looking at?"

"A stupid wookie man-bear-pig who doesn't know how to mind his own business." I slid off the horse and caught myself before falling onto my butt. My legs were going to be really sore tomorrow from all the riding, along with my ass.

He laughed. "I know about wookies, but man-bear-pigs? What's that?"

I was too frustrated to spar with him. "Go look in the mirror. I'm busy." I clomped up the steps and left him to take care of the horse. He'd taken the reins so I assumed that's what he was there for.

"You have to brush your horse out!" he shouted behind

me.

"I'll do it later!" I yelled back, banging the door behind me. I strode into the kitchen to get a glass of water. Maeve was there at the sink and it slowed me down considerably.

"Oh. Hi. I didn't know you'd be here."

Maeve looked at me over her shoulder and smiled before going back to her task. "Where else would I be?"

I went over and leaned on the nearby counter. "I don't know, actually. What do you do here?"

"Lots of things." She was snapping beans in the sink. "Clean. Cook. Take care of the chicken and gardens."

"Sounds … fun." I was totally lying.

"Actually, it's a very simple life but I find it relaxing and enjoyable. I can finish my work in half the day and that leaves the rest of it for personal pursuits."

"Oh yeah? Like what kind of personal pursuits?"

"Crocheting. Painting. Book club. I do lots of things on the side of my work life."

I sighed wistfully. "All of those things are things I wish I had time for." This time I wasn't lying. I was a total granny at heart.

She shrugged, never hesitating in her work. "So find the time."

"Ha. That's funny. Have you ever worked in a law firm?"

"Can't say as I have."

"Well, it sucks for free time. I work from six in the morning until sometimes ten at night or even later when I'm going to trial."

"Sounds like you don't even have time to breathe."

I stared out the window into the back yard. "I don't. I haven't had time to breathe since I was fifteen years old." The simple sad truth of that calmed me down completely. "I don't know why I ever thought that was something I wanted."

"Don't be so hard on yourself. First off, you were young and you were doing what you needed to do to make the most of things. And second, you're still young. You aren't stuck doing what you don't want to do. If your life isn't working for you, change it." She stopped with her bean-snapping and looked at me. "Nobody's forcing you to stay where you are in life."

"I am," I said pitifully.

She smiled. "Well, my advice is to not let *you* stand in the way of your own happiness."

"Yeah," I said, blinking a few times as the words sunk in. "That is kind of dumb, isn't it?"

"Not dumb. Safe. I get the impression you've lived a safe life."

I chuckled bitterly. "For the most part, yes. And the one time I stepped out of the safety zone, I monumentally screwed up the lives of about five people." I was tallying up the entire MacKenzie family as collateral damage.

"I doubt that." She lifted a big container of beans out of the sink and put it on the counter. "Life has a way of working out, whether it's following our plan or not. I have a feeling that you're going to look back on that time you stepped out of your safety zone, as one of the best things you could have done for yourself."

"I really wish you knew what you were talking about," I said, before I realized how rude it sounded.

She laughed. "Trust me. I know what I'm talking about."

"Have you screwed up before? Like massively, awfully screwed up?"

She nodded. "Yep. We all have. It's part of becoming a strong person." She put her hands on her hips and faced me. "I'm a strong person, Andie. But it's only because I've fought for it."

"Shine not burn," I said softly, my heart collapsing in on

itself in my chest.

She nodded. "That's right. We MacKenzie girls shine, not burn." She pulled me into a hug. "You're one of us, so you should know."

I broke into tears, clinging to her like a drowning girl to a life ring.

# Chapter Thirty-Seven

AFTER I'D CRIED MYSELF OUT and blubbered all over Maeve's very understanding shoulder, I walked up to Ian's room and fell into an exhausted sleep. I dreamed of huge groups of people witnessing my shame and condemning me for it. Visions of my mother's boyfriend accusing me of being a slut tortured my already bruised sense of self-worth. Mewling cries escaped my lips as I pictured my bosses firing me for besmirching the reputation of the firm.

It was then that I felt a warmth come over me and the darkness slip away. Like a magic spell had been cast, I went from disintegrating to safe. Alone to protected. I shifted in the bed and realized I wasn't alone anymore.

"What are you doing here?" I asked in a tear-scratched voice.

"Shhh, just go to sleep. You're exhausted."

"But what about dinner?" I wasn't hungry, but I hoped to get rid of him. I didn't deserve the care and compassion; I deserved to be punished.

"Dinner's long over. If you want, we saved you a plate, but I think you should just sleep. I kept you out in the sun too long. Sorry about that, babe."

"It's not the sun." *It's the giant crack in my heart that will never heal.*

He kissed my neck tenderly. "No, it's not the sun. It's me. I wore you out with King Dong."

I laughed in spite of myself. "Shut up."

"Fine." He kissed my shoulder. "Go to sleep."

"Go away and I will," I whispered, already falling into the twilight sleep zone where nothing made much sense and shadows of memories swirled and danced.

"I'm not going anywhere…"

It was the last thing I remembered hearing before the sun streaming in the window woke me up. It was the morning of the picnic, dawning sunny and bright. My heart felt like ten pounds of lead in my chest.

# Chapter Thirty-Eight

"WAKE UP SLEEPY HEAD! I have a dress for you to wear today." Maeve swished into my room wearing a pretty wrap-around dress covered in yellow flowers.

"What?" I sat up, my hair a rat's nest on my head. Every muscle in my body let me know that it was sore and very unhappy about being overused the day before.

She held up a blue halter neck dress. "A dress. For you to wear. Mack bought it for you in town, along with these sandals." She held up a pair of darker blue slip-ons in her other hand.

I stared at the dress's simple lines, flowing material, and low neckline. It's exactly what I would have picked myself if I'd done the shopping, perfect for a sunny day in Baker City. "I ... can't wear that."

"Why ever not?" She looked at it critically.

"Because ... what if it doesn't fit?"

She draped it over a chair and put the shoes on the floor nearby. "He looked on the tags of your clothes. I'm sure it will fit. You have a beautiful figure."

"Have you seen my butt?" I asked, swinging my legs out off the side of the bed and staring at the floor. Every square inch of my body was aching, from my scalp to the bottom of my feet. I'd never felt so wasted in all my life. *No wonder*

*Mack has such a killer body. What a frigging workout.*

She smiled; I could hear it in her voice. "I happen to know that men like bountiful figures, so even though yours could stand a few more pounds on it, I think you're going to do just fine with … the men of Baker City."

I looked up at her, my expression broadcasting the shame in my heart. "I have some bad news about the picnic."

She stopped in her fussing around the room. "Oh yes? What's that?"

"My fiancé, soon to be *ex*-fiancé, is on his way out here. I'm surprised he isn't here yet. I'm pretty sure you won't want either one of us at your party when that happens."

"Nonsense. Any friend of yours is a friend of ours." She moved some picture frames around on the dresser as if they'd be much better off being one inch more to the right or left.

"You don't understand," I explained. "He's coming to take me back but I'm going to break up with him and go back on my own. I'm canceling the wedding. It's going to be ugly."

She turned her head and grinned at me. She actually grinned, like my life falling apart was funny. I frowned, wondering why she'd be so happy about it. Maybe I'd misjudged her friendliness.

"I'm sure it'll be fine. As soon as he gets a taste of Grandma Lettie's beef brisket he'll settle right down and stay for pie. And I've made pecan and apple, so he'll be too full to give you a hard time."

Now her happiness made sense. She hadn't met Bradley yet.

I stood, shuffling over to the door. "You are living in a really nice fantasy world. Are you taking on immigrants? I'd like to move in."

She smiled, walking past me out into the hallway. "You are always welcome in my fantasy world. Or my real one for that matter." She left me, headed towards the stairs. "We could use your help downstairs whenever you're ready. We have almost a hundred people on their way and we still don't have all the tables out."

"What?!" Guilt overwhelmed me. Here I'd been sleeping all morning while everyone else worked. What an asshole.

I heard laughter and then the voices of men shouting instructions to each other coming through the front door.

"Shit," I said, going back to grab the dress and some underwear before running on tiptoes into the bathroom. *Time to shower, shave, and get with the program, Andie. You can be an asshole and break everyone's hearts later.*

I caught a glimpse of Mack coming up the stairs as I closed the door. I locked it and waited for him to come close. When the sound of his footsteps stopped outside the door I spoke, using my most commanding tone. "Don't even think of sneaking in here again, Mack. I know you're out there. I have to shower and shave so I can help."

"I wouldn't dream of interfering in that." He was messing with me, I could tell. I held onto the lock just in case he was trying to jimmy it open. "I just came up to see if you needed anything else."

"No. I'm fine." I bit my lip, wrestling with myself, embarrassed and touched that he'd gone out of his way for me. "And thanks for the dress. And the shoes. That was ... very thoughtful."

"I'm a thoughtful guy. I'll be downstairs waiting for you."

"Don't wait for me," I said, resting my head on the door.

"Don't make me wait too long this time," he said, ignoring the double meaning in my words. Or maybe he was giving me some of his own. His mouth was just a door's width away. I could picture his full lips and the feel of his tongue on mine. I rested my hand against the wood, knowing I could just let him in and feel him inside me once more before it was all over. The temptation was driving me insane.

"Why can't you just let me go?" I asked, almost pleading. This was the dumbest place in the world to be having this conversation, but that was just par for the course with me, I guess. Careless does as careless is.

"I can't let you go because you're mine. And because I can't stand to see you sad. I'm going to fix that. You sure you don't need me in there right now? I could cheer you up real quick, I promise."

I could picture the devilish smile on his face, and I couldn't help but respond in kind.

"I might be wallowing in misery, but that doesn't mean I'm going to be dead-ass lame and not help with your family's once-a-year family picnic. Stop trying to distract me."

"That's the spirit. Grandma Lettie's coming with her beef brisket, you know."

I giggled. "So I heard."

"Well hurry up, then. Those tables aren't going to put themselves out."

My heart was soaring over the teasing we were enjoying together. He made the atmosphere that had threatened to suffocate me ten times lighter, and his attitude made me believe that life could be so much simpler and uncomplicated if I just said yes to what he was offering.

I was tempted to open the door and yank him in with me, but the sound of his whistling near the stairs stopped me. It was better that we didn't do anything else to make my leaving any harder. My hand dropped away from the door and I turned around, sighing.

Stepping into the warm shower, I couldn't keep the smile off my face. I might be facing an apocalyptic event with Bradley showing up in the middle of everything and forcing a very public, very ugly breakup, but at least for now I had a pretty new dress to wear and a famous beef brisket to look forward to. *What the hell is a beef brisket, anyway?*

# *Chapter Thirty-Nine*

THE FIRST GUESTS FOR THE MacKenzie's annual picnic and rodeo began arriving around eleven in the morning. A party rental company had set up three large tents earlier to provide shade not only for the guests but also for the band that was in the process of setting up to entertain everyone with eighties rock classics. The food was set out on a long banquet table, and as people arrived, they added their dishes to the offerings. Nearly a hundred people stood in groups, laughing, smiling and talking

I found myself standing alone when several of the guests and family moved as one big group towards the front of the house. Most of my focus was on Mack and the jeans that hugged his amazing rear end and the black t-shirt that stretched across his thick back. He had his best cowboy hat on today, a light cream color with a thin black band around the top. Just looking at him had me going warm in all the wrong ways and in all the most inappropriate places. This picnic was going to last forever with him there torturing me like that, just out of my reach ... the perfect male, so close and yet so far.

I took a deep breath to calm my libido down a notch or two. That's all I could manage with him looking like he did today. It was going to be a helluva long picnic.

A huge cadillac that looked like it was built in the sixties drove up to the front gate and parked before going all the way through. Curious, I wandered over, keeping my distance from the MacKenzie clan and the many townspeople who'd already arrived. The driver's door opened and then shut, but I didn't see an actual person getting out. It wasn't until she made it up to the front of the car that I realized why.

"Grandma Lettie, I presume," I said softly into the empty air around me. Maeve and Angus fawned over her, and she accepted their hugs and kisses with some of her own. She stood less than five feet tall and had wispy bluish-gray hair that floated around her head like a cloud. Ian took the car keys from her and moved the huge vehicle off to the side, parking it out of the way.

The group of welcomers moved with her in my direction, and I shifted off to the side to give them room to get by. Mack was carrying a big oval pan with a lid on it that had come from her trunk, and I could tell by the way his muscles were bulging under his t-shirt that it was heavy.

As they drew near, Maeve leaned down and spoke in her ear. The older woman's head shot up and her eyes searched the area until they landed on me. She pointed with a bony finger in my direction and the whole group shifted trajectory, no longer headed towards the banquet table but towards me instead.

My heart began beating faster and sweat beaded up on my lip. I quickly swiped it away and stood as tall as I could before she got near. I felt like I was going before the appellate court judges with a crappy case file in hand and no pants on.

"Who's this young lady?" she asked when she was about four feet away, her watery blue eyes taking my measure. Her expression gave me no clue as to what she was thinking.

I held out my hand and stepped forward. "I'm Andie. It's nice to meet you."

She took my hand in a surprisingly strong grip and

squeezed. "Nice to meet you, too. I hear you're part of the family."

My heart stopped for a few seconds and then raced to catch up. "Ummm ... yes ... I guess I am."

I could feel Mack's gaze burning into me, but I kept my eyes locked on the old woman. Her baby blue housedress matched the white cardigan over her shoulders and white patent leather low-heeled sandals perfectly. Her hair had obviously been done special for the occasion. Even though she wasn't much bigger than a hobbit and had more wrinkles than a year-old raisin lost in the back of the pantry, she was still intimidating as hell.

"How do you like it here so far? I was told you've been here a few days." She kept a grip on my hand, so I did the same with hers, not wanting her to feel like she was hanging onto a dead fish. I kept my fingers wrapped softly around her delicate, birdlike hand, marveling in the strength I could sense there.

"I've been here two days, actually, and I like it a lot. It's gorgeous here." I wasn't shining her on, either. The beauty that Maeve had spoken of on my first night was obvious to me now. I would miss it greatly when I left.

"This place gets into your bones and never lets you go." She continued to hold my hand as she turned. "Come on over here with me and show me what you've done."

"What I've done?" My voice went up an octave, wondering if she was talking about what I thought she was talking about. *How does she know about me and Mack?*

"The food, darlin', the food." She gestured to the banquet table covered in dishes with foil on them. "What'd you make? What's your specialty?"

I breathed out a sigh of relief. "Oh, I didn't make anything. Maeve did it all."

"Don't you cook?" She looked a little bit outraged, and it was hard not to smile at her reaction.

"No, not really. I never learned."

"Well, what about your mother? Didn't she cook?"

I shook my head, not trusting myself to speak. My mother didn't do a whole lot of anything other than act as a human punching bag for life's biggest losers, but I wasn't going to tell Grandma Lettie that. I had a feeling she'd ask why my mother hadn't cut their testicles off.

"Not everyone comes from a family of great cooks, Grandma," said Mack, setting her dish down on the table. "Maybe you can teach Andie a few things."

"Sounds like I'm going to have to," she said, once again focused on getting to the table. She took careful steps, but they were solid. I had a feeling she didn't need to hold onto me, that she was just keeping me close so she could conduct her interrogation.

I glanced at Mack to find him grinning at both of us, like he was enjoying some inside joke. I stuck my tongue out at him but that only seemed to make him happier.

"Lift up the lid there," she ordered, pointing at her pan.

I did as she asked. The only thing visible inside was a big hunk of aluminum foil.

"That there's a beef brisket. Best one you'll ever taste, guaranteed. I don't mess around when it comes to brisket."

I nodded sagely. "I can see that."

She looked up at me with a frown. "I don't see how, since it's covered in the tin foil like that."

Ian snickered behind me, but I ignored him. "But I've heard. So I can imagine what it looks like." I smiled and nodded.

"You ever eat brisket?" she asked.

My smile fell off. "Uhh ... no. Can't say that I have."

"Then how are you able to imagine it if you've never even seen one?"

"I'm creative?" My face went red as Ian busted out in guffaws.

She grinned at me, revealing perfect dentures. "I like you. You're sassy."

I grinned back, relief washing over me. "I like you too. You're kind of sassy yourself."

She cackled. "You're dang right I am. Life's too short to be sickly sweet all the time, don't you think? Like that aspartame. Nasty aftertaste. Bah."

I nodded. "Absolutely. I like the real stuff. Sugar all the way for me."

She let go of my hand and squeezed my arm. "Good. You and I are going to get along just fine. She teetered in a circle and faced the clan. "Now which one of my grandsons are you here with? It better be one of my boys and not that Boog person, I'll tell you what."

Boog's mouth fell open while everyone else laughed. I dropped my gaze to the ground, too embarrassed to answer her question. Mack stepped up beside me and put his arm around my shoulders, pulling me against him firmly. "She's with me, Grandma. She's here with me."

Grandma Lettie looked at both of us critically for a few seconds and then nodded. "Good enough." Then she faced the crowd. "Boog, get me a chair, will ya? My feet are tired. I went to a barn dance last night and stayed up 'til one a.m. Now I'm too pooped to piddle."

Boog walked away grumbling, but he grabbed a chair and dragged it back anyway. I wandered away with Mack as others closed in on Grandma Lettie, standing around her like she was visiting royalty.

"Well, that was interesting," I said, the feeling that I'd just dodged a bullet soothing my frazzled nerves.

Mack took my hand and led me back over to the food table. He reached inside the big pan and removed some of the tin foil from the top. "This is what a beef brisket looks like."

I stared down at the hunk of brown meat. "Oh. It looks

... boring." I didn't know what I'd been expecting, but this sure seemed like very little to get excited about.

He laughed and then spoke in a soft voice. "Don't you dare let Grandma Lettie hear you say that."

"I *wouldn't* dare," I whispered back. "She scares me."

Mack leaned in like he was going to kiss me, but I drew back.

"What? I can't kiss you?" He looked hurt.

"No, you can't kiss me, you fool. This is not happening." I pointed to him and then me. *"We* are not happening." It felt horrible to say it, but it had to be said. The longer we played at being a couple, the harder it would be when I left. And I was leaving, papers signed or not, tomorrow.

"Bullshit it's not happening. It very much *is* happening." His good mood was quickly evaporating.

"Please don't make a scene," I said, glancing back at his grandmother.

"You're the one making a scene," he said, his tone going soft again. "I'll tell you what ... Just give me one kiss, and I'll leave you alone. Otherwise I'm going to harass you all day."

I eyed him suspiciously, pretending to hate the idea but secretly thrilled to know he would kiss me in front of his family. "One kiss and you'll leave me alone for the whole picnic?"

"No. For fifteen minutes."

I feigned outrage. "That's not fair!"

"Well, if you want to do *more* than just kiss me, that could buy you more time." He moved his eyebrows up and down suggestively.

I elbowed him in the ribs, smiling the whole time. "Go away, horn dog. No blowjobs at the family picnic."

He gestured to a big tree with a stack of rocks next to it. "There's a nice little hiding spot over there. We just have to be real quiet. And I wasn't talking about blowjobs. I have other things planned for you." He leaned in really close and whispered in his best wicked voice. "That's why I bought you a dress and not shorts."

My eyes bulged out of my head. "Stop! Someone's going to hear you." My face turned bright pink and a chill rushed over my skin, goosebumps coming out to reveal my physical reaction to his suggestion. I could picture him down there with my dress pushed up to my waist almost like it was already happening.

He put his arm around me and leaned in again. "Come on. Stop torturing me. One kiss. Fifteen minutes. Take me up on the deal now before I change the terms."

I stood on tiptoe and gave him a quick peck on the lips, pulling away before he could prepare or react.

"Oh, no way," he said, grinning like the devil he is. "That doesn't count."

"Yes, it does." I tried to hold back my grin and remain serious. "You didn't specify a certain type of kiss." My heart was ready to explode with the joy of just being stupid with him.

Then I heard a car door slam shut over by the front of the house and remembered that Bradley could come rolling down that dirt road and show up at any minute. The joy that had just threatened to overwhelm me dissipated into the hot air around us, leaving behind frustration in its wake. Some evil part of me instantly became angry at Bradley for forcing my hand like this. Maybe I'd get lucky and a semi-poisonous snake would bite him if he tried to come interrupt this day - but only the kind that would send him to the doctor and not actually kill him. Half a second later I was overcome with guilt for almost wishing that on him. He was just doing what Mack would have done in the same circumstances. *I am such a terrible person. How have I fallen so far in such a short period of time?*

"What's wrong? Why aren't you smiling anymore?"

Mack tried to move in closer. "It's because you didn't get any tongue action, isn't it?"

I shook my head, forcing thoughts of Bradley to leave my head. Until he showed up or I went back, I could pretend those problems didn't exist. I could do that for Mack, at least.

"No, that's not the reason."

"You know it is. Come on now, pretty girl. I'll give you another chance."

Being called *pretty girl* like that probably should have offended me as a strong, professional woman, but instead it warmed me to my core and made me want to go explore that little spot behind the tree. I shook my head at myself. This sexy cowboy really knew how to press my buttons and make me forget what I was supposed to be doing - namely, detaching and preparing to leave.

The sound of a loud vehicle pulling up and an even louder horn announcing the arrival of someone special distracted both of us from our silly flirting games.

"Oh, shit," said Mack, sighing as he looked out towards the main gate. His shoulders sagged low.

"Who's that?" I asked, trying to see the person getting out.

"Welcome to my nightmare," he said, dropping his arm from my back and stepping away to greet the visitor.

"Hannah Banana!" yelled Boog from across the tent area as the Barbie doll beauty came from around an old beat-up truck to join the crowd mingling by the front of the house.

"Don't call me that, *Boog!*" she yelled back, sounding like a country singer the way she said it. Then her face turned into pure sunshine as she noticed Mack coming in her direction.

Jealousy overwhelmed my thoughts and had me staring daggers at both of them. *Where are those poisonous snakes when you need them, anyway?*

"Hey, Mack! Hey, Miss Maeve. How're y'all doing?"

Hannah chirped. "Brought my blueberry tart, just like I always do, *every* year." She held something wrapped in tin foil up above her head like she was the Betty Crocker Statue of Fucking Liberty or something.

I tried to use pure brain power to tip the thing out of her hand and onto her head, but apparently I have zero psychic connections because nothing happened. She brought it down in one smooth maneuver and peeled the foil back to reveal the food beneath for Mack. Unfortunately for her, he walked right past her and towards his brother Ian who was standing off to the side.

My jealous heart plumped up to three times its normal size. *He really doesn't like her! He wasn't lying!*

"It's your favorite," she said in a singsong voice over her shoulder, not at all dissuaded by his brush-off.

"No, it's not," he deadpanned. "I'm allergic to blueberries."

"Since when?" she asked, clearly offended.

"Since the day you were born."

His insult echoed throughout the entire party and everyone went dead silent for several seconds, before the singer in the band broke the mood by working on his equipment. Even I felt a little bad for Hannah, as obvious and obnoxious as she was, when I saw her face fall.

"Mike check *one!* One, one, *one.* Mike check *two!* Two, two, *two.* Mike check three four and close the *door.* The door, the *door.* Five and *six* that's Nikki *Sixx.* Of Motely Crue and me and *you.* Mike-a, mike-a, mike-a-phone check, check, check..."

"We hear the goddamn microphone, *okay?!*" screeched Hannah, her pie trembling in her hand.

The singer banged his forehead into the microphone when he bent down and sent a squeal of feedback through the tents. Everyone either ducked or covered their ears, me included. I could still hear the ringing in my head for a while after it stopped.

Hannah turned to me when the recorded music started coming out of the speakers a few seconds later, her snarling anger going all fake sweetness and glaring sunshine in the space of two seconds. She twitched her head once to the side and then took a long-legged, high-heeled step towards me, the promise of retribution for man-stealing in her eyes.

I threw my shoulders back and angled my chin up, bracing myself for her arrival.

*Time to shine not burn, Andie.*

*And, snakes? If you're still out there? Now would be a good time to make yourselves known...*

# Chapter Forty

HANNAH STOPPED IN FRONT OF me, the music growing louder and people moving around to get some shade under the tent. The party was officially in full swing with people drinking beers and sodas while they munched on appetizers scattered around the various tables.

"So. You're still here." Her smile reminded me of a reaction to biting into a fresh lemon.

"Yes, I'm still here. But I'm leaving." I glanced around, but no one seemed to be paying us much attention anymore. Mack was watching from a safe distance with Ian, making me want to stick my tongue out at him for being such a chicken shit and leaving me to deal with her alone. He would pay later, and it wouldn't be pretty.

"You're leaving? Really?" She went from bitchy to cheerful just like that. "Oh, wow, such a bummer." Her words came out in a rush. "When are you going?"

"Tomorrow. I have work and stuff to get back to."

She nodded, pretending to go all concerned and serious on me. "Yeah, sure, of course you do. Wouldn't want all that work stuff to get backed up on you. That's just extra work, right? Plus you could lose your job. Get fired and all that. That'd be terrible, losing your job."

"If I got fired it wouldn't be the worst thing in the world, actually." Her complete happiness about me leaving her alone with my husband made me mad enough to say the words I'd been toying around with. And as soon as they left my mouth I knew they were true. Picturing myself not working at the firm anymore brought me relief. I realized in that moment that the only thing I would miss about being a lawyer in West Palm Beach would be Ruby.

"In this economy?" She scoffed. "You can't be serious. I had to take a job at the diner just to keep my apartment." She looked around casually but stopped as soon as she saw Mack. The wattage channeled through her grin threatened to take out the town's electricity.

"*Mack's* apartment, you mean." I managed a tight smile.

She turned back to me. "Oh, that's right. Silly me. I'm living with Mack now. We've been together since ...," she looked up at the sky, doing her very complicated math, "... Months now. Months and months. It's been great. He's *so* handy to have around." She leaned in and whispered conspiratorially. "And sexy too, right? Especially when he walks around in his skivvies."

I took a step back to keep myself from doing something stupid to her face. "Hannah, I think Boog wants you." I looked around desperately for the man-bear-pig. If someone didn't come over here soon and rescue me, things were liable to get ugly. Primal urges were sneaking up on me that I'd never met before. Caveman-level shit. I was almost ready to tear eyeballs out.

"Boog?" She rolled her eyes. "He doesn't want me. He just wants to harass me about something."

"What's up with you guys, anyway? Did you date before or something?"

She snorted and then laughed loudly, sounding disturbingly like a braying donkey. "I may be country, Angie, but I don't date kin. Sorry to disappoint you, city girl."

"It's *Andie*. And you guys are *related?*" My jaw dropped

open a little at that factoid. *Since when do man-bear-pigs share DNA with Barbie dolls?*

"Yeah, we're related all right. He's my half-brother."

"So your mother married a wookie?" I meant it as an insult, but apparently I don't know how to throw down country-style.

She laughed, giving me her first genuine smile of the day. "You're kinda funny, City."

"And you're kinda *not*, Country."

She studied me closely, her smile melting away. "Whaddya say we cut the crap and come to some sort of agreement?"

"What kind of agreement?" My lawyer hat went on as I waited for her terms.

"How about I agree to let Mack and you alone for the day, and you agree to get out of town tomorrow and never come back?"

"Seems like a little one-sided, don't you think?" I cocked my head to the side.

"How so?"

"Ohhh, I don't know. Maybe because you work for half a day, and I work for the rest of my life? Doesn't seem fair, does it?" Staying away from Mack forever would definitely be work. I glanced over at him and my heart strings twanged like a banjo.

Her eyebrows drew closer together. "You want me to pay you or something?"

"No," I said, lowering my voice to match her tone. I looked her right in the eye, with every badass bone I had in my body channeling the heat. "I want you to keep your talons out of my man's back, that's what I want."

Her mouth fell open and she stared at me as storm clouds gathered in her eyes.

Mack came walking up just in time to catch her reply.

"He is *not* your man! He's *my* man, and he's *been* my

331

man practically my whole *life!*"

"Oh, Jesus, Hannah ... could we not do this right now?" he asked, his voice revealing fatigue. I wasn't sure if it was just being around her that did that to him or our long day yesterday, but he definitely looked like he could use a nap. His head dipped down, causing his hat to shield his entire face from view.

"Do what? Finally tell the world the truth? I think it's time you cowboyed up, Mack, and told everyone what's really going on between us."

His head snapped up and he gaped at her. "You cannot be serious. How deluded can you possibly be? There's *nothing* going on, Hannah, and you know it! I've never laid a finger on you."

People under the tents stopped talking and started paying closer attention to us.

"Maybe you could tone it down a little," I suggested, worried about ruining the party.

I was totally not expecting her next move.

Without any warning whatsoever, she attacked, slamming her open palms against my chest and sending me back a step or two. "Maybe *you* could just tone it down, man-stealer!"

"Hey! That's enough, Hannah!" said Mack, throwing an arm out to block her from coming any closer.

I'm not sure exactly what happened to my rational, thinking brain in the split second that followed, only that something snapped inside it and caused me to see red. I got my footing after stumbling a few steps and then rushed her without a second thought, pushing right past Mack's arm and making contact against her squishy hooters with my two fists.

"I am *not* a man-stealer!" I yelled, popping her in the chest with everything I had.

She barely lost any ground before she was coming at me again. And she no longer looked like a Barbie doll; now she was like a giant killer Chuckie doll, complete with tiny knives in the form of acrylic nails.

Mack jumped between us as fingernails, arms, slapping hands, and hair began to fly. I may have screamed. She *definitely* screamed. And then there was a loud crash when my big butt banged up against the banquet table behind me and sent a bunch of dishes to the ground.

"My brisket!" crowed a brittle voice.

"There goes the blueberry tart," said Ian, not sounding very happy about it.

"Stop it, you two!" yelled Mack, wrestling first with me and then giving up to go control the Attack Barbie who had a fistful of my hair.

I was on my knees, so I punched her hard in the groin muscle to get her to release me. It worked like a charm, and as soon as I was free, I stood up straight, breathing like a bull. Tossing my hair out of my face, I gestured for her to come at me. "Come on, bitch, bring it on." I huffed and puffed, waiting for her next move. "I'm ready for you now." I held my fists up and began dancing from side to side like Mohammed Fucking Ali, grateful my lifeplan had involved over three hundred hours of kickboxing aerobics. She was pretty tall, but I was fairly certain I could give her a roundhouse to the side of the head and at least knock her silly.

"Andie?" came a startled voice from off in the distance.

My brain made the connection the minute I saw the myriad expressions move across Mack's face:

Disbelieving.

Stricken.

Angry.

"Andie what are you doing?" the man asked.

My fists dropped to my sides as I sagged inward. All the fight went out of me like air from a dying balloon, as fantasy collided with reality and left me blindsided. "Oh. Hi,

Bradley. What are you doing here?"

I never saw the fist coming until it connected with my jaw.

# Chapter Forty-One

I CAME-TO LYING ON the ground next to the banquet table, several faces looming over mine. The first one I noticed was Mack's because his was the first I wanted to see there. And his hat was taking up a lot of space and blocking out my view of anyone else.

"Hi," I said, confused and embarrassed. "Tell me I just dreamed a girl fight as part of a head injury."

"I think you got it in reverse. Girl fight first and then the head injury." He put his hand on the top of my head. "Are you okay enough to sit up?"

"Andie, what the hell is going on?" Bradley asked.

For the first time I noticed him standing off to my right, down on bended knee on my other side. His face was one giant frown.

"You're really here too?" was all I could manage.

"Yes, I told you I was coming. Jesus, would you get up? You look terrible lying there on the ground like that."

Mack shot him an angry look but said nothing, putting his hand behind my neck and sitting me up.

The world tilted a little and then went normal again. Standing in front of me were Maeve, Grandma Lettie, and several other women. They were doing what they could to get the table put back together. Maeve glanced at me and then went back to her work.

Tears came to my eyes. "I'm so sorry," I said, my voice breaking partway through. The shame was unbearable.

"Don't worry about it," said Maeve, obviously unhappy. "This is not your fault."

"Of course it's not her fault," said Bradley. "She was attacked by that woman over there. I hope she knows she's looking at a civil suit."

I held up my hand. "Stop, Bradley. I'm not suing anyone."

"Of course you are. We're not going to let some inbred criminal attack you like that."

"Man, I don't know who you are, but you'd better watch your mouth." This threat came from Ian. I glanced over and saw him standing off to the side with Boog who was looking after a distraught Hannah Banana. I don't know why I thought she looked like Chuckie before. Now she just looked pitiful, with makeup smeared under her eyes, one of her heels broken off, and her hair in frizzy clumps all over the place.

Mack got me to my feet and held onto me until I had my balance back. I nodded to let him know he could let me go and he did, stepping away.

Bradley moved in to put his arm around me. "Come on, we're leaving."

I shook him off, getting angry when he made it difficult. "No, stop. I'm not going with you."

Bradley stood there with his arms out in a frozen embrace. "What do you mean you're not going with me? You just got hit on the head. You can't travel by yourself."

"If she needs to go back, I'll take her," said Mack. He looked at me. "Or you could just not go back. You could stay."

Bradley laughed, a very snobbish unkind sound coming from his throat. "Oh, man ... do you really think a girl like Andie'd be interested in staying out here in the middle of bumfuck Oregon with you? ... Just because you've got a cowboy hat on and a swinging dick? Please. She has more class than that." He reached for me again, but I stepped out of his range and closer to Mack.

"Don't talk to him like that," I insisted, embarrassed about the fact that I'd actually considered marrying this jerk. All the times Ruby and I had made fun of him at the firm came back to me, along with all the feelings of loathing they had engendered. I realized then that I had some freakishly superhuman powers of distraction, somehow managing to trick myself into forgetting all that and actually sleeping with him for almost two years.

"You're defending him?" Bradley took a step back. "I don't get it, Andie. What the hell is going on here?"

The ladies who'd been straightening up the buffet moved closer to listen in, Maeve and Grandma Lettie at the head of the group. Angus, Ian, and Boog came over too, all of them forming a large ring around the three of us: Mack, Bradley, and me. It was like the showdown at the OK Corral, only without guns and a lot more embarrassment.

I cleared my throat, my gaze darting to the faces around me. I saw questioning looks, accusatory ones, and sad ones. The only one that mattered to me was Mack's, and of course his face was a mask I couldn't read.

"Tell him, Andie," Mack encouraged. 'Tell him what we did."

My voice caught in my throat as the tears spilled over onto my cheeks. I shook my head slowly, the humiliation of telling everyone what I'd done to both Mack and Bradley with my carelessness too much to bear.

"Do you want me to do it?" he asked gently.

I couldn't say yes. It was wrong to make him shoulder this burden. "No," I finally said through the tears that continued to fall. "I'll do it."

"Tell me," said Bradley, angry now.

"Don't be mad at Mack," I begged. "He didn't do anything wrong."

"What's going on, Andie?" said Angus, his voice calm and soft. "Whatever it is, I'm sure we can work it out."

I put my hand on my lips to keep them from quivering. Reaching deep down inside me, I pulled up the last bit of reserves I had to calm myself enough to talk. I cleared my throat and looked at Grandma Lettie. She nodded her head once and winked at me, her face completely serious. I used her confidence as my guide and then looked at Bradley so I could deliver the crushing blow to both of our hearts.

# Chapter Forty-Two

YOU COULD HAVE HEARD A pin drop when I started talking.

"Two years ago I went to Las Vegas with my two girlfriends. While I was there I met Mack." I looked over at him and my breath hitched when I saw the longing in his eyes. I had to turn away so I could continue. I focused on Bradley's angry expression instead. I owed him that much.

"We played blackjack but then we drank a lot. I'd already had quite a few cocktails before I'd met him, but then we had more, and eventually we ended up ... getting together."

"Aw, Jesus, come on, Andie, this has nothing to do with us," said Bradley. "We didn't start dating until after you met him and came back."

"Yes, it does have something to do with us. It has everything to do with us. Just ... let me tell it." I took a deep breath and looked at Maeve. Time to pay the piper.

"When we were in Vegas, we got married. At one of those twenty-four hour chapels."

Maeve's eyes opened wider and she looked at her husband. He seemed more stunned than she did.

"He disappeared for the whole damn night, thanks to you," said Ian. He was pissed.

"Shut up, Ian. Now's not the time," warned Mack.

I continued, ignoring Ian's interruption. "We hardly even knew each other, but we got married."

Mack stepped over and stood close to me, pulling my attention away from his mother's shocked expression. I could feel his arm all the way down mine and his warmth comforted me as I think it was meant to.

"It's not real, Andie. It didn't happen," said Bradley, also stepping closer. He was using his cajoling tone, trying to get me to change my mind.

"Oh, it's real, all right," said Mack, defensive. "She has the documentation to prove it, and I'm not signing any divorce papers. Not yet anyway." He looked down at me. "Not until she's absolutely sure she's done with me."

I stared at the ground.

"She doesn't need you to sign any papers, you redneck idiot," Bradley ground out.

"Hey now, there's no call for that kind of language," said Angus, his chest puffing out a little. Several of the men nearby moved closer to stand behind him.

I started feeling panicky about the situation. I had to fix things before they got out of hand. "Bradley's right. Mack doesn't have to sign the papers. I can do it without the signature if I have to." I forced myself to look up at him, even though I knew it was going to bring so much pain.

He was stricken. "You're not going to do that are you?"

"I have to," I said, my voice trembling. I wanted to vomit right there at his feet I was so sick over it.

"No, you don't," he insisted, putting his hand on the side of my face. "I told you, you can stay here. Stay with me. Be my wife in more than just words. Let me show you how much I love you."

"Am I the only person here who hasn't lost his mind?" yelled Bradley, clearly frustrated.

"No!" yelled Hannah. "You are *not* the only one!"

"Thank you!" he yelled back, looking at me. "Andie, that knock you took to the head obviously caused you some brain damage. We'll get it looked at back home, but you need to come with me *now*. No more playing cowgirl. We have a rehearsal dinner to plan, a wedding to finish, and people to pick up from the airport. Our friends and family are waiting for us back home."

I looked from Bradley to Mack, my head spinning with the choices flying around me. Lifeplan or off-the-rails-no-plan? Lawyer or rancher? City or country? The man I once loathed and then came to see a partnership opportunity with or the man I'd never had anything but fun with? The known quantity or the stranger?

Mack's hand fell away from my face and his expression became shuttered.

"I don't think she wants to go with you, city boy," said Grandma Lettie.

Bradley frowned at her dismissively before turning back to me. "You're just feeling obligated," he said, his voice much gentler than it had been. "You feel like you signed the paper and said the vows, so now you have to follow through. I know you, Andie … I know you a hell of a lot better than this hayseed does. But you don't have to do that, okay?" He got a really hopeful grin on his face. "I made some calls. It's all good news." He held his hand out for mine.

"What's good news?" I asked, wondering what he had cooking up his sleeve. Bradley was always good for a last minute courtroom surprise, and that's what this felt like.

He glowered at Mack for a few seconds before continuing. It made my heart freeze over because I knew what it meant.

"I called the Nevada State licensing department."

"So did Andie. She has a document from them," said Mack. He was nervous too. I could hear it in his voice.

"I'm not talking about *that* department. I'm talking

about the one that licenses wedding chapels."

My blood ran cold and the sound of pounding heartbeats echoed around in my head. I could hear my own hammering pulse and it was drowning out everything but Bradley's voice. He was like the great and terrible Oz, delivering the bad news.

"That place that married you? They weren't properly licensed. Your marriage is a sham. It's not real. You're not really married to this guy. See? You don't even need a divorce."

There were a couple gasps from the women and a mumbling came from Angus's group of friends.

"What are you talking about?" I asked when I could speak again.

"For a girl known around town as the discovery queen, you sure didn't do a very good job of checking your facts," he said mockingly as he moved in to take me by the elbow. "Come on. Time to go home." He looked over my head at Mack. "No harm, no foul, guy. You're single. Might as well live it up while you can."

I looked back at Mack and felt something like a knife entering my chest at the expression on his face. He was staring at me like I had done it, like I had tricked him into thinking he was married.

"I'm so sorry," I whispered as I let Bradley lead me to the front of the house.

The crowd in front of us parted and fell away. An almost clear path led from the banquet table to Bradley's shiny silver rental car. The only thing standing in our way was Grandma Lettie.

## Chapter Forty-Three

SHE FROWNED AT ME, BRINGING what looked like a hundred years of practiced shaming down on my head.

"Come on, Andie." Bradley pushed me so we could go around her. I stumbled numbly to the side.

"Are you just going to let him boss you around like that?" she asked.

I was in a fog. I could hear the words, but they weren't making sense. "What?"

"I *said*, are you going to just let him boss you around like that? Because if you are, you're not the girl I thought you were."

I looked up at Bradley and could tell he was at the end of his patience with the situation.

"Just let me talk to her," I said, trying to keep him from blowing his stack.

His grip on my elbow tightened. "No. You've talked enough. It's time to go home." He pushed on me again, but I dug my heels in, refusing to move.

"Just let me talk to her for a second. Then I'll go." I owed the old woman that much. She was going to be hurt by all this too.

He let go of my arm and stood there, hulking over me like a dark, angry shadow. "So talk."

I looked at the older woman. "I'm sorry, Grandma Lettie." It took everything I had not to bawl.

"Don't say sorry to me. Say sorry to the man whose heart you're breaking behind you."

I couldn't look back. I just couldn't.

"He'll be fine," I said, trying to convince myself as much as I was her. "Mack's an amazing man with everything going for him." I tried to smile, but my lips were trembling too much. "Now he doesn't have to worry about a crazy wedding out in Vegas that made no sense anymore, so he can get on with his life."

"Exactly," Bradley chimed in. "Let's go."

When he tried to push me this time, I smacked him lightly on the arm. "Stop pushing me, would you? I'm not done talking yet."

He put his hand on the back of my neck. He didn't squeeze, but his threat was clear enough. He leaned down and spoke softly but menacingly in my ear. "The time for talking is over. Now *get* to the car."

Grandma Lettie shook her head. "Poor girl. You are walking into the biggest mistake of your life. Why can't you see that?"

"Grandma," said Mack from behind me. "I think you'd better step aside."

The minute the words penetrated the fog in my head, my heart collapsed in on itself. Pain like I'd never known before came rushing in to fill the empty spaces. Mack didn't want me anymore, and he didn't want his family trying to convince me to stay.

The crushing blow had been delivered, and it was everything I deserved. This is what people like me should get out of life. A life of happiness and wedded bliss is for other people, not me.

"If you say so, son." Grandma Lettie stepped off to the side and disappeared from my view.

I took a step forward, guided by Bradley's hand still on the back of my neck. I was fifteen again, being pushed into a back room by my mother's boyfriend. He was going to teach me a lesson about life he said, about back-talking grown-ups and not doing what I was told. Not staying *on plan*. He undid his belt as he walked.

My shoulders heaved with the silent tears that poured out of me. My throat ached with the screams that I couldn't give voice to. I imagined I knew in that moment what a person walking down death row must feel like, saying goodbye to the light of day and entering the prison of darkness, forever paying for sins committed.

"Andie?"

Mack's voice rose above the din of the music and whispered conversations behind me.

I stopped but didn't turn around.

"I think you'd better step aside too, babe."

I stopped breathing for a full five seconds, my heartbeats slowing, slowing, slowing. The word *babe* was like a ray of light, penetrating the darkness that enshrouded me. A term of endearment so simple, but so full of meaning at the same time.

Bradley turned around, his hand falling away from my neck. "Don't even think about it, cowboy."

I heard footsteps in the dirt coming towards us, first slowly and then faster until they were running.

Bradley pushed me and I fell to my side on the ground. I was in the perfect position to see Mack make a flying tackle into Bradley, taking him down into a cloud of dirt.

# Chapter Forty-Four

THE TWO MEN ROLLED AROUND in the dirt unencumbered, everyone making room for them to fight.

"What are you doing?!" I screamed as I scrambled out of the way, not sure which of them I was even talking to. Maybe it was the bloodthirsty crowd I was appealing to, but regardless, it didn't matter. This fight was going to happen, and it was obvious no one was going to interfere.

"Stop! Okay, *stop!*" I got on my feet and held out my hands towards them, trying to see a way to get in between them.

Mack and Bradley completely ignored me, locked in an embrace that looked like a fighter's waltz, each of them taking turns hitting each other in the gut.

Maeve was suddenly at my side, putting her arm around me. "Just let them work it out," she said, pulling me back away from them.

"But it's barbarian," I exclaimed, watching as Mack landed a solid punch to Bradley's cheek, snapping his head back and making him stumble.

"Sometimes it's the fastest, easiest way for them to figure things out."

"Maybe for Mack, but not Bradley." His Brooks Brothers shirt was getting destroyed, already covered in ground-in dirt and grass stains. One of his loafers was off his foot and sitting on the outskirts of their fighting ring. I'd never seen him lose his temper, ever. It's why he was still a part of my lifeplan, or had been before I'd come out here.

She snorted. "Sorry, sweetie, but even I can see that city boy's a scrapper. He's had plenty of fights of his own, I can promise you that."

Once I paid closer attention, I realized she was right. Mack was winning, but Bradley wasn't going down easy. Every time I thought it was going to be over, Bradley came back at Mack again and caught him unawares. They were almost evenly matched, but in the end, it was Mack who had the stamina and strength to win out.

Angus, Ian, and Boog moved in to separate them when they were doing more hugging than fighting. Both of them were bleeding in the face and across their knuckles, and neither one of them could stand up straight anymore.

Maeve squeezed me once before letting go. "Come on, sweetie. Let's get your men cleaned up."

"They're not my men," I said petulantly, embarrassed she saw them that way.

"They are until you officially let them go."

I followed behind her reluctantly as the men led the fighters up the front steps and into the house. I'd thought the scene outside in front of everyone was embarrassing, but something told me this one was going to be worse. Now it was just the close MacKenzie family there to witness my shame. There would be no buffers and no running away this time.

# Chapter Forty-Five

WHEN I GOT INTO THE kitchen, Bradley and Mack were seated at the dining table. Maeve put together two ice packs and handed them over, letting them do their own dirty work of tending to their bruised faces and egos.

I walked over quietly and stood in front of the table, staring at each of them in turn.

They looked at each other and then at me. No one said a word until Angus sat down at the head of the table and gestured to the seat next to him. "Have a seat, young lady."

He sounded so much like an imposing father figure, I couldn't ignore his order. I pulled the chair out and sat down. I looked him right in the eye, waiting to hear my sentence.

He smiled. "Don't look so glum, little one. You have two good looking, strapping young men willing to fight for you sitting right here at this table."

A watery smile made it to my lips. "That's part of the problem, I think."

His smile didn't leave. "All you have to do is look them in the eye and tell them how you feel. I'm right here for you." He reached out and put his giant hand over mine, enveloping my small fingers in his warmth. My heart spasmed painfully in my chest.

I nodded, taking a deep breath and lifting my eyes first

to Mack and then Bradley. They were still angry at each other, but when they looked at me, their expressions softened.

My life flashed before my eyes, just like I'd read about it happening to people who were having near-death experiences. As I sat across the table from the two battered and emotionally broken men, I saw myself as a teenager, crying helplessly in my room after suffering a beating with a belt. My mother was cooking in the kitchen and pretending like it hadn't happened, like I hadn't just been beaten down like a piece of trash by a man who treated women like possessions. A piece of me knew she was relieved it was me suffering his ire this time and not her. It made me hate her and at the same time drove me into myself, as I realized finally that I was truly alone in the world. My father was long gone, and now I was motherless too. I had to come up with a plan. A good one. Something that would get me out of this pit of a life and back to a place where I could find love and maybe even a haven from the anger that surrounded me everywhere I went.

And so the lifeplan had been born. I picked up a pencil that day and wrote the outline down, and over the course of several months refined it until it was perfect. It got me out of that miserable place with excellent grades that translated into full scholarships to college. I disappeared from my mother's toxic influence and entered a world of my own making. A carefully crafted script brought me friends and more success in college and then acceptance to law school. Step by step, I followed that plan until I took a couple days off to go to Las Vegas. It was the first time I'd gone off-plan in ten years and look where it had gotten me.

I looked at Bradley, a man I had thought I knew who now I suspected I really didn't. Where had he learned to fight like that? And he'd mentioned mistakes he'd made, things he'd done that I would probably be asked to forgive him for. He was supposed to be my husband, but he really wasn't husband material. Not when I suffered from feelings of regret every time I looked at him.

I looked at Mack. A man I didn't quite know as well as I should but who I wanted to know more of. He had honor, strength, and patience like I could never imagine possessing myself. He shouldered blame when he didn't need to. He went out of his way not to hurt people. And the light shining out of his eyes told me that he really cared about me. Maybe if I was lucky some day, he could really learn to love me.

Mack's hand slid out across the table and waited for mine, his palm opened up.

"Andie?" Bradley sounded vulnerable, which was a first in my experience. I looked at him, begging him with my eyes to let me go. He cast his eyes down, sighing heavily. "Go ahead. I know what you want."

I looked at Angus and he just nodded, encouraging me.

Maeve was standing behind me, so I twisted around to see her. She nodded too, a tear slipping out of the corner of her eye.

I swallowed my fear and reached my trembling hand up out of my lap, putting it in Mack's. The balm of love coated my heart with its healing magic when he closed his fingers around mine. He looked over at Bradley as he put his ice pack down. He held out his free hand. "Sorry, man. I didn't mean to screw everything up for you. But she was mine first, and I'm not going to apologize for that."

Bradley stared at Mack's hand for a few seconds before taking it and shaking it hard. "The best man won. Nothing I can do about that."

His words of defeat made my heart ache for what I'd done to him.

"I'm so sorry, Bradley. I didn't mean to hurt you, I swear it."

He stood, his chair scraping out behind him. "I know. Listen, I need to get going. I have a plane to catch."

"You can stay here until tomorrow if you want," offered Maeve.

"No, thanks. I don't think that would be a good idea." He waved at me with a weak flick of his hand and then he was gone.

After he left, Grandma Lettie came in and stood where he'd just been.

"So. We got things worked out?" She looked from Mack to me.

"No, not exactly," Mack said, pulling his hand from mine.

My face went white as all the blood drained from my head and a wave of dizziness almost took me down. I saw it coming now. The big break up. The humiliation. The end. The end of me.

He reached into his front pocket and slid out of his chair at the same time. "I was going to wait and do this later, but I guess now's as good a time as any."

He went down onto his knees next to my chair and put his hand on the arm of it, pushing it out so that I was facing him.

"What are you doing?" I whispered, crying all over again. I was so confused I had no idea what was going to happen next.

He held up a small, black velvet box and smiled, his split lip starting to bleed again. I took a napkin from Maeve and dabbed at it, smiling through my tears as I tried to stave off the heart attack I could feel coming.

"Andie. Crazy girl. I met you two years ago and I fell in love with you. The minute you threw that drink on me, I knew I was done." He opened up the box to reveal a sparkling square-cut diamond surrounded by smaller diamonds that were all set in a band of diamonds. I'd never seen so much light flashing out of a piece of jewelry in my life.

"Wow, that's a beaut," said Grandma Lettie in a hushed voice.

He responded to her but his eyes never left mine. "I had to get her something that would remind her of where we met. All those lights … remember Andie?"

I nodded, unable to speak. Only sobs could come out.

"I thought we were already married, but it doesn't matter to me that we're not. I feel married to you and I want to be married to you. If you'll do me the honor, I'll take you to the courthouse on Monday and make it official." He pulled the ring out of the box and held it up. "I bought this the other day when you came into town. I was going to give it to you since we never had a chance to get one before. But now, I guess it's an engagement ring."

He took my left hand in his, holding the ring right at the end of my finger. "So, what do you say? Will you marry me? Will you join Clan MacKenzie?"

"Shine not burn?" I managed to say.

He smiled, making his puffed up black eye look even worse. "Yes. Come with me so we can shine together."

# EPILOGUE

The musicians were playing the prelude to the wedding march, and I was poised at the end of the aisle, my arm wrapped tightly through Angus's. My bouquet of white roses and baby's breath trembled in my hand. A little tuft of purple troll-doll fluff stuck out from between some of the flowers.

"You okay there, sweetie pie?" he asked, looking splendid in his black tux.

I nodded, looking out over the small crowd of people seated in white chairs on either side of the aisle I was about to walk down. Most of them were still strangers, but I knew in time they'd be like family to me.

"I'm glad you agreed to let your mom come." He looked pointedly at the left side of the aisle, near where Candice and Kelly were standing and holding their bridesmaid flowers.

I looked at the thin woman sitting in the front row wearing the purple dress. She was a stranger to me, but she didn't want to be. She'd gotten healthy and was happily single, no longer looking for a man to guide her through life.

"It was Mack's idea, not mine." I still wasn't sure it was possible for my mother and me to put the past behind us, but I was willing to try for Mack's sake.

"He's a good man. He'll do right by you, I'll see to it."

I smiled. "I'm glad I'm getting you as my father-in-law. It's like a special bonus package deal."

He patted my hand that rested at his elbow. "We're both kind of lucky, aren't we?"

I nodded. "Yeah. We are."

He gestured down the aisle with his chin. "You ready to do this?"

"As ready as I'll ever be."

Angus and I walked to the end of the aisle and waited for the beginning of the music. When it came, we took slow, measured steps up the walkway, the short train behind my dress swishing along the white runner that had been laid down over the grass in the back yard. An arbor covered in flowers waited for me, and under it was the man I would marry for the second time, only this time it would be official in the eyes of the law. Standing next to him was his younger brother and the hulking form of a man-bear-pig.

Mack wore a tux with a bolo tie and a black cowboy hat. He'd never looked so stunning, his bright blue eyes drawing me in from all the way down the aisle. He kept them locked on me, never looking away, never wavering. Just like his love for me, they shined like beacons, leading me out of darkness.

We reached the altar and Angus put my hand on Mack's arm. "Take good care of her son, or you'll have to answer to your mother and me."

Mack nodded. "I wouldn't expect or want anything less."

Angus took his seat next to Maeve who was quietly dabbing tears from her eyes and holding Ruby's hand. Ruby wore a bright red dress and her best hat, little berries and a bird dangling off the side. She pursed her lips at me and nodded slowly. Her approval made me happy. I knew I'd made her proud.

"Do you have your vows?" asked the priest.

I shook my head no, but Mack nodded.

"What?" I whispered at him, confused.

He reached into his pocket with a grin and pulled out a bar napkin.

A flashback hit me like a freight train. *The bar napkin...*

"That's..." I pointed at it, remembering the bar we'd drank our last cocktails in.

He nodded. "These are the vows you wrote with me that night."

"You *kept* them?" I whispered, tears coming again. I'd thought I was fresh out of the damn things after a week of talking and crying and laughing, but here they were again, threatening to destroy the makeup job Candice had done an hour or two ago.

"Of course I kept them. Memories are important." He shook the napkin to unfold it and nodded at the priest. "We're ready."

My mind flashed through memories that were finally coming in a huge rush, unblocked by the magic bar napkin. Mack and I had left the hotel room after having crazy monkey sex and had walked the streets of Vegas arm-in-arm and hand-in-hand, reveling in the lights and the noise and the crowds of happy people. All the while we kissed and hugged and laughed with the emotions that were overwhelming us. We found a corner of a busy street and just sat on a bench and talked and talked and talked about our dreams and our pasts and our hopes. We joked about having kids together and what we'd name them. And then he suggested that we go get married, getting down on one knee right there on the dirty sidewalk, and I said yes. We kissed the entire way there and the entire way back.

"Andie?"

Mack's voice snapped me out of my trance.

"Yes?"

"Are you ready?"

I nodded. "Yes. I'm ready."

"Go ahead with your vows," said the priest, nodding at Mack.

Mack grinned at me and began to read.

"I, Gavin MacKenzie, sexy cowboy man of Baker City,

Oregon ... being of sound mind and hot body ... do hereby declare that I love you, Andie Marks, lawyer extraordinaire, and want to be married to you until I'm so old, I either die or my pecker falls off."

"Holy shit," I whispered, my face flaming red.

Candice snorted and someone out in the crowd giggled.

Mack continued. "I will have sex with you whenever you want, and I will always give you the option to be on top if that's what will make you happy. Blowjobs will always be optional but appreciated."

I dropped my head and bit my lip to keep from laughing out loud. This was nuts. I hadn't realized until this moment just how off-plan I'd gone that night with Mack, but it was strangely liberating. Mack had set me free somehow, his love unlocking the door to my heart and freeing me to just be myself.

"I will change diapers when called for, both for our children and for you when you're old and decrepit. I will never spit in public or burp too loudly or say mean things about your friends."

Candice nudged me with her flowers. "Good one," she whispered.

"And finally...," his voice went softer, "I promise never to raise my hand against you in anger or tell you that you're useless or threaten to hurt people who you love. Ten-four, over and out, happily ever after. Those are my vows."

I was crying before he got to the end. I'd written the promises of a drunken fifteen year old falling into her first love. I could see myself ... a silly girl writing on a bar napkin as she wandered the lonely road of the past, following the beacon of light that she saw as her future. A future with Mack.

"Thank you," I whispered. I looked out into the crowd to see how badly I'd embarrassed my soon-to-be husband, and there wasn't a dry eye in the house. My mom was sobbing quietly into a handkerchief while Maeve wrapped an arm over her shoulders. Grandma Lettie was nodding her head like she was a revival meeting. *Praise the Lord.*

"And now for your vows," said the priest looking at me.

"I … didn't write any. I didn't know …"

"Just say whatever you want," said Mack. "Or you can use these." He waved the napkin between us.

"No thanks," I said, unable to keep the grin from my face. I cleared my throat. "I can do this."

"I know you can." He leaned over and kissed me tenderly.

"Hey, no kissing until after," said Kelly, tapping me on the shoulder with her flowers.

I pushed Mack away gently and cleared my throat. "Okay. Vows. Take one." I looked at Mack, trying to express with my eyes how much I loved him in that moment. "I promise to be faithful to you. To always listen to you when you want to talk. To have sex whenever you want, wherever you want." His eyebrows went up at that, and I continued, a smile refusing to leave my face. "I promise to learn how to cook a mean beef brisket, to rope a calf, and ride a horse. I'll stick around for as long as you'll have me. And I promise to be as good a mom to your kids as I possibly can."

A tear came out of each of Mack's eyes and his lips quivered just the slightest bit. "Thank you." He mouthed the words before turning to face the priest.

"Well, I guess that about does it then," said the man in front of us. "Does someone have the ring?"

Ian leaned in and handed the gold bands to Mack. Mack gave me his and held out mine.

"Please place the bands on your future spouse's finger."

A wave of warmth washed over me when Mack slid the band over my knuckle and settled it onto my finger where I knew it would reside until the day I died.

He closed his fingers over mine as I finished pushing his

ring onto his finger.

"I now pronounce you husband and wife. You may kiss your bride, cowboy."

Mack grinned and bent down, blocking my view of the guests with the wide brim of his hat.  "I love you, Andie MacKenzie," he said, as he lips came up against mine.

"I love you too, Gavin MacKenzie," I said, pressing my lips to his.

**Want to get an email when my next book is released?**
**Sign up here:** http://eepurl.com/h3aYM

## ABOUT THE AUTHOR

Elle Casey is a prolific American writer who lives in Southern France with her husband (who sometimes wears a kilt), three kids (who never stop moving), Hercules the wonder poodle (who sleeps next to her side for every word typed), Monie the bouvier (who also never stops moving), and a few other furry creatures (don't ask). Her favorite things are red wine, pretty much anything with sugar in it, and sexy books. If she has all three around her at the same time, please do not disturb ... the writer is busy creating. In her spare time she writes new adult and young adult novels (you can find her Women's Fiction work under the pen name Kat Lee.) She publishes at least one novel per month and has been accused of being a cyborg for her ability to consistently turn out captivating stories with characters that stay in readers' heads long after the book is closed. She neither confirms nor denies this accusation.

### *A personal note from Elle ...*

If you enjoyed this book, please consider leaving positive feedback on Amazon, Goodreads, or any book blogs you participate in. More positive feedback means I can spend more time writing! Oh, and I love interacting with my readers, so if you feel like shooting the breeze or talking about books or your pets, please visit me. You can find me at ...

www.ElleCasey.com
www.Facebook.com/ellecaseytheauthor
www.Twitter.com/ellecasey

**Want to get an email when my next book is released?**
**Sign up here:** http://eepurl.com/h3aYM

# OTHER BOOKS BY ELLE CASEY
*\*= Coming Soon*

**(New Adult Romance)**
Shine Not Burn
Rebel*
Hellion*
Trouble*
Trainwreck*
By Degrees*
Don't Make Me Beautiful*
**(YA Paranormal Romance)**
Duality, Volume I (Melancholia)
Duality, Volume II (Euphoria)
**(YA Urban Fantasy)**
War of the Fae: Book One, The Changelings - *FREE!*
War of the Fae: Book Two, Call to Arms
War of the Fae: Book Three, Darkness & Light
War of the Fae: Book Four, New World Order
Clash of the Otherworlds: Book 1, After the Fall
Clash of the Otherworlds: Book 2, Between the Realms
Clash of the Otherworlds: Book 3, Portal Guardians
My Vampire Summer
My Vampire Fall*
Aces High (co-written with Jason Brant)
**(YA Post-Apocalyptic)**
Apocalypsis: Book 1, Kahayatle
Apocalypsis: Book 2, Warpaint
Apocalypsis: Book 3, Exodus
Apocalypsis: Book 4, Haven
**(YA Action-Adventure)**
Wrecked
Reckless

# ACKNOWLEDGMENTS

First, a shout out to the book bloggers who feature my books on their websites. Thank you! Without you, readers would have a really hard time finding me in the ginormous pile at the online retailers. To Sarah Welsh, Theresa Veraa, Craig, and Margaret ... my beta readers and proofreaders ... thank you! Your feedback was immensely helpful to me, especially with this being my first romance novel. A big hug to my husband who is such a great inspiration when it comes to writing sexy scenes. To my readers who are the reason I write. Thank you so much for investing your time and money in my work. I am grateful to you every day of my life! And last, not least, to my children who are very understanding with me when I tell them that Mommy has to write.

Made in the USA
Lexington, KY
06 July 2013